DISAPPOINTMENT CRASHED THROUGH HER, AND ALONG WITH IT AN ODD SORT OF RELIEF. MAYBE THERE REALLY WERE THINGS PEOPLE WERE BETTER OFF NOT KNOWING, NO MATTER HOW MUCH THEY MIGHT THINK THEY WANTED TO. MAYBE –

Skyler burst into tears.

And as her mother's arms went around her, more gently this time, holding her, rocking her a little, Skyler's pain was eased a bit and the emptiness inside her was filled by the love she could feel flowing from Kate.

For the moment, at least.

For in her heart, she knew she would never entirely be free of her yearning to know the story that, now, only her real mother could tell.

Someday, she thought. *Someday I'll find you ... or you'll find me. Someday I'll know.*

TRAIL
OF
SECRETS

Eileen Goudge

A SIGNET BOOK

SIGNET

Published by the Penguin Group
Penguin Books Ltd, 27 Wrights Lane, London W8 5TZ, England
Penguin Books USA Inc., 375 Hudson Street, New York, New York 10014, USA
Penguin Books Australia Ltd, Ringwood, Victoria, Australia
Penguin Books Canada Ltd, 10 Alcorn Avenue, Toronto, Ontario, Canada M4V 3B2
Penguin Books (NZ) Ltd, 182–190 Wairau Road, Auckland 10, New Zealand

Penguin Books Ltd, Registered Offices: Harmondsworth, Middlesex, England

First published in the USA by Viking 1996
First published in Great Britain by Michael Joseph 1996
Published in Signet 1997
1 3 5 7 9 10 8 6 4 2

Printed in England by Clays Ltd, St Ives plc

To my dear friend Andrew,
who fights the good fight.

ACKNOWLEDGMENTS

This work truly has been a labor of love in so many respects. Mostly because it gave me the opportunity to explore the fascinating—and very divergent—realm of professional horseback riding ... and to live out one of my fondest fantasies: namely, riding on patrol with the Mounted Police of New York City. Special thanks to Deputy Inspector Kathy Ryan and Sergeant Brian Flynn for that unforgettable thrill. Many thanks also to the following:

Tom Smith, of the New York City Mounted Police, a true officer and gentleman, from whom I learned much, not only about the unit, but about modern-day chivalry and our frequently unsung heroes in blue.

"Scotty," formerly of the New York City Mounted Police unit, who is now enjoying a well-earned retirement in a pasture where he can graze to his heart's content.

Michael Page, former Olympic silver medalist in the three-day event, who was gracious enough to provide useful information on show jumping ... and who, even more graciously, gave me a lesson in jumping I won't soon forget.

Lindy Kenyon, equestrienne par excellence, who was kind enough to vet the horse and show-jumping scenes for accuracy.

Dr. Lucy Perotta, director of the Neonatal Intensive Care unit at Beth Israel Hospital, for taking time out of her busy schedule to answer my questions, and for allowing me to hang out with her for a morning. For every ailing baby in this world I would wish a doctor as compassionate and wise as Dr. Perotta.

Dr. Robert Grossmark, for his invaluable input ... and, in particular, for his guidance concerning group therapy.

Bill Hudson, of Hudson, Jones, Jaywork, Williams & Liguori, for being the ultimate good neighbor and freely lending me his expertise on the ins and outs of child custody hearings (at the expense of his vacation time!).

Pamela Dorman, Audrey LaFehr, and Al Zuckerman for their useful editorial comments.

Dave Nelson, who works tirelessly behind the scenes to make it all happen.

Angela Bartolomeo, my loyal assistant, who facilitated the writing of this book through a particularly trying time in my life.

Nancy Trent, my friend and publicist, for adding the razzle-dazzle.

John Delventhal, stable master of the Gipsy Trail Club, for teaching me that there are no shortcuts to being a good rider ... and for instructing me in the art of buying horses. I thank him especially for being an unfailing advocate of those who cannot speak for themselves.

Happy families are all alike;
every unhappy family is unhappy in its own way.

—Leo Tolstoy, *Anna Karenina*

Prologue

Ellie shivered in the perpetual high noon of the Great White Way, clutching the collar of her borrowed coat as she hurried home from work. *And then there was light,* she thought. Everywhere light—blazing from neon marquees, flashing off the mirrored siding of nightclubs, glaring from the cars streaming down Broadway.

But it was a cold light. Even in Euphrates, Minnesota, in the blue heart of winter, with the cow ponds frozen solid and the pastures a vast salt lick of snow, she had never felt this cold. In her cheap nylon uniform and her sister's too-small coat, she imagined her bones snapping like twigs in an ice storm.

Only her breasts, swollen with milk, seemed to radiate a dull heat. She felt them start to prickle—time to nurse. She quickened her pace, turning the corner onto Forty-seventh Street, her whole body aching now for her baby as she made her way toward the derelict apartment building near the end of the block in which she shared a tiny walk-up with her sister.

Had she left enough formula with Nadine? Her sis-

ter, she thought with a sigh, wouldn't think to go out
and buy more. Ellie pictured Bethanne fussing, her
sweet doll's face going all red and crumpled as she
squirmed in Nadine's arms. Ellie hugged herself, pretending it was Bethanne she was holding, comforting.
All evening, in fact, perched on a high stool in the
stuffy ticket booth at Loew's State on Broadway and
Forty-fifth, punching out tickets and palming change
through the slot, she'd had this feeling—a persistent
unease that niggled at her like some sort of mental
hangnail.

What if that slight flush in her daughter's cheeks
that she'd noticed earlier today meant Bethy was coming down with something? Measles or mumps or . . .
or maybe even smallpox. Ellie felt her insides lurch;
then she immediately got a grip on herself.

People don't get smallpox these days, she told herself
firmly. *Besides, she's had her shots. So just calm down
and stop fretting. You have bigger things on your
plate—starting with how on earth you're ever going to
save up enough money to move into your own place.*

On her earnings as a ticket taker, even though she
put aside every nickel that wasn't for food or her share
of the rent, it looked like maybe she'd be hanging
curtains in her very own kitchen sometime, oh, around
the turn of the next century. But just thinking about
it—a place she could fix up, with space for a second-
hand crib and a real honest-to-goodness mattress (as
opposed to the lumpy sofa bed she slept on at Nadine's)—perked her up some. She actually felt herself
lift up off the pavement, as if her sneakers had suddenly developed extra spring.

She *was* going to make it happen somehow. Find a
better job. Find a way to go to college. Maybe even
find herself a husband somewhere along the way
(though she wasn't putting any eggs in *that* basket). It
just might take a while, that's all. And the one thing
she had plenty of was time. She was only eighteen,

for heaven's sake! Though she couldn't remember the last time she'd felt anything even close to being a teenager.

Passing under a street lamp, Ellie caught her reflection in the mirrored panel of a display window. She saw a tall, broad-faced girl with the strong cheekbones and fair hair of her Scandinavian forebears—a girl you'd expect to see on a billboard along I-94 at the Minnesota–Wisconsin state line, dressed in a dirndl and puff-sleeved blouse, welcoming visitors to the North Star State and reminding them to buckle their seat belts for safety.

She smiled ruefully, stepping around a starburst of broken glass on the sidewalk. God, she was so far from being that image of apple-cheeked milkmaid it wasn't even funny. Little more than a year ago she'd been valedictorian at her high school graduation, and now here she was, a *mother*. As much as she loved Bethanne, sometimes it just didn't seem possible to Ellie that she could be *anyone*'s mother.

Jumbled memories of the night she'd given birth crowded into her head: the emergency room with its moaning, jabbering press of bodies, followed by the labor ward with its rows of curtained beds and onslaught of probing hands and cold instruments. Then there had been only the swelling rhythm of her pain; and at last, mercifully, her baby, sliding from her in a gush of biblical proportions.

As her tiny daughter was handed to her, wrapped in a white cotton blanket like some wondrous gift, Ellie had wept. The feeling that rose up in her was like the cyclones that occasionally ripped through Euphrates, tearing away the roofs of henhouses and tossing pickup trucks ten feet into the air like Tonka toys. Her joy was both awesome and terrifying.

In that instant, as completely as a jar of preserves dropped into boiling water, Ellie's future had been sealed. She had become a grown-up. Time to stop cry-

ing over spilt milk. Jesse wasn't going to marry her,
and Mama and Daddy weren't going to beg her to come
home—not after the fit Mama had thrown, quoting
every curse in the Bible before literally hurling the
Good Book at her. Except for Nadine, who was hardly
able to care for herself, much less be of any help to
her, Ellie was on her own.

But despite Ellie's newfound self-reliance, a hard
kernel of fear grew with each passing day. Leaving
her baby with Nadine six nights a week while she
worked the evening shift at Loew's was hardly any
kind of a life. But what choice did she have? She
couldn't afford a baby-sitter on her salary, and Nadine
would at least make sure nothing bad happened to
Bethy.

*Are you so sure about that? What about when she
has her men friends over—would she even hear
Bethy cry?*

A sour, cottony taste filled Ellie's mouth as she hurried home, her heart seeming to contract with each
step. She tried to form a picture of her four-month-
old, quietly asleep in her makeshift bassinet ... but it
was no good. She couldn't shake this awful, clutching
feeling that something bad had happened ... or was
about to.

The last time she'd felt this way, Ellie recalled, was
the day she told Jesse she was pregnant. As soon as
the shock wore off, he'd sworn up and down and sideways that he loved her, God knew he loved her more
than anything or anyone on earth ... but what was he
supposed to do, give up going to West Point and stay
in Euphrates his whole life? They'd get married after
he graduated, he'd promised. In four years, he'd have
his commission, and they could live anywhere—maybe
even Germany. They would travel all over Europe.
Their child would grow up speaking several languages.
Everything would turn out better this way, she'd see.

Ellie had caught the gleam of desperation in his eye,

and somewhere in the mist of her wishful longing, an icy bead of anger formed. She'd thought: *When pigs fly.*

The reality was that Jesse had put her behind him in more ways than one the minute the taillights of his Corvette blinked over the rise where Aikens Road forked off toward the interstate. He'd answered only one of her letters, and the only time he phoned was just after she'd come home from the hospital with Bethy, when he'd offered her no apologies, only the vague promise of money that had yet to arrive.

To hell with Jesse, she thought with sudden vehemence. To hell with all of them—all those sanctimonious souls in Euphrates who'd turned their backs on her, and that included Mama and Daddy. A year ago, when she was marching up to the podium at the Masonic Lodge in Bloomington to accept first prize in the Minnesota-wide Bernice T. Little Poetry Competition, she hadn't needed anyone to tell her who or what she was. And she didn't need it now.

Ellie became aware of a heavyset man with a fedora pulled down over his brow strolling toward her along the nearly deserted sidewalk. He slowed almost to a stop, eyeing her speculatively. Ellie, her heart pounding, darted past. This area, just west of Times Square, she thought bleakly, was no place for a woman to be out walking alone at eleven o'clock on a weeknight. She shuddered, and pulled her coat more tightly about her.

You could always go on welfare, said a voice inside her head. A voice so calm and rational she was hard pressed to argue against it.

The money wouldn't be much less than what she was making now. And it would be only for a little while, until she could find a better job, enough to pay for day care for Bethanne as well as the night classes at City College she'd marked off in the dog-eared bro-

chure she carried everywhere with her, folded over in
her purse like a talisman.

Abruptly, her mother's face rose in her mind—
Mama's narrow-eyed expression whenever she happened to catch sight of their next-door neighbor, Mrs.
Iverson, taking out the trash or shooing one of her
ropy-haired kids off to school; the way Mama's blue
eyes slid over the stoop-shouldered woman in her
faded housecoat like a knife scraping cold leftovers
from a plate.

"Doing without is one thing," she'd sniff, "but the
day you catch me in line for government handouts
you may as well put a gun to my head and pull the
trigger."

Welfare would be even more humiliating than taking money from Jesse's father, Ellie thought. She
winced, remembering Colonel Overby offering to
write her a check, how the words had dropped from
his thin-lipped mouth like tacks onto the polished
hardwood floor of his study. She'd felt sure she would
die of shame on the spot. It had taken every speck of
starch in her spine to pull herself up and look him
square in the eye. She'd asked only for enough to
cover bus fare to New York and a thousand dollars
to tide her over until the baby came. Watching him
make out the check with quick, stabbing jerks of his
pen, wearing a disdainful expression that said how little he thought of her—not so much for getting pregnant as for being too proud and ignorant to ask for
more—she'd felt so sick to her stomach she thought
she might lose her breakfast right there atop his
scrolled walnut desk.

No, welfare was out of the question. She wouldn't
take any more handouts. The only thing worse would
be having to depend on a passel of boyfriends, the
way Nadine did.

Boyfriends? Admit it, your sister is a whore.

Well, at least Nadine had managed to keep from

getting knocked up, Ellie was quick to remind herself. Besides, her sister had taken her in when nobody else would, so what right did she have to judge her? That would sure enough be the pot calling the kettle black.

Even so, in her heart Ellie knew she wasn't anything like her sister. Hadn't Daddy always said they were as different as peas from corn? Growing up, Ellie had spent every spare moment down at the Euphrates public library, her nose buried in a book. Nadine, on the other hand, could usually be found at the Ben Franklin on Main Street, sampling lipsticks and debating over shades of nail polish with names like Coral Sunrise and Mocha Madness.

But the day Nadine boarded a Trailways bus for New York City, not even a heavy layer of Coty foundation could hide the shiner Daddy had given her after catching her down at the creek with her jeans off, and Clay Pillsbury riding her like a bull in rut. That had been four years ago, and the only show of repentance in Nadine was that now she wasn't giving it away for free.

It wasn't like that with Jesse, Ellie was quick to tell herself. But did that make her better than Nadine ... or just a whole lot dumber?

She was passing a shabby storefront with "Madame Zofia's" in faded letters above the crudely painted outline of a hand when she noticed a black Town Car idling at the curb a short distance away. Recognizing its license plate, she felt the brush of a cold finger against her spine.

Monk, she thought.

The oddly sedate, almost preacherlike black man showed up once a week, rarely staying more than an hour or two, always carrying away with him an envelope stuffed with bills—his cut of Nadine's earnings.

The man gave her the creeps. It wasn't just that what he did made him lower than slime—it was the way he *looked* at her with those dark, hooded eyes of his that took in everything and gave nothing back. Eyes that said, *I don't know what it is you're good for yet, but when I figure it out I'll be coming round to get my share.*

Ellie hung back, breathing a sigh of relief when she saw the car glide away from the curb. At least she wouldn't have to speak to him. Thank God for small favors.

Even so, her heart was thudding as she bounded up the broken stone steps of her building and let herself in through the front door marbled with graffiti. She climbed the stairs to the sixth floor, careful to avoid catching her toes on the curling rubber guards, yet only dimly aware of the sounds that drifted from behind dead-bolted doors: muffled voices, the mutter of TV sets, the squeal of a chair leg on linoleum.

The door to Nadine's apartment stood open a crack, as if Monk had been in a hurry when he left.

"Nadine?" Ellie called, her voice pitched an octave higher than usual.

She scanned the dreary living room, with its Naugahyde recliner crisscrossed with duct tape, and the fold-out sofa that had left a permanent ache in the small of her back. In one corner Ellie had strung a curtain fashioned from a ruffled bedsheet. Not much in the way of a nursery, but it had to do until she got her own place.

Ellie was pulling the curtain aside to check on the baby when she was distracted by the sight of Nadine, standing in the doorway to her bedroom, one hand cupped gingerly over the right side of her jaw. She was a mess, with one eye swollen shut; she stared at Ellie with the glassy fixedness of someone deeply in shock. Nadine's hand dropped heavily to her side, and Ellie gasped at the swollen, purplish melon distorting the lower half of her sister's thin, pretty face.

"That son of a bitch," Ellie swore, fury sweeping through her. "He did this to you, didn't he?"

She started toward her sister, but Nadine shrank away, clutching the front of her flame-colored kimono as if it were the only thing holding her up, and making a low whimpering sound deep in her throat.

"Coud't shtop him. I tried, but he woud't lishen ..." The mangled voice that emerged from Nadine's swollen lips made Ellie think of summers when they were kids, sucking on Popsicles until their tongues were frozen.

She felt frozen now as she stared at her sister, trying to absorb the mush of words tumbling out of her. *"Hit me when I tried to get her away from him ... said he'd hurt her too if I didn't stop ... Ellie ... I swear ... I swear it washn't my fault. ..."*

Comprehension descended on her with the swift brutality of the fist that had rearranged her sister's face: *Bethanne ... something's happened to my baby.*

Ellie sprang forward with a savage moan and grabbed Nadine by her shoulders. Her thumbs dug into the sockets of a collarbone that felt as if it might snap in two like a dry turkey wishbone, but she didn't care if she was hurting her sister. All she cared about was her baby.

"What are you trying to tell me? *What?*" Ellie cried.

Nadine's good eye rolled like that of an animal caught in a trap.

"The baby," she croaked.

Ellie, her heart squeezed to a stop, took a reeling step backward. The room went gray and fizzy, and she was seized by a queasy lightheadedness. Reflexively, she brought her knuckles to her mouth and bit down hard, tasting blood. The pain catapulted her back to full consciousness.

With a low cry, she darted over to the makeshift curtain, yanking it hard enough to tear it loose from the length of wire anchoring it to the wall at either end. The curtain collapsed with a sigh, revealing the

wicker basket on the floor, one she'd lined with flannel
and trimmed with lace from an old slip of Nadine's.

The basket was empty.

Ellie stared in disbelief. It was as if she'd stepped
onto a carousel, the room slowly spinning and tilting.
She felt herself lurching to one side, and threw her
hand out against the wall to keep from losing her balance. This wasn't happening, she told herself. This
wasn't—

"Where is she?" The words were torn from her
throat like a scream of terror.

She spun about just in time to catch sight of Nadine's slow, elevatorish glide down the doorjamb. Nadine landed with a thump on her tailbone, her legs
splayed out in front of her like a discarded doll's.

"Monk," Nadine wheezed. "He sesh he knows thish
guy . . . some lawyer who finds babies for people who
can't have their own. He tole me blue-eyed babies get
the mosh money." She began to whimper.

"Where is he? *Where did he take her?"* Ellie was
so frantic she didn't realize she was standing over her
sister with both fists raised until Nadine flinched and
scooted her rear end back as far as it would go.

"Don't know," Nadine squeaked.

"What do you *mean*? You know where he lives,
don't you?"

Nadine shook her head. "He wouldn't take me
there . . . said it might get me in trouble."

Her kimono had fallen open, leaving her breasts
bobbling. But Nadine wasn't bothering to cover herself. She *was* a doll. A stupid, useless doll.

Ellie turned away from her sister. The police. She'd
call the police. They'd help her. They'd find Bethy
for her.

But the prospect of dialing, then trying to explain
it all to some disembodied, possibly suspicious voice,
defeated her even as she was was madly scrabbling
for the phone by the sofa.

A wave of terror knocked her back on her heels— terror mixed with rage that that monster even *imagined* he could get away with taking her child. She threw her head back and let loose an anguished howl that seemed to rip the flooring right out from under her. Then she was vaulting toward the door, shoving aside a chair, knocking over a floor lamp that reeled drunkenly before it toppled to the carpet.

Minutes later, half out of her mind, her cheeks icy with tears she hadn't known she was shedding, Ellie found herself running down Broadway in search of . . . she didn't know what. Help. Salvation. Anything. Anyone.

She was vaguely aware of coat sleeves brushing against her, a din of voices and traffic sounds, neon light firing at her from every direction.

She felt a warm, sticky wetness soak the front of her blouse.

Blood, she thought in a strangely detached way. *This is what it feels like to be shot in the heart.*

But it was only her milk letting down.

Somewhere in all this madness, a baby was crying. A baby that might be hungry. A baby she prayed was hers.

CHAPTER 1

Northfield, Connecticut, 1980

There were times when she could forget. Moments. Hours. Sometimes a whole day would go by and Kate would realize as she was brushing her teeth or easing into bed that it had not once entered her mind—the terrible secret that was as deeply lodged in her as the steel pins in her shattered left femur; a secret accompanied by a shame that, like the pain in her leg and hip, ebbed and flowed in darkness.

Today was one of those days.

Standing at the Stony Creek Farm schooling ring fence, watching eight-year-old Skyler, astride her bay pony, sail over a course of cross-rails and oxers and vertical jumps, Kate Sutton felt not only proud, but, well . . . blessed.

My daughter, she thought. *Mine.*

She remembered Skyler at age two, first time in the saddle, her tiny feet barely reaching the stirrups at their highest notch. From that day on, she couldn't be pried off. As if all along—*Who could doubt it? Just look at her!*—Skyler had been destined for this. To be *her* child, and grow up at Orchard Hill, with its

century-old stone stable, its acres of green to be galloped across and its boxwood hedges to jump.

And what luck that Stony Creek—one of the finest
riding schools in the country—was situated only a few
miles from their place, at the north end of the meadow
where Willoughby Road forked off toward the village.
With Skyler practically living here every summer, and
on weekends the rest of the year, Duncan MacKinney
had become almost a second father to Skyler—as he
had to Kate growing up. Though you'd never know it
to hear him barking orders at her now.

"Release! Shoulders back! You're hanging on his
bloody neck!"

The former Olympic gold medalist, tall, whippet-
lean, with a mane of graying red hair crowning a frame
grown more imperial with each passing decade, stood
straight as a flagpole in the center of the ring.

Skyler, her small face grim with concentration,
shifted sideways a bit and shortened her left rein,
cutting Cricket in a diagonal across the ring. At four-
teen-two hands, the spirited pony would have been a
handful for someone twice Skyler's size—aggressively
forward, and forever trying to ride off the bit. Skyler,
though, had him perfectly in hand. She sat erect, her
narrow back slightly arched as she guided the pony
with hand and leg movements so subtle they would
have gone unnoticed by an eye less practiced than
Kate's.

The picture Skyler made in her boots and breeches,
with her hair tucked up under her helmet, brought a
smile of recognition. At home, among her collection
of faded ribbons and trophies, Kate had photos of
herself on her first pony, looking very much as Skyler
did now—long-legged and slim as a crop, head high,
with her gaze set on some distant horizon as if antici-
pating that something wonderful would be waiting for
her when she got there.

These days, whenever she looked in the mirror, instead of peering anxiously at tiny wrinkles and gray hairs the way another thirty-six-year-old woman might, what Kate saw was the unremarkable brown of her hair, while her daughter's was the pale gold of a Grimm's fairytale child, and her own gray-green eyes in a John Singer Sargent face that bore no resemblance to Skyler's.

I thought I knew what lay ahead, but I didn't have a clue . . .

"He was half a stride short on that last jump." Skyler's clear, piping voice punctuated the August heat that had settled over the ring like an upended bowl. "It felt like he was rushing it."

"Try it again. Bring him around at a working trot," ordered Duncan with a maestrolike swoop of his long arm, stirring the dust that hung in the air, as still as the shade of the beech tree under which Kate stood. "Easy does it. Nice and collected. You're hanging on the bit—loosen up."

"I'm taking that one." Skyler pointed toward an ascending oxer at the far end of the ring—three horizontal poles at ascending heights spaced no more than six inches apart.

Kate, with a sharp intake of breath, judged the highest of the oxer's three poles to be between four and five feet.

"Over my dead body." Duncan's face, long like the rest of him and weathered the color of an old girth strap, was ruddy with outrage.

"I can do it." There was nothing defiant in the way Skyler stood up to him. She was stating it simply as a matter of fact. "I've jumped every other one. It's not that much higher than the triple bar."

"When I *say* you're ready is when you'll be jumping anything higher than my kneecap," he thundered.

Skyler laughed, sending a shiver up Kate's spine. Kate knew that laugh—not insolent, as Skyler's teachers at school insisted. It was just Skyler's way, when

brought short by some well-meaning but clearly misguided adult, of showing that she knew better.

But too often there was a gap between what Skyler
believed she could handle and what she actually *could.*
An image flashed through Kate's mind: Skyler darting
across the avenue in midtown Manhattan during rush
hour to rescue an injured pigeon. Six years old, dodg-
ing cars and taxis, ignoring her mother's screams as
Kate dashed after her.

Now it was Duncan whose shouts Skyler was ignoring as she brought Cricket around in a direct line with
the jump. Head up, measuring the pony's stride, giving
him the correct signals—she was so damn *good,* it
didn't seem fair to hold her back. Even as Kate's own
cry of "Don't!" fought its way free of her throat, she
was aware of a familiar tingle spreading through her,
a ghost of the adrenaline rush she used to get when
approaching a jump.

But along with the remembered thrill, the old terror
shot a cold bolt through her chest. She gripped the
fence so tightly that she could feel its rough edges
driving tiny splinters into her palm.

Kate sucked in a deep breath of air seasoned with
the smell of manure and tan bark. *Four and a half
feet,* she told herself. At last month's Pony Club rally,
in the under-twelve jumper class, Skyler had taken a
vertical almost that high. And she not only just made
it over, but added a red ribbon to the blue she'd won
in the point-to-point.

Kate nevertheless found her eye straying to the cane
propped against the fence post where she stood. Made
of plain mahogany, it was sturdy and unpretentious.
It didn't draw attention to her physical limitations; it
merely served as a reminder of the crippling accident
that had resulted, through a bizarre flip-flop of fate,
in their adopting Skyler. A kind of talisman.

But no talisman was going to protect her now, she
thought, watching in helpless, terrified awe as her

daughter urged her pony in to the oxer. Kate, her heart in her throat, watched Skyler lean forward slightly, one hand grabbing a handful of mane, the other forming a bridge with the reins across the pony's crest. Her heels were down, and her little acorn of a bottom rose just enough for a child's fist to have comfortably fit between the saddle and the leather seat of her breeches.

But the damn pony wasn't focusing. With the jump half a stride off, he picked up with a sudden burst of speed ... rushing it ... then braking inches from the first rail and cutting sharply to the left.

In horror, Kate watched her eight-year-old cannon from the saddle, and fly headfirst into the wing stand with a sickening crack.

For a long, dreadful moment, Skyler didn't move. Then, in a quick movement that was more a spasm, she rolled into a sitting position. Her helmet was off, Kate saw. Its chin strap must have popped with the force of the impact.

Kate's paralyzed heart squeezed out a beat. "Don't move!" she yelled.

But Skyler was already on her feet, tottering unsteadily. She took two steps before collapsing, her slender form folding downward with a weird grace, like a dress slipping off its hanger.

Kate fumbled with the latch and was through the gate. Ignoring the pain that sluiced through her left leg like kerosene, she ran ... faster than she would have believed possible, her shadow lurching out over the tanbark. Faster even than Duncan, whom she could see out of the corner of her eye loping in her direction.

By the time she reached the small figure lying unconscious near the center of the ring, Kate's leg and hip were on fire. It would have been agony just to lower herself into a chair, but without a moment's hesitation she was on her hands and knees.

Skyler, sprawled on her back, looked queerly flattened somehow . . . and so pale, her mouth an ashy thumbprint in a face the color of bleached bones. An angry red knot the size of a crab apple was forming just below her hairline. Kate, too stricken even to cry out, rocked back on her heels, a hand flying to her chest.

Please . . . O dear God let her be all right . . . please . . .

She was only peripherally aware of Duncan dropping down beside her as she stroked Skyler's hair where it had come loose from its ponytail. She smoothed back wisps as fine as goose down from Skyler's temples. "Sky. Listen to me, baby. You're going to be okay. Do you hear me? *You're going to be just fine.*"

She fixed her gaze on her daughter's still face, willing Skyler's mouth to twitch in the smile that always gave away her game of pretending to be asleep.

"Let me have a look."

At Duncan's clipped command, Kate shifted her gaze to the gaunt form hunkered alongside her. She watched as he expertly ran his hand down the limp arm angling from the sleeve of Skyler's blue-and-yellow Stony Creek Farm T-shirt. His silver-blue eyes, in the creased leather of his face, were bright and hard as buckles.

"Nothing broken." His gravelly voice with its Highlands cadence revealed not even a hint of the panic he surely must be feeling.

In the same way she'd often seen him run his hand down a horse's leg, feeling for a swollen knee or fetlock, or a hot hoof that might lead to lameness, Duncan applied feather-light touches to Skyler's rib cage and legs. Kate, calmed by the gentle motion of the trainer's knotted brown hand, felt her heartbeat slow a bit.

"She'll be fine. She *will.*" Kate heard in her own voice a desperate need to convince herself.

But there were no assurances to be had, and she knew it.

Kate instead found herself anchored by Duncan's steady gaze. "She's a hardheaded one," he said with gruff gentleness. "Like her mother. She'll come out of it all right."

It was that promise Kate clung to as the ambulance shrieked down Hickory Lane under the drowsy shade of spreading oaks, past Constable landscapes of horses and cows grazing in sunlit fields.

God, don't take her from me, she prayed even while cursing the winding road, unpaved in spots, preserved in all its rustic charm by her grandfather and Will's when they'd built their adjoining estates.

Staring down at her daughter's pale, still form strapped to the gurney, it all came rushing back—eight years ago, the morning Kate had innocently dropped by the Stop & Shop for a quart of milk ... and had walked away with a lifetime's supply of heartache. On her way out of the store, glancing at the newspapers stacked below the bulletin board, a frightening headline had caught her eye: PLEASE DON'T HURT MY BABY!

Furtively scanning the story about a distraught young mother whose baby girl had been kidnapped the week before, Kate had grown so dizzy that one of the checkers, Louise Myers, had insisted on escorting her to the employees' lounge. But even sitting down, with a wad of paper towels soaked in cold water pressed to her forehead, Kate had felt her head spin as she refused to accept what her heart knew: the baby girl she and Will had taken home with them just days ago—the blond, blue-eyed angel they'd fallen instantly, passionately in love with—didn't belong to them after all. Their lawyer claimed she'd been found abandoned in a Lower East Side tenement with no birth certificate, no papers of any kind, to identify her; but in truth she was the child of a woman who very much wanted her back.

A closer look at the grainy photo of mother and child that accompanied the article had only confirmed Kate's suspicion.

Oh, how easily deceived she and Will had been! Too dazed by their good fortune to look any further than the sweet-faced infant swaddled in a pink blanket. More questions might have led to answers they didn't want to hear. And, anyway, why should they have doubted their lawyer? Grady Singleton wasn't some sleazy Hell's Kitchen practitioner; he had offices on Wall Street and had come highly recommended by Kate's father. And the document he'd showed them seemed legitimate—an order signed by a judge.

Instead, gazing rapturously at the pink bundle in her arms, Kate had told herself, *She was meant for us all along.* Four years before, when she'd fallen from her horse going over a vertical at the Hampton Classic, she'd done more than smash her leg. She'd lost the baby she was carrying as well. After the surgery, when she'd been told she would never have another child, Kate had fallen into a depression so deep that whole days would go by when she couldn't get out of bed. Back then, she would not have believed she could ever feel this blessed.

They named her Skyler, after Kate's grandmother, Lucinda Skyler Dawson.

A sharp swerve drove Kate's shoulder into the side of the ambulance with a painful thump. She sat up straight and looked out the window. They'd passed through the village with its quaint Victorian-style shops and eateries, and were fast approaching the south side of town, where the parklike grounds of Northfield Community Hospital loomed like an oasis.

At the red-curbed emergency entrance, the ambulance lurched to a halt. Then hands, so many hands, stirring the air around her, adjusting straps, lowering the collapsible stretcher, lifting, pushing. Hands under

Kate's elbow, steadying her, as Skyler's motionless form was whisked down a fluorescent-lit corridor.

Watching her daughter disappear from view, Kate stopped short as abruptly as a bird smacking into a windowpane.

Leaning heavily on her cane to blunt the spur of pain that had settled into her hip, she had to force herself to move, slogging her way through what felt like knee-deep ditch water as she made her way past the half-dozen or so patients clustered near the admitting desk. Behind the counter, a heavyset woman in a light-blue smock coat was helping an elderly man with a form that seemed to be taking him forever to fill out. Kate felt like screaming.

Mercifully, she was spared from doing so by the appearance of a second clerk, a curly-haired young woman with a chipped front tooth. As soon as Kate uttered her last name, nodding wearily in response to raised eyebrows, and saying yes, *that* Sutton, she was briskly escorted down the hall. When she was younger, it had bothered Kate a great deal, the obsequiousness of the villagers. But she was used to it by now, and at this moment profoundly grateful to Will's great-grandfather, Leland Sutton, for having bequeathed to the township, along with an endowment of three hundred million, the land on which Northfield Community Hospital had been built.

But no amount of family influence could protect Kate against the panic that mounted with each labored step as she neared the waiting area outside Radiology. Limping past cozy groupings of sofas and chairs, she lowered herself onto the molded plastic seat of a pay phone as if it were a lifeboat.

Will. She had to reach Will somehow.

Kate struggled to remember the complicated codes for England before giving up and dialing the operator, to whom she recited the number for the London office of Sutton, Jamesway & Falk.

No answer. When she remembered the five-hour time difference, she called the Savoy, but Will wasn't at his hotel either. Hanging up, Kate wanted to put her head down and cry.

If only someone would tell her what was happening. It was bad, she knew. But just *how* bad?

Fear surged in on a riptide. *I'm being punished. I kept quiet even after I knew she'd been stolen. Now she's being taken away from* me.

Kate had no idea how long she sat there in her tanbark-flecked khaki trousers and red-and-white checked shirt, hands knuckled over the curved handle of her cane. It could have been minutes or hours. When the sandy-haired doctor in the white lab coat appeared before her, she blinked in surprise, as if she'd been caught napping.

Skyler's injury, Kate was informed in a somber tone, had resulted in an epidural hematoma. She would need immediate surgery to relieve pressure on her brain.

As she and and her daughter were whisked off in a LifeFlight helicopter, Kate felt as if she'd been plucked up by a cyclone like Dorothy. It might have been some mythical land where witches and monsters dwelled that they were being ferried to, not Langdon Pediatric on East Eighty-fourth Street in Manhattan.

Dr. Westerhall, the pediatric neurosurgeon, was there to meet them when they arrived. Compact, barrel-bodied, with clipped gray hair, he made Kate think of a general striding briskly along a corridor of the Pentagon. His firm, dry handclasp was like an injection of some strong sedative. Lulled by the confidence in his voice, she had difficulty absorbing what he was saying about the techniques and risks involved in this type of surgery. She merely nodded, as if she'd understood every word, all the while thinking, *I don't care how you do it, just save her, goddammit, save her.*

Two hours later, Kate sat on the sofa in the waiting

area across from the nurses' station on Eleven West, sipping a cardboard cup of vending-machine coffee she didn't want—it was just something to do.

She'd tried calling Miranda, but had gotten the damn machine instead. Then she'd remembered the estate auction in Greenwich, at which Miranda planned to bid on a Hunzinger chair that had caught her eye in *Arts and Antiques Weekly*. She had to be on her way there now, hurrying madly because she'd waited until the last possible moment before giving up on Kate, who'd promised to be back in time to take over at the shop.

Kate briefly considered calling her mother, but couldn't seem to muster the energy. Mother would just make this harder for her, demanding to know what was being done, and by whom, and was this Dr. Westerhall *anybody they knew*? In other words, was he one of the elite Park Avenue specialists sought out by her circle of friends?

Kate couldn't have stood it. She had only enough strength for Skyler.

"You must either be a masochist or have a cast-iron stomach."

Kate looked up into a pair of startling blue eyes in the pretty face of a fair-haired young woman in a pale green dress. She looked vaguely familiar, with her striking cheekbones and rather square jaw. Did she work here? She wasn't wearing a smock or a badge, but her upbeat tone and the warmth of her smile immediately eliminated her from the ranks of the distraught parents Kate had seen drifting about like ghosts.

With a weary sigh, Kate set her coffee cup down on the low table in front of her. "I wasn't really drinking it," she said.

"Can I get you something else? A cold drink maybe?"

Kate sensed she was about to receive some sort of

news ... and prayed it wasn't going to be bad. Why else would this woman be hovering over her so solicitously?

"No, thank you," she said.

"I'm Ellie Nightingale ... psych department. You're Mrs. Sutton, aren't you?" The young woman put out her hand, which felt firm and capable in Kate's grip. "Dr. Westerhall thought you might need someone to talk to."

Kate felt herself stiffen. Did the surgeon know something he hadn't told her ... something that might cause her to fall apart?

Reason quickly asserted itself. Any news that bad, Dr. Westerhall would have delivered in person.

"It's not *me* I'm worried about ... it's my daughter," Kate said, unable to keep a sharp note from her voice.

"I'd be worried, too."

Ellie Nightingale's response, though far from encouraging, was so refreshingly honest that Kate felt herself relax the tiniest bit. "You don't sound like a shrink," she said with a small smile. Upon closer inspection, Ellie didn't look old enough to be one, either. She couldn't have been more than twenty-six or -seven.

Ellie shot her a wry grimace. "I'm doing an externship here for my master's. If I ever *do* start sounding like a shrink I promise I'll rethink my career—something where the *P* in Ph.D. doesn't stand for *pompous*." She sat down in the chair across from Kate, smoothing back shoulder-length hair the rich color of polished oak. A pair of dangly earrings swayed from her earlobes. "Feel like some company?"

"Not particularly," Kate told her, mildly taken aback by her own lack of manners.

Ellie must have caught her expression, for she smiled and said lightly, "Don't worry, I'm not offended."

"I don't mean to be rude."

"You're not. You're a mother, is all. You must be scared sick."

Kate looked at her as if seeing her for the first time. It was a surprise, finding someone so straightforward in a hospital, where everyone talked either down to you or over your head.

"My daughter is going to be *fine*," she stated. Softening, she added, "But thanks. I appreciate your concern."

"Would it help you to know that I think Dr. Westerhall is absolutely the best there is?" Ellie sounded sincere enough. "He performed the same operation on one of my husband's babies just last week, and the little guy is going home tomorrow."

Kate looked at her, confused.

"Paul's a resident in the NICU—neonatal intensive care unit," Ellie explained.

"I see."

She saw Ellie look at her cane. Unlike most people, who looked away quickly rather than embarrass her with their curiosity, the young woman gazed at it frankly.

"How did it happen?" she asked.

For a foggy second, Kate thought she meant Skyler; then she realized Ellie meant *her* injury. "Riding accident," she said. When she saw that Ellie's attention hadn't wavered and that she wasn't asking merely to be polite, Kate went on. "I was competing in the Hampton Classic—it was going to be my last show for a while. I was four months pregnant, you see." She took a deep breath. "It had been raining, and the grounds were muddy. My horse slipped and went right through one of the fences. I don't remember much after that. . . . I'm told he came down on top of me. Smashed nearly every bone in my leg."

"It's a miracle you didn't lose the baby."

Kate opened her mouth to correct the misunderstanding, to say that Skyler was not the baby she'd been expecting, then realized she'd already said far more than this perfect stranger needed to know.

Instead, she merely nodded.

Something was tugging at the back of her mind—something she couldn't quite put her finger on. She couldn't shake the feeling that she *did* know this woman, and not from here. From another time ...

"Do you have children?" Kate asked to be polite, though she wasn't terribly interested one way or the other.

A shadow seemed to pass over Ellie's pretty, high-cheekboned face. "I did ... a daughter." She didn't elaborate. Clearing her voice, she sat back and said brightly, "Paul and I plan on starting a family when he's finished his residency and I'm done with school—but that might be a while."

Suddenly, it struck Kate. In her mind, she saw the clipping, now a yellowing relic tucked away in a seldom-opened book in her library at home. A name she'd buried just as deep in her own memory surfaced with a sharp sting of recognition.

Ellie. That young mother's name had been Ellie, too. Different last name ... but she hadn't been married then.

I had a daughter. ...

Dear God ... *could* it be?

No, of course not, Kate told herself. Such coincidences happened only in movies and paperback novels. Granted, there was a resemblance. But the news photo had been grainy, and eight years had passed since then. The girl whose anguish had been so vividly captured in that shot might not look anything like that now.

And ye: ...

Kate thought of her silent prayers over the years, her pleas for God's forgiveness for what she'd done, the terrible sin she'd committed in keeping Skyler from her true mother. How she'd longed for some way to know what had become of that young girl.

As Kate stared at Ellie Nightingale, she became aware of a peculiar tingling sensation spreading across her scalp. She pressed a hand to her throat, where a pulse was jumping wildly.

Stop this, she scolded herself. *You're overwrought, that's all. Imagining things. In this city alone there must be hundreds of women in their twenties named Ellie.*

Yet at the same time, absurdly, Kate thought of that old chestnut of a horror story circulated at every slumber party of her junior high years: a girl alone at home on a dark night hears noises, and runs about locking and bolting every door and window in sight ... only to realize the escaped lunatic is *in the house.*

Had she been fooling herself into thinking she could hide from something there was no escaping from—something that quite possibly was destined?

Gripped by a sudden, morbid need to know, Kate found herself blurting, "Do you mind my asking what happened to your daughter?" She held her breath, feeling it quiver like something small and defenseless tucked under a folded wing.

Ellie didn't answer right away. She crossed her legs, then uncrossed them. Finally, folding her arms over her chest, she replied in a soft voice, "She was kidnapped."

Kate felt her heart become still as glass. "I'm sorry." She spoke in an almost inaudible whisper. "It must have been awful for you."

"It was like the end of the world." Ellie gave her a look of such exquisite sorrow Kate wanted desperately to back away, as if from a fire she'd started that had flared out of control.

Ellie passed a hand over her face, as if adjusting a mask that had tilted askew. While Kate sat utterly still, her heart poised on the brink of shattering, the young woman in the pale green dress, who quite prob-

ably was the mother of her daughter, rose to her feet
with a contrite look.

"Listen, I have to go," she apologized. "But if you
need me for anything, I'll be around the rest of the
day. You can have me paged."

An odd, etherlike calm invaded Kate, which she recognized in some distant part of her mind as quite possibly the onset of hysteria. It took every shred of will
she possessed to keep all her crumbling pieces pressed
into some semblance of a whole.

"Thanks. I just might," she lied.

Even while she sat there, stricken with remorse for
what she'd robbed this woman of, Kate thought, *If she
tried to take Skyler back now, I'd stop her any way I
could.* For she had plucked from the tree of knowledge, and could no longer lull herself into thinking
Skyler's real mother was safely hidden in some faraway place. She would have to guard her daughter
against this smiling blond woman who—*Oh, how
could I have missed it?*—looked so much like Skyler.
Even while a part of her longed to sink to her knees
before Ellie and beg her forgiveness, Kate wanted her
gone . . . out of their lives for good.

She flinched as Ellie innocently said, "If I don't hear
from you, I'll stop by tomorrow and see how your
daughter is doing. She'll be out of the recovery room
by then, I'm sure."

Before Kate could protest, she was gone. Watching
her round the corner, tall and leggy as Skyler would
one day be, Kate slumped back. She felt drained and
flat, as bloodless as a chalk outline on a carpet.

If only Will were here, she thought.

Yes, and what help would he be? a peevish voice
carped.

Her mind flew back to the long-ago day when she
had confronted Will with her suspicions about Skyler's
real mother. Her principled husband—the man who
once showed a dinner guest to the door for telling a

crude racist joke. Will had grown so violently upset
by the idea, the very *idea* of Skyler belonging to someone else, that without a word he'd turned his back
on Kate and walked out the door. He'd returned the
following morning, unshaven, disheveled, fixing her
with red-rimmed eyes that seemed to accuse her of a
crime she had no memory of committing. "We won't
talk about this ever again," he'd said in a voice of
such deadly quiet that she'd felt her blood turn to ice.

And they hadn't. Will tended to business; under his
shrewd management, the real estate firm founded by
his father had tripled its revenues over the last decade.
He was also a good husband in most ways, loyal and
considerate . . . even if she was often left frustrated by
his unwillingness to discuss anything that was bothering her for which he didn't have an instant, concrete solution.

So that she alone had been left to tend the eternal
flame of their unspeakable crime. She alone had
kept watch.

And now it was up to her to ward off the destiny that
had found its way in through the locked door of her silence and was threatening what she cherished most.

Somewhere around eight that evening, Dr. Westerhall
appeared like a tired angel in wrinkled green scrubs,
and delivered Kate from her purgatory. Skyler had
pulled through the surgery, he told her, and showed
every indication of making a full recovery. Kate,
weeping with exhaustion and relief, tried once again to
phone Will in London. Almost before she had finished
telling him about Skyler, he was racing to catch the
next plane home.

He arrived early the following morning, and the moment he strode into Skyler's private room on the ninth
floor, in the carpeted, antiques-furnished Thompson
Pavilion, Kate felt her body sag with relief. She'd

spent the previous night on a lumpy cot next to their
daughter's bed, and every bone and muscle ached.
Now, as she looked into her husband's worried face,
suddenly she couldn't bear another moment of enduring this on her own.

"Oh!" she cried. "Oh, Will, thank God you're
here." She hugged him, not minding the strong odor
of an unshowered man who'd been in a nervous panic
for the past eight hours.

Will's eyes were bloodshot, and his suit looked
every bit as slept-in as her own rumpled clothes. But
what a welcome sight! His dear face with its strong
features and the faint scar over one eyebrow where
he'd accidentally been struck, at age nine, with a garden rake wielded by the precocious seven-year-old girl
next door—the same girl he would one day marry.

"Jesus, to think I was sitting in that goddamn club
sipping brandy with Lord What's-His-Face, and all I was
thinking about was how I could get some kind of a
commitment from him on this City Island project . . ."
He stopped, scrubbing his face with one hand.

The City Island Riverview project, Kate knew, was
one of the biggest that Will's firm had ever handled—
a multimillion-dollar development that would entail
tearing down and rebuilding a huge section of waterfront. Financially, the firm was in deep, *too* deep—
and now it seemed as if the British investment group
they'd been counting on might back out. How it must
have looked to the Brits, Will running off in the middle of negotiations! Only now, with Skyler out of the
woods, could Kate allow herself to spare a pang of
worry about what it might mean for the firm—and for
them—if this deal fell through.

She helped him off with his jacket, saying quietly,
"There was nothing you could have done. Anyway,
the important thing is she's going to be okay." Kate
couldn't even bring herself to speak the words Dr.
Westerhall had used, phrases like "no permanent

damage" and "every indication of unimpaired motor skills." Just the *idea* of any damage or impairment was unthinkable.

Will was looking anxiously at their daughter, who was asleep in the bed, an IV line attached to her arm, her head turbaned in gauze that made her look like the world's smallest rajah.

"Has she come out of it yet?" he asked in a hushed voice.

"A few hours ago, but she was pretty groggy," Kate told him. "I just held her, and she fell right back to sleep."

Will went over and sank down in the chair beside Skyler's bed. Ever so gently, he brushed her forehead—the part of it that wasn't bandaged—before leaning forward and dropping his cheek onto her small sun-browned hand. Tears stood in his eyes.

Kate waited several minutes before stealing up alongside him and placing her hand on his shoulder. "Remember the very first time I put her up on a horse?" she remembered aloud. "She couldn't have been more than two. The look on her face . . . it was Christmas in July. She screamed when I tried to take her off. She would have stayed in that saddle for hours, just being led around the ring on a longe line."

He looked up at her, blinking hard. "Kate," he said, his voice breaking.

Her fingers convulsed, grabbing a handful of his shirt. "I know, I know. But she's all right now."

She thought briefly of telling Will about Ellie, but just as quickly rejected the idea. He would only accuse her of imagining things, and even if he *did* believe her, what good would it do for both of them to worry? No, better simply to let Will do what he did best— take charge of concrete situations, ask the right questions and get solid answers.

Now, by the sudden determined set of his face as he stood up, she could see that that was exactly what he planned on doing. "I'd like to have a word with this Dr. Westerhall," he said in his most commanding voice. "I put a call in to the chief neurologist at Boston Children's Hospital on my way in from JFK. We may want to fly him down for a consult." He started for the door.

"I don't know if that's really nec—" Kate started to protest.

Will made a familiar leveling gesture with his hand. "Look, Kate, I'm sure Westerhall is competent, but it wouldn't hurt to have a second opinion." He spoke quietly, with a confidence born of years of knowing what he wanted, and usually managing to get it.

If only he could be that good and strong in other ways, she found herself wishing. *Ways that have more to do with healing than with fixing.*

The instant Will was out of the room, she stretched out on her cot, intending to close her eyes just until he got back. She was so tired. More tired than she remembered being after any of her four operations, when she hadn't believed it possible there could be enough bones in her leg and hip for all the steel pins required to hold them in place. As she drifted asleep, she thought, *But I survived . . . and so will Skyler.*

Kate was jerked away by a familiar sound—the voice that from the very beginning, when it was nothing more than a cry, never failed to snatch her from the soundest of sleeps.

". . . Eight," she heard Skyler pipe. "My birthday's the week before Mickey's. She's my best friend." The words were slurred, as if she were still half-asleep.

Kate jerked upright, brought instantly to full consciousness by the sight of her daughter propped nearly upright against a throne of pillows . . . and the slender blond woman who was perched on the bed beside her.

Kate watched Skyler take a tentative sip from the cup of water Ellie Nightingale held to her daughter's lips. *I'm dreaming this,* she thought. But no dream had ever affected her this way, gripping her heart and bringing a rush of stinging acid to her throat.

Skyler saw her sitting up and gave a wan smile. "Mommy." She was very pale, with purplish bruises under her eyes, her voice little more than a froggy whisper.

"Oh, sweetie." Kate lurched forward with a muffled cry, gathering Skyler to her as gently as she could manage.

"I hurt, Mommy. I hurt all over." Skyler quivered in her arms, sounding as if she was trying hard not to cry.

"It's okay, baby," Kate soothed, close to tears herself. "You're going to be okay, I promise. Everything's fine now. You fell and hurt yourself, but you're going to be all better in no time."

"I know. That's what *she* said." Skyler smiled at Ellie, and drooped back against the pillows.

Kate tried not to stare, but she couldn't help it. *They look so much alike.* God, didn't the woman see it? How could she not?

"She was just waking up when I stopped in," Ellie told Kate. "I didn't want to disturb you."

"It was nice of you to remember us," Kate thanked her, mentally blessing her mother for the early training that enabled her to keep even her most powerful feelings under wraps—a talent that came as automatically to her as breathing.

"My pleasure." Ellie placed the plastic drinking cup on the table next to the bed. Her smile, as she looked over Skyler's head at Kate, was almost wistful. "She's really a very special little girl. You're lucky to have her."

Kate's heart did a long, slow free fall. "Yes, I know." She saw that Skyler was trying to say something, and she leaned close to hear.

"Mommy, is Cricket okay, too?"

"He's absolutely fine." She hadn't the slightest idea

if the pony was all right or not; she hadn't given him a moment's thought.

Satisfied, Skyler let her eyes drift shut. "Mommy . . . ?" she murmured, not finishing the sentence.

"I'm here," Kate choked. "Daddy, too. He'll be back any minute."

Ellie got up and smoothed her skirt—today she was wearing a pale gold top and a blue skirt that perfectly matched her eyes. The light glanced off a gold hoop earring as she dropped her head to one side to tuck a stray wisp behind her ear.

Skyler muttered something . . . something that sounded like "Don't go," and for a stricken instant Kate didn't know if she meant her or Ellie.

"I'm glad everything worked out all right for you," Ellie told Kate on her way out.

Kate took the firm hand Ellie offered her, and allowed herself the dangerous luxury of meeting Ellie's frank, compelling gaze. She felt the circle closing, wrapping as tightly about her as a noose. They were joined in some awful, immutable way, just as she had always, from the beginning, feared they would one day be.

While her every cell screamed *Leave us alone, don't ever come back!,* she found herself remarking in a voice pitched low with barely restrained passion, "She's very precious to her father and me. I would die if I ever lost her."

"No, you wouldn't," Ellie said with the simple conviction of someone who knew all too well. "But I'm glad you won't have to find that out."

Kate gave a grim smile, and, hating herself as thoroughly as she'd ever hated any human being, buried the knife that only she could see deep in Ellie's heart.

"Not if I can help it," she said.

CHAPTER 2

On Skyler Sutton's seventeenth birthday, two things happened.

The first was that she lost her virginity, in the boathouse of her parents' summer place on Cape Cod, to Prescott Fairchild, a sophomore at Yale and the son of old family friends. She cried a little, and bled a lot ... but on the whole, she decided, it had been a pretty good experience, considering she wasn't in love with Prescott.

The second thing, entirely unrelated (or so she thought), was that she stopped wishing on candles, and made a vow instead: to find out the whole truth about her mother.

Over the years, Skyler had been consumed with longing to know about her real mother. She'd fantasized about a strange woman appearing at her front door, sobbing and saying it had all been a ghastly mistake; she'd only meant to leave Skyler alone for a minute while she dashed to the store. The story Skyler invented was that her mother had been hit by a speeding taxi on her way home and had spent months in a coma, only to regain consciousness and find her baby daughter gone for good.

Other times, Skyler saw herself tracking the woman down . . . and being given the cold shoulder. Her mother would look at her with dead eyes and say she wanted no part of her, she *never* had.

Either way, Skyler had to know what lay behind the story she'd been told, gently and lovingly, by her parents when she was six: that she'd been found abandoned in a tenement by a mother who'd left no forwarding address.

When she was little, her fears had taken the form of nightmares, from which she'd awake in a cocoon of twisted damp sheets, flailing and sobbing. Nightmares about being left alone . . . wandering a dark street, calling for her mother . . . being chased by shadowy dark figures. She'd outgrown the bad dreams, but they'd been replaced by something even worse: the awful suspicion that her parents were keeping something from her, something too dreadful for words.

Skyler had seen it in Mom's eyes—something deep and furtive and fraught with pain. She'd sensed it, too, in the way Daddy always became too busy to talk whenever the subject of her adoption was raised.

But no matter how bad it is, it can't be any worse than being in the dark.

The thought entered her mind as she was squatting on the concrete floor of the Stony Creek stable, winding an elastic traveling bandage about her horse's left leg. The sun hadn't yet come up, and even though the weather was mild she found herself shivering. It had been exactly one week since her birthday. And in exactly three hours she would be competing in the junior jumper division at the Ballyhew Charity Horse Show in Salem, a half hour's drive from Northfield. But that wasn't what was making her so nervous. What had Skyler's stomach in knots was wondering how she was going to approach her mom.

She had been putting it off until after the show; with her nerves already stretched to the breaking point, Skyler didn't dare risk a scene that might upset them both. Besides, she'd waited all these years. What was one more day?

Even so, her hands moved with unfamiliar awkwardness, and her stomach felt like a wet rag being wrung out. She couldn't stop thinking about the Big Talk she had planned on having with her mom tonight.

What had happened with Prescott, she admitted now to herself, probably had something to do with bringing all this to a head. Afterward, lying under him in the cool of the boathouse, staring up at the reflected water shimmering across the pitched ceiling, she'd felt an odd connectedness to her real mother. Had it been like this for *her* the first time? Had she been a teenager, whose only mistake had been to get pregnant?

Skyler fastened the bandage just below the hock, then straightened and delivered a pat to her horse's rump. This early, the stable was nearly deserted, except for Duncan and one of the grooms, whom she could hear whistling off in the hayloft. Watery sunlight leaked through the chinks in the barn door where some of the boards didn't quite meet, and the dust-streaked window over the feed bins glowed a pale amber. A bucket rattled somewhere. At the far end of the double row of stalls, she could hear the stamp of hooves, and Mickey swearing—her friend's horse was notorious for jerking his head when she was putting on his halter.

Skyler walked in a slow circle around her own horse, tethered by cross-ties to the scarred tongue-and-groove walls on either side of the grooming area. Chancellor, his mane tightly braided and his chestnut coat brushed to a polish, cast a reproachful eye at her as she reached up to straighten his head collar. He knew what all this fuss was about, and there was nothing he disliked more than being trapped in a horse

trailer and carted to a show over miles of twisting
country road. He scraped a hoof over the concrete
floor indignantly, and tossed his head hard enough to
rattle the cross-tie chains.

"Look, it's no good getting yourself all worked up ...
you're going, and that's that," she scolded affectionately. "Besides, you're not the only one who's nervous. You think *I'm* not scared shitless?"

The A-rated Ballyhew Charity Horse Show was the
most prestigious she'd ever competed in. She and
Mickey would be up against some of the best jumpers
in the area. They couldn't afford a single misstep.

"Trailers are out front. You about ready?"

Mickey, leading her Appaloosa, emerged from the
gloom of the corridor that ran between the double
row of stalls. In her breeches and denim shirt rolled
up at the sleeves, an unlit cigarette stuck at a jaunty
angle in a corner of her mouth, she looked older
than seventeen.

"Chance is having second thoughts," Skyler told her
friend, watching his ears flatten as she tossed a traveling blanket onto his back.

"I would be, too, if I were him," Mickey challenged
with a husky laugh as she lit her cigarette with a
smudged old Bic lighter. "Carousel's going to whip his
ass and he knows it." Her dark hair was its usual
tousled mop, and her eyes, the rich blue-black of
plums, regarded Skyler with amusement.

"Oh, yeah? Who took first in the green hunter division at Twin Lakes?"

"That was only because Carousel threw a shoe."

"That's not all he threw, the way I remember it."
Skyler laughed, recalling how the Appaloosa had gone
into a bucking frenzy and tossed Mickey into a hedge.

But Mickey's grin, far from sheepish, seemed to
flash with challenge. *"You're* the one who's running
scared, admit it. You know I'm going to leave you in
the dust."

They'd been like this since their Pony Club days, but if anyone else had dared taunt either of them that way, he or she would have had two females to fight off instead of one. She and Mickey had practically grown up together at Stony Creek, and Skyler loved her the way she would have loved a sister.

"Keep talking—maybe you'll convince yourself," Skyler tossed over her shoulder as she pushed open the wide double doors and led her horse out into the yard.

Two pickups with Kingston trailers hooked to their rear bumpers idled in the parking area just beyond the gravel turnabout. The drivers of the trucks were leaning against the fence, smoking cigarettes and drinking coffee from foam cups. Skyler paused to take a breath of air fragrant with cut grass, looking out at the tree-lined horizon, over which the sun was just now rising. Its golden light sparkled off the dew in the pasture, and lent the weathered outbuildings the mellow glow of buttered toast. In the schooling ring, where a boy in shorts and tank top was hosing down the tanbark, a fine mist of droplets had sent up a perfect, storybook rainbow.

Skyler experienced a moment of utter serenity before the thought of her real mother, like a blister rubbing on her heel, intruded.

"I wonder if she's still alive."

She hadn't realized she'd spoken aloud until Mickey tipped her a slanted gaze through a drifting scrim of cigarette smoke. "Who?"

"My real mother." Skyler's tone hardened. "The one who thought I was such a precious darling, she decided to leave me as a present for the landlord."

"What made you think of *her* just now?"

"I don't know." Skyler paused, feeling that queer wringing sensation in her stomach again. "I guess I can't help wondering what she would think if she could see me now. I mean, would she be proud of me? Would she even *care*?"

Mickey gave her a long, measuring look as she sucked on her cigarette and sent a lazy stream of smoke up into the cool blue of the sky that would be searing hot by midday. This wasn't the first time Skyler had shared with her friend her innermost thoughts about her real mother . . . and it wouldn't be the last. Mickey understood that there could be no answers to questions that held no logic.

"It could be worse. At least you got two out of three," she said with a sanguine shrug. "My own flesh-and-blood parents don't give a shit about me, but you have a mom and dad who think you walk on water."

Skyler thoughtfully stroked the clipped silk of Chancellor's neck.

The bitter truth was that with every jump she soared over, every ribbon she went after, it wasn't just the desire to win spurring her on—it was her mother. As if Skyler could somehow prove to her—the woman who'd fed her, changed her diapers, rocked her to sleep . . . then just walked away—that she *was* worth something.

As she and Mickey led their horses over to the waiting trailers, Skyler felt Chancellor start to pull back.

"Give it up, Chance," Skyler growled as she tugged on his lead line.

But when they reached the aluminum ramp propped against the rear gate of the first trailer, Chancellor put on the brakes. He stood there looking at her until Skyler dug into her pocket with a sigh and produced a stub of carrot. Holding it in front of him, she didn't let him have it until he'd been coaxed up the ramp into the trailer.

She thought then of Mom—would she be so easily coaxed into revealing what she'd hidden so well all these years? Climbing into the backseat of Duncan's dusty Wagoneer alongside Mickey, Skyler sent up a silent prayer that she would succeed in getting her mother to open up.

On their way to Route 22, driving through the main street of the village with its white clapboard shops and Victorian-inspired street lamps, she waved to Miranda, who stood outside the former carriage house that was Mom's shop, watering the impatiens in the cast-iron planter. Miranda, model-thin and outfitted, as always, like an ad in a J. Crew catalogue, waved back. She was used to holding down the fort in the summer and fall while Kate followed the show-jumping circuit as Skyler's own one-woman cheerleading squad.

This morning, Kate had gone on ahead to nail down a good seat in the stands. Skyler smiled to herself, unable to remember a time when her mom hadn't been there for her. Like the time Mom had volunteered nearly every flower in her precious garden for the float Skyler's Brownie troop had fashioned for the Veterans Day parade. And after Skyler's operation, when she'd been bedridden for more than a week, Mom had spent hours and hours reading to her and helping her put together a scrapbook of horse pictures from magazines.

Mickey's right; I am *lucky,* she thought. And not just because she had terrific parents. Growing up here, she'd had every advantage as well, without being spoiled.

Northfield, just twelve miles northwest of Greenwich with its mansions and four-car garages, was the kind of place where money played itself down rather than showed itself off. None of the parents of the girls Skyler had gone to school with drove fancy European cars or cared particularly about designer labels. They turned their noses up at the faux-English country decor that was the current vogue, and would have stayed home rather than tow a heap of monogrammed luggage around Europe. They plopped catsup bottles down on fine antique dining tables, and tromped over two-hundred-year-old Turkish rugs in mud-caked riding boots. No sofa was off-limits to the dogs that spent an equal amount of time lolling about barns and pastures. And the talk at the dinner table wasn't about who was worth more than whom, but about a three-year-old filly that showed a lot of promise, or who had won the cup at Gladstone, or whether or not Lake Placid would be rained out again this year.

What made her own mom different, in Skyler's mind, wasn't just that she walked with a cane, but that she had suffered. The pain was always there, showing in the fine lines around her eyes and mouth, glinting behind every smile like the point of a very sharp knife. Mom never complained, or even spoke of it ... but then, she was good at keeping secrets.

What secret is she keeping about my real mother? What horrible thing is responsible for that dark look behind her eyes whenever I raise the subject?

Staring out the car window at the countryside rolling past, Skyler hoped with all her heart that she was doing the right thing in opening this particular Pandora's box.

The Ballyhew Charity Horse Show, held every August, was famous as a showcase for new talent. And by midday, both Skyler and Mickey had done well enough in the preliminaries to be up for the timed amateur-owner/junior jump-off.

As Skyler rode her horse out of the warm-up ring, she was less nervous than she'd expected to be. Skyler scanned the packed bleachers, hoping to catch sight of Kate. But there were too many people, and Chancellor was dancing around, making it hard for her to focus.

She trotted him over to the white-fenced events ring, with its cleverly designed jumps, and dropped back in the saddle, squeezing Chance to a halt just short of the bustle of activity by the in-gate—half a dozen grooms tightening girths and checking snaffle bits, trainers giving last-minute advice, riders guiding nervous horses in circles. The air was a dirty brown cloud of dust stirred by prancing hooves and pacing boots, the heat already unbearable though it wasn't even noon yet. In the distance, the pristine buildings and rolling green pastures of Ballyhew Farm shimmered like a tantalizing desert mirage.

Skyler leaned forward to stroke Chancellor's neck. He was edgy ... but so was she. A pulse leaped in her temple and she squeezed her eyes shut, willing it not to settle into a headache. Silently she urged, *Listen, Chance, this is the big one. We've got to ace it ... so take no prisoners, okay?*

She'd shown him last season, earning ribbons at A-rated shows and taking fourth place in the Maclay hunter seat equitation class at the Northeast Regionals. But at six, he was still young, and had a tendency to spook. Small, too. At fifteen-three hands, no more than an overgrown pony.

The thing was, Chancellor could jump. Boy, could he ever.

Skyler smiled, remembering the day, two years ago, when he'd first arrived at Orchard Hill. The Dutch-bred gelding that had been her fifteenth-birthday present had kicked down the door of his stall, shot out into the yard, and leaped a six-foot hedge.

But jumping in the field or schooling ring was a far cry from competition, she knew. And the shows they'd competed in so far had been a breeze compared to this.

In the preliminaries, Chancellor had picked up only three faults, for a refusal in the Six Bars, placing them among the nine who'd qualified for the jump-off out of a field of thirty-seven. If they won this—*Please, God*—she'd have enough points to enter the Zone I finals in South Hadley in September.

"Number eighteen, Lucky Penny, ridden by Amanda Harris ..."

The blaring of the loudspeaker sent Chancellor into a frenzied jig. Skyler shortened the reins, keeping him in a tight frame with her legs. There was no need to check the jumping order on the bulletin board by the in-gate. They'd posted the draw an hour ago, and she'd pulled second.

"We're next," she whispered.

Under her velvet-covered hunt cap, Skyler's scalp felt as if it were on fire. That stupid accident when she was eight had screwed up her wiring somehow; too much excitement put it on overload.

It didn't help, either, sitting out under the broiling August sun in a riding costume designed for the misty cool of England: breeches and black boots, a fitted navy gabardine jacket over a crisp white blouse with a monogrammed choker collar on which she'd pinned a small diamond brooch in the shape of a horseshoe.

She took a deep breath, and glanced over at Duncan, who stood planted in front of the bulletin board. He was squinting at the course diagram, his blue eyes screwed nearly shut, running a gnarled hand through the shock of gray hair that made her think of smoke drifting from a chimney. As if he didn't already know the course backward and forward . . . as if he hadn't walked it with her, measuring the number of strides before each jump, testing the rails in their cups, kneeling to feel the footing.

Now, catching her eye, he strode over, and without a word set about readjusting the curb chain on her bridle. Watching him, Skyler felt a prick of exasperation before she reminded herself that if it hadn't been for Duncan's careful schooling and eye for detail she probably wouldn't be here.

"He was having trouble with that last triple combination in the Fault and Out," Duncan told her. "He'll go for the corner on the nine-B oxer. Keep him dead center, if you can." His fierce blue eyes studied her a moment; then, as if satisfied with what he saw, he gave her a crisp nod.

"I'll do my best," Skyler said.

Anyway, it wasn't the triple that was worrying her. Her eye was on seven, a wall with a little liverpool in front of it—a rectangle of glistening blue, twelve feet long and two feet wide. A snap if your horse didn't happen to be deathly afraid of water.

As a colt, Chancellor had nearly drowned in a cow pond. Ever since, anything that looked, smelled, felt, or sounded like water had made him balk unless he could drink it from a bucket. She worked him all last summer, taking him over the creek below the stable, again and again, until June's trickle had risen to cover the stones in the bottom of the creek bed. Still, she never knew. . . .

In the opening class, the liverpool was the one jump Chancellor had refused. The same jump Lucky Penny was now taking with ease.

The bay had posted only two faults so far, for a hind foot knockdown on the triple spread. A clean jumper, but not a particularly fast one. As he cleared the last jump and passed through the timing beam at the exit gate, his time flashed on the electronic scoreboard overhead: 40.789seconds.

"Number thirty-eight," the announcer blared as Lucky Penny pranced from the ring, tossing his head. "Skyler Sutton on Chancellor . . ."

Skyler was as conscious of every eye in the bleachers and judges' box as if a spotlight had been turned on her. Two thousand spectators, looking at her, waiting for her to impress the hell out of them.

I have to win, she thought. Not just because it would prove that she was good . . . . but because it would be a good omen. If she took home the blue ribbon today, Skyler told herself, then nothing she found out about her real mother could be so terrible.

Duncan circled Chancellor one last time, checking

him from noseband to cantle before giving Skyler a nod. Granting her one of his rare smiles, he said gruffly, "Remember, it takes hard work to get lucky. You've worked hard. Now get lucky."

Not just lucky, but fast, she thought. *I've got to be faster than anyone.*

At the blare of the klaxon, Chancellor was through the gate like a missile shot from a silo. The first jump, a three-foot fence, he took as easily as a child skipping rope. Cross-rails; a double oxer: the chestnut soared over both with inches to spare.

You can do it, Chance . . . that's it. One more . . . now another . . .

He cleared the number five, a vertical sponsored by Grand Union Market, dressed up to look like a produce stand. His hooves had barely touched down when she squeezed him forward, urging him into the next jump, a wall topped by two rails. Going over it, he ticked the top rail with his foreleg, and it rattled in its cups. She felt a split-second flash of panic. But the rail held. *Yes.*

Coming at the next fence at too sharp an angle, Chance slewed to the right, and as he landed she had to pull him back, get him back on stride. More precious time lost. Skyler could feel it as acutely as she felt the sun that had papier-mâché'd her blouse to her back: each fraction of a second like blood draining from a severed vein.

She fixed her sights on the next jump—number seven. *Okay, here we go, fasten your seat belt—*

But as they approached the fence with its liverpool, Skyler felt the rolling cadence of his hooves shortening, bunching. *He knows . . . he's putting on the brakes. Oh, God.* The water loomed, and she thought, *Come on, Chance, you can do it. Come on.*

Using thigh and calf muscles she hadn't known she was equipped with, Skyler gripped with all her might, leaning over his neck, propelling Chancellor forward with a will that was almost physical—a thing he must have felt as surely as the boot legs pressing into his flanks, for all at once, blessedly, there it was, he was picking up his stride. Then rounding his back, springing up and over the gleaming rectangle of water, forelegs tucked under, bringing them home free.

The rest of the course seemed easy by comparison. Even the triple combination Duncan had warned her about—a staircase followed closely by two alternating oxers—didn't faze Chancellor. He sailed over them and galloped past the timing beam as if swept by the ocean wave of the crowd's roar.

A clear round!

On the scoreboard, Skyler caught a red flare of numbers out of the corner of her eye: 32.845 seconds. If no one else came in clear with a faster time, she'd be in first.

"He's a heartbreaker," called out one of the grooms at the exit gate, burly Russ Constantini. "That'll be a tough one to beat."

Skyler, still high on adrenaline, prayed he was right . . . that no one would better her time.

Allison Brentner, on her white Thoroughbred stallion, Silver Spurs, came in next at 34.032, posting six faults. Three refusals eliminated Good and Plenty, ridden by Nate London, in fourth. A fast run by Merry Maker was marred by sixteen faults, leaving his rider-owner, Anna MacAllister, in tears as she dismounted.

As Duncan and his head groom, Craig Losey, led Chancellor over to the stabling area, Skyler remained at the fence. Mickey was up next, and Skyler didn't want to miss this.

But something was wrong—the black gelding trotting into the ring wasn't Carousel, and the prissy-looking man astride it was *definitely* not Mickey. Skyler, feeling anxious, scanned the horses and riders in the warm-up ring. Where in God's name was Mickey?

After a brief search of the parking area and

grounds, she located her friend under one of the tents that served as a makeshift stable. But Mickey wasn't alone; the veterinarian was with her. Dr. Novick, a heavyset woman with a sandy braid as long and thick as a palomino's tail, was hunkered down in front of Carousel, gently palpating his right fetlock.

"Feels like a splint," she said.

Mickey stared at the vet, white-faced, looking as if she'd just picked herself up off the ground after a bad spill. Carousel's leg would heal in time, Skyler knew, but a bad splint could put him out of competition for months.

Skyler placed a gentling hand against the Appaloosa's flank and asked the question Mickey was too stricken to voice. "How bad is it?" She didn't have to ask how it had happened; stress injuries like this one were more common than not among horses trained four and five hours a day before an event.

"I'd keep him turned out the rest of the season." Dr. Novick rose heavily to her feet with an audible cracking of her joints. Under the open-sided tent, the air was hot and stuffy, and the muffled roar of the crowd drifted toward them.

"What about blistering him?" Skyler had spent the past few summers working part-time at the Northfield Veterinary Clinic, which had given her some experience in this area.

"Could help—but mostly what he needs is a dose of good old-fashioned rest." The vet's deeply tanned face creased into a basket weave of lines. "Sorry. Wish I could offer you a miracle cure."

Skyler pressed her cheek into Carousel's neck, which smelled of the baby oil Mickey used to make his dappled coat shine. "Hear that, boy? It's Club Med for you," she murmured, feeling sick with disappointment for her friend, but knowing Mickey would resent any display of sympathy that might push her over the edge into tears.

The gelding snorted, turning his head to give her an affectionate nudge. Dr. Novick smiled, and said, "You're good with them.... I've seen you with your horse. Some of these kids ..." The smile dropped from her face. "Well, maybe you wouldn't go so far as to call it abuse, but they might as well be out taking a spin with their daddy's car for all they care about their horses."

"I'm going to veterinary school after college," Skyler told her. It had been her father who'd insisted on Princeton first, arguing that a liberal arts degree would give her a more well-rounded education.

"If you don't wind up killing yourself first." Dr. Novick hefted her medical bag. "You're all nuts, you know. Getting busted up time after time, and going back for more."

Who would know better than I? Skyler thought ruefully. A fuzzy image surfaced, of a white hospital room, nurses drifting in and out.

She looked over at Mickey, who was wearing what Skyler called her No Trespassing expression—her face bolted shut, her dark eyes revealing about as much of what was going on under that tangle of black curls as a stretch limo's tinted one-way windows.

Mickey wouldn't cry, she knew. She'd smoke a cigarette as if she were about to burn down someone's barn with it, and she'd swear like a stable hand until whatever was killing her was out of her system.

"He was limping when he went into the warm-up ring," Mickey told her miserably. "I had them switch me with Evan Saunders so I could have his leg looked at."

She hunched forward in the old hunt jacket that was too tight across her bust even after being let out, cradling her right elbow in her left palm as she chewed on her thumbnail. Mickey had had two clear rounds in the preliminary classes, and a better-than-good shot at a ribbon in the jump-off. Now her whole summer

would be ruined. And this was their last season before
they'd be eighteen and no longer eligible to compete
in the junior division.

"Damn," Skyler swore.

"You're telling me," Mickey groaned. "Now all I
have to do is explain to my father why he should pay
six months' board on a horse that can't be ridden.
He's already shitting a brick over the alimony Mom's
lawyers are sticking him for."

Skyler kept her eyes averted from Mickey's. She
knew how much this had meant to her friend—not
just winning a ribbon, but showing her asshole of a
father that she could ride well enough to qualify for
the open classes in the money division. . . . If she won
there, the purses would stop his squawking about the
fortune she was costing him.

She had a sudden inspiration, but waited a moment
before speaking, allowing herself to imagine the full
spectrum of possible consequences. She could end up
screwing herself. But what were best friends for?
Wouldn't Mickey do the same for her?

"You could ride Chance," Skyler suggested mildly.

Mickey cast her a startled look. Hope flared briefly
in her eyes, then immediately was quenched. "Forget it."

"Shut up and just listen to me, will you? You've
ridden him before; you know him. All you have to
watch out for is that liverpool jump."

Mickey's hands curled into fists at her sides. "And
you know me," she said in a voice that could cut glass.
"I jump to win. I'll do whatever it takes."

Skyler met her look with one equally defiant.
"Prove it."

A long moment passed during which Skyler considered the very real possibility of Mickey taking the blue
ribbon. She wanted that ribbon as much as Mickey
did. The difference was she didn't *need* to win, not for
financial reasons at any rate. She already had every-

thing—a good-sized trust fund, a cottage left to her by her grandmother, a horse worth as much as a nice house in a good neighborhood.

Everything but a history.

From the show grounds drifted the reverberating sound of the loudspeaker. "Number thirty-two, Black Knight, ridden by Melody Watson . . ."

Black Knight, posted in ninth, would be the last to jump if Mickey didn't get her butt out there in the next fifteen minutes. And it would take that long just to tack Chancellor up again.

She watched Mickey's expressive face conduct a brief war with itself. Then her friend took a deep breath and said, "Okay, you're on."

It was unusual, sure. But nothing in the AHSA rule-book, as far as Skyler knew, specified that a rider couldn't switch horses midway through the competition, even up to the last minute. At the judges' tent, there were some raised eyebrows, but as Skyler watched Mickey take Chancellor through the in-gate, it was merely her own good sense she questioned. Her time on Chancellor was still the one to beat, and Mickey was the only other jumper on the junior circuit who routinely cost her ribbons.

I must be crazy, Skyler groaned inwardly. She thought of Mom up there somewhere in the bleachers, and could only imagine what she must be thinking.

Skyler reminded herself once again that Mickey would have done the same for her. Yet she couldn't help feeling a touch of superiority when Chancellor's hind foot rapped the top rail going over the first fence, which he'd taken so beautifully with *her* on his back. Mickey was in her usual into-the-fray form. She jumped like no one else, chin nearly resting on the gelding's crest, elbows sticking out, her rear end up high enough to be spotted on the radar screen of an air traffic control tower. Lucky for her that in this sport how you looked when you jumped didn't count either for or against you. All that mattered was that you made it over.

And Mickey was flying.

God, just look at her! Chancellor was halfway through the course already, taking the liverpool jump with only the briefest hesitation. At the Grand Union fence, when it looked as if he'd crash straight through, Mickey brought his head up sharply and practically hurled him over. The last triple combination nearly cost her another knockdown, but as she sailed over the third element and through the timer beam, the results of her clean run flashed on the scoreboard like the cocky grin now lighting Mickey's face: 32.805.

Faster than Skyler's time by less than one-tenth of a second.

Skyler didn't know whether to cheer or cry.

Minutes later, in the winner's circle, poised between Mickey and Chancellor, ribbon in hand, she had a sudden vivid flash of Mickey and her, at age thirteen, bending over the toilet in her bathroom puking their guts out following an orgy of Boone's Farm Apple Wine and Entenmann's chocolate chip cookies.

"That'll teach you to be so nice next time," Mickey muttered under her breath as cameras flashed and minicams whirred. Tears stood in her eyes as she grinned at Skyler.

Skyler fished a handkerchief from her jacket pocket and handed it to Mickey. "Your nose is running."

"Thanks," Mickey grunted, furtively swiping at her eyes.

"Don't thank me. I just wanted to make sure you'd be around for zone finals so I can whip *your* butt."

Though she didn't regret her act of selflessness, Skyler wasn't altogether sure she was glad Mickey had won. She would have liked it even better if *she* had been the one holding the blue ribbon up to the cameras aimed their way, Skyler admitted to herself. But being second-best wasn't the end of the world.

The only showdown she had no intention of losing was the one she planned on having with her mother tonight.

And for *that,* she thought grimly, there would be no blue ribbon ... only more heartache. Because Skyler had a feeling that, in this case, the truth would be more hurtful than the lies.

At supper that evening, Skyler could hardly eat.

In the large, high-ceilinged dining room at Orchard Hill, which Kate had made less formal with stenciled walls and a pine cabinet filled with bright Mexican pottery, Skyler felt so tense she couldn't believe her parents hadn't picked up on her mood. But judging from the way Daddy was going on about his latest project—a former police precinct in SoHo that he was turning into luxury apartments—and from the bright look of interest on Mom's face, Skyler concluded wryly that she was not, after all, the center of their universe.

Daddy was stressed out; she could tell from the tone of his voice. There was a lot riding on this SoHo project, she knew, and a lot had gone wrong already: a union strike, some contractor screw-up, and now there appeared to be a problem with the zoning. Lately, more and more, Skyler had come across her parents speaking in low tones about money. She gathered that the firm was in debt, but wasn't Daddy always saying that with real estate uncertainty was "the nature of the beast"? She couldn't imagine anything really terrible happening.

Skyler tuned out their conversation. Instead, she rehearsed in her mind what she was going to say to Mom later on.

It would be no use trying to get her father to open up to her, she'd decided. You couldn't discuss personal things with him ... things that had you worried or scared. He loved her without reservation; she never doubted that for a moment, but it had always been her mom whom Skyler had confided in.

Abruptly, she interjected, "Did you hear about Torey Whitaker?"

"She's getting married, that much I know," Kate replied, looking up calmly from her plate of cold poached salmon and saffron rice.

"That's not all—she's having a baby." Skyler watched her parents exchange surprised glances. "I ran into her sister at the show today. Diana told me her mom is going nuts trying to see how fast she can pull together a wedding."

"If I were they, I wouldn't be too quick about it." Her father dabbed at his mouth with his starched napkin. "That young man of hers strikes me as being a little too comfortable with the idea of rich in-laws."

"I saw Marian Whitaker at the Stop & Shop the other day," Mom said thoughtfully. "She did tell me they were buying the kids a house as a wedding present ... but, oh, dear, a *baby*." She shook her head, a smile tugging at her lips. In a voice rich with irony, she added, "I can't imagine why Marian didn't mention it."

"It won't matter once they're married," Skyler said.

"Depends on who you ask." Her father chuckled. "I'll just bet old Dickson is having a coronary over this."

Skyler couldn't get over it, how Daddy seemed to get more handsome with each passing year. Her friends were always saying he looked like a movie star, though he scoffed when she told him so. "Next thing you know they'll be putting me in a wax museum," he liked to joke. But with his square-cut features and his thick hair the color of the pewter mugs lining the fireplace mantel at his back, he looked more distinguished than old. Not that fifty was so old, she was quick to remind herself.

"Sky, you've hardly touched a thing!" Mom cast a

pointed look at the plate on which Skyler's food sat, mostly uneaten. "Are you feeling all right?"

"Just a little tired, I guess," Skyler said, dropping her eyes. "The show really knocked me out."

In the car on the way home, Mom had commented mostly on things like the difficulty of the course, which riders the judges had seemed to favor and why, and the people she'd run into who remembered her from the old days. But now she looked at Skyler and said, "You know, I was really proud of you today."

"I could have been better," Skyler disagreed. "I was a little slow on that first jump."

"I meant what you did for Mickey," Kate said softly.

Skyler felt herself flush, and muttered, "It wasn't that big a deal."

Daddy, as usual, wasn't tuning in on their exchange; instead, he was looking out the French windows at something that had caught his eye near the patio. Frowning absently, he observed, "Those damn moles are really making a mess of the lawn. Kate, I thought you told the gardener to put out more traps."

"I'll speak to him again," she said evenly. In an obvious effort to change the subject, she turned to Skyler and asked brightly, "Are you seeing Pres tonight?"

Mom didn't have a clue that she and Prescott had become lovers—Skyler could tell just by the tone of her voice.

"He said he'd drop by," she replied indifferently. "A friend of his invited us to a party, but I'm not sure I'm up to it."

Right now, she wasn't sure she was up to a confrontation with her mother, either. In fact, she felt more than just tired. She felt as if she might throw up.

Would it be fair to rock the boat? To hurl her doubts and accusations into the calm that surrounded her?

Skyler had always thought of her home as almost magical, like the lands people escaped to in storybooks. She loved Orchard Hill, with its acres of open fields and its stone stable that first-time visitors often mistook for the main house until they reached the huge old colonial half a mile of winding road beyond it. Inside, there were no vast rooms, only lots and lots of cozy ones, where overstuffed sofas and chairs with needlepoint pillows and hand-crocheted afghans beckoned like so many warm, plump laps.

Everywhere Skyler looked she saw evidence of Kate's deft, loving touch—a spray of gladiolus reflected in the mirror over the mantel, a sweet carriage clock chiming on the sideboard, the collection of antique cookie jars occupying a shelf in the china cabinet.

Skyler was suddenly more afraid of what she might lose than what she stood to gain.

Something bumped Skyler's leg, and she leaned down to scratch a silky ear, which was quickly followed by a cold black nose poking out from under the starched tablecloth. Belinda was such a beggar. Really, it was disgusting how spoiled she'd gotten, Skyler thought, tearing off a chunk of bread and slipping it to their Labrador.

At that moment, Vera appeared to clear the table—all one hundred and eighty pounds of her in a flowered smock, her plump brown face wearing a frown of disapproval as she glanced at Skyler's untouched plate before whisking it away.

"I think I'll change, just in case," Skyler said, excusing herself. She really didn't feel like going out ... but depending on how things went with her mom, afterward she might not feel like staying home either.

Upstairs in her bedroom, Skyler slipped out of her shorts and T-shirt, and pulled on a purple silk chemise and a pair of Levis worn white at the knees. While Belinda watched from her throne of needlepoint pillows on the settee at the foot of the bed, she stood back to study herself in the mirror by the dresser.

But no matter which way Skyler angled the oval of glass, what was reflected back at her remained basically the same—her face with its square jaw and cheekbones like broad curved blades, her tapering body with hips so narrow they made her look almost boyish. And her hair! It was so thick the blunt ends just wouldn't lie flat, no matter how much mousse she used.

She wondered, as she always did, if she'd inherited her looks from her mother—and if so, would she recognize the woman should she happen to bump into her on the street?

A discreet knock was followed by Kate appearing in the doorway, announcing, "Your father and I thought we'd drive into Greenwich for a movie. If you and Pres feel like joining us, you're welcome. We won't be leaving for another hour."

Skyler regarded Kate's reflection in the mirror, feeling a rush of love for the mother who, in matters of the heart, had never denied her a thing. "No, thanks— I think we'll invite our friends over for a wild party instead, and break out every bottle of wine in the cellar," she said, deadpan.

"As long as no one spills anything on the carpets," Kate said mildly. "Oh, and the '72 Montrachet? Save some for Daddy. He says it's the last case."

"You're impossible," Skyler laughed, turning to face Kate.

"So I've been told."

Kate crossed the room and sank down on the settee next to Belinda, who grunted at the intrusion and refused to budge. She'd hardly needed her cane at all tonight, Skyler had noticed. Mom was having one of her better days—which meant she'd be in the mood to talk. Skyler's stomach turned a slow cartwheel. Her gaze fixed on Kate's guileless green-gray eyes in her lightly freckled face that never seemed to age.

"Mom ..." Skyler began softly, walking over to where she sat. "You wouldn't keep it from me, would you, if there was something really important I needed to know?"

Kate smiled and cocked her head. "What would make you ask a thing like that? Have I ever kept anything from you?"

"Not that I know of."

"Well, then ... there you go." Kate stroked Belinda's ear, draped like a silky black mitten over one knee.

"You'd tell me even if you thought it would upset me?"

Kate was looking at her curiously now, and a faint pink blush had crept into her cheeks. Her answer this time came more slowly, and seemed far more considered. "That would depend on the situation, I guess." She paused, then asked gently, "Sky ... what is this all about? What is it you want to know?"

Skyler struggled a moment with herself, unsure of whether to continue. *Curiosity killed the cat,* she thought, stifling a helpless giggle. Nonetheless, like floodwater risen past its high mark, the dark brew of hope and dread she'd so long held inside came bursting through.

"Tell me about my mother."

She watched the color drain from Kate's cheeks, and her eyes grow enormous in the pale valentine of her face. Skyler felt a panicky urge to snatch back her words, but it was too late.

But Kate's voice, when she spoke, was calm, patient, even a bit surprised. "My goodness, what is there left to tell?"

"Yes, I know. You told me I was abandoned ... but what I don't know is *why.*" To her dismay, Skyler realized she was on the verge of tears. "How could a mother just walk away from her baby without at least leaving a note? How could someone like that just ... just vanish into thin air?"

In a queer, flat voice, Kate said, "It's hard to understand sometimes, the things people will do." Her eyes seemed to burn into Skyler's. "Darling, what brought all this on all of a sudden? Was it something someone said to you?"

"No one said anything. No one *had* to. And it's not something that came on all of a sudden. Ever since you told me—what was I, six?—I haven't stopped thinking about it." A tear slipped down her cheek.

"Sky ... I'm sure she had her reasons."

"She *left* me!"

"I doubt that either of us could possibly imagine the kind of circumstances that would make a mother do a thing like that."

But what Skyler couldn't imagine was any set of circumstances, no matter how desperate, that would have made Kate give her up.

With a sob, she sank to her knees before her mother, burying her face in the warm lap that had never once refused her. Despite the wave of love and gratitude that flowed through her, Skyler felt more sure than ever that Kate was holding something back.

"Mom ... please ... tell me. I won't hold it against you that you kept it from me. I promise. Whatever it is, I can handle it. Nothing could be as awful as not knowing."

Kate pitched forward, gathering Skyler to her in a fierce embrace. Skyler could feel her trembling, but only very faintly, a sensation like the humming of an instrument just after it's been played.

When she finally drew away, it was with a tired, pained smile. Carefully, almost fussily, she rearranged the sofa cushions behind her, and sank back.

"Darling, why didn't you come to me sooner? I had

no idea! Of course, I don't blame you for wondering. There's so much we don't know...."

As Skyler searched Kate's innocent, clear-eyed expression, a sliver of doubt worked its way into her mind. Oh God, suppose there really *wasn't* anything more?

"What about the police, didn't they look for her?" They'd been through this before, several times over the years, but the desperation welling up in Skyler was like nothing she'd ever felt.

"Naturally there was an investigation," Kate told her, showing no sign of impatience at having to explain this all over again. "We were told the police had questioned the neighbors, but no one knew anything. Apparently the apartment wasn't even in your mother's name. She'd been living with a friend, or a sister—I'm not sure which—and after she—your mother—went away ... her friend disappeared, too."

"What about a note? Didn't she leave *anything*?" Skyler was aware of her voice rising, teetering on the edge of shrillness.

"Nothing that could be traced, I'm afraid." Kate's hands knotted in her lap, and her green-gray eyes filled with tears. "If you want me to confess that I hoped and prayed your mother would never be found—all right, then. There wasn't a day that went by when I didn't thank that woman in my prayers for not coming back to you. I know how awful that must sound ... but, you see, I loved you so much. I just couldn't have imagined giving you back. *That's* the truth, darling, the only truth that matters."

What Skyler believed was that what Kate was telling her was as close to the truth as she would ever get. The road ended here. If there was more, she wouldn't hear it from Kate. Disappointment crashed through her, and along with it an odd sort of relief. Maybe there really were things people were better off not knowing, no matter how much they might think they wanted to. Maybe—

Skyler burst into tears.

And as her mother's arms went around her, more gently this time, holding her, rocking her a little, Skyler's pain was eased a bit, and the emptiness inside her was filled by the love she could feel flowing from Kate.

For the moment, at least.

For in her heart, she knew she would never entirely be free of her yearning to know the story that, now, only her real mother could tell.

Someday, she thought. *Someday I'll find you . . . or you'll find me. Someday I'll know.*

CHAPTER 3

Ellie Nightingale sat in the meeting room at the Gay Men's Health Crisis on West Twentieth, where every Tuesday evening, from six to eight-thirty, her AIDS group convened. It was still a few minutes before six, and not all the members had arrived. She settled back in her chair, and looked around her—at the coffee urn on the rickety table in the corner, where Roy Pariti was trying unsuccessfully to steady the foam cup in his trembling hand as he filled it; at the sofas and chairs pushed into a rough circle, where several early comers sat chatting quietly among themselves. Behind her, the radiator hissed softly, though the room would have been warm enough without it—unusually so for late October. On the wall to her left someone had stuck a poster advertising the AIDSWalk, a reproduced photo of two hands clasped in brotherhood.

Ellie had formed the group four years ago, not long after going into private practice. On the heels of her five adrenaline-fueled years at Bellevue, and two at St. Vincent's working half-time while building her practice, it had turned out to be just what she'd needed. Sometimes, in the midst of her jam-packed schedule—which had grown to include thirty private patients, as well as a Thursday-night couples' group— she tended to lose sight of what it was all about. But here, in this room, every Tuesday evening, she felt everything she knew and believed in come together in an intensely vital way. There was something special about this group of dying men, all of them soldiers in a war in which there was no winning side. A war they were fighting as hard and with as much dignity and good humor as they knew how.

Back in the late eighties, doing her postdoctoral work at Bellevue, she'd witnessed the front lines first-hand. In the open wards, she'd seen things that had shocked her into a new awareness: men with AIDS dying slow, excruciating deaths without a single friend or family member ever visiting; men ostracized by other patients fearful of being infected, and kept at arm's length by the hospital's staff. Her paper on the subject, "Dying on the Moon: A Study of the Ethical Issues Involved in the Treatment of AIDS Patients," had created a mild controversy within the medical community when it was published in *American Psychologist.* Many were outraged by the parallels she'd drawn to the leper colonies of the nineteenth century; others were spurred into a more compassionate approach.

But out of the fire had come this group. It had started with a dozen men; and though most of the original members had since died, their number at the moment stood at ten. The faces changed from year to year, but the raw emotions that poured forth every week never abated. New members sensed it immediately, almost as soon as they walked in: This was a safe place, a place where no one would judge or condemn them. Here, there was comfort for the dying in learning how best to live.

Tonight, as she scanned the room, Ellie found herself counting heads. Only one was missing. Then she remembered—Evan Milner had gone into the hospital on Monday. She made a mental note to drop by Beth Israel later in the week and see how he was doing.

At the same time, Ellie found herself imagining a far different hospital scene, one that involved life, new life, not death.

"Any day now," Christa's obstetrician had said. A baby. After all the years of dead ends and disappointments, it was finally going to happen. Ellie felt a surge of joy that caught briefly, like a kite in the wind ... and then spiraled downward.

If only she could relax and stop worrying! Christa wasn't like the others, she told herself. These past few months, they'd talked on the phone nearly every other day, and the bubbly teenager had shown absolutely no sign of having second thoughts. But until the baby actually was *here,* how could she possibly be certain whether or not—

Ellie caught herself. *Get a grip,* she commanded. A favorite saying of Georgina, her friend and former supervisor at St. Vincent's, popped into Ellie's head: "Don't pay interest on trouble you haven't even borrowed." Good advice, she thought. Wasn't there trouble enough in her life without going to the bank for more?

She looked up at the assembled group, smiling in what she hoped was a reassuring way. These men had their own plagues of Egypt to cope with, she told herself. They didn't need her locusts on top of everything else.

Nicky Fraid, wearing a red beret at a rakish angle on his nearly bald head, was the first to speak. Looking around him, he noted Evan Milner's absence and quipped dryly, "And then there were nine."

"Nine little HIV-positive Indians ... and you can bet they won't be singing *that* version in kindergarten." Adam Burchard gave a short laugh, thrusting out a jaw so cleanly shaven it looked polished, as he worked loose the knot in his conservatively striped tie.

There was a mutter of laughter, followed by a silence that was broken only by a ragged coughing fit. Peter Miskowski, a former cardiac surgeon whose sunken chest made Ellie think of archive photos of the liberation of Bergen-Belsen, was bent over nearly double, a fist screwed to his mouth as if it were the only thing keeping him from toppling to the floor. The others glanced at him in sympathy, but no one reached over to thump him on the back, or even put an arm around his quaking shoulders. Eventually, the coughing subsided.

Then a raspy voice from the far side of the room spoke. "I dreamed last night that I was on stage again. Dancing. It was opening night and every seat in the house sold out ... but when I looked out into the audience, no one was there. Just rows of empty chairs. I didn't know whether to feel relieved that now no one would notice if I fucked up ... or like a dumb shit who'd fallen for the world's biggest practical joke."

Ellie looked affectionately at the thirtyish, red-headed man in the chair to her right. Even before he got sick, she thought, few would have pegged Jimmy Dolan as a ballet dancer. The pug-nosed, wise-cracking son of an Irish cop from Canarsie, he looked more like a scrappy kid from the neighborhood, the kind you'd expect to see hanging around a basketball court looking to pick up a game. But he had style as well as grit. Several years ago, she and Paul had seen him at the Joyce Theater, and the memory that stood out in her mind was of little Jimmy Dolan hurtling across the stage, teeth bared, his pale, muscular body flashing like a fire opal under the lights.

"What happened then?" Daniel Blaylock wore a nervous smile. Dan, fortyish, heavyset, with the gut of hard-working guy who liked to knock back a few beers after work, was the least symptomatic of the group, and also the most frightened of getting really sick.

"Nothing. I woke up." Jimmy smiled, but from this angle, Ellie could see his troubled expression and the pockets of shadow that had collected in the hollows of his eyes. "It's the same every morning. I open my eyes—and it hits me. For about ten seconds, I *know* ..." His eyes closed, and his jaw knotted.

"What do you know?" Ellie asked softly.

He opened his eyes, and smiled ... a slow, almost beatific smile that lit his winsome, wrecked face. Despite the professional distance she managed to maintain for the most part, Ellie felt wrenched.

"That I'm dying," Jimmy replied in a flat voice.

Roy Pariti steadied his foam cup with both hands as he lifted it to his lips. "What I'm wondering is what the fuck we're even *doing* here?" he said, his angry voice flaring. "So we sound off, air our feelings ... what's the point? What do we get for it? A paragraph in the obit column, if we're lucky."

Every eye turned to Roy, a former activist and a Stonewall veteran whose red bandanna, knotted about his graying ponytailed head like a bloodied bandage, made him look like a survivor of the world's oldest war. But it was Jimmy's gaze—calm, steady, focused in a way that called attention to itself—that brought everyone scooting an inch or two forward in their chairs.

"It's like dancing," Jimmy said in a quiet voice that matched his intense expression. "You do it because you can't *not* do it, and it hurts a lot of the time, yeah, but you keep going, you keep busting your ass, because otherwise there'd be no reason for even *being*." From his ferociously blue eyes shone a kind of acceptance that filled Ellie with both admiration and envy.

All these years, she thought, *and I still can't accept the terrible thing that happened to me.*

The image of pregnant Christa once more intruded,

and Ellie offered up a brief, fierce prayer: *God, I'm sorry to put it this way, but you owe me. No one deserves this more than me. No one.*

Directly across from her, Brian Rice began to weep softly into his cupped palms. Quiet, slope-chinned Brian, whose horn-rimmed glasses and conservative suits often made him the butt of friendly teasing. In the two months he'd been with the group, he'd hardly spoken except to offer an occasional insightful comment. Now Ellie found herself turning toward him, alert and sympathetic.

"It's Larry," Brian choked into his hands. "He moved out yesterday. Couldn't take it anymore, he said. I don't blame him. I don't know if I'd want to live with me now, either, if there was any way out."

Ellie caught the hardbitten expressions on several faces. They all listened intently as Brian haltingly described how he and Larry had met and fallen in love. How Larry had stood by him when he was diagnosed, with never a hint of accusation as to how he might have caught the disease. And how Larry now was leaving him for someone else . . . someone young and handsome and *healthy*.

Everyone, it seemed, had a similar story of rejection or betrayal . . . everyone except Jimmy, who remained silent throughout.

The group all knew about his friend . . . his *straight* friend, who'd stood by him since they were kids growing up together in Brooklyn, and would be there at Jimmy's side at the end. They didn't need to be told that, whatever the betrayals Jimmy had suffered, there would always be Tony.

Nicky, who'd recently moved in with his parents after breaking up with his lover, was the first to invoke Tony's name. Fingering the AIDS ribbon pinned to his denim jacket, he turned to Jimmy with a hard gleam in his eye. "Your friend—the cop—doesn't *he* ever get sick of it?" he asked belligerently. "Hauling your ass to the doctor all the time, running your errands, checking in on you to see if you're okay?"

Jimmy shrugged, his expression an odd mixture of tenderness and exasperation. "Tony? He acts like nothing's changed. Like all this"—he threw out an arm—"is just something that'll eventually blow over. He keeps saying stuff like, 'Jimmy, when you're better, we're going on that camping trip we talked about, just you, me, and the mosquitoes.' " He sighed. "It's hard, sometimes, you know, staying up around him, acting like a couple of mosquito bites would be my worst problem."

"What do you think would happen if you told him what you're telling us?" asked Erik Sandstrom. The tall, articulate Fordham professor's one eccentricity, as far as Ellie could see, was his seemingly endless collection of wristwatches. This week's was an aviator watch with a tiny airplane attached to the minute hand.

A faint smile touched Jimmy's lips. "Lay it on the line with Tony? Listen, you're talking about a guy who walks through shit every day of his life and never lets it get to him. The man is a *cop,* for chrissakes. Not just a cop, but a *mounted* cop. When I was a kid, I had these toy soldiers on horseback. It was like . . . *make-believe.* And he's living it. You're gonna hammer it into a guy like that his best friend is dying?" Tears stood out in Jimmy's eyes.

Ellie thought about the man who, in the eight months Jimmy had been with the group, had not missed a single Tuesday. Tony was always there, waiting for Jimmy in the reception area when the group let out, his green Ford Explorer parked at the curb outside.

"Are you sure it's Tony you're protecting?" she asked.

Jimmy was silent.

"There's a certain amount of risk involved here,"

Ellie went on. "Trusting someone you care about to respond in a way that you won't feel let down."

"Let me tell you something about Tony." Jimmy leaned forward, and for an instant she clearly saw the dancer he'd been—lithe, athletic, nearly shimmering in his passion. "When I was diagnosed, you know what my old man said? He told me it was my own fault, I'd brought it on myself, the way I live. He did everything but spit in my face." The group had heard it all before, but they sat quietly, letting him finish. "And here's Tony, hanging with me in the hospital every day, every goddamn *day,* when my own family won't even send a lousy bouquet of flowers. FTD? You know what it stands for? *Fuck That Dick-Sucker.*" He fell back exhausted, his chest heaving. "Jesus, what am I getting all worked up for? I got exactly what I was expecting from them. Nothing. My old neighborhood? They're all like that. Out in Canarsie, they still talk about rolling queers."

The men were silent, each lost in his own bitter memories.

"The thing with Tony is ..." Jimmy spread his hands in a helpless gesture. "People see us together and they think ..." He swallowed hard, his Adam's apple riding up and down the pale stem of his throat. "Tony's okay about it, though. Never even bats an eye. He lets them think what they want, even though it's got to bother him."

"The dude's cool, what can I say?" Armando Ruiz, the lone Puerto Rican of the group, flashed a grin that sat crookedly on his delicate-featured face. Speaking for all of them, no doubt, he exclaimed, "Shit, man, we could *all* use a few more friends like that."

"Yeah." Jimmy's tamper-proof smile was back. "I worry about it, though. About how's he's going to handle it when I'm not around anymore."

A picture flashed across Ellie's mind, of a pink baby blanket crumpled in the bottom of a wicker basket. It was always the same image, never more, just that blanket, stuck there like the underpinning of a deeper story that wasn't being told. Sometimes, in her dreams, she frantically pawed the blanket, searching for her baby, madly searching against hope or reason. But the blanket would only grow in size, its folds swallowing her up like some kind of horrid burrowing maze she could never find her way to the end of. She always woke from those dreams with damp eyes, and a strangled cry wedged in her throat.

Ellie pushed the image away. After the baby came, Christa's baby, the nightmares would stop. And the ache of her loss, though it would never fully go away, would lessen.

"I'm lucky, I guess," Jimmy went on. "I mean, hey, guys I've been with, some of them go their whole lives never finding out what it's all about."

The discussion shifted then from how it felt to be left to what it was like doing the leaving. They talked about honesty, and how far you needed to go in being truthful with friends and family about death. And the usefulness, at times, of play-acting, of pretending everything was going to be okay.

Ellie ended the group, as she always did, by going around the circle of chairs and giving each man a brief hug. She knew that many of her colleagues would have considered it unorthodox at best, outright unprofessional at worst, but she'd found there was often more therapeutic value in the human touch than in any words she could have offered. Moreover, she didn't give a damn what anybody outside this room thought about her methods.

Jimmy fell into step with Ellie as they were leaving. They chatted about a new dance company Jimmy was particularly excited about and thought she'd enjoy seeing. He promised to try to get her and Paul house seats for the opening performance.

Tony, as usual, was waiting in the reception area.

He rose from the couch, dropping the magazine he'd been leafing through. In tan chinos and an open-neck shirt he was unmistakably, unapologetically Brooklyn born and bred. There was no way big swarthy Tony Salvatore could have been mistaken for a relative of redheaded Jimmy, but the arm he slung around his friend's shoulders showed an affection as easy and familiar as any brother's.

Still waters, Ellie thought. Where Jimmy, with his frenetic energy, seemed to spin out in every direction, Tony was as steady as a piling anchoring a skiff. Everything about him solid, dense, defined. The way the muscles in his arms moved like tightly wound machinery, even the way his coiled black hair molded his finely shaped head. His features were strong; they wore a kind of watchfulness that was reassuring rather than off-putting. He put on no airs, asked for no quarter. He didn't need to.

"Hey, Dolan, you're not gonna believe this, but just now this rookie shows up and decides to give me a ticket for double-parking." Tony made an abrupt, in-your-face gesture with his free hand. "So I tell him I'm a cop, too, Troop B, Mounted Police, and you know what he says? He says, 'You and that talking horse, Mr. Ed.' So I say to *him,* as he's pulling out his book, 'Yeah, the commissioner's daughter is a big fan of our horses, always coming by with carrots, and you know Mr. Ed, you can't shut him up.' "

Jimmy laughed. "No shit. He let you off?"

"Not only that, he's keeping an eye on the car till I get you outside."

"You're priceless, man."

"I must be, the way Paula keeps hitting me up every paycheck. Aren't ex-wives supposed to go away once you've given them everything you've got?" Tony rolled his eyes, but the good-humored smile hadn't left his face.

"You're just lucky you two didn't have any kids . . .

you'd be paying child support up the wazoo," ribbed Jimmy.

Tony's expression darkened, but only for an instant. Then he shrugged his quintessentially Brooklynese shrug, and said, "Yeah, sure, I guess so."

A sudden chill took hold of Ellie. Lucky not to have kids? God. She couldn't imagine ever feeling that way.

All at once, she felt the collective weight of it pressing down on her ... the years of fertility tests and surgical procedures, followed by more years of adoption agencies, dead ends, and disappointments.

This time I won't walk away empty-handed, she told herself with a confidence she wished she felt.

Ellie brought Jimmy back into focus, and smiled. "You'd better be off before your friend runs low on goodwill with the department. I'll see you next Tuesday."

"If I'm still around," said Jimmy, flashing her a grin.

"What? You want to kid around about a thing like that? What are you, some kind of fucking ghoul?" she heard Tony affectionately scold his friend as they were heading outside. "That medicine you been taking has scrambled your brains. What you need, buddy, is some fresh air. When we take that camping trip ..." His words were cut off by the front door thumping shut behind them.

Ellie followed them outside a few minutes later, deciding to walk rather than hail a cab. Her office was only eight blocks away, and the exercise would do her good, maybe even burn off some of her restlessness. But even though she had no other appointments that evening—only some paperwork—Ellie found herself hurrying along Ladies' Mile, which she usually took at a leisurely stroll. She loved this stretch of Sixth Avenue, which had been the hub of high-society shopping a hundred years ago, and which had more recently seen a conversion of its white elephant department stores into fancy shops, but tonight she hardly glanced at the window displays.

Ellie was thinking of the answering machine on the desk in her office. In her mind, she saw its red message light blinking. Could one of the messages be from Christa? The teenager had promised to call the minute she went into labor—

Brought to a halt by a sharp stitch in her side, Ellie stared sightlessly at the artful display in the window at Bed, Bath, and Beyond until she'd caught her breath and the pain had subsided. How many times had she set her heart on a baby, only to be disappointed? This time she had to be sensible, not get too excited until she was absolutely certain the adoption would go through.

Paul is right, she told herself. *We've been through this too many times to leave ourselves wide open to more heartbreak.*

But Paul didn't know what it felt like to have your own child ripped away from you. He couldn't even begin to imagine what it was like to have a piece of your heart cut, and the rest of it left to bleed for a lifetime. How could she *not* long to fill that vacant place inside her?

The memories came pouring forth again then, like dark oil on even darker waters. Weeks. It had taken weeks to get a single lead on Monk—a stray clue that had dead-ended in an empty apartment, a see-no-evil super, no forwarding address. The police, with no one left to question, had turned their suspicions on her. Had she told them *everything* she remembered about that night? Had she been under the influence of alcohol or drugs? Was it possible she'd done something to her baby, then panicked and tried to cover it up by claiming Bethanne had been kidnapped?

An infant was found in a trash container, wrapped in newspaper and badly decomposed.

Even now, more than twenty years later, Ellie began

to shudder uncontrollably as she relived her terrible journey down into the bowels of the morgue, where she'd glanced at the tiny gray corpse long enough to see that it wasn't Bethanne before promptly throwing up in a wastebasket.

And then, not more than a month later, like a sick joke or a recurring bad dream, traveling those same subarctic corridors, this time to positively identify the body in question.

Nadine, dead of a drug overdose.

Her last and only witness. The one person who could have backed her up . . . helped her identify Monk.

She hadn't thrown up that time, though later she would wish she had. She'd done something that would haunt her all her life, even more than the sight of Nadine's still, white face laid bare by the peeled-back shroud of plastic.

Ellie had slapped her.

Even now, all these years later, she could feel the cold sting of her sister's dead flesh against her palm, flesh that had looked like marble but that yielded with a horrible rubbery clap that would forever echo in her head—just as it had in that grim, tiled chamber and in the shocked faces around her.

I hated you, Nadine. I hated you because you were weak and took the easy way out. I could barely crawl out of bed each morning to face the newspapers that were calling the kidnapping a hoax, and the crank calls accusing me of murdering my baby. Sweet Jesus, don't you think I wanted to die too?

But she hadn't died, had she? She'd survived . . . barely. Ellie smiled faintly, remembering her bald, milky-eyed boss at Loews, aptly named Mr. Friend, who had taken pity on her, promoted her to night manager. But how she'd managed to keep up with both her job and a full courseload at City College, she would never know. Insomnia, she thought. She

couldn't sleep, thinking about Bethanne. Those years
were ones she barely recalled, except in a kind of
haze, the kind that comes over you at four in the
morning when you've been studying since two.

As she walked briskly down Sixth Avenue on a
pleasantly warm October night more than twenty
years later, Ellie found herself growing angry at her
husband for being unwilling to go the extra mile with
her now. She wanted to shout out at him even though
he wasn't there to hear her. Oh, they'd discussed it.
Argued, fought, wept over it. But Paul was adamant.
This was the last time, he'd said. He'd had it. If this
one didn't work out he couldn't see his way through
to trying again.

Oh, but it's going *to work out,* she argued passionately in her head. *Don't you see, Paul? We're finally
going to get what we've always wanted. To be a family.*

Ellie was out of breath by the time she reached
the narrow thirties-vintage building near the corner of
Twelfth Street and Sixth Avenue in which she rented
a small one-bedroom apartment that had been converted into office space. She rode the creaky old elevator to the fourth floor and let herself in. Dropping her
handbag on the sofa, she strode across the room to
her desk, an old rolltop that clashed splendidly with
her Eames chair and Klee prints. She punched the
message button on her answering machine.

The first two messages were from patients, calling
to reschedule. Then one from Paul telling her not to
expect him home until late, he'd be tied up in surgery—something about an emergency case helicop-
tered in from Roslyn. The last call was from Christa.

"Ellie, it's me." Christa sounded as though she were
crying. "There wasn't no time to call you before the
baby came, it happened too fast. Ellie, you gotta get
over here. . . ."

Ellie was out the door before the machine had
clicked off on Christa's last choked sob. Something

was wrong. Terribly wrong. Just the sound of Christa's voice, hesitant, scared, pleading, filled Ellie with foreboding. As she pelted down the fire stairs, panic lodging in her heart like a bullet, she thought, *God . . . oh, God . . . it's happening all over again. . . .*

St. Vincent's Hospital was only a block away, but her body was burning up, her lungs on fire, by the time she reached the emergency-room entrance.

Christa's room—the private room Ellie had arranged for in advance—was on the fifth floor. As Ellie burst in, out of breath, she was impressed by how cheerful it looked. A bouquet of yellow mums in a vase on the nightstand. A balloon stamped with IT'S A BOY! tied to the foot of the bed. Then her gaze took in Christa—and the sullen-faced boy hunched in the chair beside her bed.

Christa was sitting up, her arms folded tightly over her chest. Her face was swollen and blotchy from crying, and when she saw Ellie she broke into a quavery smile.

"Ellie." Her eyes flooded. "You should see him. He's so beautiful. Would you believe it? Eight pounds, three ounces!" She shifted her weight, wincing as she did so. "I wanted to call you before, but after my water broke there wasn't time."

"It's all right," Ellie reassured her. "The important thing is that you're okay, and the baby's okay."

A boy! Oh, wait until I tell Paul! Her frantic mind raced with joy despite the threat she could sense in the boyfriend's glowering stare.

"There's just one thing. . . ."

Christa's muddy brown eyes, in a face as round and soft as the Little Debbie cupcakes Ellie had tried to wean her from during her pregnancy, seemed to plead with Ellie. She wound a hank of mousy hair about her forefinger, a nervous habit of hers. The pink polish on her nails was badly chipped, Ellie saw, and she wore the usual array of silver rings, one on every finger.

"What Christa's trying to say is, me and her, we're getting married." The boyfriend—Vic was his name—rose to his feet. He struck a cocky stance, his pimpled chin up, the scuffed toe of one boot propped on the edge of the chair he'd been sitting on.

For the first time, Ellie really looked at him, and she didn't like what she saw. He was the same age as Christa, just sixteen, but there was something much older in his narrowed eyes and in the cast of his sallow face. Something that made her think of a gunfighter squaring off before a duel.

Ellie waited, not saying anything, knowing that to argue or offer unwanted advice would only give him the fight he was looking for. Instead, turning back to Christa, she said pleasantly, "I'm sure you'll be making lots of important decisions about your future ... once you're back on your feet." She smiled. "After all, you just had a baby."

Christa caught her lower lip between her teeth, and nodded. But Ellie didn't know if she was agreeing that she needed to postpone making any important decisions, or simply acknowledging that, yes, she'd had a baby.

"Not *a* baby. *Our* baby. We're keeping him."

Ellie heard the barely repressed fury in Vic's voice, and it was everything she could do to keep her eyes trained on Christa. "What do *you* want?" Ellie asked her, this young girl who had sat with her feet up on Ellie's living room sofa more times than Ellie could count, devouring fashion magazines and wrinkling her nose when Ellie brought her a glass of milk instead of the Pepsi she'd asked for.

Christa looked down and began feebly plucking at the blanket that covered her legs. "I don't know," she said in a barely audible voice.

"What d'you mean you don't know!" Vic exploded. "We got it all worked out. We're gonna live with my mom till we can get a place of our own. Shit, what's the point of me finishing school ... I can take that job down at my brother-in-law's Sunoco station." Vic paced back and forth alongside the bed, repeatedly forking blunt fingers through his longish dishwater-blond hair.

Ellie fixed him with her calmest gaze, and said quietly, "If this is what Christa wants then I'm sure she won't have any trouble speaking for herself."

Vic bent over so his head was nearly level with Christa's. "Listen, I don't want you thinking this is something I *gotta* do," he said in a low, wheedling voice. "You don't want me, just say the word, I'm outta here." He paused a beat and fixed Christa with a plaintive look. "So . . . you want to get married, or what?"

Christa's head remained down, and now a tear plopped onto the back of her wrist. "I guess so," she mumbled.

Ellie remained rooted to the spot, her heart growing huge in her chest, each beat sending out a great throbbing wallop that shook her rib cage. Suddenly, every tiny thing about the room became magnified somehow, as if by a powerful microscope—a faint yellowish stain on the pillow at Christa's back, the irritated patch of skin above her wrist where she was absently rubbing at her plastic ID bracelet, a pitcher of water that had left Donald Trump, featured on the cover of the magazine underneath it, with a puckered wet halo.

Ellie wanted to scream, to grab Christa by the shoulders and shake her for being so spineless. Where had Vic been throughout her pregnancy? When she'd gone for her doctor's appointments, who had driven her there? The time Christa woke up in the middle of the night with stabbing pains, whom had she called?

It took every ounce of restraint for Ellie to remain calm. She looked hard at Christa, so hard the force of her gaze caused the teenager at last to drag her head up and meet Ellie's gaze.

"Is this really what you want, Christa?" she asked.

"I guess so," the girl repeated dully.

"I just want you to be absolutely sure, that you know what you'll be getting into. You're only sixteen, Christa. For God's sake, don't rush into anything!" Ellie stopped herself, realizing how she must sound— like someone with more than Christa's best interests at heart.

Oh, it wasn't fair! She *did* care about Christa. But what she cared about most was the baby ... and her own stake in all this. Could anyone blame her for that?

Christa stared at her with swollen eyes, and nodded listlessly. "I know," she said. "But, the thing is, me and Vic—we're, like, a family now." She spoke in a hushed, apologetic voice. "I'm sorry, Ellie. Really, truly, I am. I never expected it to turn out this way."

Ellie felt dizzy. This wasn't happening. It couldn't be. This dough-faced girl was robbing her of the baby she'd already begun to think of as her own. The baby she had a crib for at home, set up in a nursery with pale blue walls, with clouds painted on the ceiling.

"Don't decide right now," Ellie urged, no longer attempting to hold back. "Christa, you just had a baby! You're feeling emotional, and that's under-standable. But a baby ... it's a huge responsibility. I know. I ... I had a baby girl when I wasn't much older than you." Ellie was aware of tears coursing down her cheeks, but she didn't bother to wipe them away.

"What happened to her?" Christa's eyes were huge in her whey-colored face. Ellie hadn't told her before about Bethanne; she hadn't wanted to burden Christa with all that.

"She was taken from me." As soon as Ellie said the words, she knew she'd said the wrong thing. She saw

Christa's head jerk back in surprise, and then her eyes cut away to Vic, with whom she exchanged a panicky glance.

They're thinking it was my fault somehow . . . that I wasn't a good enough mother. Oh God, why did I say anything?

At that moment, a stocky gray-haired nurse breezed in, wheeling a Plexiglas isolette in which an infant lay cocooned in a white blanket. Ellie caught a glimpse of a red, squashed-looking face crowned by a thatch of dark hair. Her heart tipped sideways like an overfull glass spilling warm liquid throughout her chest. Then she saw Christa look away, as if from something she wasn't ready to confront, her expression growing remote and sulky. A small flare of hope went up in Ellie. *Maybe it isn't too late. . . .*

"Well, goodness, what do you know? The whole family here to meet you," the nurse chirped at the slumbering infant. She wheeled the isolette around and parked it beside Christa's bed, wearing a congenitally cheery smile. "Would you like to hold your son, or shall we give Grandma first crack?"

Clearly, the woman had seen her share of teenaged moms accompanied by mothers still young enough to have given birth themselves, but even so, Ellie had to hold her breath to keep from screaming out, *You've got it all wrong . . . he's mine!*

Tension hung in the air. She stared hard at Christa, who remained still, her gaze averted, her hands twisting in her lap.

Then the unexpected happened.

Vic, his hard young face abruptly melting into an expression of awkward tenderness, stepped forward and gingerly lifted the baby from the isolette. Holding the small white-wrapped bundle in the crook of his skinny arm, he gazed down in wonder, a smile playing at his lips.

Watching them together, Christa burst into tears.

Vic brushed the fingers of his free hand over her wobbling red face. "Damn, Christa. Don'tcha see? We can't just hand 'im over to some stranger like ... like he's some kinda fucking door prize." His voice cracked a little, as if he were a boy on the verge of adolescence.

Christa's response was to sob harder.

The baby opened his eyes and began to squall, too, in small choking bursts.

"You think he's hungry?" Vic asked, wearing a frown of uncertainty.

Christa, looking as nervous as a kid in a store trying out a toy behind the manager's back, allowed him to transfer the baby into her arms.

"I don't know what to do," she whimpered. Her eyes darted between Vic and Ellie, who stood at the foot of the bed, barely able to breathe, much less move.

Vic grinned and pointed at the front of her gown. "You got what he wants, don'tcha?"

Christa bit her lip, and this time her gaze remained firmly fixed on Ellie. In the teenager's soft, round face, there was a look of desperate pleading edged in defiance.

She wants me to give her my blessing, Ellie realized with a sickening jolt. But she wouldn't ... *couldn't.*

Ellie opened her mouth to protest, to scream that *she* deserved this baby more than either of them. What kind of a home would he have with Christa? She'd destroy him, ruin her own chances at a decent future. Not to mention what this would do to Ellie and Paul.

I don't know if we can survive this. The thought rang in her head as clearly as if spoken aloud.

Ellie, like an animal caught in the glare of onrushing headlights, watched helplessly as Christa pulled her gown up and brought the squalling infant to her breast. The girl gazed down at him in awe, one chipped pink nail resting against his cheek as he snuffled and rooted. Vic bent over the two of them, mother and son, his face transformed.

Ellie might have been invisible.

She saw herself, as if in a dream, becoming wonderfully elastic, arms stretching out, out, scooping the baby up. Her breasts tingled with milk long dried up, like the phantom limbs she'd heard amputees tell of. She could actually *feel* him, the weight of his bottom in the cup of her palm, the tiny pistoning arms and legs, the dark tuft that would spring silkily against her palm like a kitten's fur when she ran her hand over it.

A great wail was building in her, a thing she seemed to have no more control over than she would a train rushing toward her. A cry built of all the years and years of searching, of longing, that had culminated in yet another loss.

Ellie did the one thing she would not, in a million years, have imagined herself doing.

She ran.

As the wail broke loose into the hands clamped over her mouth, she ran as if her life depended on it, looking straight ahead but not seeing where she was going, white coats, gurneys, wheelchairs, rushing past her in a blur.

And all the while a single thought flogged at her brain: *How am I going to tell Paul? How will we get through this?*

The summer Ellie and Paul met, she had finally earned enough college credits to graduate. The year was 1979, and as she'd done every year since her tragedy, she'd marked it with a birthday other than her own: Bethanne would have been almost seven. She herself had been twenty-five going on ninety, working a day job as a receptionist in a law firm and going to school at night. Her life had become a time clock into which she did little more than punch in and punch out. No men, no social life other than occasionally grabbing

a sandwich or a cup of coffee with one of the girls
from work.

Paul changed all that.

It had started with Alice Lawson, whose desk was
catty-corner to Ellie's, inviting her to a Fourth of July
party out at her parents' house in Forest Hills. Ellie
had declined at first, with the excuse that she had too
much studying to do. But Alice had eventually worn
her down. It wasn't until Ellie arrived at the house, a
bowl of potato salad balanced awkwardly in the crook
of one elbow, that she realized the reason for Alice's persistence.

"Come on ... there's someone I'd like you to
meet." Alice, her eyes sparkling with suppressed glee,
grabbed Ellie's arm.

The backyard was crowded with people standing
about in clusters with drinks in hand, and perching on
the picnic tables and chairs scattered over the lawn
and patio. Against the tall wooden fence was a table
laden with platters of food covered in plastic wrap.
The deliciously smoky smell of sizzling meat hung in
the sultry air.

Paul Nightingale, an old school friend of Alice's,
was over by the barbecue with a group of men. He
stood leaning against the side of the house, one
scuffed loafer parked on the edge of the planter in
front of him, a large hand wrapped loosely about the
beer bottle propped on his knee. Ellie's first impression as Alice introduced them was merely of a lanky,
nice-looking man with sandy hair and slightly crooked
features. At second glance, she noticed his glasses, the
steel-rimmed kind that gave him the look of a modi-
fied Berkeley radical—which, she discovered later, was
where he'd gotten his undergraduate degree.

After a few minutes of stilted conversation, Paul
dipped his hand into the cooler at his side and offered
her a dripping beer. "You're not enjoying this very

much, are you?" he observed mildly. "Being around a bunch of people you don't know."

"No," Ellie confessed.

He smiled, and she saw that the tiny crease below the right-hand corner of his mouth that she'd thought was a dimple was actually a scar. "To tell you the truth, neither am I." He leaned closer and confided: "Alice twisted my arm to get me here for the same reason she twisted yours."

Ellie had felt her face redden, as if she'd been standing in the hot sun too long. She didn't know what to say, so she said the first thing that popped into her mind: "I don't normally do this kind of thing."

Paul cocked his head, his smile broadening. "What? Barbecues . . . or fix-ups?"

"Either," she told him, not caring if it sounded rude.

But unlike the other men who'd had the dubious pleasure of being brushed off by her, Paul seemed more intrigued than anything else. He stood there, smiling at her as if she were a road sign in some foreign language that he was trying to puzzle out. Finally, he tipped his beer back in a long swallow, and returned his smiling gaze to her burning face.

"What would you rather be doing?" he asked.

Ellie was so taken aback by what appeared to be genuine interest on his part that for a moment she couldn't think of an answer. At last, she broke into a hesitant smile. "I've always wanted to see the fireworks at Coney Island on the Fourth of July."

Without a beat of hesitation, Paul answered, "You got it." He relieved her of her half-drunk beer, stashing it alongside his on the grass next to the cooler.

Ellie was too surprised to resist as he gently tugged her through the throngs of people, and winked at Alice.

On the long subway ride to Coney Island, Ellie learned that Paul was a second-year resident at Langdon Pediatric Hospital in the West Eighties. He, too, had put himself through school. He'd made it through Berkeley and then Cornell Medical School on student loans, part-time jobs, and gallons of coffee. Like her, he scarcely had the free time to leaf through a magazine, much less go out on dates. She laughed when he told her that the last time he'd taken a woman to a movie, he'd fallen asleep in the middle of it and woken up afterward to discover she'd left without him.

They had other things in common. Paul loved jazz; any free time he could carve out from his crazy work schedule she would most likely find him down at the Village Vanguard, he told her. Ellie told him how she'd felt listening to Billie Holiday the first time, when she was fourteen ... as if she'd discovered buried treasure. Her parents, of course, didn't approve of that kind of music, so she'd had to play it very softly on the record player in the room she shared with Nadine. Ellie even found herself confessing to Paul something she'd never told anyone—how she would sometimes turn off all the lights while the music was playing, and leave a cigarette burning in an ashtray, making believe she was in a smoky nightclub.

Paul laughed so hard, she thought he was making fun of her . . . until he grabbed her hand and squeezed it.

By the time they reached Coney Island, she felt as if she'd known him forever. But it wasn't until she passed out cold on the boardwalk that she quite literally fell in love.

They were still catching their breath after a ride on the Cyclone, making their way along the crowded esplanade toward the hot dog stand by the ring toss concession, when Ellie glimpsed out of the corner of her eye a woman hurtling past, screeching, "Betsy, where are you? Betsy! *Betsy! Oh, God, has anyone seen my little girl?*"

The woman, she recalled with crystal clarity, was clad in pink shorts that revealed a pair of wobbling

thighs burned even pinker by the sun. Her dyed blond
hair stood out in frantic-looking scribbles around her
white face. She held one hand clutched to her heart,
as if she'd been stabbed. In the other was a pair of
child-sized rubber beach thongs.

All at once it hit Ellie, a flock of memories that
spiraled up like black crows from a telephone post.
She remembered the world going grainy, like the old-
time sepia photos she'd seen advertised on a sign
board they'd passed a ways back—COSTUMES NO
EXTRA CHARGE! Then every light on Coney Island,
even the fireworks, blinked out at once.

Swimming back to consciousness, she found herself
on her back on the warm splintery planks of the
boardwalk, blinking up at a ring of curious faces. She
started to panic; then one of the faces emerged into
the foreground. It was a familiar face, a *good* face.
Paul. He was shooing away the others, somehow managing to shield her from their peering eyes as he did
so. Ellie remembered laying there, staring at the heels
of his Weejuns—which, she'd noted dully, were worn
down at a sort of slant—and feeling profoundly grateful to him.

Only after he'd helped her to her feet and over to
a nearby bench did embarrassment creep in. She put
her head between her knees as he instructed, more to
hide her burning cheeks than to dispel her dizziness.
Even Paul's light touch on the back of her neck did
nothing to alleviate her awful sense of exposure.

"Feel like talking about it?" he asked softly, as if
he'd read her mind.

Ellie shook her head, the ends of her hair whipping
her kneecaps. Cupping her hands over her face, she
compounded her humiliation by starting to cry. Paul,
bless him, didn't try to console her. He just sat there,
warm and solid at her side, the tips of his fingers resting against the nape of her neck.

Finally, she was able to lift her face to his, and

confront the look of awkward puzzlement she was certain he must be wearing. But instead, she'd found an expression of warm concern, and a sad, faintly knowing gleam in his slate-colored eyes. Paul, she realized, was himself no stranger to loss. And it was because of that that she felt able to trust him with the awful secret burning a hole in her heart.

She told him then about Bethanne ... and how it was all her fault. She should never have left her baby in Nadine's care. She should have known something bad would happen. If she hadn't been too damn proud to go on welfare, her little girl would still be with her.

The self-recrimination she'd held in for so long burst forth like the fireworks exploding with muffled *bruumps* way out over the languid water. And all the while, Paul never once tried to argue with her, to alleviate her guilt with reassurances. He simply held her hand, only occasionally tightening his fingers about hers. When she finished, he lifted her hand and gently kissed her palm in a gesture she could only have described as courtly.

"I knew you were strong, but I didn't know why," he said. "Now I do. It's all that weight you've been carrying on your shoulders." He looked at her, his gaze steady and thoughtful. "Maybe you're strong enough now to let it go."

Ellie looked back at him just as a burst of fireworks shot scattered red filaments of reflected light across the lenses of his glasses. He understood ... in a way that went beyond her having to explain in any more depth what she'd gone through.

Instead of turning her face away, she did something that until that very moment she could never have imagined herself doing, never in a million years. She brought his hand to her cheek, and held it there, trusting him with her silence just as she'd trusted him with her secret.

Ellie had no recollection of how long they had sat

there on that bench, comfortably holding hands, each
lost in thought. Much later, she learned that years before Paul had lost a younger brother to leukemia. And
he'd decided to specialize in neonatology partly out
of wanting to spare as many families as possible the
grief his had gone through.

The thing Ellie remembered most clearly about that
summer night was a singular revelation: the heart
she'd believed dead had life in it after all. Stranded
amid the streams of milling, squawking revelers, she
had never felt so close to anyone as she did to Paul.
There was wonderment in her discovery, as if she'd broken off a branch of a long-dead plant and discovered a
trace of green at its quick. There was pain, too . . . the
pain of awakening from a long, fitful slumber into the
world of the living, where she would surely be hurt
again.

But above all, she had felt relieved.

No longer would she have to bear her burden alone.
She'd felt it then as strongly as if it had already been
decided. She and Paul would be lovers. More important, they would be friends.

And God knew that what she needed most in the
world, after her long solitary trek through the wilderness, was a friend.

Ellie was in bed fully dressed, with the bedspread
clutched about her like the shawl of an old crone in
a fairy tale, when she heard Paul's key in the front
door of their garden-floor apartment on West Twenty-
second Street. It was after midnight, but she hadn't
closed her eyes once, not even for a minute. She sat
up, shivering.

Paul appeared in the doorway, a lanky silhouette
that seemed to hesitate before he crossed the room
and sank down on the bed. He took her in his arms,
holding her tightly. He didn't say anything; as she
poured out the story he only made a sound deep in

his throat that might have been a moan . . . or maybe
a suppressed sob. When she finally pried herself free,
she saw that his eyes were wet. Gently, she removed
his glasses and set them on the small night table by
the bed.

We still have each other, she told herself. A line
corny enough to be stitched into a sampler, but true,
so true. Then why didn't it comfort her now? Why
did the bleak look in his slate-colored eyes fill her
with a terror more chilling than any she'd experienced
so far?

She looked around her desperately, as if by clinging
to the familiar she could banish her fear. This room,
with its mission bed and plain cherry dresser, its bright
splashes of color—her Picasso posters, the antique toy
carousel on the sewing table in the corner, a hand-
blown Lundberg vase of deep cobalt with a scattering
of stars across its surface.

When she allowed her gaze to return to Paul, it
struck her how tired he looked; not just sleep-
deprived, the way he'd been throughout his residency,
but deeply, fundamentally exhausted. His long face
with its chronically amused smile was devoid of
humor. And was it her imagination, or was there more
silver than brown in the wavy hair that curled down
over the collar of his rumpled shirt?

This time, it was Ellie doing the consoling as she
slipped her arms around him. "I wish I had an answer," she whispered hoarsely into the curve of his
neck. "But all I have are questions. Why? Why *us*?"

"It seems like the more you want something, the
less likely you are to get it." Paul's voice was cynical
and hard.

"You make it sound as if there's no point in going
on." She felt her tears welling up again.

He stroked her back. "There is, of course there is.
I love you. Christ, Ellie, I love you so much that sometimes—" His voice seized up. Taking a deep, steadying

breath, he said, "I miss it, that's all. How it used to be, before we got caught up in all this craziness. All those weekends we used to spend antiquing in the country—remember that inn in Vermont where the bed broke, and we were laughing so hard we couldn't stand up? But forget about weekends ... right now I'd settle for an evening out. When was the last time we sat through a set at the Vanguard or the Blue Note without you ducking out to dial home and check your messages? When was the last time we went to a *movie,* for chrissakes?"

Ellie couldn't blame him for being frustrated. Who could? Not after what they'd been through: an obstacle course with no end in sight. There was no medical reason for her infertility, the doctors had concluded, which had only made her and Paul cling to hope longer than they probably should have. Then a new type of ultrasound showed the uterine cysts other tests had failed to reveal. Paul was there at her side when they wheeled her into surgery, and his was the first face she laid eyes on when she came out of the anesthetic. They'd waited three months before trying again, as ordered. Then ... nothing. By the time they began hesitantly to talk of adoption, eight years had passed.

Their first serious prospect, a shy, freckled girl from Kentucky named Susie, spoke with them several times over the phone before they flew her out to meet them. Ellie remembered being nervous, but the meeting had gone well, or so she'd thought. A week later, their lawyer informed them that Susie had decided on another couple—churchgoers living in a suburban tract house with a backyard big enough for a swing set.

But Susie had been only the first of many disappointments. In between, there had been weeks, months, years of placing ads, being given the once-over by skittish teenagers, but mostly just ... waiting.

That was the worst part. And the not knowing if what you were waiting for would ever come.

Then, a year and a half ago, Denise had tumbled into their lives like a gift. Denise was six months pregnant, a bubbly college sophomore with a level head and clear views on what was best for the baby she felt she was too young to raise on her own. Ellie and Paul had hit it off with her from the start. In her seventh month, Denise even asked Ellie to be her Lamaze coach . . . and Ellie had been so excited she had rushed out that day and ordered a crib and dresser for the nursery.

Then, two weeks before her due date, Denise's mother, with whom Denise had been at bitter odds, arrived suddenly on the scene. Mother had prevailed upon Denise to keep the baby, even offering to help with childcare so Denise could finish school. The girl had stood firm at first, insisting that the decision had been made, and that she wasn't backing down. Then the family pastor was brought in, as well as entreating aunts, uncles, cousins. Eventually Denise caved in.

Ellie had been too shattered even for tears. It was a good six months before she felt strong enough to pick up the pieces and try again. Eight weeks after that, they found Christa.

"Paul, it's not going to be like this forever," she told him now, in the semidarkness of their bedroom.

"How do you know?" He wasn't challenging her, simply asking. "Where is it written that pain and suffering is just something you have to go through to get what you deserve? Most of my patients, they're not even fully formed, and they suffer more than most of us endure in a lifetime. Even with all that technology has to offer, a lot of them don't make it." He paused, his throat working. "The baby we operated on tonight—a twenty-six-weeker—he probably won't live to see tomorrow."

"But a lot of them *do* make it."

"At what cost? I'm looking at this little scrap of a human being on the operating table, and I'm asking myself, Is there a price that's just too damn high? Then I come home to find out this healthy baby, this baby we had everything pinned on, all our dreams— *we even knew what school we were going to enroll him in*—that it was just another illusion."

He slumped back against the slatted headboard with a deep sigh, and picked up her hand, splaying her fingers over his knee, where the denim of his jeans was worn a lighter blue. He ran his thumb over her knuckles, lightly pressing it into their soft hollows.

Ellie shivered, feeling so cold . . . a cold she was certain no amount of heat or blankets could ever thaw. "Oh, Paul . . ."

He held her once more, cradling her while she wept. In the way that the smell of baking bread always brought to mind warm feelings of home, even though hers had not been so warm, the scent of Paul—musky, old-corduroyish, faintly soapy—at once made her feel utterly, unconditionally loved.

She remembered the first time they'd made love, exactly one month after her epiphany on the board-walk at Coney Island, how she'd clung to him after-ward and cried, the last of her defenses melting. Opening up to Paul, becoming vulnerable again, had been like turning a key, unlocking the chamber in which her emotions had been kept in cold storage.

Now, with her face against Paul's neck, she found herself whispering, "He weighed eight pounds, three ounces."

His only response was to hold her tighter.

She took as deep a breath as she could with him nearly crushing her, and said, "Paul, I w.. t to keep trying. I don't want it to end this way . . . with us giving up."

His arms slackened without letting go. "Ellie, I don't think this is the time—"

"Yes, it is," she told him with more firmness than she'd been able to muster in hours. "Because otherwise I don't see how I can bear it."

"It's funny," he said, pulling away. "I was just thinking the same thing, only the other way around. If I thought we'd have to go through this again, I don't know that I'd be holding up so well now."

"Oh, Paul, how can you say that?"

"I can't help how I feel, Ellie."

"What about how *I* feel?" she cried. "Dammit, Paul, we're talking about something that's going to affect the rest of our lives!"

"Ellie, I'm tired," he said quietly. He regarded her for a moment with his naked bloodshot eyes before retrieving his glasses from the night table. As if in putting them on, he was somehow placing a barrier between them. "It's not just today. It's not just about Christa changing her mind. I'm just . . . tired. Tapped out. No more gas left in the tank."

"What are you saying?" They'd had this discussion before, but now it was no longer about what *might* happen. They had reached a crossroads, and there was no backing away from it.

"I'm saying that if you want to keep on trying to adopt you'll have to do it alone." It hurt him to say it, she could see that.

She stared at him, at the face she'd have been able to identify in the dark, merely by touch, at the fine lines around his eyes that hadn't been there a year ago, the set of his wonderfully crooked mouth that seemed to smile less and less these days. This wasn't just about the two of them; it was about Paul being director of the NICU at Langdon, too—the tiny babies even his most heroic efforts couldn't save, the hours spent conferring with the ethics committee, playing God in a place where it was a struggle just to retain one's humanity. It wasn't that Paul didn't care. He cared *too* much.

Ellie recognized all that, and while her heart ached for him, while she clearly saw his side, none of it seemed to matter. She could have been standing in the middle of a road with an eighteen-wheeler bearing down on her, and if running for safety had meant relinquishing all hope of ever having a child, she'd have taken her chances on the driver spotting her in time.

It wasn't even as if she had a choice. Not even a will of iron—something she'd often enough been accused of having—could have prevented her from reliving the nightmare again and again, each baby she saw on the street or in the supermarket swamping her with unbearable yearning. Bethanne was all grown up, she'd tell herself. She'd try to picture her daughter as a young lady, but it was no good. To Ellie, Bethanne was, and would always be, the sting in her eyes when she caught the sweet scent of baby powder, or heard a toddler's merry laugh, or watched a mother take firm hold of her child's hand crossing the street.

"I dreamed about her last night," she said softly. "I actually saw her, Bethanne. *Him*, too. I saw myself running after him, but whenever I got close he'd be another block ahead of me. Then I lost him in the crowd." Tears flooded her eyes, but she blinked them back. "I never told you this, but sometimes, after the dream, I can feel my milk letting down."

He touched her hand. "Ellie." Just that, her name, soft as a caress, only sadder, carrying all the sorrow of the world.

"I can't stop," she told him. "Even if I wanted to. I have to keep trying."

"You can't replace Bethanne," he told her.

"This isn't just *about* Bethanne anymore," she said impatiently. "Paul, I'm forty. There isn't much time left. If I stop now ..."

" 'Am I not better to thee than ten sons?' " His mouth flickered with the ghost of his old, ironic smile.

"First Samuel, chapter one, verse eight." Growing up in Euphrates, she'd had the Scriptures pounded into her, but never had she imagined the plight of poor, childless Hannah would one day be hers.

"I hate this," he said through gritted teeth. "I feel as though I'm asking you to choose, and I know that's not fair. But I can't help it, Ellie. I wonder if I enter into this equation at all—if I'm not just some convenient backdrop for this drama of yours."

She felt the icy core at her center seeping into her blood.

"You can't believe that," she answered softly. "God, I don't know how you could even *say* it."

"When was the last time we made love?" he demanded hotly. "With Christa, we've been on pins and needles for the past month, so worried she'd change her mind if we weren't there for her every second we hardly dared leave the apartment except to go to work. Ellie, we can't even hold a conversation without me feeling like you're listening with one ear for the phone."

Ellie felt a rush of contrition . . . and also of fear.

What if Paul made good on his threat? What would it be like, waking up every morning to an empty bed . . . rushing home to share a triumph concerning one of her patients and not finding him there . . . aching for his touch in the loneliness of the night?

I need you, Paul, she wanted to say to him. *In a hundred and one ways you're there for me . . . consoling me when I'm down, even if a backrub is all you can do to make it better . . . offering advice when I'm in doubt, but never unless I ask for it . . . even doing little things, like bringing me coffee in the morning, and remembering to turn your socks right side out when it's my day to do the laundry.*

There was no questioning the depth of her bond with Paul. But Ellie also understood now what it was like for some of her patients, those in the grip of an

inexplicable obsession. Was she becoming like them,
losing control of her life, alienating those closest to
her?

Not at all, a calm voice advised. *What you want is
the most natural thing in the world. What nearly every
woman wants.*

"I can't promise it'll be any different," she told him.
"Only that it won't go on forever. There *will* be an
end to it."

"When? *When*?" All the anguish she felt was reflected in his eyes, and in the almost painful pressure
of the fingers digging into her shoulders.

Suddenly, it all seemed so clear. When you stripped
away everything else, it was as simple and pure as
a child's drawing. *Elementary, my dear Watson,* she
thought, a smile touching her lips. Why couldn't Paul
see it? How perfect it all could be if they could just
hold on a little longer?

"When I get a baby," she said.

CHAPTER 4

There was no viewing window onto the Henry Carter Deacon Neonatal Intensive Care Unit.

As he strode through the swinging entrance doors, Dr. Paul Nightingale, director of the NICU, mentally blessed—and not for the first time—the compassionate soul who'd placed Deacon a floor above the regular nursery. At present, the unit was responsible for fifteen preemies, each one requiring a small ground-control station of equipment, technology, and medical expertise. Life was tenuous for these tiny patients, and tough on the doctors and nurses who cared for them. It was even tougher on the parents. But at least when visiting they were spared the viewing window downstairs, with its panorama of healthy full-term babies.

Paul headed for the deep stainless sinks to the right of the entrance. The sign fixed to the wall over the Exidine dispenser read: "Before You Visit Your Infant Remove All Jewelry and Scrub to Elbows with Brush for Two Minutes." As he was scrubbing, he caught a glimpse over his shoulder of one of the mothers, Serena Blankenship, hovering over the Number Three warmer. Like the nurses on Deacon, she wouldn't have had any jewelry to remove; not wearing any no doubt had become routine after three weeks.

"Bad night," muttered Martha Healey, jerking her head in Serena's direction.

Martha stood by the cluster of desks on the far side of the fat red stripe that divided the floor into two sections—nonsterile, and reasonably sterile. Anyone who hadn't scrubbed first wasn't allowed across that line, which Martha and the other nurses guarded as fiercely as any border crossing.

"Theo's bilirubin is up," Martha added somberly. "He doesn't look good."

"Has she been here all night?" Paul asked with a pointed glance at Serena.

Martha nodded. Tiny, almost waiflike, with her pixieish ginger bob, she looked as if she ought to be hawking Girl Scout cookies door to door, but she was the best kind of NICU nurse, in Paul's opinion: passionately devoted to "her babies," and a terror to slipshod interns. The junkie moms, Martha had even less sympathy for. She'd greet them at the entrance with fire in her green eyes, and a voice that antifreeze wouldn't melt, prepared to uphold to the death the restraining order taped to their baby's warmer.

"I tried to get her to take a break," Martha told him. "At least put her head down in the conference room if nothing else. She won't budge."

Paul made his way through the thicket of isolettes on rolling tables, each one accompanied by an almost frightening display of computerized equipment—cardiac monitor, pulse oximeter, ventilator. He nodded to the nurses in cranberry-pink scrubs jotting notes in files, administering meds and feedings, changing diapers and weighing them to measure urine output. At Theo Blankenship's isolette, he paused to check the settings on the computer monitoring oxygen flow. Fifty percent—up two from yesterday. Damn. It was the old catch-22. The vent that *caused* the BPD that had left

Theo's thimble-sized lungs so scarred would only get worse with the increase in oxygen, but without it he wouldn't be able to breathe.

"He's worse, isn't he?" A soft voice punctuated the hiss of ventilators.

Paul looked up into anxious eyes the pale, washed-out blue of the scrubs he wore. Yet there was nothing about Serena Blankenship that would suggest even a hint of unsteadiness. Christ, the woman couldn't have slept more than twelve hours total in the three weeks Theo had been here, and on top of that she was still recovering from a C-section. No husband to spell her, either. She ought to be a basket case.

He certainly was. These past few weeks, since the debacle with Christa, he and Ellie had gone about their routines, trying to pretend nothing was wrong, not talking about it simply because there was nothing more to say. But Paul felt like if he breathed in too hard, he'd discover there was no more oxygen left in the atmosphere. It was a little like bolting the door against a cyclone. Too little, too late.

Where do you go when there's no room for compromise? What do you do when you love your wife so much you'd do just about anything for her—anything but sign the death warrant on your own marriage?

If only he could somehow persuade Ellie to stop. Rescue her, in a way. Paul's mind formed an unlikely image of his wife trapped in a tower, and he in Prince Valiant garb scaling it at risk to life and limb. His mouth hooked up in a mirthless smile. Fat chance of his rescuing the likes of Ellie. She'd laugh him off the ramparts.

But the thought persisted—it was a holdover from his student days as an activist with the SDS, inciting campus peace marches and sit-ins and draft-card burnings, a time when he'd believed with all the passion in his student's heart that the war in Vietnam could be ended if they all yelled hard enough—that this

thing, this *obsession* of his wife's, was the dragon of
his fractured fairy tale. If he could slay it, Ellie would
be free of its evil enchantment.

He became aware that Serena was staring at him,
politely waiting for his reply. He focused on her, for
the first time seeing her not as a mother but as a
woman. She was pretty, but in a way that didn't demand his attention. With her even features and
sweetly rounded chin, she could have been any one
of a thousand women over the years smiling at him
across a counter or a desk, there to help him fill out
a form, cash a check, apply for insurance. Her honey-
colored pageboy looked as if she brushed it religiously
one hundred strokes every night. She wore a simple
beige wool dress with low-heeled shoes, her only jewelry the tiny gold knots in her ears. He could see her
wearing exactly this outfit to attend a PTA meeting
or accompany her son's class on a field trip to the
Museum of Modern Art. Except that if Theo didn't
pull through, there would be no PTA meetings or
field trips.

Paul consulted Theo's flow sheet: IMV 60, Pressure
20/5, bilirubin up to 8, urine output just under .7 cc's
an hour. He examined the tiny scrap of flesh, almost
too small to be considered human, much less to carry
the unwieldy name of Theodore Haley Blankenship.
The baby was still jaundiced, his skin the color of
weak green tea, the flesh around his navel, where a
tube fed into his umbilical vein, swollen and irritated-
looking. The notation in Theo's chart, left by Amy
Shapiro, the resident on call last night, was no more
encouraging. "Hospital day 14 for this 700-gram 26-
week preemie with severe BPD and 2 episodes of oli-
guria in last 10–12 days now on vent settings of pres-
sures 20/5, oxygen at 50%."

Paul felt something catch inside him. Most of the
time he managed to keep his patients at an emotional
arm's length, but this one was different. It was some-

thing about those eyes that seemed to track him like tiny blue beacons. Or maybe it was Serena, coming day after day even when all she could do was tape photos, facing in, to the Plexiglas side of Theo's isolette—snapshots of grandparents, of her house in Roslyn with its overgrown flower garden and friendly-looking golden retriever, even one of her ex-husband, who as far as Paul knew had not once visited.

"It doesn't look good," he admitted. He met her quietly anxious gaze. "Why don't we step outside where we can talk?"

She followed him out into the corridor, and down the hall a short way to the conference room, which was more commonly used as a place for exhausted residents and parents to grab a few winks. Some long-gone misguided optimist had decorated it in Easter-egg colors—pale yellow walls, Scandinavian table and chairs, a low couch upholstered in green and blue stripes that showed the stains of coffee spilled by unsteady hands. At present, there was an unused isolette shoved against the wall and a metal filing cabinet in one corner with a box of plastic tubing stashed on top.

Paul watched Serena settle on the sofa, her legs crossed primly at the ankles. The only sign of her tension was the ramrod straightness of her back. In the glare of the recessed lights, he saw the bruised-looking circles under her eyes, and thought of Ellie. These days, she looked beaten, almost mugged. And, yes, in a way they *had* been robbed. God, did she think for one minute he hadn't wanted that baby, too?

Maybe that's what made Theo so special. Just as Christa's baby had been the end of the line for Paul, the tiny infant in the next room was Serena's last hope. She'd confided in Paul the other day that her pregnancy had been a miracle—after years of infertility, the happy result of IVF, which Paul knew from his and Ellie's experience had only a thirty percent success rate at best. He wondered if all that running back and forth to specialists, the tests, the hormone therapy, the surgical procedures, then the waiting, the interminable waiting for the results of pregnancy tests that over and over proved negative—if all that had contributed to the defection of Serena's husband.

"He looks awful," she said in a voice pitched a note higher than usual. "Be honest with me—what are his chances?"

Paul considered his approach carefully. He wanted to be very clear, very direct ... but not brutal. "Theo is failing," he told her gently. "His lungs just aren't mature enough. He's also weakened from his surgery. Even now that it's patched, his heart just can't keep up, and that's causing his kidneys to fail."

She stiffened. "Are we talking DNR?" Over the past few weeks, Serena had become nearly as well versed in the terminology as one of the unit's interns.

Codes were so much easier than the actual words. "Do not resuscitate." The reality—standing by and merely watching as transparent flesh turned blue, a tiny fluttering chest grew still—was even worse. In this case, he found even the thought of it deeply disturbing.

Paul tried not to let in the murky thoughts that had plagued him ever since Theo had been brought here—thoughts about Theo being born on the same day as Christa's baby. Like a sign from heaven. Everything but Charlton Heston's voice, amplified by an echo chamber, commanding that he save this tiny, sick child in lieu of being father to his own.

Jesus, what a sentimental jerk, he thought.

Yet he was quick to say, "I don't think that's indicated just yet. I'd like to give it another day or two. Then maybe go to Protocol One. That's—"

"I know," she interrupted him. "Leave him on the respirator, but no CPR, no drugs." Blotchy patches of red stood out on Serena's pale cheeks. "You're asking me to think about it, Dr. Nightingale. If you want to know the truth, for the past three days I've thought about nothing else. I don't think I could sleep if I tried."

"You really should," he cautioned. "I could prescribe something, if you like."

Serena shook her head. "No, I want to be awake in case—" She stopped, and the pale blue of her eyes dissolved in a shimmer of tears. He could see how hard she was struggling to maintain control, and was moved. Finally, in a constricted voice, she asked, "Is there anything more you can do for him, anything at all?"

She was asking him for a measure of hope, no matter how scant. But hope was an analgesic they were pitifully short of on Deacon. Paul could do no more than lean forward and take her hands in his, attempting to warm her icy fingers with his own.

"The one thing I can tell you is that I've been surprised before," he answered, careful not to imbue his words with more than their face value. "Babies the entire staff has given up on sometimes pull through. It doesn't happen often . . . but it happens."

"Are you saying Theo could make it on his own?"

"Anything is possible."

She frowned, drawing her hands away and folding them in her lap. "Why don't you just say it? *Theo isn't going to make it.*" Overcome, Serena slumped to one side, burying her face in the crook of her elbow. Her shoulders convulsed in spasms, coupled with a gasping sound so desperate it caused Paul to flinch. When she finally lifted her head, it was all he could do not to shrink from the naked, ravaged face of her grief.

"In my professional opinion," he said as gently as he could, "there is very little likelihood of Theo recovering."

"I want him made DNR," she said, her voice a strangled whisper. "I don't want him to suffer. He's been so brave." She gave a choked sob, but somehow managed to go on. "There *is* something left to give him—an end to his suffering. I want him to have that."

An image swam into Paul's mind: Dr. Merriweather, his aged, pipe-smoking physical diagnosis professor at Cornell. "What do people fear most?" Merriweather had asked the class of ninety wide-eyed medical students. "Is it death, do you think?" A forest of hands had gone up. But the old imp had merely chuckled, saying, "You have much to learn, my young friends."

Over the years of his internship and residency and fellowship, Paul had come to understand what Merriweather had meant. Death wasn't the bogeyman; suffering was. When the pain simply became too much, the prospect of death could seem as welcome as a pickup pulling onto the shoulder of an endless dusty road, and a friendly hand waving you on board.

Every professional instinct in Paul urged him to support her in what had to be the most difficult decision of her life. But something buzzing in the corner of his brain—something as small and possibly irrelevant as a fly bombarding a windowpane—told him not to give up. Not just yet.

"I'd like to give it another day," he told her. "If there's no improvement, we'll talk again tomorrow." He could see that she was wavering, wanting to trust him against her own better judgment.

Is that what I'm doing with Ellie, too? Hoping she'll do an about-face when I know that's like hoping Theo will pull through?

"All right." Serena sighed, dabbing at her eyes with the Kleenex he offered her.

"In the meantime, I'd like you to get some rest." He held up a hand to stop her protests. "Just for a few hours. I'll have one of the nurses wake you if there's any change."

Paul walked away feeling more troubled than he had in years. He'd always been so damn scrupulous about not letting his ego get in the way of what was best for his patients. Always aware of the fine line between fighting an uphill battle and what threatened to become a quixotic one. Had he lost all perspective here? Was he committing the unpardonable sin of letting his private life color his professional decisions?

Back on the unit, Theo, looking up at him from the sheepskin pad that cushioned a body devoid of any fat, seemed to reproach him. Paul carefully peeled back the bandage on his chest and listened with a stethoscope smaller than a child's toy one to the heart he'd assisted in patching. *Listen, little guy. I'll make a deal with you. Show me you can do it. One more cc of urine, and I promise not to give up on you.*

Paul was examining the Melendez baby, born at twenty-nine weeks addicted to methadone, when he heard the ping of a cardiac alarm. He ignored it. Alarms were always going off on Deacon, and it was usually just a matter of a practiced tap delivered to the monitor or to the baby. Out of the corner of his eye, he saw Martha hurry over to Theo's isolette. But despite her ministrations, the line on his cardiac monitor remained flat. Theo's heart had arrested.

Christ.

"Code?" Martha asked, her anxious eyes meeting his.

Paul raced over, and checked to make sure the vent was working. It was.

"Let's just make sure the tube is in." He extubated, and using a laryngoscope and stylet, inserted a fresh plastic tube. Switching to a bag vent that would give him a higher pressure, he listened for sounds of breathing. Nothing. "Pull up a syringe of epinephrine," he ordered. "And get X-ray up here. I want another blood gas run, too. Here, you take over bagging him," he told the nurse who'd joined them, a heavyset Jamaican with large, competent-looking hands.

Gently but hurriedly removing bandages and patches,

Paul placed his hands around the Lilliputian chest with
its jagged red scar, his fingertips meeting in back
with plenty of room to spare. He began pressing down
with his thumbs in a gentle rhythmic motion. *Easy
does it.* He counted the compressions, his eyes on the
monitor, where he could see the waves of activity he
was generating.

He's got the whole world in his hands. Paul heard
the words of the spiritual in his head, and at this moment it seemed as if the whole universe did indeed
rest in his hands. There was only this—the flexing of
tissue-thin cartilage under his fingers, the rhythm he
counted under his breath, the artificially undulating
red line on the monitor.

After a couple of minutes, he stopped and waited
five seconds. *Come on, dammit, I can't do this forever.*

But the line once again flattened. The tiny chest, on
which he could see the red marks left by his thumbs,
had stopped moving.

He began pressing again, a hundred and twenty
compressions a minute. *Come on, come on.*

His thumbs began to ache, then grow numb. He felt
a thin trickle of sweat crease one temple. Another
pause. No activity. Shit.

"Do you want me to take over, Doctor?" asked
Martha. Her voice implied that he ought to give up
altogether.

He ignored the question. "Give me another tenth
of a cc of epi," he snapped.

He was aware of Martha and the other nurse ex-
changing a glance as Martha injected the epinephrine
into Theo's endotracheal tube, and he wondered, on
some detached level of his brain, if he had, in fact,
passed the extreme limits of medical viability and was
well into the realm of *deus ex machina.* Even Jordan
Blume, the resident now peering over Paul's shoulder,
shaking his head, seemed to be saying "Enough is
enough. Let the kid go."

Paul couldn't have explained it to them—any more, he guessed, than Ellie could ever really explain to him her burning need to keep on with her quest for a baby. This was just something he had to do.

But if no activity showed in the next minute, he would have to call off the code. No matter what he felt, Paul couldn't subject Theo to such a futile, ghoulish effort.

Now. He let up with his thumbs. *Beat, damn it, beat.* Nothing.

His mind raced. Had he overlooked anything? Was there something else he could do? Something that might have led directly to the arrest, other than just a general failing of Theo's bodily systems?

"Might be a pneumothorax," he conjectured aloud.

In a desperate last-ditch effort, he yelled, "Hit the lights and let me have a transilluminator." Holding the stainless-steel device to Theo's chest, he saw it, a glowing patch of red where oxygen had become trapped. He grabbed the angiocatheter, and inserted the needle to which it was attached. Within seconds, the deadly pocket of air had been released.

He wasn't aware he was holding his breath until he saw Theo's chest give a feeble jump and the monitor's red line begin to spike on its own. Then the air emptied from his own lungs with a rush that left him slightly dizzy.

Martha let out a whoop, but was instantly sobered by the look on Jordan Blume's sallow hound-dog face. "We're not doing him any favor," muttered the young resident. "He'll die anyway."

"Maybe," Paul said when he could trust himself to speak. "Let's give Theo a chance to decide that for himself."

He remembered his promise to Serena, but saw no point in waking her just yet. The crisis, for the moment, had passed. He would talk to her after his rounds.

An hour later, Paul found her sound asleep on the
sofa in the conference room, one arm curled protec-
tively about a throw cushion as if she were cuddling
her baby in her dreams. His throat grew thick, and he
felt frighteningly close to collapse himself. Delayed
reaction, he thought. He hadn't let himself mourn, not
once, since the tearful call from Christa, home from
the hospital and confirming that she was keeping her
baby. Maybe he'd been afraid Ellie would take any
sign of grief on his part as proof that he was in this
as deep as she.

Serena woke with a start the instant he dropped his
hand onto her shoulder. She sat up, blinking, looking
both alarmed and ashamed, like a sentry caught sleeping at her post. Pushing her fingers through her hair,
she croaked, "Theo?"

"He had an episode," Paul said evenly. "About an
hour ago. There wasn't time to call you. His heart
failed, but we managed to rescucitate him. He's comfortable at the moment."

"Oh, God." She cupped a hand over her eyes as if
to shade them from a light that had suddenly become
too bright. But when she looked up at him, the light
seemed to come from her. "Tomorrow," she said, un-
nerving him with her brilliant, anguished gaze. "If he's
worse, or even the same, I want it to be over. I refuse
to let him go on suffering."

Suddenly, Paul was seeing himself at ten years old.
Wrestling with his little brother on the lawn, then
watching eight-year-old Billy double over on the grass,
heaving and clutching his stomach. "Billy, you little
doofus!" he'd yelled. "I told you not to eat the whole
box." But then Paul had realized that this was something more serious than Billy getting sick from eating
too many chocolate-covered raisins. Looking down at
his brother's convulsed white face, Paul, screaming for
their mom, had felt a shadow pass over him, like the
one scudding over the grass at his feet. He couldn't

have put the feeling into words at that time, but he remembered it a year later, when Billy died from leukemia.

Only now the something he couldn't put his finger on was whispering *Wait, wait.*

"Tomorrow," he promised.

"It's taken her a year to put it together," Georgina informed them, leaning so close the wet rim of her glass brushed Paul's sleeve. Her vivid blue eyes looked out at Paul from a face webbed with fine lines. "Traveled all over Europe, camping on sidewalks with her Nikon. Have you ever seen anything like it?"

Paul hadn't. And if Ellie's friend hadn't bullied them into attending her niece's photography exhibit, he could have lived without it. But the exhibit, in a loft on Twenty-fifth and Sixth, was walking distance from their apartment, and as Ellie had pointed out, they'd be doing Georgina a favor. Not that he didn't find the show interesting and avant-garde—all the clever photos of department-store mannequins in every possible guise and setting. Trouble was, Paul was so beat that if he could have leaned up against one of the loft's support pillars, he'd have been asleep in less time than it took to snap a picture.

He looked about him at the crowd of sixty or so— mostly people he didn't recognize—milling among pedestals, set at varying heights, on which stylized mannequins posed. Georgina was crowing about what a stroke of genius it had been, getting the owner of this mannequin showroom to lend her niece the space, even if the far-from-fashionable address had kept some people away.

"I like the one of Harrods," Ellie was saying. "It really does remind me of London."

"Exactly." Georgina reached up to tuck behind her ear a wisp that had come loose from her long silver braid. "Do you know that Alice had to practically bribe a bobby into letting her stand in the middle of traffic to get that shot? Her husband nearly had a heart attack when he heard. It was their honeymoon, you know." She chuckled, and sipped her drink.

Georgina was wearing one of her ubiquitous caftans, this one gold silk with a batik pattern that made him think of prehistoric cave paintings. Heavy Indian-looking earrings stretched her earlobes, and the squash-blossom necklace draped about her neck looked as if it weighed enough to topple her. But looks were deceiving, Paul knew. Just last summer, in celebration of her eightieth birthday, Georgina had gone trekking in the Himalayas.

"That reminds me of *our* honeymoon," Ellie recalled, turning to Paul with a wistful little smile. "Remember our taxi driver on the way to the Louvre— the one who got into a drag race with his friend?"

"I remember you telling him off in very bad French," Paul said.

"He was lucky I didn't tell him off in English."

Watching Ellie, Paul thought, *God, does she have any idea how beautiful she is?* In her tailored chocolate suit and a silk blouse the color of *caffè latte,* she ought to have looked no more than chicly professional, like window blinds adjusted to let in only some of the light, but her stylishness revealed only a fraction of her beauty.

All at once, in spite of everything that had come between them these past few weeks, he wanted her. Desperately. He felt like a teenager on a first date, lusting after someone unattainable. Did she want him, too? They hadn't so much as kissed in almost a month ... but tonight she'd seemed more like her old self, relaxed, even a bit flirtatious. God, he'd give anything right now to be home in bed with her.

"Oh, that reminds me," Georgina cried, latching on to Ellie's wrist with a piratical hand. "The symposium in Lucerne next month, will you be joining us? Please say you will. I was talking to Henry about your AIDS group. He thinks it'd make a wonderful topic."

Ellie hesitated. "Can I let you know later in the week?" she hedged. "My schedule is awfully full at the moment, but I'll see what I can do."

"It's an excuse, you know," Georgina said, and for a stricken moment Ellie looked as if her bluff had been called. She relaxed a bit as the old lady scolded, "How long since either of you took any time off? This would be the perfect excuse for sneaking off afterwards to some secluded Alpine auberge."

"Right now, I wouldn't say no to a Holiday Inn in Secaucus," Paul joked. But he could tell from the look Ellie darted at him that she wasn't fooled.

But he put on a bright smile—maybe even believing it was possible for them to pick up the pieces of their life and go on—and said, "It sounds wonderful. I really *will* try, Georgie."

"Good. Now go on, a quick look around for politeness' sake and you're off the hook," the old lady trilled. "You've done your duty just showing up, and that's all my brilliant niece should expect from her first show—enough body heat to keep the chill off."

"Was it that obvious?" muttered Paul as they threaded their way through the bodies clustered around each exhibit. "I *feel* like I could do with a month's sleep, but I'd hate to think I'm walking around looking like Mr. Personality here." He nodded toward the bored-looking male mannequin at his elbow.

Ellie took a step back, appraising him with eyes that held the first genuine sparkle he'd seen in weeks. "You look old-money elegant. I especially like the button missing on your coat. Very understated."

"I didn't have time to sew it on," he said, glancing down at his muted plaid sport coat with the fondness he reserved for his very oldest clothes.

She touched the spot on his jacket where the button

was missing, smiling up at him. "How would you like to buy me dinner at the fanciest restaurant in the neighborhood instead?"

Paul struggled to keep his lust at bay. It was just like the old days, Ellie flirting and him falling for it. Even the tired lines around her mouth seemed to have eased. And she hadn't spoken a word about adoption, not since the night they'd argued about it. Was it possible that, with a little perspective, she was having second thoughts? Or was he just kidding himself?

He took her arm, giving her his sexiest Jean-Paul Belmondo smile. "I thought you'd never ask." Had she guessed how much he wanted her ... enough to skip dinner and take her home this very instant? Maybe, but he knew enough to take it slowly, make her feel properly seduced.

At the Ballroom, two blocks away, they stuffed themselves with tapas and got drunk on sangria listening to flamenco guitar. Paul forgot how tired he was, and even managed to keep from thinking too much about Theo. He simply allowed himself to feel happy, even knowing that tomorrow morning would most likely deliver more than a hangover and Friday's mail.

The mood held as they made their way home on foot, arms slung companionably about each other's waists—until a sudden cloudburst sent them scurrying the last block and a half to their brownstone.

"Oh, shit, my new shoes will be ruined!" Ellie cried, glancing down in dismay at her suede pumps as she ran.

Paul didn't stop to think. Spotting the puddle below the curb just ahead of them, he turned toward Ellie, and with a single mighty effort scooped her into his arms. She let out a squeal that was half delight, half warning—after all, she was not a dainty woman—then threw her arms around his neck and buried her face against his shoulder.

Paul, even while cursing himself for neglecting to take better advantage of his YMCA membership, found himself caught up in the overblown heroism of his act. He knew it was silly, but damn if he didn't feel, well, *Arthurian*. What was very real, though, was the wonderful heft of Ellie in his arms, her heat warming him through their layers of wet clothing. God, could she feel how much he wanted her?

"You're crazy, you know that?" She laughed breathlessly when he set her down on their stoop. "You could have thrown your back out."

"Now that would have been a shame . . . considering what I have in mind," he teased wickedly.

"Now what could that be?" A smile played at her lips.

The instant they were inside, she was kicking off her shoes, laughing as she whipped her head so that her wet hair flicked him with cold drops. Taking her in his arms and kissing her, Paul tasted lipstick and spices . . . and something more, a sweet yielding that made him catch his breath.

He fumbled with the buttons on her coat, feeling the way he had the first time he'd kissed a girl on her doorstep—Jean Woollery from Holy Cross, who'd discreetly palmed the gum she'd been chewing then was so flustered she'd ended up accidentally plastering it to the back of the jacket of his good blue suit. Except now, with Ellie, he didn't feel like a kid with a hard-on. Along with the damp heat their wet clothes were giving off, he was swamped with memories—of the time they'd made love in the cramped bathroom of a 747 bound for Orly; of stumbling into the kitchen at two in the morning to find Ellie, stark naked, blissfully eating a peach, her breasts sticky with the juice dripping off her chin; of sitting at the living room window during last winter's blizzard, holding hands while they watched flashes of lightning turn the street below into a glass snow dome.

Ellie wriggled out of her clothes, laughing, tossing them into a sodden heap by the door. Looking at her, naked except for her rope of pearls, water trickling down her neck and breasts, he wanted her more than ever. More than he could express.

He dipped his head, licking the raindrop that shivered like a tiny jewel from one nipple. She trembled, and up close he could see that her skin was pricked with gooseflesh. Lightly, she touched the top of his head. *Yes,* the gentle pressure of her fingertips seemed to say as he drew circles with his tongue. *Like that. Like before* . . .

Before they'd gotten so wrapped up in tilting at windmills they'd lost sight of what had made them want to be a family in the first place. Before they'd started counting days to the middle of her cycle. Before the answering machine that, even with the phone set at its quietest ring, would cause her to tense beneath him. Before they forgot how to do this . . . to *play.*

"Here?" She lifted an eyebrow as he drew her to the center of the living room, in front of the Stickley sofa, which now held his own clothes, hastily lobbed over its back.

"Too cold?" he asked, kissing one eyelid, then the other.

"Mmm. Not anymore." She tucked herself around him as if to seal off any gaps where cold air might get through.

He caught their fractured reflection skimming across the coffee table's glass top as he lowered her onto the carpet. Lying on her back, with her wet hair spread out around her head, and the light from the hall fixture leaving half her face in shadow, Paul almost, *almost,* believed they could pull it off, put Humpty Dumpty together again.

He took her sooner than he'd intended, not because he couldn't hold back, but because Ellie, as he was moving his mouth down her belly, grabbed his head with both hands, gently pulling him back up, then opening her legs and arching her hips to take him into her. She was as wet inside as out, he discovered with a small chill of pleasure—gloriously, sumptuously ready for him.

Paul moved slowly, cautiously, because now he *was* holding back. God, it felt good. Wanting something, wanting it badly, but knowing it was within his grasp, knowing he could pluck it from its stem whenever he wished. She had her legs wrapped about him now, her wonderful hips—she thought they were too wide— thrusting with a new urgency that gave him that last little push over the edge.

It was so acute, it was almost painful, the final letting-go. It took him by the throat as he clutched her, frenzied, his face pressed into the wet mist of her hair, feeling her strain beneath him, hearing her hoarse cry of release mingling with his own.

Afterward, as they lay tangled together, one of his knees wedged uncomfortably against the leg of the coffee table, Paul could feel her trembling. "Cold?" he whispered, and felt her shake her head. Then, with dawning horror, he realized she was crying. He lifted himself onto one elbow and looked down at her, touching the spot over her temple where a tear was vanishing into her damp hair.

"Ellie?"

"I'm sorry." Her voice was small and fierce, the way she sounded when the one she was most angry at was herself. "I swore I wasn't going to do this. God, I'm such a broken record."

He tensed. *Jesus, no, not now.*

Rather than answer her, he placed his arms around her, hugging her tightly.

"I can't, Paul. I tried. I even talked to Georgina about it. But it's no good." She spoke into the side of his neck, her words muffled. "I can't stop thinking about it."

"Ellie, don't. Not now."

He drew away, pulling himself onto his knees. Shivering, rocking back on his heels, he stared at her, and all at once he didn't like what he saw: the stubborn set of her mouth, the way her eyes looked back at him, bewildered by his inability to see what she so clearly did.

"Paul, I talked to Leon today. He said he'd put out some feelers . . ."

"Without even *telling* me, you talked to him?" Leon was the lawyer who'd found Christa for them.

Paul stood up so suddenly the blood rushing from his head made him dizzy. He was conscious now of his nakedness in an unpleasant way, a way that left him feeling awkward and exposed. He snatched up his pants and tugged them on, hardly noticing they were still damp. Hot anger rose in him like a blister.

He couldn't shake the feeling of somehow being . . . ripped off.

Ellie sat up, crossing her legs, making him think absurdly of an overgrown flower child at a summer love-in. "I'm telling you now." Her calm infuriated him even more.

"Telling, as opposed to *discussing*? Sure, I get it. What I want doesn't factor into this one iota."

"I wish you didn't have to see it that way," she said, looking desperate and pained.

"Why?" he demanded. "Because you want me to be as much a part of this as you—or because it'd all be so much tidier if I just went along?"

She winced, and he saw something dark flare in her eyes.

"Was that a question . . . or just a cheap shot?" she asked in her most coolly professional tone.

"I'm sorry," he apologized. "It *was* a cheap shot.

But dammit, Ellie, don't you get it? If this is about us being a family, how can you just ignore how I feel?"

For a long moment he .was trapped by her steady, thoughtful gaze, until finally she spoke. "I thought you *wanted* a child," she said softly. "And not just to make me happy."

"I do ... but not as much as you." Paul felt something shift in him, a realization that went much deeper than the one he'd spoken aloud. "Jesus, Ellie, this is it, isn't it? We've painted ourselves into a corner."

"It looks that way." He could see she was struggling not to cry.

"So where do we go from here?"

"Your call."

"As if it'd be as easy as me just walking out the door." He heard the bitter irony in his voice.

"Maybe it is." Her gaze was flat, unflinching.

"Are you *asking* me to leave?"

"Maybe it would be for the best."

He stared at her, her words not registering at first. It didn't seem possible, after what they'd just done together. After all the times they'd made love, which, if they'd been strung together, would have formed a rope of pearls ten times longer than the one looped about Ellie's neck. He watched in disbelief as Ellie rose gracefully to her feet, her eyes glittering with wounded anger.

He took one last, hard look, his eyes blurring with what might have been exhaustion, but was more likely the tears he'd been staving off like some macho asshole. He thought of Serena Blankenship, making a decision he knew had to be killing her, but one she felt she had no choice in making. DNR. *Do not resuscitate.*

"If you need to reach me, I'll be at the hospital," he told her, grabbing his shirt and jacket and heading for the door.

Deacon had no concept of day or night. The sun never rose or set there, and the nurses, respiratory therapists, and residents never went home, only changed faces with each new shift. Yet it seemed to Paul as he entered the fluorescent-lit room that babies, even ones as small and fragile as these, knew the difference. At three in the morning, they seemed to be slumbering more deeply, their breathing less troubled somehow, their monitors quiet.

An illusion probably, he told himself, brought on, no doubt, by his own troubled patch of sleep in the residents' lounge. Approaching Theo's warmer, he felt his gut tensing. What would he find? Bilirubin through the roof? Oxygen up?

Theo was awake. His bright blue eyes, underlined with creases that made him look like the world's tiniest professor, seemed to fix on Paul with a sanguine expression, as if to say, *Well, now, what have we here?*

"Hey there, little fellow," Paul murmured, touching a tiny palm and feeling it curl about his fingertip like an embryonic starfish. He felt a tiny seed of hope crack open inside his chest.

Theo's color was better, not quite so yellow, and Lee Kingsley, the duty nurse, had recorded on his flow sheet a urine output of one and a half cc's an hour— way up from yesterday's. Blood gases slightly improved. Results of the ultrasound were encouraging, too. No bleeds. Paul stared at the numbers, blinking as if trying to bring them into focus. He simply could not fathom what he was seeing.

Fucking unbelievable. Not quite a miracle, but a significant improvement. Theo's kidneys were functioning. His bilirubin was down. His oxygen setting was unchanged.

Theo, all on his own, was getting better.

Paul felt as if his oxygen levels had suddenly shot up, making him giddy, almost buoyant. "Hang in there, buddy—you're doing okay."

Theo regarded him with that wise-professor look. *Oh, yeah?* he seemed to say. *Well, you look like shit.*

Paul felt his mouth forming a goofy smile even as his eyes filled with tears. *How the hell is a guy supposed to look when he's just walked out on his wife?* The truth was it was taking every ounce of resistance he possessed to keep from calling Ellie and telling her that to stay apart would be a disastrous mistake.

But everyone had thought it was mistake to save Theo . . . and look at him, not quite out of the woods, but bearing due north.

A memory came to Paul suddenly—his mother holding vigil at Billy's bedside, knitting a blanket that seemed to go on forever. He could almost hear the clicking of her needles as she furiously purled and stitched, as if by her ceaseless activity she was somehow keeping her son alive. In the end, nothing could save Billy. But the blanket, ah, the blanket—a blend of yarns the rich color of a sunset, an almost celestial thing he would never have expected from a woman who favored Betty Crocker cake mixes and wore a pillbox hat to church every Sunday. It was that blanket that had kept Paul warm, nights when he'd been feverish and his own bedcovers weren't enough to keep out the chill. In his mind, he could see it draped over the back of Mom and Dad's sofa, in the house on the beach at Montauk where they'd moved when Dad retired.

He wouldn't call Ellie. But he wouldn't stop believing something good might come of this, either.

She could still change her mind.

Or he could change his.

"Dr. Nightingale?" A softly plaintive voice caused him to whirl around.

Serena Blankenship, in a somewhat wrinkled print dress, stood staring at him with punch-drunk fixedness. Her honey-colored hair was ruffled with sleep, and she held her hands tightly clasped in front of her in a way that made him think of a reluctant bride clutching her bouquet.

"Paul," he corrected gently. "Please call me Paul."
It seemed silly to stand on formality after all this time.

"Paul, then." Her mouth flickered in a tentative
smile. "Has ... has there been any change?"

Paul took a breath, warning himself that it would
be a huge mistake to let her get too optimistic when
Theo's prognosis was still far from good. Nevertheless ...

"Actually, there has," he told her in an even voice.
"He's showing some improvement. I wouldn't get too
excited just yet.... Let's give it a day or two. But
based on what I'm seeing, it's very possible he's turned
a corner."

Serena stared at him for a long moment before
bursting into tears.

Paul stepped forward and took her in his capable
arms, thinking of Ellie as he did so, remembering how
helpless he'd felt in the face of his wife's raging grief.
Only Serena's were tears of celebration. Her tiny window of hope had widened just a fraction, enough to
allow her a glimpse of a future she hadn't dared imagine. Was it selfish of Ellie to want the same? No, he
thought sorrowfully. She had as much right to motherhood as Serena. More, even. If he could have given it
to her, he would have, just as he'd somehow managed
to keep Theo alive. But he couldn't. Physically, mentally, emotionally, he just couldn't. And, oh, Jesus,
that hurt.

As he held Serena under the false noon of the fluorescents, accompanied by the soft beeping of monitors
and the sighing of vents, Paul wondered for a brief
moment who was comforting whom.

Oddly, he found himself thinking of the child his
wife had lost ... the baby girl who would be a young
woman if she were alive today. He saw her in his
mind, a woman who looked very much as Ellie had
when he'd first met her. Was she as determined as
Ellie? As strong and loving and passionate?

He hoped to God that if nothing else, wherever and whoever Ellie's daughter was, she carried somewhere deep in her heart the knowledge that her mother had loved her and wanted her every bit as much as the woman weeping in his arms wanted her baby son to live.

CHAPTER 5

June 1994

"Look! Lookit the horsies!" The little girl in the pink shorts and Care Bears T-shirt tugged on Skyler's hand and pointed into the thick of the parade making its stately way up Fifth Avenue under the blistering June sun.

Skyler smiled down at five-year-old Tricia, struck by her uncanny resemblance to the young Mickey; with her mop of curly dark hair and huge brown eyes, Tricia looked more like Mickey's daughter than her niece. Following the little girl's rapt gaze, Skyler caught sight of the horses: four enormous bays ridden by mounted policemen in short-sleeved uniform shirts and jodhpurs, moving single file between the blue police barricades and the periphery of the parade. Pressed in alongside Mickey and seven-year-old Derek, Tricia's brother, on the curb at Fifth Avenue and Fiftieth Street, Skyler had a pretty clear view of the parade. A high school marching band was approaching now, its members outfitted in crimson and yellow. They were playing what she guessed to be the Polish national anthem, loudly and not very well, but she cheered them along with the rest of the crowd that jammed the sidewalk.

When Mickey had invited her along this Saturday to help show her niece and nephew around the city, Skyler had agreed mainly as a favor—Mickey would have had her hands full otherwise, looking after two little kids. Left to her own devices, though, Skyler would have preferred a day of doing absolutely nothing. She was still recuperating from the round of parties and family celebrations that had followed her graduation from Princeton two weeks ago. And the day after tomorrow she'd be starting her regular part-time summer job at the Northfield Veterinary Clinic, not to mention training heavily for the Wilton Classic, which was taking place in just two weeks.

But the excursion—they'd already "done" the Empire State Building and Rockefeller Center, and were heading over to F.A.O. Schwarz after this—was turning out to be a lot more fun than she'd counted on. For one thing, Tricia and Derek were both adorable, small and fleet-footed as monkeys. For another, minding the children had kept her from thinking too much about Prescott.

Pres—oh, God, what am I going to tell him?

Shading her eyes against the brilliant sun, Skyler watched a contingent of folk dancers in bright, puffy-sleeved costumes whirl past. But she wasn't really seeing them; she was thinking of the hurt look behind her boyfriend's tight smile when he'd dropped her off at her house last Saturday night. But what had she said that was so terrible? He should have given her more warning! Asking her out of the blue to marry him, what did he expect? Once she'd gotten over her initial shock (which actually shouldn't have been such a shock, considering they'd been going together, off and on, for the past five years), Skyler had done something she was famous for—she'd acted on what

Mickey had long ago dubbed her terminal foot-in-mouth disease, blurting, "What for?"

Now, Skyler found herself wincing anew, imagining how it must have sounded. Of course, she'd all but tripped over herself explaining that she hadn't meant it the way it had come out. She just hadn't expected to get married so *soon*. They were barely out of college. She'd be starting veterinary school at the University of New Hampshire in the fall. He'd be in law school. What was the big rush?

No rush, Prescott had assured her in his quiet, steadfast way. They wouldn't have to set a date for the wedding; it could be years from now, if she liked. He'd just feel better knowing they were engaged. Things wouldn't have to be any different than they were now ... except she'd be wearing a ring.

Skyler had promised to think about it.

She was supposed to give him her answer tonight, but she still hadn't made up her mind. All she knew was that a week of agonizing over it had left her feeling slightly queasy, with a low-grade headache that wouldn't quit.

Oh, why did Prescott have to go and mess up a good thing? She loved him, there was no question of that. Even better, they loved the same things—horses, dogs, opera, anything to do with France. Not to mention that their families were so close it was almost as if they were related. The Fairchilds vacationed with the Suttons every summer on Cape Cod, and the Suttons often shared the Fairchilds' box at the opera.

But something was holding Skyler back. Something she couldn't explain, even to herself. Deep down, she couldn't help feeling that marrying Prescott would be a little like marrying ... well, a *brother*.

Skyler became aware of a small hand tugging on hers, but this time it was a moment or two before she could fully focus on Tricia's animated, olive-skinned face. "I want to pet the horsie! Please, Skyler, can I pet the horsie?" squealed the little girl as another pair of mounted policemen trotted into view.

"Not now . . . maybe after the parade," she answered.

At her elbow, jockeying for a better view, stood Mickey, in cut-offs and a tank top, with her hands resting on the sunburned shoulders of her nephew in front of her. Derek, a slightly taller version of his sister, wearing baggy shorts and a Knicks jersey, was staring with glassy-eyed, slack-jawed awe at the policemen riding past, as if witnessing something on the scale of his favorite cartoon superhero coming to life.

Mickey shot an amused glance at Skyler, and in a low voice said, "He's been going on and on about wanting to be a policeman ever since he learned to talk. My uptight brother, Mr. Bonds Trader, is starting to think he's got a problem. Wait till Derek starts in about *mounted* police."

"Don't laugh . . . if I flunk out of veterinary school, I may apply for the job myself," Skyler joked.

Mickey gave a throaty chuckle. "Sure, I can just see it: Officer Sutton, on the job. You'd fit in about as well as caviar on pastrami and rye."

Skyler didn't respond. Mickey was only kidding, sure . . . but at times she could cut a little too close to the bone. In this case, she was right on target. *I would stick out like a sore thumb,* Skyler thought glumly.

Why should that bother you? drawled a voice in her head, a voice with disturbingly distinct Fairfield County inflections. *You'll end up marrying Prescott, you know you will . . . eventually. And the most un-Fairfield-like thing you'll be doing is treating horses for bog spavin and laminitis.*

Skyler wanted to argue against that voice. She'd gone through most of her life without questioning what many considered to be her birthright, but Princeton had cured her of that—four years of living in dorms with girls who named-dropped shamelessly; of snooty eating clubs; of hidebound traditions. Even the town of Princeton had irritated her. With its upscale shops, pricey restaurants, and gracious tree-shaded houses, it was just another version of Northfield. By the time she graduated, Skyler was left wondering uneasily if what wealth mainly brought you was a ticket to a theme park where everything was picture-perfect and everyone seemed content—a theme park franchised across the country in only the most exclusive areas, so you could move from town to town and never feel out of place.

That wasn't what Skyler wanted. Just lately, she'd felt a restlessness in herself, a pulse, flickering below the surface, that she couldn't put her finger on. And maybe that was why she wasn't leaping to get engaged. And why at this moment she felt a sudden impulse to join the group of spectators off to her right who'd broken into a spontaneous little dance.

"I have to go pee-pee," whined Tricia.

"I'll take her," Skyler volunteered. "I know where every ladies' room in Saks is. I used to hide out in them whenever Mom took me shopping for new clothes."

But Mickey wasn't listening to Skyler; she was too busy staring at the mounted policeman reining his horse to a halt in front of the police barricade fifty feet or so from where they stood. She gave a low whistle. "God . . . check out the arms on that one. He looks like he eats bricks for breakfast."

Skyler was used to Mickey making such comments, but secretly believed her friend's interest in the opposite sex was excessive. Nevertheless, her gaze was drawn to the cop in question. *Oh, my,* she thought. His build brought to mind the young Marlon Brando in one of her favorite old movies, *A Streetcar Named Desire.* His bronzed skin had been darkened by the sun to deep umber on his arms (which, she had to admit, were pretty impressive). She couldn't see much of his face under his visored helmet and sunglasses, but he didn't look as if he'd have any trouble getting a date.

The impression, though fleeting, stuck in her mind as she turned, holding Mickey's niece tightly by the hand, and began making her way through the crowd toward the marble-framed entrance to Saks, not more than a dozen feet back from the curb.

Skyler hadn't gone more than a few paces when she happened to glance back over her shoulder ... and spotted what Mickey, caught up in the spectacle of the parade, was oblivious to: seven-year-old Derek ducking under the blue barricade in front of him. He was heading straight for the police horse Young Marlon Brando was, at that moment, bringing around broadside in an effort to contain a herd of rowdy teenage boys. The cop couldn't have seen monkey-quick Derek bearing down on him.

Oh, God! Derek's going to get trampled. Skyler's heart vaulted into her throat.

Without thinking, Skyler gave Tricia a push in Mickey's direction and darted after the little boy, who was inches from a broken bone or a kicked-in head. A woman loaded with shopping bags stepped in front of her. An enormous man jabbed her with his elbow as he lit a cigarette. Skyler came down on someone's toes with the heel of one Docksider, and was chastised by a loud screech. The instant she spotted an opening in the wall of bodies, she ducked through it and under the wooden barricade.

Someone else must have seen Derek, because suddenly a woman screamed, *"Watch out!"*

Skyler saw the cop twist around in his saddle to see what the commotion was about, breaking contact with his horse's mouth as he did so. The big bay skittered backward—and now, oh, God, Derek was *underneath* him.

That was when one of the teenagers, a gangly bullet-headed kid who obviously didn't know the first thing about horses, decided to play Arnold Schwarzenegger. Yelling like a cowboy and waving his arms, he tried to scare the bay into backing away from the little boy. *Idiot.* The horse flattened his ears and tossed his head. The cop was holding him on a short rein, and everything would have been fine if one of Schwarzenegger's dimwit friends hadn't chosen that moment to lob a soda can at the poor frightened beast.

Skyler watched the can bounce off the bay's flank in a bullet flash of reflected sunlight. She felt a fine mist of Coca-Cola spray her face as she lunged forward, snatching the seven-year-old, now frozen with terror, from under the horse's dancing hindquarters.

Derek let out a wild shriek, and the bay reared. In that instant, as Skyler glanced up at the cop, she caught a fractured glimpse of the sun skating off his blue-and-white helmet, and the muscles in his powerful dark forearms knotting as he threw his weight forward. A moment later, he was sprawled on his backside on the pavement.

Skyler watched in horror as his panicked horse charged headlong into the precise formation of flag-toting army veterans that now spanned the avenue between Forty-ninth and Fiftieth streets. The uniformed men broke rank and scattered, one of them stumbling on a steam grate and nearly falling on his face onto the curb. Another gray-haired vet, this one marginally more spry, took off after the horse, but ran out of breath after only ten seconds or so.

Skyler turned to a stylish blond woman in an expensive-looking dress. "Watch him," she ordered, prying Derek's arms from around her neck and handing him over.

The big bay was already halfway down the block, stirrups flapping, reins flying, when Skyler took off in pursuit. Lucky for her, the horse, hemmed in by people on all sides, wasn't able to get up to a full gallop, and was instead going in frantic circles. Her heart racing, she slalomed her way through the throng of bodies tearing every which way.

By the time she could get anywhere near him, the bay had slowed down, just a hair. He was heaving, she saw, and flecks of foam stood out around his bit. With a deep breath and a silent prayer, Skyler lunged forward—and barely, just barely, managed to snag the reins. Out of instinct born of years on horseback, she grabbed a handful of mane and, with a running hop, catapulted herself into the saddle. Finding her seat and sinking back, she let her breath out between her clenched teeth in a hissing rush.

"Ho, there . . . easy boy, easy does it," Skyler crooned. She gathered up the reins and squeezed him tightly with her legs. The horse, obviously well trained, at once slowed to a trot.

Skyler, watching the crowd before her part like the Red Sea for Moses, and hearing the cheer that went up, wondered what all the fuss was about. God, you'd think she'd done something really amazing! A flush rose into her cheeks as she cut the heaving, lightly lathered bay in a diagonal across Fifth Avenue to meet the dismounted cop, who was limping toward them with a sheepish expression. His smile was half grin, half grimace, and in the dark lenses of his aviator glasses miniature reflected suns wheeled and flashed.

It wasn't until she was sliding down from the saddle, a bare sole slapping onto pavement hot as blacksmith's iron, that she realized she'd somehow lost a shoe in all the excitement. *Great, just great,* she thought as the horse, recognizing its owner, broke away and trotted over to him, leaving her to balance on one foot in her shorts and Princeton T-shirt, feeling as stupid as a flamingo lawn ornament.

"That was some stunt," the cop acknowledged, reaching up to pop the chin strap on his helmet. "You impressed the hell outta me, and that's saying something." Noticing that she was barefoot, he belted in a voice that she was certain would have carried the length of Fifth Avenue, "Yo, anybody see this lady's shoe?"

Moments later, a bearded man in plaid Bermuda shorts rushed forward, brandishing her Docksider as if it were a piece of vital evidence at a crime scene. The cop flashed her a grin, and with a wink managed to drop to one knee and slide it onto her foot even while maintaining a grip on his horses reins. The crowd cheered and hooted, and somebody yelled out, "Hey, Cinderella, how's the fit?"

"I feel ridiculous," she muttered.

"And I feel like a jerk for getting thrown, so I guess that makes us even." He shot her a wry look that held more than a dash of wounded male ego. Up close, she judged him to be in his late twenties, maybe thirty. But the toughness of the life he no doubt led, not to mention the gun in the holster on his hip, somehow made him appear older.

"It wasn't your fault," she assured him. "It could have happened to anyone."

"Easy for you to say. You're not a cop."

"No, but if I had a dime for every time I've been thrown I could walk into Saks right now and buy myself a new pair of loafers."

He regarded her with undisguised amusement. "Would you settle for a beer instead? I'll be off duty in a couple of hours. Hey, it's the least I can do." He sounded sure of himself, without coming across as cocky. She liked that.

Watching him pull off his dark glasses and helmet, Skyler became aware of a queer feeling threading its way up from the pit of her stomach. Up close, the likeness to the young Marlon Brando was even stronger than it had appeared from a distance. Yet, upon second glance, she saw that the resemblance wasn't so much physical as the general impression he left. He was the kind of man who defined rough-edged sex appeal.

Not, she quickly assured herself, that it was of any interest to her. After all, she had Prescott, who was no slouch himself in the looks department.

Yet she couldn't tear her eyes from the cop's face. His brown eyes—so dark they were almost black—met hers in a look of equally frank admiration. She stared in fascination at the fine droplets of sweat caught gleaming amid his dense black curls. A tiny crease just below one corner of his full mouth that might have been a dimple gave the faint impression that he was aware of what she was thinking. An uneasy thrill scribbled its way up her spine, and a favorite expression of her grandmother's leaped into her head: *Bold as brass.* Unlike most of the guys she knew, Prescott included, there was nothing whitewashed about this man's strong Roman nose and well-defined brow . . . nothing that had been lost or blurred through generations of "good breeding."

"Tony. Sergeant Tony Salvatore." He stuck out a blunt, tanned hand. As she shook it and introduced herself, Skyler was intensely aware of the hard buttons of callus on the fingers wrapped firmly about hers. "Listen, don't worry. I'm not hittin' on you or anything. It's just . . . I feel like I owe you."

"You don't owe me a thing," she argued. "Honestly."

"Okay. How 'bout we chalk it up to my own sense of fair play, then?"

Skyler hesitated. And just then, looking into his knowing eyes, she had the uneasy sense that he was seeing something beyond her polite refusal, something that smacked of a scrupulous attempt to avoid appearing snobbish. *God, he probably thinks I think I'm too good for him.* And on the heels of this came a rush of shame that such a thought should even have entered her mind. Flustered, she added a bit too brightly, "Well, if it would make you feel better, I don't see how I can refuse."

I'm not a snob, she told herself, *really I'm not.* It was just that she'd never before had the opportunity to get to know a guy like Tony Salvatore.

Yeah? Well, what's stopping you now? challenged a voice in her head that sounded suspiciously like Mickey's.

Prescott, for one, she argued staunchly.

Nonetheless, Skyler found herself staring at his English riding boots, custom-made from the looks of them, and polished to an ebony gloss. The gun on his hip. His badge, glittering on the front of his shirt, just below his shoulder. What *would* it be like to date a cop? she wondered.

"You free around four?" he inquired. "There's a bar a block or so from the barn, on Forty-second and Ninth. Mulligan's. You know it?" Seeing her hesitate, he quickly added, "Look, if it's out of your way, we could meet in your neighborhood."

She was at once struck by the unwelcome vision of Tony at the Red Quail, the bar in Northfield that did its best to pass for a quaint English pub. "Mulligan's is fine," she replied firmly.

"Catch you later then," Tony said with a small wave as he gathered up his horse's reins and swung himself into the saddle with the easy grace of a man half his weight.

As her gaze skimmed along the gold stripe that ran down the leg of his breeches and disappeared into his boot, she felt a small pulse of electricity. *Tell him you can't meet him after all,* the sensible interior voice advised. *Tell him you just remembered something you have to do.* It wouldn't be a complete lie. After all, she was meeting Prescott at Le Cirque at eight, and she had a lot of thinking to do before then.

It was Mickey, in the end, who provided her with the rationale she was looking for. As they were heading uptown, Derek and Tricia firmly in hand, she turned to Skyler and said, "You know what would be really great? If you could get the guy to give these two a tour of the police stable next time they're in town. Derek would think he'd died and gone to heaven."

Derek, seemingly none the worse for wear despite having nearly gotten trampled, tipped his head up at Skyler with a look of wide-eyed expectation. "The *police* stable? Really?" he crowed. "That'd be *awesome.*"

"I'll see what I can do," Skyler replied with a breezy authority that was in direct contrast to the vague uneasiness stealing through her.

Inside, she was thinking, *What in God's name am I getting myself into*?

Exactly two hours later, after seeing Mickey and the kids off at Grand Central, Skyler was pushing her way through the heavy, brass-handled door of Mulligan's Tavern near the corner of Forty-second and Ninth Avenue.

"An Adventure in Slumming," by Skyler Sutton. The silly, self-conscious thought took hold as she hovered near the entrance, letting her eyes grow accustomed to the murky dimness. A TV glowered like a baleful eye from above the mirrored bar. It was tuned to a baseball game, which was being followed with avid interest by the noisy, mostly male crowd occupying the bar stools and nearby tables. The crack of a bat was followed by wild cheering, and a hail of fists thumping against marine-varnished surfaces gone milky with age.

If Pres were with me, he'd ask what the score was, then snag us a couple of beers as if there were nothing at all out of place in us being here. Because Prescott— despite the two-hundred-dollar loafers he wore without socks in the summertime, the gold-and-stainless Rolex, the vintage MG his parents had given him as a graduation present—truly wasn't a snob. Which, she thought miserably, made her a real bitch for wondering if maybe she was entitled to more than what Prescott had to offer.

A familiar face surfaced amid the smoky gloom. Tony, she saw, had changed into jeans and a faded blue polo shirt that showed off his muscular arms and torso. She was struck once again by that rogue pulse of electricity, like a hot-wired car engine kicking in, and had to remind herself that this was *not* a date— just a thank-you drink.

"Beer?" he offered. "Not that there's much choice. The wine they serve here could pass for lighter fluid." He took her elbow and steered her over to a table near the back, where it wasn't quite so noisy.

"Sounds good," she said. "A beer, I mean."

Tony disappeared, returning a few minutes later with two frosty bottles of Heineken. "Listen, I don't know if I officially thanked you." He dropped into the chair opposite hers. "I know a lot of mounted cops who couldn't have pulled that off as easy as you." She watched him take a long swallow of beer, his Adam's apple sliding up and down in a throat thickly corded with muscle. As he dropped his chin, his dark eyes met hers in smiling comradeship. "You really know horses." It wasn't a question, merely a statement of fact.

"I've been riding almost as long as I've been walking," she told him.

"You must live somewhere near a stable, then."

"I grew up in Connecticut," she told him. "Northfield. It's just a little north of Greenwich. There's a riding school not far from my parents' house, where I board my horse."

"Your own horse, huh?" She caught the flicker of his eyelids, the ever so slight widening of his smile, with that little mocking tuck at the corner. Then he said, "Wish I could say the same about Scotty. He's assigned to me, but Mounted horses are strictly police-issue."

"I've had Chancellor since I was fifteen," she told him. "He's getting a little old for competition, but he doesn't know it yet. You should see him go over a jump."

"You jump in shows?" *Now* he sounded impressed.

She nodded, then said, "Only the summer circuit so far. I'd have to make a career out of it if I wanted to compete in the winter circuit, too." She sipped her beer. "What about you ... have you always ridden?"

He grimaced. "You wouldn't think so from what happened today, but yeah, I've been around horses most of my life. My uncle has a farm upstate where I spent summers as a kid. Ever since I can remember, the only thing I ever wanted was to someday earn my living on horseback. And here I am. Been with the Mounted for eight years. Before that, I was a patrol officer with the Tenth precinct."

"Sounds like you know your way around." Skyler, realizing that her comment might have sounded like a come-on, found herself blushing.

"I do okay." There was nothing even remotely suggestive in his voice.

"Do you make many arrests?" she asked, suddenly curious to know more about him.

"When I was with the Tenth, sure. Not so much these days. For one thing, city people are scared of horses. That's why we use them for crowd control—there's no better threat than sixteen hands of horseflesh coming at you. New Year's Eve? All five troops—you're looking at a hundred and twenty officers—turn out in Times Square for the big event. I tell you, it's something."

"I'll bet." *And if every male cop looked like you, you'd probably have an all-woman riot on your hands.*

Skyler sat back, a small, abashed smile touching her lips at the unladylike thought. She'd been hanging around Mickey too long, she told herself. Either that, or all her agonizing about whether or not to get engaged had unhinged her. Couldn't she have a perfectly respectable drink with a man without fantasizing about him leaning across the table and kissing her?

The imagined kiss sent a bolt through her that was as real, and yet as transient, as summer lightning.

Another burst of raucous cheering erupted at the bar, bringing a somewhat chagrined smile to Tony's handsome, animated face. "This isn't your scene," he acknowledged ruefully. "I should've known better, taken you someplace nicer. I've been coming here for so many years, I guess I stopped noticing what a dive it is. Ever get that way about something—so stuck in one place you don't really see it anymore?"

"More often than I'd like." The thought of Prescott crossed her mind, but she quickly shut it out.

"Another beer?" Tony pointed at the bottle on the table in front of her, which Skyler was a bit surprised to note was empty.

She watched him amble over to the bar, where everyone seemed to know him. Several of the men greeted him with hearty slaps on the back, and a beefy guy with a receding hairline threw a bill down on the bar when the beers he'd ordered came, shaking his head vehemently when Tony tried to refuse. Finally, with a good-natured shrug, Tony simply snagged the necks of the two bottles with one hand, mouthing something that sounded like "Catch you next time."

As he was making his way back to their table, Skyler noticed that he was limping a little. "Does it hurt much?" she asked.

"Nothing an Advil and another one of these won't cure." He grinned as he thunked the beers down on the table. His teeth were very white against the deep umber of his face, she observed a bit dreamily.

"When I was eight, I almost got killed falling off a horse," she told him.

His grin faded abruptly, and he gave a low whistle. "No shit."

"It was a jump I had no business going over, but I was determined to prove that I could."

"Now, why doesn't that surprise me?" He tipped his chair back, regarding her with heavy-lidded amusement, his sweating Heineken propped on one denimed knee, forming a damp circle that she couldn't seem to pry her eyes away from.

With an effort, she drew her gaze back up to meet his. "I guess you could say I'm not afraid to take chances."

"That makes two of us."

Skyler, unsettled by the direction in which this conversation seemed to be drifting, found herself striking a prim posture she vaguely remembered from some etiquette class back at Miss Creighton's School for Girls: spine straight, shoulders back, hands folded in front of her. But she couldn't suppress a tiny smile as she penciled an imaginary cartoon bubble over her head with the caption *Goodness gracious, what would Prescott think?*

Sensing her withdrawal, Tony said admiringly, "If you hadn't taken a chance this afternoon, somebody might've gotten hurt."

Embarrassed, Skyler shrugged. "I happen to know my way around horses, that's all. But that's not hard when you've spent more time in Wellingtons than in high heels. My mom has an antique store now, but she used to jump competitively—that's how I got into horses. My dad's a lawyer. He wouldn't get near a horse if you paid him. He thinks I'm crazy, wanting to be a veterinarian ... but he's never stood in the way of anything I really wanted."

"Smart guy. Probably knows he'd get mowed down if he tried." Tony chuckled, bringing his chair back onto all four legs with a muffled thud against the worn floorboards.

"Well, at least he won't have to support me," she joked.

"Hey, who knows, you might wind up supporting him," Tony laughed.

Skyler laughed, too, but his teasing remark had brought to the surface a half-baked worry she'd been shoving to the back of her mind for months. There was nothing specific, nothing she could put her finger on . . . but lately she'd observed her parents conferring in whispers, their conversations breaking off the minute she walked in. She knew that her father's firm had suffered some major reversals with the bottoming out of the real estate market in the eighties, and there had been some talk of the firm downsizing. But there wasn't any real cause for concern, was there?

Tony, she realized, was looking at her curiously. Fearing that he might have picked up on her thoughts, Skyler blushed. "My dad isn't the problem," she confided. "It's my mom. I know she's disappointed that I'm not making a career out of jumping."

"Sounds like a part of you wants that, too."

"Sure . . . but the life can get pretty inbred. A lot of the people who ride the circuit year round do it simply because they love it and can afford to . . . even if they don't win the big purses.

"Doesn't sound so bad."

"Oh, it's not! But, you see, there's something not quite, well, *real* about it." Partly fueled by the beer she'd consumed on an empty stomach, and partly by a spark of totally unexpected anger toward Prescott for abruptly changing the rules on her in mid-game, Skyler added heatedly, "I'm not like *them*. I know how to say all the right things, how to fit in . . . but inside I'm . . . I'm different."

"What makes you think that?" he asked evenly, his gaze growing more keen.

"I don't know. I've always thought it had something to do with me being adopted." She took in a breath against the little downbeat she felt in the pit of her stomach whenever she talked about it. "You see, I wasn't exactly handed over to my parents in some nice, clean hospital. I was abandoned. They guessed I was around three months old."

"What about your mother—she ever turn up?"

"No. The police tried to find her . . . but eventually they gave up."

It never failed to surprise her, the dull little ache she felt each time she fingered that particular bruise. Shouldn't she have gotten over it by now? she wondered. Would it haunt her the rest of her life?

She became aware of Tony's dark eyes fixed on her, as if waiting for her to go on. But she'd said too much as it was. Skyler dropped her eyes, staring at a helix of cloudy, overlapping rings on the tabletop. When he switched the conversation to himself, she felt the tension in her body unravel at once.

"I used to *wish* I was adopted." Tony's voice was low and hard. "That way, at least, I wouldn't have had to worry that I'd turn out like my old man."

"That bad?"

"Pop spent more time in bars than at home," Tony reminisced darkly. "Which I guess you could say was a blessing, considering that when he did make it back to our place, he was usually too busy busting it up to notice."

"I'm sorry." She didn't know what else to say.

"I'm over it," he said in a brusque tone that implied otherwise. But the shrug he gave just then was that of a true survivor—someone who didn't let life's hard knocks get him down for long. "He died when I was fourteen. Managed to get himself shot in the line of duty. Did I mention he was a cop? Only good thing he ever did for us, leaving Ma that pension."

"I guess nobody gets exactly what they want," she said softly.

"You can say that again."

Skyler stared at the two empty bottles in front of her. When had she drunk that second beer? She couldn't recall even picking it up, but her head felt loose and swirly, so she must have. She settled deeper into her chair, which seemed to be gently listing to one side.

"Do you have brothers and sisters?" she asked him, trying to keep him talking.

"Three sisters, four brothers . . . and Jimmy."

"Who's Jimmy?"

"Jimmy Dolan, my best buddy. We grew up on the same block. Been like brothers ever since. Guess I've always sort of looked after him." In the faint amber glare cast by the neon Molson's sign on the wall, the distinct planes of his face gleamed with sudden intensity. "Jimmy, see, he's gay. And out in Canarsie, you might as well be crippled, 'cause either way you're sure as hell gonna wind up on crutches." Tony's eyes grew hard, and she saw the flicker of a muscle in his jaw.

Skyler thought about sprightly Mr. Barrisford, who owned the antiques store across the street from Mom's. The whole town knew he was gay, but most people were too polite to let on. The unspoken consensus was that if he always wore a fresh carnation in his buttonhole, and spoke with an accent, it had more to do with his being British than anything else.

"Where's your friend now?" she asked.

"In the hospital with pneumonia." A sudden fierce look turned the affable man across from her into a stranger she wasn't sure she wanted to get to know. "Dolan's got AIDS," Tony explained. "I don't know how much more time he's got, but let me tell you, if there's a place in heaven for guys who had to go through hell to get there, he'll have front-row seating."

Skyler found herself putting her hand over the rock-hard fist clenched on the table in front of him. "It's got be tough on you, too."

"Yeah. The thing is, I don't let on to him that I know how bad it is. I figure he's gotta have at least one person he can kick back with, where he doesn't have to listen to taps being played in the background." He shook himself, as if suddenly remembering where he was. "Christ, listen to me. You don't even know me, and here I am crying in my beer."

"You weren't crying," she corrected him. "Anyway, that only applies when it's yourself you're feeling sorry for."

Tony grinned. "No complaints in that department . . . unless you want to get me started on my ex-wife."

"You were married?" For some reason, that surprised Skyler. She'd have pegged him as a bachelor.

"Four years."

"What happened?" she found herself asking, even though it was none of her business.

"Paula?" He shook his head. "The thing with her was she never got why a guy who made it through law school was happy just being a cop."

Skyler tried to hide her surprise. *Law school?* She didn't doubt he was smart enough . . . yet somehow she couldn't imagine him as a lawyer going off to work in a suit and tie. But with Tony Salvatore, she suspected, there was a lot more than met the eye.

"What made you decide not to practice law?" she asked.

He stared off into the distance. "After I got through killing myself to get my degree and pass the bar—working night tours, taking classes at St. John's four days a week, studying in between—it hit me that what it had all been about for me was the challenge . . . not whatever reward was supposed to come out of it." He shrugged. "Guess I just didn't have it in me—the duplex in Manhasset, the Beamer, the charge account at Bloomingdale's. That whole scene was what Paula wanted, and she couldn't forgive me for not giving it to her."

"There's nothing wrong with being a cop," Skyler said, with a bit too much conviction.

"Yeah—except when you're too busy talking about yourself to notice you're chewing someone's ear off." He grinned, and rose languidly to his feet. "Come on, let me get you something to eat, or a cup of coffee, at least. There's a diner down the block that's not half bad."

She took in his full measure—the way the cuffs of his faded jeans fit over the tops of his cowboy boots as snugly as gloves; the dull gleam of his belt buckle, feathered with so many scratches it had the look of burnished silver; his polo shirt with its subtle shadings of blue to darker blue in the places where his chest strained against it. At the same time, Skyler realized, in her half-intoxicated state, that it wasn't food she wanted. It wasn't another beer or a cup of coffee, either. What she wanted was simple, really. And at the same time, hopelessly, foolishly complicated.

She tried to scour away the idea forming in her mind by concentrating on Prescott instead. After dinner, they planned on staying over in the city, at Daddy's pied-à-terre on Central Park West. They would make love, as they always did, enthusiastically, with a good deal of thrashing and moaning. And for a minute or two afterward—never longer than that—she would feel strangely flat, like a false note played on a violin, before she once again convinced herself that Prescott was everything she could ever want in a partner.

But it was no good thinking of Prescott. He wasn't what she wanted right now.

What she wanted was . . .

"Would you like to go to my apartment instead?" she blurted. "Actually, it's my dad's . . . but he's not using it right now." She felt suddenly weightless, as if her chair had dissolved and left her suspended in midair.

Tony cocked his head, a thumb hooked over the

waistband of his jeans, smiling down at her as if not quite sure how to take her offer. Skyler, in a heated rush of understanding, imagined how she must appear to Tony. In his eyes, she was every rich girl who had ever screwed her tennis pro, or sneaked behind the barn with one of the grooms. God, what had made her open her mouth?

But Tony, she observed gratefully, didn't appear to be passing judgment on her. He wasn't leaping to accept her offer, either. "I don't think that would be a good idea," he said slowly.

"Oh?" She kept her voice light, even though she felt as though she was burning up.

"Listen, I'll be straight with you," Tony said with an even candor she found maddening. "You're a beautiful, classy woman . . . and I haven't been with anyone since Paula. But I don't want to mess with you. It wouldn't be nice."

Nice? For God's sake, *she* was the one who'd propositioned *him*. How dare he treat her as if she didn't know what was good for her?

"Give me one good reason," she challenged, in too deep now to pull herself out. What was that expression of Duncan's? In for a penny, in for a pound.

"All right." His gaze remained steady, his nearly black eyes seeming to cut right through to the heart of the fire consuming her. "For one thing, I'll bet you a weekend in Atlantic City you've got a boyfriend you're not telling me about."

Skyler felt as if she'd been busted, right here in this dingy bar, by his cop's knowing eyes and straight-shooting mouth. She looked down quickly, so he wouldn't see the look of shame dawning on her face.

"He's got nothing to do with it," she muttered. "Look, forget it. Forget I even offered."

Tony was silent for so long, she figured he was as embarrassed as she was. Maybe she should just leave. Get up right now and just walk—

She looked up, and found Tony staring at her with a new expression—one that engulfed her in wicked longing. As if warring with himself, he closed his eyes and shook his head. When he looked at her again, he was smiling ruefully, as if at some private joke. "Look, I'll drive you uptown," he said. "It doesn't have to be anything more than that, okay?"

"Deal." Skyler rose on shaky legs. She had never felt anything remotely like this with Prescott, and it shocked her.

His car, a green Ford Explorer, was parked on the next block. He made room for her on the passenger seat by sweeping it clear of old newspapers, coffee containers, a police-issue truncheon that looked as if it had been chewed by a dog. The whole drive up to Sixty-second and Central Park West, he didn't speak a word to her. By the time they reached her father's building, Skyler was in a state of near panic, thinking that their flirtation was going to end any minute. At the same time, she felt strangely relieved.

But instead of just dropping her off, Tony surprised her by pulling into a parking space that had miraculously appeared in front of the building. As he followed her into the marble-tiled lobby, she had to fight to keep her gaze averted. If she looked at him—if she so much as *looked* in his direction—she would pass out on the spot. They rode the elevator in silence, without touching or even glancing at one another, and by the time they reached the twelfth floor, Skyler's legs were so wobbly she could hardly stand.

It wasn't until she was fumbling with the various locks on the front door of 12-C that she risked a glance at Tony . . . and was struck by the full measure of what they were doing. He wasn't being stand-offish, as she'd first thought. In his heavy-lidded eyes as black as a lunar eclipse, in the almost rigid way he held himself, she saw a man who hadn't been to bed with a woman for longer than he would have thought possible. Tony wore the look of a starving man afraid to take a single bite because after that there would be no stopping him.

Letting herself inside, Skyler felt a delicious shudder course through her. *This is a dream,* she thought. *And in dreams, anything can happen.* She dropped her purse and keys onto the small Chinese table by the door, and, without prelude, slid her arms around Tony's neck. She could feel her heart climbing up her throat, and her breath growing short.

With an oddly boyish tentativeness, Tony put his arms around her waist, and bent to kiss her.

That was where the boy ended and the man took over.

All at once, she felt his hunger . . . felt him holding back, wanting more even as his tongue found its way into her mouth.

It's never been like this with Pres, she thought as he tipped her head back, threading his strong, blunt fingers through her hair. She didn't have to pretend to be in love with Tony. She didn't even have to *like* him. . . .

She just had to *have* him.

He moaned, and she could feel how much he wanted her as he backed her against the wall and pressed himself against her. His hands moved down her sides, taking in the shape of her, his thumbs pressing into her waist. She felt the button on the waistband of her shorts catch on something—his belt buckle, probably—and then a skittering sound as it popped loose and hit the parquet floor.

Then his hand was between her legs, and even through her shorts the heat of his palm was making her feel naked. God, could he feel how wet she was . . . how desperately she wanted him?

Shame dug into her.

How would Pres feel if he walked in on you right now?

But she didn't care about anything beyond the sensations she was drowning in. All she could think about was this man who was kissing her, and how in just a few more minutes he would be inside her. And how there would be no predicting what came after that. With Tony, she sensed a dangerous undercurrent, a riptide the breadth and strength of which she could only guess at.

With a deep, shuddering sigh, Skyler undid the buttons on his shirt. Something glinted up at her—a silver medal nested in the haze of soft black hair that covered his chest. She traced its raised design with her fingertip.

"St. Michael," he murmured. "The patron saint of cops."

She watched him take off the rest of his clothes, surprised that a man's nakedness, all on its own, could give such pleasure.

He was dark all over, except for his thighs and the uppermost sections of his arms, where the sleeves of his uniform shielded him from the sun. Just below his right nipple, extending almost to his navel, a jagged scar creased his flesh.

"Gunshot wound," he told her matter-of-factly. "St. Michael must've been looking the other way that day."

"How—" she started to ask, but he hushed her by putting a finger to her lips.

She concentrated instead on the thick mat of hair covering his chest. Between his legs, too—God, she'd never *seen* so much hair. So much *everything*.

"My turn," he said in a strangely thick voice as he began to undress her.

Skyler felt a wave of spiraling faintness, like steam rising from a puddle following a summer thunderburst. She was too dazed to do anything but stand there as he tugged her T-shirt over her head and unzipped her shorts. Not until he was struggling to unhook her bra did her arms float up, her fingers dance over his to help him with the clasp.

The way Tony was staring at her as she stepped away from the crumpled heap of her clothing, Skyler might have been Venus alighting from the half-shell. She felt a self-conscious laugh bubble up in her throat, but it was quenched the instant he caught her breasts in the callused cups of his palms. He groaned, and she felt a shudder pass through him. "Jesus, you're beautiful," he whispered.

But it wasn't just his rough thumbs playing over her nipples that excited her so much. It was the sight of her pale breasts against his dark skin, the tiny jewels of sweat winking in the hair that covered his broad chest, and the tattoo—a heart set in a garland of leaves—twining about the thick band of muscle along his upper arm. Tony felt so different from Prescott, so marvelously wild and uncharted, that she sucked in her breath, as if she'd just looked down and found herself teetering on the edge of a steep cliff.

Even his texture was alien—scratchy where Prescott was smooth, the muscles in his arms dense and bunched as a boxer's. And his smell, cleanly sweaty, faintly horsey, like saddle leather after a hard ride.

Bending at the knees, he grabbed her by her ass cheeks and picked her up off her feet. As she wrapped her legs around him, she felt just how excited he was, and began to tremble. Then he was carrying her into the living room, tipping her onto the sofa, into the trapezoid of light that fell over the carpet from the picture window that overlooked Central Park, where the sun was setting in a sullen blaze. She felt the fine weave of the upholstery pressing into her back as he lowered himself onto her, then moved down, kissing her between her legs.

Skyler found herself arching and squirming in a way that was embarrassingly undignified . . . but she couldn't help it. Couldn't stop the waves of almost

agonizing pleasure that each flick of his tongue sent
through her. Couldn't stop ... oh, God ... God ...
was she really coming this way? With a man she barely
knew? The pleasure of it spiked through her like
warm oil.

But afterward, when she tried doing the same thing
to him, he caught her lightly by the shoulders and
pulled her up so that she lay facing him. "No," he
said, turning her onto her back and straddling her with
his knees, arms braced on either side of her neck. "I
want to be inside you when I come."

"What about what you just did to me?" she asked
with a lightness that didn't dispel the quiver in her
voice.

He laughed softly. "That was just for starters." A
band of light lay in a thick stripe across his chest,
setting fire to the St. Michael's medal swaying hypnoti-
cally from its almost-too-delicate silver chain.

She thought of something that snapped her out of
her daze. "How do I know if ... if it's okay?" she
asked, because, of course, these days you *had* to.

But Tony didn't seem bothered. "I meant what I
said, about not being with anyone since Paula," he
said with that frank gaze of his that had witnessed
many things much worse than a sheltered girl's embarrassment. "But it doesn't mean I wasn't *thinking* about
doing it. Anyway, seeing how it is with Dolan, I figured it wasn't something to fool around with. So I had
myself tested. If you need proof ..."

"No." If it were written in blood on parchment
paper, she couldn't be more sure of Tony's honesty.
"I'm okay, too, about ... that. Student health services
these days cover just about everything. You don't have
to worry about me getting pregnant, either. I, uh, I
took care of it already."

Earlier in the day, in anticipation of her evening
with Prescott, she'd inserted her diaphragm. Just in
case she agreed to get engaged after all, and they de-

cided to celebrate. But suddenly realizing how it must have sounded to Tony, she felt her cheeks flare.

Tony, though, merely looked amused, as if she were a little sister who'd surprised him with dinner when he hadn't known she could cook. Holding her face lightly cupped in his hands, he kissed her deeply, the taste of her still on his lips and tongue. She felt a thread of saliva trickle down her chin, and didn't know whose it was, didn't care. She was as excited as if she hadn't already come, more so, as if that had been just the warmup before the main show.

Skyler felt an instant of panic as he entered her. He was so ... God, the *size* of him. Not that Prescott had been exactly *small* ... but this ... she could feel him all the way up inside her, each thrust bringing a stabbing little ache. But if it hurt, she hardly noticed. She was so hot, if the building had been on fire she wouldn't have felt it. She came again, an explosion so intense that her head reeled with the stars doing a crazed dance behind her closed eyes.

And then Tony came too, noisily, arching back with a yell that made the cords in his neck stand out. Beads of sweat dropped from his forehead onto her face like tiny hot kisses, and she found herself climaxing all over again.

"God!" she cried as he collapsed on top of her, spent. "Is it always like that with you?"

"Too rough for you?" He rolled off her, frowning with concern.

"No—oh, no. It's just ... I'm not ... well, I've never ... ," she stammered, thinking that anything she said right now would probably be better left unsaid.

"Yeah, I know what you mean." He grinned. "Like I said, it's been a while." With a tenderness that contrasted sharply with what they'd just done, he drew her with the crook of his elbow into the humid curve of his neck, where she could feel a pulse thumping.

Now what? Skyler wondered with a mounting sense

of panic. It was getting late, and she was due to meet Prescott in a couple of hours. But she couldn't just ask Tony to leave.

Mainly because she didn't *want* him to leave.

With a sense of incredulity coupled with a growing chagrin, Skyler realized that what she wanted was for him to make love to her again. After five minutes or so, she rolled over so that she was half on top of him, one long bare leg slung over his. She felt very decadent—like an experienced woman in a foreign film. Was *this* what Mickey had been trying to describe to her all these years, ever since they started their periods and started noticing boys? Even Mickey, for whom sex was as much a thrill and challenge as the speed stake event in an A-rated show, couldn't have experienced love-making more exciting than this.

"Tony . . ." Skyler murmured in his ear, taking hold of him with her right hand and lightly stroking.

He groaned, and she felt him start to stiffen again.

Even though she'd initiated it, Skyler was a bit startled. "I didn't know a man could recover so quickly," she remarked with a little laugh.

"You don't know me," he said, and grinned.

They made love two more times before Skyler finally swam up from the depths of her erotic haze and saw that somehow an hour and a half had elapsed—and that she had only twenty minutes before she was due to meet Prescott.

Pres! Oh, God!

She started to sit up, but Tony gently pulled her back down again, burying his face against her neck. She clung to him for a moment, suffused with his scent and the heady glow of their lovemaking, before gently drawing away. She wanted to ask him to *stay,* not to go, but if she didn't say something she'd be late. And that wouldn't be fair to Prescott, who had never done a single thing to hurt her.

Fortunately, Tony rescued her from the awkwardness of having to ask him to leave. With a glance at his watch, he jumped to his feet and began tugging on his jeans. "Jesus, will you look at the time? And I promised Dolan I'd stop by and see him before visiting hours are over. I'd better haul ass if I'm going to make it." He cut a glance at her as he was buckling his belt. "Okay if I call you sometime?"

Skyler caught the hint of uncertainty in his voice, and wondered if Tony had the same reservations as she about their getting any more involved than this. Was he as reluctant to get in over his head in waters that could prove turbulent?

As she scribbled her number on the back of an envelope she'd found on the table next to the couch, a prudent voice in her head lectured, *Just what exactly do you think you're doing here? What's the point of seeing him again? Even if you decide not to marry Pres, even if you go so far as to break it off altogether with him, what could possibly come out of what just happened with Tony that would be about anything other than you getting royally laid?*

That she wouldn't mind. But if they repeated what had happened this afternoon often enough, they might actually fall in love. What then?

It wouldn't be his law degree you'd be thinking about when you brought him home to meet your family. You'd be noticing them notice his St. Michael's medal, and the way he drops his "ings" and if he happened to take off his shirt, that tattoo on his right tricep.

Skyler was at once overwhelmed with guilt. Oh, what a hypocrite she was! All that looking down her nose at Princeton's social scene ... what had that been except a way of feeling superior to those snobs? Thinking she was better than girls like Courtney Fields, who was famous for making snide cracks about the scholarship students in their dorm—the way they dressed, talked, ate. Well, look, at her. She wasn't

even as good as Courtney, because at least Courtney
was up-front about how she felt.

Skyler kissed Tony on the cheek as he was leaving,
with a chasteness that was almost comical after what
they'd just done. Maybe he wouldn't call her after all.
Maybe he would just chalk this up to an afternoon of
fabulous sex, and simply move on. Part of her hoped
he would. Another part longed to see him again.

He was almost out the door when she called,
"Tony?"

He turned, and in the wedge of light from the hallway she thought she saw something flicker in his eyes,
something dark and unreadable. Then he flashed her
his ready grin—a grin that might have seemed arro-
gant on someone else, but on Tony fit as perfectly as
the snug jeans riding low on his hips.

"Relax," he said, as if he'd read her mind. "Nobody
got hurt, that's the main thing. We had a good
time . . . and that's all. Ain't nothing in the world
wrong with that."

As the door clicked shut behind him, Skyler felt
suddenly, magically clearheaded. It was as if on his
way out Tony had switched on some unseen light
source. What had been dim before was now illumi-
nated. She knew now the answer she had to give Prescott. She couldn't marry him—not now, not ever.
Hadn't she known that for some time? Wasn't a large
part of the reason she went to bed with a perfect
stranger a need to prove to herself what her heart had
been unwilling to admit?

What she hadn't counted on was Tony himself. The
things they'd just done . . . the glimpse he'd given her
of things as yet undiscovered. And, oh dear God, the
state he'd left her in: breathless, her pulse racing as
she leaned into the door, listening for the distant
whine of the elevator descending to the ground floor.

CHAPTER 6

"Central Park Conditions Car ... ten-thirty ...
Pedestrian was robbed on Sixty-fifth Street
Transverse ... perp headed northbound from
Heckscher Playground . . . Hispanic, around five-
eleven, mustache ... He's wearing black pants, green
sweatshirt. . . ."

Sergeant Tony Salvatore was patrolling the south-
west corner of Central Park with big Duff Doherty,
when the alert leaped out from the ceaseless staticky
squawking of the radio on his belt. He squeezed his
horse to a halt and brought the radio to his mouth,
responding: "Armed?"

"Perp displayed a revolver," crackled the dispatch-
er's voice.

"Oh, Christ," swore Doherty, trotting up alongside
him. It was midday on the hottest Saturday in July so
far, and great moons of dampness darkened the blue
fabric of his uniform under his arms. His wide, freckled plank of a face was lightly greased with sweat.
"These guys, I tell you they got no respect. He
couldn't have waited until I was off?" After his last
detail, up in Washington Heights taking part in a
sweep of illegal street vendors, he'd pulled this post—

Central Park South to Seventy-second, from Fifth to Central Park West—with a big fat smile on his overgrown Dennis-the-Menace face. Doherty's wife was due to give birth any day, and he didn't need his blood pressure to go any higher. Now this.

"Guess nobody told him it's not polite to mug before dark," Tony cracked, not without a tightening in his own gut.

They'd just crossed West Drive at Sixty-seventh and were heading east along the pathway that traversed the north end of the Sheep Meadow. Despite the sodden heat, Tony felt charged, his blood surging at high tide. Central Park, with its eight hundred forty-three acres spanning the heart of the city from Fifty-ninth to 110th, was like an urban frontier, one that never failed to bring out the cowboy in him. For every manicured lawn, there were pockets of wilderness in which all manner of murder and mayhem could, and did, transpire; for every paved pathway, an outcropping of schist jutted like a granite fist. And, boys, let's not forget the Ramble—thirty-seven acres of wooded hills that were a magnet both for bird-watchers and for gays looking for action. Harlem Meer, too, was one place you didn't patrol at night without your hand on your holster.

At the moment, however, as Tony scanned the open stretch of green that was Sheep Meadow (where, once upon a time, sheep had actually grazed), he saw nothing more threatening than the nascent sunburns that by evening would be agony to the white-limbed city dwellers lolling about on beach towels and picnic blankets—mostly kids plugged into Walkmans, or sprawled on their bellies with a book. Not much action here, Tony noted, except for the Frisbee tossers and a vagrant rummaging through a trash receptacle.

His eye picked out a young couple entwined under a sycamore, engaged in activity that would have been illegal if they hadn't been fully dressed. An image flashed through his mind—a diamond of sunlight on a pale curve of hip. And he thought: *Skyler.* The things they'd done that day . . . Christ. After nearly a month, the memory had faded some, but its power remained, like the aftermath of a dream he couldn't shake. At least once a day, even at unlikely times like this, he found himself turning it over in his mind, like the souvenir of a trip he barely remembered, except how good it had been.

Yeah, sure, he'd called her a couple of times. But their conversations over the phone had had all the exaggerated naturalness of two people straining their hardest to keep from saying what was really on their minds. And the vague plans they'd made to meet for coffee or a drink had, for one reason or another, failed to materialize. A change in his schedule; a summer cold; a forgotten appointment remembered. Last week, when she phoned to ask if he would mind giving the niece and nephew of a friend of hers a tour of the barn, he'd been surprised. After all this time, he hadn't expected to see her again.

Tomorrow was the big day. He'd arranged for Skyler and her friend's kids to meet him at the barn when he got off duty at three-thirty. No big deal, right? An hour or so of showing them around, and they'd be on their way. So why was he breaking out in a sweat that had nothing to do with the perp he was on the lookout for?

You know what's bugging you, pal? You wish it'd been nothing more than a fuck, but somehow it wasn't. You want to forget her, but you can't.

Maybe because he knew good and goddamn well that for her it *had* been just a fuck. Fun and games, courtesy of the boy-your-folks-would-shit-a-brick-if-he-moved-in-next-door. And, well, yeah, he resented it. He resented the hell out of it—which made *him* the horse's ass, because he'd known the score and nobody'd twisted his arm.

Tony pushed Skyler from his mind, which was
harder than it should have been. He had *real* business
to take care of right now, he told himself. Enough of
this personal bullshit.

Fifty yards ahead, where the path fanned out in a
T-junction, a bronze statue of two eagles devouring a
ram shared the tree-shaded spot with a Sabrett hot
dog vendor. Tony reined in his horse and considered
which direction to take. The perp could have gone
either way. Or he might be nowhere in the vicinity.

"I'll head up by Rumsey Playground," he told Doherty. "You check out the lake. He might've ducked
under the Terrace."

"You got it, Sarge."

As Doherty rode north in the direction of Bow
Bridge, Tony cut his horse to the left, onto the path
that opened onto the Mall and then curved up behind
the Naumberg Bandshell. *Guy's probably halfway to
the Bronx by now,* he speculated. Sure, they had their
share of radio runs, but most of them weren't the stuff
TV movies are made of. Drunks and vagrants, the
occasional troublemaker or pickpocket.

Not that being a mounted cop didn't have its moments. Like the ten-thirty on Forty-seventh couple of
months back. He'd been the first officer to arrive on
the scene—a jewelry store that'd been hit by a pair
of armed robbers just moments before. He found the
owner's wife sprawled on the floor, bleeding from a
leg wound. The owner himself, a Hasidic man whose
black beard had stood out like ink scribbles against
the paper whiteness of his face, had cast frightened
eyes toward the front door. One of the punks had
gotten away, but the other had been drunk or high
and not so quick—

Tony remembered how he'd dashed outside and then
spotted the perp, a skinny white kid making his way
along the crowded sidewalk toward Sixth Avenue with
a pistol dangling from one hand. But as Tony was

swinging himself into the saddle to give chase, his left
boot had somehow gotten tangled in his stirrup. Just
then the kid had spun around, and as his feverish eyes
locked with Tony's, he'd raised the pistol. His aim was
a bit wobbly, but true enough to raise the tiny hairs
on the back of Tony's neck. If Scotty had chosen that
instant to bolt, if he hadn't remained stock still ...
Jesus. He didn't like to think what might have happened. Looking back, it was sort of comical—there
he'd been, hopping on one foot, struggling to keep his
balance while at the same time reaching for his gun.
"Police! Put down your weapon!" he'd bellowed, and
fortunately the doped-up kid had obeyed. But it
wasn't until the kid was flat on his belly on the pavement, hands behind his head, that Tony was able to
disentangle himself and breathe a sigh of relief.

And crowd control? Like it wasn't tough enough
keeping a tight rein on an animal Scotty's size on city
streets booby-trapped with things that might set him
off—an umbrella snapping open, a gust of wind kicking up a sheet of newspaper, steam rising from a grate,
the sun glinting off a piece of broken glass or a
chrome hubcap. On top of that, you're trying to hold
back a noisy, shoving tide of bodies. Even with the
entire force deployed, every one of the hundred and
twenty officers from their five troops, there inevitably
were the assholes who decided to get cute.

The memory brought to mind last month's Polish
parade ... and the picture Skyler had made chasing
after poor Scotty, tall and slim in her white shorts,
with her long legs pumping and her pale gold hair
whipping about her head—a picture very much like
one in a book of Roman mythology he had at home,
of Diana the Huntress. He'd never met another
woman like Skyler, not even the female officers he
worked with, who lacked for nothing in the bravery
department. There was just something about that po-
tent combination of sexiness, brains, and competence,

with a dash of daredeviltry thrown in, that both slayed him and turned him on beyond belief.

Tony's mind was jerked back to the present by a flash of movement at the outermost edge of his field of vision. He straightened, scanning the chain-link fence that ran the length of the Rumsey Playground. Probably a squirrel, he told himself. Central Park was a real zoo, with whole colonies of gray squirrels and flocks of pigeons and sparrows, not to mention dogs of every breed busy walking their owners. In addition, the paths were crowded with old people out for a ramble, parents pushing strollers, joggers and in-line skaters in bicycle shorts and knee pads zigzagging through.

Then Tony spotted him, not twenty yards away—a slight man in black jeans and a green hooded sweatshirt. He was running along the grassy verge that sloped between the fence and the path Tony was on, one hand cupped over the front of his waistband, where Tony made out a bulge that definitely wasn't his belt buckle.

Tony grabbed his radio. "Mounted Portable . . . I have a possible on the perp from Heckscher Playground, south end of Rumsey headed east in the direction of East Drive."

"Possible" became "You bet your fucking ass" as the perp caught sight of Tony and without breaking stride reached under his sweatshirt to produce the gun tucked in his waistband. *Jesus.*

Slapping a hand to his holster and yanking free his own revolver, a Smith & Wesson .38 that saw far more action at the firing range up in Rodman's Neck than in the line of duty, Tony felt a drop charge of adrenaline explode through his system—a taut, wired, pulse-pounding sensation that in anyone without his training, not to mention his love of danger, would have translated into panic.

"Freeze!" he bellowed.

The perp only ran faster.

Tony watched a white-faced mother cast a startled glance over her shoulder before snatching her baby from its stroller; a teenage girl in cut-offs stumbled and caught herself against a litter basket.

Park benches, wrought-iron lampposts, the striped umbrella of a refreshment stand, flicked past like moving scenery on a stage where Tony, even while spurring his horse to a canter, seemed to stand still. He itched to break into a full gallop, but that would have presented its own dangers: there were too many people, and not all of them were as swift as the ones jumping out of his path.

Through the trees ahead, from a distance of fifty yards or so, he caught a fast but good look as the perp cast a frantic glance over his shoulder: greasy long hair, droopy mustache, squinty eyes—a fucking *bandido* right out of Central Casting. Except the gun in his hand wasn't some antique six-shooter.

"Police! Drop your weapon!" At the same time, Tony gave Scotty a quick jab with his spurs.

The big bay picked up speed at once, streaking through the grove of trees shading a whimsical statue of Mother Goose astride a goose in flight. Good old Scotty, who, despite being a little spooky at times, always came through when it counted. Tony, his eyes never leaving the figure in the black pants and green sweatshirt flashing among the trees half a city block ahead of him, felt himself, with each gliding thrust of his pelvis, sink deeper into the saddle that was worn to his shape like a favorite easy chair. Branches tore at his face and made a skittery scraping sound as they combed along his helmet. A damp, ruptured smell rose up around him as the earth beneath Scotty's hooves broke open and scattered in grassy little clots.

Under the sweat-dampened fabric of his uniform, Tony could feel the puckered scar along his chest begin to heat up, glowing like the embers of an almost-dead fire.

But deeper, in his bones, what Tony felt was cold. The distance between him and the fleet-footed figure he was chasing was closing, but the guy still had a good thirty yards on him. Watching the perp plunge into the stream of joggers and bikers eddying along East Drive, he prayed: *Christ, don't let me lose him.*

Abruptly, the creep swung around, his gun aimed at Scotty ... and before Tony could take proper aim, his eardrums were assaulted by a cracking report. The bullet tore out a chunk of the maple tree on Tony's right, scattering bits of bark like shrapnel, and setting off a shock wave of screams as passersby scattered for cover.

Tony's stunned heart took a brief leave of absence before swelling up to fill his whole chest. Then he swore under his breath, "You stupid *shit.*"

Scotty, his head jerking up in panic, skidded and almost stumbled, then picked himself up and was off again, flying across the road with a hollow clatter of his borium-studded shoes that Tony could have sworn, from the heat sizzling up through his legs, had struck sparks. He hit the grassy verge on the far side at a full gallop, charging down a green slope dotted with trees, through which Tony could see the gleam of the Conservatory Water below ... and the perp headed straight for it.

Shade-dappled benches filled with people tilted into view. On the pond, a regatta of model sailboats, amazingly lifelike, cut lazy figure eights across the silvery surface. It was almost shocking, like an obscenity scrawled in ugly black paint across a painting, to watch the perp shatter the bucolic landscape with a flying jump that sent fans of dirty water spraying up on either side of him.

The drowsy bench-sitters were screaming now, ducking behind trees and racing for the bushes. In his state of hyper-alertness, even the smallest details stood out. Tony watched a hastily tossed aside grape Froz-Fruit sketch a slick purple comet's tail across the paving stones to his right. A young woman in yellow striped shorts was sobbing as she struggled to untangle her setter's leash from the bench leg to which she'd tied it. A mallard flew across his path in a startled explosion of feathers.

As they drew closer to the pond, he felt Scotty adopt the balky, almost backpedaling stride of a horse on the verge of shying. "Don't even *think* about it," Tony muttered under his breath.

His blood flogging his face and neck with each hoofbeat, Tony threw his horse into the water with such force that for an instant it felt as if he were actually *lifting* Scotty with his legs.

The pond couldn't have been more than three feet deep, but on horseback it was like plowing through quicksand. A model tugboat swirled into Tony's path, and was swamped. A few feet away, the perp, his sweatshirt pasted to his torso and his hair hanging in greasy, wet strings, swatted aside a jaunty sailboat, sending it smashing into the stone embankment.

"Fuck you, asshole!" screeched the raggedy, drenched creature.

It took only a glimpse of the gun clenched in the guy's fist for Tony's instincts, sharpened to a fine point by years of patrolling the streets on horseback, to spark a reaction. Simultaneously digging his heels into Scotty's flanks and throwing all his weight back, he felt a thousand pounds of dripping, quivering horse rear like a tidal wave. A fine net of droplets seemed to hang in the air, spinning mad little prisms of colored light. The screams from the embankment, when they reached his ears, seemed muffled, as if coming from underwater. But the sickening crunch of bone as Scotty came down on the cowering heap before him was as clear and sharp as the sound of dry kindling snapped in two.

In the split second it took for him to draw both his breath and his gun, Tony was leaping off his horse and splashing over to where the perp, amazingly still conscious, hunkered in a crablike crouch, cradling an arm that looked like something that had been taken apart and put back together the wrong way. Blood dripping from a gash on his forehead bloomed like some ghastly pink rose on the pond's scummy surface. Dark eyes glittered up at Tony, full of hate that seemed to spew out at him like the mouthful of filthy water that hit the side of his neck. Tony glanced down and saw the gun that had come too close to rearranging his guts. Its glimmered at the murky bottom near his submerged boots.

"Looks like you picked the wrong asshole to fuck with," he remarked mildly, with a proud glance at Scotty, who was rewarding himself with a nice long drink.

The perp screamed when Tony cuffed him.

Minutes later, when Doherty rejoined him, looking flushed and out of breath, followed by backup in the form of a half-dozen patrol officers and an ambulance, the perp was still yelling. They'd take care of him at Bellevue, Tony thought. And once his broken arm was in a cast, they'd take care of him even better at Central Booking.

After dropping Scotty off at the barn, Tony spent the remainder of the afternoon waiting at Bellevue for the perp to be released, then booking him and filling out a complaint for the DA's office. By the time he made it back to the troop office and signed out, it was almost nine-thirty. And he still had an hour and a quarter's drive ahead of him. Not even the thought of the overtime he'd logged was enough to improve his mood.

By the time he pulled into the driveway of his small

white frame house on a quiet back street in Brewster—eighty miles north of the city, in sleepy Putnam County—he was so beat it was all he could do just to heat a can of soup and then stagger into bed. When the alarm awakened him at five a.m., with a mouth full of cobwebs and eyes that felt as if they'd been rubbed with sandpaper, he could have sworn he'd been asleep no more than ten minutes at the most. Then he was up and on the road again, a mug of coffee he grabbed at the deli wedged between his knees and the seat of his Explorer, booking south on 684 to make a seven-thirty roll call.

As he drove, a single thought cleared a pathway through the gritty layer of sleep that clung to him like a hangover: *Skyler . . . I'm seeing Skyler today.*

It was Sunday—a day civilized people went to church, lingered over the *Times,* played golf, phoned their loved ones. Tony couldn't remember the last time he'd had a Sunday off. Normally, he didn't mind his crazy schedule, but with temperatures due to soar into the nineties, the *last* thing he'd need at the end of this particular Sunday's tour was the storm of emotion Skyler's visit would inevitably rake up in him.

Skyler Sutton. Even her name sounded expensive, for chrissakes. Adopted or not, she bore the surname of people who could trace their ancestors a lot farther back than Ellis Island. *What she spends on clothes in a year would put me in hock for the rest of my life. And I'm still paying off Paula's Visa and Amex.* Not, he would venture to guess, that Miss Skyler Sutton didn't come umbilically attached to a trust fund that would probably put any guy she married in clover for the rest of his life.

Tony stopped his thoughts from progressing any further down that path. What did any of it have to do with *him*? He sure wasn't the kind of guy she'd ever get serious about. And as far as that went, he had better things to do with his time than jerk around trying to fit in where he didn't belong and didn't *want* to belong.

Even so, remembering how she'd felt in his arms sent a surge of electricity through him. Her cool, honeyed beauty, which wasn't as cool as it appeared on the surface; her bad-girl laugh, which was in such contrast to the rest of her. Christ, it had been good ... the best ever. But what were they talking about here? A lifetime commitment? For her, it had been nothing more than a roll in the hay with Lady Chatterley's gamekeeper. For him, the champagne launch, after a long self-imposed dry spell, of his new life as a divorced man.

Fuck her, he thought. And then a nasty little voice in the back of his head chimed, *You already did that, remember? The problem is, you want to do it again.*

Tony, through sheer force of will, somehow made it through the morning and the better part of the afternoon without letting on to the officers under his command that he had anything more pressing on his mind than getting home to a cold beer and an easy chair in front of the TV. But by the end of his long, hot tour—he'd posted Times Square, a beast this time of year—the effort of climbing the stairs to the troop office above the stable left him winded, and wishing he'd remembered to pop an Advil for the stiffness in the small of his back that still bothered him.

He glanced at his wristwatch—Swiss Army with a built-in compass and a wide leather strap. Quarter after three. Skyler and her friend would be here in fifteen minutes. Shit. He needed this like he'd needed Paula with all her high-flying dreams.

At the same time, Tony felt a traitorous rush of heat to his groin. It left him with a hard-on he had to douse with a mental cold shower before he could push his way through the metal door at the top of the stairs.

The second floor was divided into two sections—the gymnasium-sized room, facing the street, that housed the headquarters for the entire Mounted Unit, as well as the deputy inspector's and lieutenant's offices; and the Troop B office in back, which was windowless and half the size, and which branched off into the male and female locker rooms where at the moment Tony could hear the twelve officers just off the seven-to-four clumping around, yelling over the hiss of showers, slamming locker doors.

At the Wheel—the desk and gray metal filing cabinet that in a less utilitarian setting might have been called a reception area—the desk sergeant, Bill Devlin, greeted him with a heartiness that made Tony wince.

"Hey, Salvatore, heard you took a plunge the other day. Guess that's one perp who won't want to be invited to your next pool party." A beefy guy two years short of retirement, with more Troop B war stories than anyone, Devlin chuckled at his own joke.

"Yeah, well, he's gonna be kind of tied up for a while," Tony quipped back as he signed out and headed for the locker room.

Time for a quick shower and a change before Skyler arrived. Just because he wasn't going to be making love to her, he reasoned, didn't mean he had to smell like a month on Rikers Island.

Dressed in faded jeans and a Mounted T-shirt bearing the logo "The Last of the Light Cavalry," Tony was downstairs in Scotty's stall, giving him a brisk rubdown with a towel—rubdowns were something the big guy loved more than sugar—when Skyler showed up.

"Anybody home?" he heard her call.

Just the sound of her voice went through him like a shot of whiskey. The sight of her, poised on the other side of the metal gate that closed the stable off from the sidewalk, was even more intoxicating. She was wearing off-white cotton slacks cinched around the waist with a drawstring, and a loose, filmy blouse the color of her eyes that seemed to float about her.

Her pale gold hair was pulled back in a ponytail, and she wore no jewelry except for a plain leather-banded watch. On the heels of the lust he was engulfed by, Tony was struck by how tired she looked ... the kind of hollow-eyed tired that doesn't come from just a night or two of missed sleep. Was she sick? Was that why she hadn't wanted to see him before this?

All at once, he felt chagrined for having judged her so harshly. More than that, he was seized by a new tenderness toward her, an impulse to take her in his arms and make whatever was wrong with her better.

Cool it, man, Tony cautioned himself. *Whatever's ailing her, she don't need you to fix it. She's got her Ivy League boyfriend for that.*

"I'd roll out the red carpet, but the only carpet around here is the one you're standing on." He cast a teasing glance at the scattering of hay on the sidewalk at her feet.

Skyler laughed. "Don't worry—Mickey and I are used to it."

Tony turned his attention to the dark-haired, Gypsy-eyed young woman standing just beyond Skyler, holding a child's hand in each of hers. The boy and girl looked too much alike not to be brother and sister—both were small and slender, with summer tans that had left them the mellow amber of maple syrup. They filed in shyly as Tony unlatched the gate to let them in.

Tony immediately crouched so that he was eye level with the boy. "Your friend here tells me you're planning on becoming a police officer," he said, repeating in an easy conversational tone what Skyler had confided to him over the phone.

The boy nodded, his eyes wide.

"Well, then," Tony said, "looks like I better show you what's in store for you." He put out his hand and shook the little boy's. "I'm Tony. What's your name?"

"Derek," the boy said in a voice barely above a whisper.

"We don't have any Dereks in the unit, so I guess we could use one," Tony observed solemnly, and was rewarded by the kid's face lighting up like the tree in Rockefeller Center at Christmastime.

With a crackling of his knee joints, Tony stood to greet Skyler's pretty, darkhaired friend, and smile at the little girl peeking shyly out from behind her blue-jeaned legs. "Nice kids," he said. "You look after them a lot?"

"Not as often as I'd like. They're my brother's kids, and John and I don't see eye to eye on a lot of things," she told him, and stuck out her hand. "Hi, I'm Mickey. We're going to be old friends whether we meet again or not. Believe me, Derek's going to be talking about nothing but you for the next ten years. John will never forgive me for this." She flashed him an unrepentant grin that was almost blinding against the olive cast of her pretty, ripe-featured face.

Tony spent the next forty-five minutes showing the four of them around. The kids' reactions, which grew from timid curiosity to boisterous enthusiasm, made him forget the cold beer waiting in his refrigerator at home. The little girl, in particular, hit a soft spot. When he lifted her to get a better view of Doherty's horse, Commissioner—a black gelding standing over seventeen hands, with a scar running the length of his nose that made him look like a gang leader—she fearlessly put her arms around the horse's great neck and laid her cheek against his. Tony could have sworn he saw old Commissioner wink at him over the girl's curly dark head.

Derek, busy scooping up handfuls of sweet meal and running around with it to every one of the twenty-five horses in the stable, made him think of his own nephew, seven-year-old Petey, who never got tired of pitching horseshoes in the backyard with his Uncle

Tony. Kids. They were something, all right. Tony felt
a tug of wistfulness, wondering what his life would be
like now if that missed period Paula had been so
freaked out about when they were first married hadn't
been a false alarm.

He was careful not to look over at Skyler; he didn't
want her to read his thoughts. Let her go on believing,
as she no doubt did, that he was no more than a big
tough cop with a taste for beautiful women. Neither
of them needed to spoil the illusion by throwing in a
dose of reality—extras like his wanting more out of
life than just an occasional bed partner ...

*That so? Well, you're sure as hell barking up the
wrong tree with this one, Salvatore.*

When the bucket of sweet meal was emptied and
every horse had been duly petted and admired, Tony
ushered his visitors upstairs. In the troop office, they
pressed in around the display case stocked with
Mounted memorabilia, everything from a plaster bust
of a horse to photos of old regiments. There was even
one of Michael Jackson posing with a Mounted officer.

"You ever shoot at people?" Derek asked in an
awed voice.

Tony thought about yesterday's little drama, and
answered, "Not if I can help it."

There was a whole list of things he tried to avoid
when he could help it—like getting drunk the night
before a seven-to-four; visiting or calling his mother
when he was down; and allowing himself to get in
over his head with any woman who didn't accept him
exactly as he was, clay feet and all.

He sneaked a glance at Skyler, who looked a little
less drawn than when she'd arrived. There was a pale
dusting of color in her cheeks, and the bruised-looking
circles under her eyes weren't quite so pronounced.
When she stood with her back to the lighted display
cabinet, he could see just the barest glimmer of her
breasts through the filmy cotton of her blouse and was

seized by a hunger for her that was close to agonizing. Damn, why did she have to be so desirable? What was it about her? Why did it drive him crazy just to be in the same room with her?

At that moment, big lumbering Duff Doherty emerged from the locker room, pink and shining from his shower, and wearing a vaguely sheepish expression as he nodded at Tony. Doherty, he knew, felt a little guilty that he hadn't been around to help make yesterday's collar.

Seizing the opportunity, Tony grabbed Doherty's arm and took him aside. In a low voice, he asked, "Listen, would you mind showing my friends around the tack room? I need a few minutes with this lady here." He gestured toward Skyler.

Doherty winked knowingly. "Sure thing, Sarge."

Tony didn't bother to enlighten him about Skyler not being his girlfriend. Let Doherty think what he wanted. The married cops (the ones who weren't cheating on their wives, that is) lived vicariously through guys like Tony, imagining they went out with a different woman every night. Not, he was quick to remind himself, that he hadn't had his share. In fact, he had a date this coming Saturday with a woman he'd met through a friend. Jennifer. She owned and managed her own boutique, and was a knockout to boot.

Trouble was that now, looking at Skyler, he couldn't remember whether Jennifer's eyes were brown or blue, whether her hair was short or shoulder length . . . or whether she had the adorable habit of every so often running the tip of her tongue between her lips, as Skyler was doing now.

When they were alone, the office miraculously deserted for the moment, he turned to face her. As her blue eyes—vivid with an emotion he couldn't name— met his, he felt as if an invisible hand had reached down inside him and rearranged his guts. This feeling

she stirred in him, it was bigger than just horniness.
Bigger than it had any business being, given that he
and Skyler were virtual strangers.

"You were great with them," she told him. "I can't
thank you enough."

"My pleasure," he said. "They're good kids."

"You seem as if you've had a lot of practice."

"Growing up with six siblings, believe me, you learn
early." He watched the corners of her tense mouth
curl up, and felt disproportionately pleased. At the
same time, he sensed even more clearly that something was troubling her. Sticking his neck out, he ventured, "Listen, Skyler ... are you okay? If you'll
pardon me for saying so, you look like hell."

"Flattery will get you nowhere." She forced a smile,
but her face had closed against him as abruptly as if
a windowshade had been yanked down.

"Hey, you're not sick or anything, are you?" Sick
wasn't the word for it; she looked like death warmed
over.

"I'm fine, but thanks for asking." Polite but distant,
with a touch of frost.

Something that went against his every instinct refused to let Tony drop it at that. Jesus, what did he
care if she'd stayed up late a few nights in a row? Or
maybe it was a fight with her boyfriend—what business was that of his? Still ...

A group of three male officers arriving for the four-
to-twelve burst into the room just then, arguing loudly
about baseball scores as they headed for the locker
room.

Tony touched Skyler's arm. "Come on ... there's
something I forgot to show you."

The farrier's room was on the ground floor, at the
far end of the east wall, behind the row of box stalls.
It was deserted, just as Tony had known it would be;
the Mounted Unit's blacksmith made the rounds of
all the troops, and wasn't due here again until next

week. As Tony drew Skyler into its dim coolness, stopping beside a tree stump on which an anvil perched like some relic of a former age, he caught the faint, burnt smell of hooves, and of hot iron long since cooled. Along the wall hung various tools and instruments; a blackened leather apron was draped over a hook by the foundry. From the tack room at the opposite end of the barn drifted the murmur of voices. Doherty was great with kids, and would have those two mesmerized with his war stories.

Tony turned to Skyler with a solemn expression.

"Look, if something's the matter, you can tell me. I like to think"—he cleared his throat—"that we're still friends, okay? I mean, what happened ... it doesn't have to happen again, if that's what you're worried about."

She blushed, reminding him of what he already knew—that underneath that layer of frost there was enough heat to scorch the hide off any man she allowed close enough.

"Whatever it is, it's got nothing to do with you," she told him, not unkindly.

"Sure," he said mildly. "Neither does ninety-nine percent of what goes down in this city."

"I'm not your *job*." He could see her polite mask beginning to curl around the edges. Then suddenly the whole mask caved in, and her blue eyes filled with tears. "I'm sorry ... it's just ... I've had a really rough week. I know you're trying to be nice, but really, there's no reason for you to be involved. You'd only wish you hadn't—" she broke off as Joyce Hubbard, one of the female officers, poked her head through the doorway.

"Hiya, Sarge," she greeted him. She was all legs and russet-brown hair down to her shoulder blades. "Heard you really hung that collar of yours out to dry. Nice going." Her eyes cut over to Skyler, and Tony caught the flicker of a question behind her smile.

Joyce, he knew, had a thing for him. And to be honest, he wouldn't have minded, except . . .

Except what, you dope? What are you waiting for? Joyce is in your league, and she's made it clear she's interested What do you need, an engraved invitation?

"What was that all about?" Skyler asked after Joyce had gone.

"Nothing much," he told her. "I collared a guy in the park the other day. I'll tell you about it sometime. Not now. You look like you could use some good news for a change. That, and a friend."

"A *friend* . . . oh God. My mother used to call it that when she was in high school." A high, thin laugh whistled out of her, a laugh that teetered on the edge of hysteria. All of a sudden Tony had the sinking feeling he really *shouldn't* have pressed her so hard. He watched Skyler sag against the wall, arms folded against her stomach as if she were holding in place a precariously stitched-together piece of fabric that might rip apart at any second.

"Sorry, you lost me." Tony shook his head.

"Oh, shit. I'm sorry . . . forget I said anything." Skyler drew in her breath in a shaky attempt at regaining control.

That was when it hit Tony. *"My little friend's here, so it looks like you won't be a daddy after all,"* he was hearing his ex-wife announce, in her bitchiest voice, after that one pregnancy scare of theirs.

The floor that had held him up nicely back then was now opening up to swallow him. "You're not saying—" He dropped his voice to a whisper. "Your boyfriend, right?"

She glanced away from him. "Look, forget it, I've got to go. Mickey's going to think you've got me locked up or something." She flashed him a thin, bright smile that might have fooled a judge in the Miss America Pageant, but not him. He caught her arm as she was brushing past him.

"You're right about one thing—this isn't the place," he told her. "Can I meet you somewhere later on?"

"I'll be with Mickey and the kids the rest of the afternoon," she told him.

"What about after that?"

"I'll be tied up." She hesitated, then added, "Besides, what would be the point?"

Tony felt his blood rising, pounding like surf against the inside of his skull. Christ, what *was* the point? She'd just handed him the perfect out. Why didn't he just take it?

But what if *he* was the father? He couldn't just let her walk away.

What do you owe her? A quickie in the sack, no hard feelings.

The face of his father loomed in Tony's memory— Pop's watery, red-rimmed eyes and the web of broken blood vessels spread over his cheeks and nose like a map of the hell he'd put them all through. He remembered the night he'd nearly had to wrestle Pop off a bar stool to get him to come home. He'd been twelve at the time. From that moment on, he'd sworn he'd never be like Pop.

Better to be no father at all.

And anyway, what was he getting so worked up about? Maybe she wasn't pregnant after all. Maybe her period was just a little late . . .

Either way, buddy, you're not going to be out buying cigars.

Maybe not, Tony thought, but the face he confronted in the medicine-chest mirror each and every morning was not one he had ever turned away from in shame, and he wanted to keep it that way.

Tony, his gaze fixed on Skyler with an intensity that matched the giant's fist clenched about his chest, replied calmly, "I almost got killed yesterday. There'd have been no point to that, either."

* * *

They met in Central Park an hour or so before sundown. Skyler was waiting for him by the gabled gingerbread entrance to the Dairy, and they strolled from there over to the carousel, where they were lucky enough to find an empty bench. The area was crawling with kids and moms and nannies . . . which struck him as ironic in light of what they were facing.

"Are you sure?" Tony asked her after they'd been sitting a while in silence.

Skyler screwed her eyes, as if trying to bring him into focus, like someone coming out of a darkened room into intense sunlight. "Yes, I'm sure," she said in a tone that implied, *Would I be dragging you into this if I weren't?* "I took one of those home tests. Actually, I took three different ones. The clerk at Duane Reade must have thought I was operating a clinic." She gave a hollow little laugh, adding, "I feel so stupid. I really don't know how this could have happened."

"You tell me," Tony replied with an evenness that was at odds with the wild bucking of his heart.

"Oh, don't worry, I'm not going to stick you with this," she snapped, obviously mistaking his tone for something else. "I can handle it on my own."

Yet for all her ferocious independence, she looked oddly vulnerable to him at that moment. It struck him that the wildly self-assured young woman who'd rescued his horse and bedded him all in an afternoon might not be the Diana of Roman myth after all, but someone all too human.

Tony felt a tug of compassion . . . and something more. Something that made him think of a line from a song, "It's that old devil moon in your eyes. . . ."

Except the devil moon wasn't in his eyes; it was somewhere below his navel. Looking at Skyler, seated straight and tall on the bench, a mild breeze sending wisps of pale hair blowing across one cheek, her fingers knitting restlessly in her lap, Tony thought he had

never wanted anything so much in his life as he
wanted right now to take her in his arms.

"It's not about you being able to handle this on
your own," he said, choosing his words carefully. "I
just want to know what we're looking at here."

"I don't know." She slumped back against the
bench, staring sightlessly at the carousel wheeling before them, its mirrored panels flashing a cold steely
light, its bright tinkling music a weird counterpoint to
their tense conversation. A nearby vendor, hawking
everything from popcorn to Ben & Jerry's ice cream,
had attracted a cluster of teenagers, a number of them
couples with their arms linked around each other's
waists. Tony couldn't shake the feeling that, in spite
of the things they'd done on the couch in her father's
apartment, he and Skyler were virtual strangers. And
now this lovely stranger, who had somehow gotten
under his skin, was turning to him and saying softly,
"It still hasn't sunk in all the way. I keep thinking it'll
somehow just . . . go away. Like a bad dream."

"My sister Trudi, she said that about her youngest
when she found out she was pregnant. With four already, she needed another kid like a hole in the
head." He offered her a crooked smile. "But you
know what? He turned out the best of the bunch. Just
made altar boy at St. Stephen's . . . and knows how to
raise hell, too."

"Are you suggesting I should keep it?" She narrowed her eyes at him.

Tony felt his hackles go up. He thought of the stable
near his place in Brewster where they bred prize Ara-
bians. One of the mares had gotten loose and had
come back pregnant by a hack stallion. The mare's
owner, shaking his head as he shared the tragic news
with Tony, had sounded much the way Skyler did now.

"I'm not saying anything," he told her. "Jesus, what
am I, an expert on the subject all of a sudden? I
couldn't even make a go of marriage, much less kids."

He watched her eyes tracking the flattened shadow of a bicycle as it rippled over the path at their feet. "I know I don't want to be married yet," she stated matter-of-factly.

"Feel the same about having a kid?" he asked softly.

A sad, sweet smile touched her lips, and she brushed a wisp of hair from her cheek. "I keep thinking of those fairy tales where an ordinary girl has a spell bestowed on her—like temporary magical powers, or some kind of enchantment. It's wonderful . . . but at the same time terrible. Because now she has this huge responsibility." Skyler paused. "Maybe it has something to do with being adopted. I feel like I've been given this extraordinary thing for reasons that make no sense to me, and I have to figure out what to do with it."

For Tony, it was a lot more personal than cosmic. This conversation—the whole possibility of being a father, whether fulfilled or not—was having an effect so mind-blowing that it was a moment before he realized what he was feeling: loss. As soon as it hit him, he sat back, thunderstruck. *This woman I barely know is carrying my kid, and she has absolutely no intention of including me in whatever plans she's making for it.*

He remembered now how excited he'd been about the prospect of Paula being pregnant . . . and how he'd had to keep a lid on it, knowing Paula didn't share his enthusiasm.

"When you've got it all figured out, let me know." He didn't try very hard to keep the anger from his voice.

"If you want." A line formed between brows that were several shades darker than her hair. "You know, it's funny, because I know an abortion makes the most sense. But when I start thinking about it, I get really upset. I don't know why, really. I'm not religious or anything. And I believe every woman has a right to

decide for herself, absolutely. Maybe it's because . . .
I mean, in a way, isn't that how my real mother
thought of me? As an inconvenience . . . as something
to just get rid of." Her frown deepened, and tears
glittered in her eyes.

"Does that mean you see this kid having parents,
getting christened, the whole nine yards?" He spoke
slowly, cautiously.

She blinked, and swiveled to face him. "I don't
know what it means. I'm really upset right now, so
I'm probably not making much sense. You wouldn't
be here if I'd thought twice before opening my big
mouth." She took in his expression, and said, "Sorry.
It's just that I just don't see any reason for dumping
all this on you. I mean, we hardly know each other."

"Relax. I'm not gonna ask you to marry me," he
told her gruffly. At the same time, he couldn't help
thinking, *Why* this *woman? Why not someone he could
have asked?*

Skyler stood up, and he noticed she was a bit shaky
on her feet. As he rose alongside her, Tony stifled his
impulse to steady her. Instead, he just looked at her.

"Well," she said, clearing her throat. "I'd better be
going." She gave him a smile that was as valiant as it
was false. "Listen, if it helps any, I think you're a
really nice guy. I'm sorry you had to get mixed up in
all this."

Tony seized her arm. He didn't know what made
him do it. Instinct, he guessed. Like the little boy on
the carousel he could see now, leaning away from his
wooden horse, reaching for the brass ring he hadn't a
prayer of snagging. Tony wasn't prepared for the
shock of her bare, sun-warmed flesh under his fingers,
and how it tore through him like fire through a Hell's
Kitchen tenement. Nor was he ready for the look she
gave him, defiant and at the same time oddly
beseeching.

"Call me," he said. It wasn't a request.

Slowly, she nodded, her expression grave.

Tony heard a frustrated squeal, and glanced over to see that the carousel was slowing, the little boy crying because he hadn't been able to catch the ring. When he looked back, Skyler was moving with a frank, determined gait along the tree-lined path that meandered in the direction of Central Park West, her pale gold hair flashing in and out of the shade like a coin at the bottom of a wishing well.

Nothing about her gave the slightest suggestion that she was in any way up for grabs. But her unavailability only made him want her all the more . . . and not just in bed. Slowly, it dawned on Tony that as improbable as it might seem—no, downright *delusional*—what he was feeling right now bore a striking resemblance to being in love.

It had been a long time. Even with Paula, in the beginning when it had been good between them, he'd never felt anything close to what Skyler evoked in him—blood that ran hot and cold, a hard-on that wouldn't quit, and a dull ache in his gut that he feared was just the opening act for the main attraction ahead.

He was a cop, accustomed to every kind of emergency and distress, but for the first time in a very long time, Tony felt out of his depth, and miles from anything that came close to resembling solid ground.

Skyler shivered and wrapped her arms about herself. It had to be close to eighty degrees, and she felt as if she'd stepped under an icy waterfall, one that was roaring in her ears, dragging her down. *God, why did I tell him?*

If only the baby had been Prescott's.

But if Pres was the father you wouldn't be walking away right now, you'd be making wedding plans. Would that really have been better? Aren't you in deep enough as it is?

This way at least, whatever she decided, it would be *her* decision.

What about Tony? Shouldn't he have some say in this?

Skyler glanced over her shoulder, and caught a brief glimpse of him, standing in the middle of the path, studying her, thumbs hooked over the front pockets of his jeans. With his sloe eyes and mouth a shade too full, his T-shirt that defined every muscle, and the scuffed toes of his cowboy boots, he looked very much like someone her mother might have warned her to keep away from.

A curious thrill stole through Skyler. A thrill that had less to do with what her mother would or wouldn't have wanted, and more to do with what Skyler herself felt for Tony. She couldn't make sense of it. The pull he exercised over her was undeniable—a force so powerful it was almost celestial, like that of the moon over the tides. Back there, sitting on that bench, she'd thought she might die from wanting him to hold her.

The father of my baby. She explored that amazing thought the way she might have a wisdom tooth working its way up through her gum. Not feeling too much pain from it yet, but knowing it could wind up knocking her flat on her back.

She felt a sudden, curious lightness at her center, as if her vital organs had been pushed aside to make room for the baby growing inside her. *Baby.*

Panic washed through her in an icy torrent.

Skyler found herself lightly coated in a layer of glassy sweat. A sudden cramp in her belly nearly caused her to double over. She stopped, supporting herself against a tree trunk, sharp little arrow-tips of bark digging into her palm.

I don't have to decide just yet, she told herself as she stepped onto the little access road that wound past Tavern on the Green. *I still have another week or two.*

Her heart, though, wouldn't stop its fear-charged hammering.

She thought of those silly astrological predictions in the tabloids, and imagined hers reading, "Powerful forces beyond your control make it necessary that you exercise extreme caution in the next few weeks."

She turned onto Central Park West, crossing the street at the light. Her father's apartment was only a block away, and suddenly the thought of a cool shower and a change of clothes seemed the answer to her problems—for the moment, at least.

It wasn't until she was going up in the elevator that she remembered the last time she'd stayed at Daddy's: the day she'd been with Tony.

God. If only she'd known.

She closed her eyes, sagging against the elevator's walnut-paneled interior. And, suddenly, freeze frame, his image leaped into her mind. Tony. Standing in the path, half in shade, those dark hooded eyes giving nothing away, a bright blade of sunlight cutting across one arm—the arm with the tattoo of a heart entwined with vines. A cop, sworn to safeguard all good citizens against danger, who could do nothing to protect her from the terror engulfing her now.

What am I going to do? It would be selfish to even pretend I could raise a child on my own.

She thought of her parents then, and how this would affect them. When the shock of learning she was pregnant wore off, they would quickly get used to the idea. Daddy, especially. He never got tired of teasing her about how much he was looking forward to being a grandfather. Mom would be less vehement ... but Skyler was already imagining the quiet longing in her eyes that would be so much harder to withstand.

Mom. Oh God.

How am I going to tell her I'm not going to keep the baby?

Skyler truly wanted to die . . . because then she

wouldn't have to face the quiet longing in her mother's eyes, the lingering hurt of a lifetime without the houseful of children she'd wished for. And, of course, the worst part was that Mom, who Skyler was positive had never knowingly hurt a single soul in her entire life, was about to be hurt by someone she loved and trusted more than anyone in the world.

CHAPTER 7

"Kate, do you want me to phone New Orleans and see what's holding up that shipment?"

Kate, kneeling beside the Eastlake dresser she'd picked up at yesterday's estate auction in Rhinebeck, tried to tune into what Miranda was saying. "Hmmm? Oh, that. No rush. It's only been ... what? A week. A mirror that fragile, it could take a day just to crate it."

She slid out a drawer and examined it for signs of recent repair, running her thumb along the dovetailed joinery. At last, she looked up at Miranda, seated at the Edwardian partner's desk in the far corner of the cozily cluttered shop, sorting through the paperwork piled on the leather blotter in front of her. From her vantage, Kate could chat with Miranda while at work in the small back room, doing what she loved best— the sanding, staining, and polishing that brought hidden treasures into the light and made them shine.

Miranda, she saw, was frowning at her with a mixture of exasperation and concern. "Kate! It's been over a *month*. You were in New Orleans at the end of June, and you picked up those diamond earrings for Skyler, for her graduation, remember?"

Dear fussbudgety Miranda, Kate thought. More a mother than a store manager, though she didn't look like either—tall, thin (as in, "You can never be too rich, or too thin"), her glossy forever-auburn pageboy anchored by a headband that perfectly accessorized her outfit. Today she wore pleated taupe trousers, together with a saffron knit top and a matching cardigan, draped over her shoulders.

Kate also noticed that Miranda was wearing the Victorian stickpin she'd given her for her forty-ninth birthday in April, and was pleased to see it hadn't ended up in a drawer. As much as Miranda loved antiques, the two of them were often at odds when it came to buying them. Miranda favored arts and crafts and mission oak, while Kate leaned more toward Victorian and art nouveau. The result was a shop crammed with an eclectic mix that somehow worked, and was probably the reason Antiquities could afford to stay open even in the winter, long after Northfield's tourists and summer-home weekenders had migrated back to the city.

"Oh . . . has it been that long?" Kate brushed a wisp of hair off her forehead and sat back on her heels.

"Honestly, Kate!" Miranda scolded. "You've been like this all week—mixing up phone numbers, misplacing invoices, forgetting appointments. Mrs. Teasdale waited an hour for you yesterday, and I *know* you told her two o'clock, because I heard you." She sat back in the leather-cushioned Victorian swivel chair, regarding Kate with a keenness sharpened by the experience of raising her four children on her own. "It's Skyler, isn't it? You're still down about her moving out."

Kate carefully slid the drawer back in and hoisted herself to her feet with the help of her cane, brushing invisible dust from the back of her skirt. "Well . . . yes, in a way," she admitted, poking her way across the threshold of the workroom. "It was so sudden, that's all. I just wish she'd given us some warning."

"Remember, Anne was only eighteen when she moved in with her boyfriend," Miranda pointed out. "If you'll recall, I spent months on the verge of hysteria—it's a time in my life I don't look back on fondly," she added dryly. "But, you know, in the end it turned out not to be such a terrible thing. Look at Anne now, with her three beautiful children."

"If I thought I'd at least be getting a grandchild out of it, I might not be so upset," Kate joked—a remark that would come to haunt her in the weeks to come.

Miranda clucked. "Skyler is twenty-two going on forty. She'll be fine. And it's not as if she'll have to forage for nuts and berries. Didn't you tell me your mother left her that cabin free and clear?"

"Oh, yes. That's not the problem."

"Then what is?"

"It's just . . ."

Kate stopped. How much could she tell Miranda? They'd been friends for over thirty years, but there were some things you didn't tell even your closest friends. Miranda was partly right; Kate *had* been feeling a bit bereft these past few weeks, ever since Skyler had announced out of the blue that she was moving into Gran's cabin. Gipsy Trail was only a twenty-minute drive east of Northfield, and Skyler shuttled from the veterinary clinic to Duncan's—where she was training for the upcoming Hampton Classic—and back home again, almost every day. Still, she seemed farther away than when she'd gone off to Princeton.

But that was only a piece of the whole picture. What Kate found more disturbing than Skyler's abrupt move was the *reason* behind it. Skyler had to have picked up on the tension around their house . . . the sense of some disaster just around the bend. Their daughter couldn't have failed to notice that Will was almost never home these days, and that when he was, he was usually buried in paperwork, or on the phone with clients. Even the cottage on Cape Cod, where they'd gone every Labor Day weekend since Skyler was a baby, would remain shuttered and empty this year.

What a waste! Kate thought. Maybe she would go without Will this year. See if Skyler could get away for a few days.

But escaping wouldn't solve anything, she realized. For wasn't that what she'd been doing all along?

For months, she and Will had carried on as if nothing much was out of the ordinary. If Will was feeling crunched at work, Kate had reasoned, it was because the real estate market itself was in a slump. That was to be expected from time to time. He was just having to work a little harder than usual to make up for it.

Except Kate knew there was more to it than that. And last week, her suspicions had been confirmed. Will had been on the phone with his accountant, Tim Bigelow, so deep in hushed conversation he hadn't noticed the door to his den standing open. She had paused in the hallway, caught by something she'd overheard—a phrase that had leaped out at her like a real-life attacker materializing from what she'd been convinced was merely a shadow on the wall.

"Jesus, Tim, if we go Chapter Eleven . . ."

A fragment lifted out of context, but it had been enough to pierce her with dread.

So why not just confront Will and say you know the firm is in trouble, more trouble than he's admitted? a voice in her head asked. *Offer to help in any way you can?*

But what could she offer except moral support? Antiquities brought in a nice little income, but quite honestly the reason she'd opened the shop in the first place was because it gave her an excuse to do what she loved best: shop for antiques. "Kate's hobby," Will affectionately called the shop, always making her bristle a little. Still, it was ludicrous to imagine that her

contribution to the family finances could rescue them
from serious financial difficulty.

Even with the monthly check she received from her
grandmother's trust, her total income covered household
expenses only. It wasn't nearly enough for the upkeep
on Orchard Hill, their BMW and Volvo, Skyler's horse,
the cottage on Cape Cod. Not to mention first-class
airfare, dinners in expensive restaurants, Will's tailor-
made suits, and her passion for antiques and art.

But how bad could it be? she reassured herself. Sutton, Jamesway & Falk had been in the real estate
business for more than forty years, and Will's father
was one of its founding partners. Not only had the
firm weathered the ups and downs of the market, but
over the years it had grown large enough to occupy
an entire floor of an office building, owned by the
firm, on Park Avenue and Forty-eighth.

True, it had never wholly recovered the millions lost
in the seventies when the City Island deal fell through.
And more recently, Will and his partners were feeling
the backlash of the eighties boom—coops sitting half
empty, midtown office buildings begging for tenants,
upscale shopping centers few could afford to shop in
anymore. A smaller firm might not have been able to
survive such losses ... but Sutton, Jamesway & Falk?
For it to go under would be like—well, like the Epis-
copal church she and Will attended closing down.

How bad could it be?

Bad enough to have reduced her husband to a
shadow of his former self, she admitted grimly. Bad
enough to keep him away from home for days at a
stretch, working late every night and staying over in
the city to dine with prospective clients. And like a
shadow, Will appeared gray and flattened somehow.
He'd lost so much weight that his suits hung on him
as if tailored for a man two sizes larger.

If only she had something more to offer him than

neck rubs and mugs of herbal tea! If only she had the
nerve to at least face what was going on!

And what, pray tell, is going on? that hectoring voice
spoke up.

Kate forced herself to look at the facts. Judging
from what she'd overheard, the firm might actually be
on the verge of going under.

Oh, dear . . .

She felt a clutching sensation in her chest that sent
her hand flying to her heart in an unconscious parody
of a Victorian lady on the verge of swooning. She saw
Miranda looking at her curiously, and with an effort
forced her hand to her side. No, she couldn't share
her suspicions with Miranda. It wasn't that her old
friend wouldn't understand; Miranda would surely be
as supportive as she was discreet. That wasn't the
problem, Kate realized. It was her own sense of what
was fair and proper; her old-fashioned adherence to
putting the horse before the cart. She couldn't tell
Miranda what was going on at home for the simple
reason that she had yet to confront Will.

You must speak to him, the voice in her head insisted. *Make him tell you everything.*

"My grandmother started losing her marbles when
she was around our age. It must run in the family,"
Kate said, skirting Miranda's probing with a manufac-
tured lightness that left her feeling like the worst kind
of imposter.

"Well, now, *there's* a comforting thought." Miranda
arched a perfectly plucked and penciled brow, but she
was smiling.

"I've never thought of myself as middle-aged, so
maybe I skipped that part and now I'm just getting
old," Kate said with a thin, forced laugh.

"Speak for yourself," replied Miranda with a sniff,
but the desired effect had been achieved. Her attention shifted from Kate's problems to whatever she was

rummaging for among the papers on her desk. "Now, where did I put that customs form?"

Kate returned to the dresser in the workroom, noticing a loose piece of molding that would have to be reglued. The veneer was a bit cloudy, too; she'd have Leonard refinish it as soon as he was done stripping the settee he was due to deliver later today. She'd have him look at the wobbly leg on that chair against the wall, while he was at it. Oh, so much to be done!

She looked at a pair of silver candlesticks nestled in paper straw that had arrived with the same shipment from Rhinebeck. They were Georgian, with engraved triform bases and stems supported by Chinese men in flowered coats. Caressing them, Kate felt the thrill that lovely old things always brought her. Maybe simply because they *were* old, she thought, liking the idea of her precious lamps and clocks and chairs and vitrines enduring through the ages despite how delicate they seemed.

Enduring, yes.

Kate felt a stab of inexplicable longing.

The sly voice in her head insinuated, *It's not just the firm you're worried about, is it? There's another can of worms you've made a point of not opening.*

She thought of the unacknowledged distance that lately had occupied the bed she shared with Will like a cold, unwelcome guest, one they were both too polite to ask to leave. Did Will have the slightest idea how it pained her? Did he imagine that in not disturbing her, even to curl up against her, he was doing her any kind of favor? Oh, if only she could find the courage to—

"Have you seen the silver polish?" Kate called over her shoulder, interrupting her own thoughts. Edging her way past chairs wedged end to end, dressers and end tables cloaked in dust, a glass-front bookcase missing several of its panes, she moved resolutely to the old steamer trunk where she kept her odds and ends—dust cloths, tins of polish, loose finials, knobs off drawers long since relegated to the trash heap.

Kate felt a hand on her shoulder, and looked up in surprise to find that Miranda had stolen up behind her. "Kate, if it's anything I can help with . . . I hope you know you can come to me. I'm often lousy at giving advice, but I'm a terrific listener."

"I know," Kate told her, quickly turning her head so Miranda wouldn't see the tears in her eyes.

"Excuse me—but could you tell me something about those chairs in the window?"

A young woman peered around the angled bookshelves that separated the office and work area from the rest of the shop. She was around thirty or so, pretty in a well-bred understated way, wearing uniformly faded jeans and a pressed cotton shirt with an Hermès scarf artfully tucked inside the collar. Grateful for the interruption, Kate hurried over to assist her.

The woman, who introduced herself as Ginny Hansen, was in the throes of renovating the old Sprague house on the corner of Washington and Chestnut. Kate looked over the wallpaper and upholstery samples the woman had brought, and helped her pick out a fabric for the set of six Sheraton chairs she'd admired. Kate advised her about drapes as well, and talked her out of a sideboard she suspected would be too cumbersome for that dining room.

"You've been so nice," Ginny gushed as Kate was making out the receipt. "It's almost like having my mother here . . . she's so good at knowing what goes with what. She would *love* this store." Ginny paused, catching her lower lip between her teeth. "Would you like to stop by some time and see what my husband and I have done?"

"I'd be delighted," Kate told her, and meant it. "Here's my card. Call me anytime."

Since she'd been a young woman herself, she'd had this effect on people. Something in her face, perhaps,

like the cheerful sign hanging in the front door that
read, "Yes, we're open!" Or maybe it was the cane
that made her seem more approachable; suffering was
supposed to make you more compassionate. Still, the
older she got, the more uncomfortable Kate felt with
the idea of herself as a sort of silver-haired sage.

*Is it because you know the truth—that you're not as
honorable and upright as you appear?*

The memory came, as it always did, on the back of
a dull pain that started in her side and worked its way
down into her hip, where it flared into hot, jagged
agony. *Ellie.* Kate could see the woman in her mind,
flaxen head bent close to Skyler's bandaged one, the
resemblance between them so striking that anyone
might have spotted it. Where was Ellie now? Had she
had the children she'd wanted? Had the memory of
her own lost daughter faded with the years?

*That would suit you nicely, wouldn't it? Then you
wouldn't have to feel quite so guilty.*

Kate clamped down hard on the dark thoughts swirling through her mind. It was no use going down *that*
particular blind alley. She knew its every brick and
paving stone, its every looming shadow and blackened
doorway. There was no end to it, and no going back.
Better not to go near it at all. She busied herself instead with the tarnished candlesticks she'd been about
to polish before Ginny Hansen came in.

The rest of the day passed in a blur. The delivery
of the crate from the Goldberg Gallery in New Orleans arrived in the midst of Miranda's phoning to see
what had become of it. Old Mrs. Otto dropped by,
wanting Kate to make an offer on a silver tea service
she insisted was Georgian but which Kate could
clearly see was late Victorian. Leonard arrived with
the refinished settee, and took away the Eastlake
dresser and a Biedermeier writing desk Miranda had
bought last month at an auction in Maine. Butler, their

store cat, presented Kate with a bloody mouse. And in the midst of it all, Skyler showed up.

Kate, delighted and more than a little relieved, rushed over to greet her. They'd exchanged words— not *angry* words exactly, but certainly voices had been raised—over Skyler's decision to move, and Skyler had been distant and cool these past few weeks.

Kate hugged her. "Darling! Why didn't you phone and let me know you were coming?"

"I didn't know myself until a few minutes ago. I was on my way home from the clinic, and I just thought I'd drop by and see how you were doing. Hi, Miranda! Hey, there, Butler ... miss me?" She bent over to pick up the big black cat twining itself about her leg.

Skyler sounded perfectly fine, cheerful even, but Kate could clearly see that something was wrong. In the weeks since Kate had last seen her, Skyler had grown thin and pale. And look how the bones in her face stood out! It was all Kate could do not to cry out in alarm, to demand at once to be told what was wrong. Instead, she cast an anxious glance at her watch. Nearly five—not too early to seize this opportunity and insist that Skyler come home with her for supper. Then, when they were both settled on the porch with glasses of iced tea, maybe Skyler would confide in her.

One thing Kate was certain of: whatever had prompted Skyler to move out, whatever was making her look so ill, was more serious than Kate had first assumed. She felt a kernel of panic form in her stomach, but was careful not to show it. She mustn't let Skyler know how worried she was; that would only drive her further away.

Kate took a surreptitious inventory of her daughter, standing by the door with Butler now lolling in her arms like a great sack of jelly beans. She was wearing jeans that were way too big, Kate observed, and a baggy cotton sweater that seemed far too heavy for

the oppressive August heat. A dusting of face powder
didn't quite hide the dark crescents under her eyes,
and her smile wouldn't have fooled a child of five.

"What about that old refrigerator of Gran's ... did
you get it working?" Kate asked, trying to sound un-
concerned. "If you've changed your mind about letting
me get you a new one, there's still time to run over
to Sears before they close. Then," she threw in casually, "we can pick up some goodies at the Marketplace
and take them up to the house for an early supper."

Skyler rolled her eyes. "Mom, I didn't come to look
at refrigerators. Anyway, the old one works fine—it's
just the freezer, and I hardly use it anyway." She
hooked her arm through Kate's. "How about letting
me take *you* out for dinner?"

"Another time," Kate said, patting her daughter's
hand. "Your father's working late again tonight, and
I thought it'd be nice, just the two of us at home
where it's quiet. I want to hear about everything that's
going on with you."

Something was terribly wrong. She could *feel* it.
Skyler was *so* quiet. Driving through the village, Kate
kept her eye on her daughter, who remained sunk in
her thoughts, even as she smiled and nodded in response to Kate's strained chatter.

As she turned into the Marketplace's parking lot,
Kate suppressed a sigh. She would have to be a bit
more patient, that was all. Skyler, who all her life had
done things in her own way and in her own time,
would eventually open up.

Kate's spirits lifted when she spotted the old hand-
cart the store owners had bought from her a few
months back; it sat parked in front, freshly painted
and overflowing with geraniums and impatiens. She
would have to make a point of telling Mr. Kruikshank
how nice it looked.

Inside, the store achieved a rustic look—there was
barnwood siding, and bushel baskets in place of plastic

bins. Kate maneuvered her cart down aisles piled with glistening produce and past deli cases of gourmet salads and pasta dishes, purposely buying more than she alone could eat in a month. It was an act of defiance that she recognized as pointless. But she could at least have the satisfaction of imagining the wonderful family meals they all might share, couldn't she?

They took home four large shopping bags and a net sack of baby yellow Finns for the potato salad Kate planned to make later in the week. But at dinner, Skyler only picked, pushing her plate aside when Kate tried to tempt her with more. Kate felt unreasonably disappointed and had to squelch an impulse simply to order her daughter to finish her supper.

Afterwards, they settled out on the back porch, on the Victorian wicker chairs Kate had upholstered in William Morris fabric. They sipped iced tea and nibbled on tiny local strawberries sweet as gumdrops. Their Lab, her muzzle gray with age, padded out and settled at Skyler's feet with a groan of contentment. Kate spent a minute watching Skyler run her bare toes over Belinda's scruffy black coat before turning her gaze to the view beyond the porch.

The sun was setting over the distant hills, igniting the treetops afire and mowing a path of gold down the center of the fields where horses had grazed when Kate was a young girl, growing up at Orchard Hill. Where the land sloped down to meet the orchards, Kate caught a glimpse, through the branches of apple trees studded with thimble-sized green fruit, of the old stable's moss-stained stone façade. They had kept Skyler's first pony there, before she began taking lessons at Stony Creek Farm. Kate remembered that pliant old Shetland mare, whose only bad trait had been a tendency to ride too close to the fence in what Kate had suspected was a halfhearted attempt to scrape loose her young rider.

Lord, I can take it if Will's firm goes under. I sup-

pose I would find a way to go on even if I lost Will. But, oh, I couldn't bear it if anything should happen to my daughter—

The thought, shocking in its intensity, seemed to swoop down out of nowhere. Kate set her glass of tea down on the table beside her chair. Her hand, she saw, was trembling. And she felt weak enough to be grateful that she was sitting down.

Kate darted a glance in Skyler's direction, but her daughter was staring past her, at some distant horizon visible only to her.

Was she thinking about Prescott? Kate had heard from Nan Prendergast that he'd gotten engaged—to a girl he'd been friendly with at Yale. By now the whole town must know. And even if Skyler wasn't in love with Prescott, it had to be a blow, only two months after breaking off with him, to discover that she was so replaceable.

Kate herself was far less disappointed about Skyler not marrying Prescott than everyone (including Nan Prendergast) assumed. She'd always known Skyler wasn't passionately in love with that boy. And when you got right down to it, what could be more important more than that?

But be careful, my darling, because once you've known that kind of love, you won't ever be content with less. She felt a pang, thinking of Will and how it had been when they were first married. How they would often stay in bed for an entire morning, exploring each other's bodies as if mapping uncharted territory. And how once, after making love, she had broken down and wept in his arms with the intensity of their passion ... and with the certain knowledge that she must never, ever let go of it.

But somehow she *had* let go. Or it had somehow gotten misplaced along the way. Kate, staring at a doe that faded in and out of the pool of shadow surrounding a stand of distant elms, found herself almost wishing she felt a greater sense of loss ... for that would have meant there was a spark still amid the ashes. But the pain in her heart had been blunted over time to a vague, dull yearning.

In the next instant, however, all thoughts of Will were blasted from Kate's head. There was a sudden, sharp intake of breath beside her, and Skyler said: "Mom, I'm pregnant."

For a moment, her daughter's words seemed to float just under the surface of Kate's consciousness, like the faint sounds of encroaching dusk—the low growl of a tractor on its way home from the fields, the chirring of crickets, the hiss of a water sprinkler. Then it hit her.

She sank back in her chair, feeling as if someone had dropped onto her lap, pressing into her so hard the old wicker creaked in protest.

It was an effort, but she forced herself to look at her daughter and ask in what would have passed as a reasonable tone of voice had she ·been able to breathe, "Prescott?"

Skyler's mouth screwed itself into a tight line. "No."

Kate refrained from grilling her. She wasn't altogether sure she wanted to know the answer to *that*, not yet at least....

"How—how far along are you?" she asked instead.

"Nine weeks."

"Oh, Skyler ..." Kate, her eyes welling, leaned forward and took hold of her daughter's cool, limp hands. So *this* was what her daughter had been keeping from her.

Skyler wore the deep scowl that meant she was on the verge of tears herself. "I know, Mom, I know. Believe me, there's nothing you can say that I haven't already said to myself." She turned a pair of stricken, red-rimmed eyes on Kate. "Do you hate me?"

"Hate you? Oh, sweetie—" Kate warred in silence against the sob that was fighting to tear loose. Swallowing hard, she stated with flat, hard-won calm, "The important thing right now is deciding what we're going to do about it.''

Along with a sense of purpose came control. Kate felt her spine straighten. She couldn't afford to fall apart now any more than she could have on that long-ago day when Skyler had almost died; she had to remain strong for her daughter.

Skyler sat back, withdrawing her hands from Kate's. "Mom," she said quietly, but firmly, "this isn't a decision I need you or Daddy to make for me."

Kate sat back, feeling both confused and hurt. How could Skyler just sit there and pretend this didn't involve her? Why, it was simply absurd to imagine—

A voice as clear and pure as running water broke in: *She's right. I have to stop trying to run her life.*

Suddenly, Kate was remembering the days when she was newly pregnant . . . the wonder of it all; a life growing inside her. For days after her doctor had given her the good news, she'd walked about in a mist of happiness, like a sailor at sea following the distant wink of a lighthouse. The baby inside her was that light, and she its lighthouse. She could feel it shining inside her, a steady, muted glow holding the promise of safe harbor . . . and of a new beginning.

And yet as much as she'd loved and wanted that baby, and as hard as it was to imagine any woman *not* feeling the way she had, what mattered most of all was the daughter seated beside her now. The child, not of her womb, but of her heart.

Please, Lord, give me the strength to do right by her.

"The baby . . ." she began, her throat seizing up again. "The baby I was carrying when I had my accident—I never would have let them operate if there had been even a slim hope of saving it." She paused, struggling with herself until she felt calm enough to go on. "But . . . but every situation is different, and you're not me. If you've made up your mind to . . . to end it . . . I'll stand by your decision."

Skyler heaved a deep sigh and looked past her, out to where the rolling fields folded into the deepening shadow of the treeline.

"I'm not going to have an abortion, Mom," she said softly. "I . . . I've decided to give the baby up for adoption."

"Give it up?" Kate was too numb to do more than echo Skyler's words.

"I've thought it over," Skyler went on in the tone of someone who must get it all out, and *quickly,* while she is still able to. "For the past three weeks, I've done nothing but think it over."

Kate felt something explode inside her like a jar exposed to too high a temperature. "But you—you—you can't just give it away!" she cried in outrage. "A baby isn't a puppy or a kitten! Your own flesh and blood—how could you even *think* of doing such a thing?"

"Mom . . . don't." A shaft of light from the setting sun caught Skyler full in the face, and her brimming eyes blazed silver.

Kate fell silent at once.

"I know it'll be hard when the time comes." Skyler's voice trembled as she spoke. "I also know it'll be the best thing for the baby. I'm just not ready to be a mother."

"Daddy and I would help. I could take care of the baby until you feel ready." Kate heard the note of pleading in her voice, but couldn't seem to stop herself. "Oh, darling, you *must* reconsider. We'll work out some arrangement we can all live with. Of course, we will. We're a *family.*"

Skyler shook her head, the grave expression not leaving her face. "I know you, Mom. You'd insist that I move back in. And with me in school, you'd be the one taking care of the baby most of the time. I'd wind up feeling twice as guilty—for not being there for my child, and for sticking you with the work."

"I wouldn't mind," Kate insisted with too much vehemence. "Besides, I'd have Vera to help, and we could always hire a nanny."

"Mom . . . no."

Kate started to protest, but the look on Skyler's face stopped her. Instead, she said, "Why don't we discuss it later, when all this has had a chance to sink in?"

"All right," Skyler agreed. "But it won't help. I'm not changing my mind. I just need to know if I can count on you and Daddy to . . ." She faltered, her voice close to breaking. "I don't know . . . to be there for me, I guess."

Kate stood up, feeling lighter, stronger, than she had any reason to. Drawing her daughter into her arms, she murmured into the silky warmth of Skyler's hair, *"That* is one thing I can promise absolutely."

She could feel, in the quivering tautness of her daughter's back, that Skyler was trying hard not to cry. With an effort, Kate withheld the motherly pats and murmurs that flowed from her core as naturally as blood from a beating heart.

She wondered how she was going to tell Will, and what his reaction would be. Would it draw them together in some way, or merely push them farther apart? Would this be the catalyst to clear away their unspoken fears and resentments—or the straw that would break the camel's back?

One thing Kate knew for certain: she could no longer sit back and wait for—well, for whatever it was she'd been hoping would happen on its own.

She had to act.

She had to tell Will about Skyler . . . and she had to force him to tell her if what she feared about the firm was true. Otherwise, how could she, in all honesty, offer the kind of reassurance Skyler would need if she were to even consider letting them take care of her child?

Kate once again felt the pull of something deeper and stronger than anything she could put a name to, an unseen tide sweeping her along, toward a destination she was only dimly aware of. The only thing she knew was where and how her journey had begun—nearly twenty-two years ago, on a freezing November day when she'd gathered close to her hungering heart the baby that had been stolen from another woman's arms.

Kate heard the muffled creak of Will's footsteps on the stairs and glanced at the clock beside the bed. Eleven-thirty. She closed the book she hadn't been reading, and switched off the radio she hadn't been listening to. The one thing she'd had no trouble with this evening was staying awake. She doubted if even a pill would put her to sleep now, the way her heart was racing.

Am I strong enough for this? she fretted. *Do I really need to know the truth about our finances when I haven't yet recovered from Skyler's bombshell?*

Kate had been doing some serious thinking over the past few hours, and she'd come to the conclusion that, as much it might pain them to do so, she and Will had to step back. Skyler would never come to her senses with her parents breathing down her neck; she was far too stubborn. She needed a long lead if there was to be any chance of her coming to the right decision on her own.

To calm herself, Kate looked around her, at the room that was her safe haven from the world. Her gaze took in the burled Viennese armoire with its pair of kissing doves carved above the doors . . . the matching Hunzinger chairs flanking the windows that overlooked her rose garden . . . her collection of beaded reticules on the far wall above the pale blue Linkrusta wainscoting. In the piece *Country Living* had done on Orchard Hill last spring, a whole spread had been devoted to the master bedroom alone. "A Victorian gem," the writer called it. But like a gem's cold gleam, the loveliness of the room never quite made up for the lack of warmth in bed each night as she lay there, missing Will, missing his arms around her. . . .

The door eased open and her husband appeared in the wedge of light that fanned over the threshold. Kate had an instant in which to study his unguarded face, and what she saw did not encourage her. How tired he looked! He was gray and stoop-shouldered, the skin around his eyes puckered and creased.

And yet Will's unwavering sense of purpose—the air of authority he brought to even the smallest of tasks—somehow came through. It was in the way he strode across the room; and in the precise way he removed first his shoes (careful to insert their corresponding shoe trees before stowing them away in the closet), then his tie (which he thoughtfully hung up instead of slinging onto the back of a chair). There was even a defined order in the way he emptied his pockets—first the wallet, then the Mark Cross key chain, then the sterling card case, and finally the loose change.

"I would have phoned," he told her, padding over to kiss her cheek, "but I thought you'd be asleep. I hope you weren't waiting up for me."

With a sigh, Kate settled back against the pillows. "I couldn't have slept if I'd tried," she told him honestly. "It's been one of those days."

"Tell me about it."

He smiled the smile of someone who lately has had nothing but days like that, giving her shoulder a distracted squeeze before moving away. Watching him undress—carefully, methodically, brushing the lint from his jacket before hanging it in the closet—Kate felt a sudden, unreasonable urgency. A need to relieve herself of this burden before it burned a hole right through her.

"Will . . . ?" she began hesitantly, and waited for

him to stop what he was doing and turn around. But Will continued to go about his business as if she hadn't spoken. Gathering her courage, Kate addressed his back instead, as he stood before the highboy dresser, poking first his right leg, then his left, into a pair of freshly ironed pajama bottoms. "Will, we need to talk."

Slowly, wearing only his pajama bottoms, he turned to face her—a fifty-two-year-old man with thick pewter hair and mustache, who was still handsome enough to warrant second looks from women half his age. Up until just recently, he'd worked out four mornings a week at the gym, and it showed in the broad ribbons of muscles in his chest and arms, which didn't match the present droop of his shoulders and the deep grooves of exhaustion etched on either side of his mouth.

"Sorry, Kate. I've been so wrapped up in my own stuff lately I haven't paid much attention to you." He came over and sat down on the foot of the bed. "Was there something in particular?"

His response threw her for a minute. But then, wasn't that what had always impressed her about Will? No matter how tired or busy he was, he never hesitated to take on yet another task if he thought it would serve a useful purpose.

But am I just another task? she wondered. *Another loose end to be tied up?*

"Skyler stopped by this evening," she began hesitantly. "She had some . . . some upsetting news." Kate pulled in a breath that was like dragging water into her lungs. "Will, she's pregnant."

A moment of silence followed in which Will simply stared at her, his blue-gray eyes stark with disbelief, his mouth below his neatly trimmed mustache working as he struggled with this new, impossible concept.

"Pregnant?" he bellowed at last. "But that's im—"

"It's not impossible," Kate interrupted, feeling a bit

annoyed at having to state the obvious to a man so intelligent.

"But—"

Kate braced herself. "That's not the worst of it. She's decided to give the baby up for adoption."

An apoplectic flush was creeping up Will's neck and suffusing his face, and for a panicky instant Kate feared he was on the verge of a heart attack. But he now was leaping to his feet, suddenly a foot taller than he had been a moment before.

He reached for the Princess phone on the nightstand beside Kate. "I don't care if I'm waking that boy out of a sound sleep or not. He's going to hear from me, and he's going to hear loud and clear. If he thinks for one minute—"

"This has nothing to do with Prescott," Kate informed him with a calm that surprised her. "He's not the father."

"Jesus God Almighty! *Who,* then?" Will dropped his hand and turned a pair of baleful, bloodshot eyes on her, as if this were all her fault somehow.

Nettled, Kate shot back, "I don't know . . . and I don't believe we *need* to know at this point. What matters most right now is Skyler, helping her get through this."

"I can tell you one thing: she's not giving my grandchild up for adoption. *That* is out of the question." Will, with a dismissive chopping motion of his hand, began pacing alongside the bed, raising furrows in the nearly threadbare Aubusson carpet that had been in Kate's family for over a hundred years. "She'll move back in with us, of course. We'll turn her old room into a nursery, and she can take the guest room." Kate could see by the way his pacing slowed, and by the thoughtful look dawning on his face, that he was beginning to warm to the idea. "The Ellises won't be needing their nanny in another year or so, and Godwin tells me the woman is wonderful with the kids."

"Will, it's too soon," Kate told him gently. "She's not ready to be persuaded. We have to give her time. Once she's really thought this over, I believe there's a good chance she'll come around on her own."

"What is there to think over?"

"She has her reasons ... and for now we just have to respect them," Kate told him. "It isn't just that she feels she's not ready to raise a child"—her eyes cut away from his—"I think it also has to do with ... with believing her mother walked out on her. Sky being afraid she'll be like *her*. But that *isn't* the way it happened. If she only knew what really—"

"Stop it, Kate." Will swiveled around, his face ashen, his hands clenched so tightly that all the veins and tendons in his neck stood out in furious relief. In a low voice, as if the words were being ripped from him, he hissed, "Stop romanticizing it. How do we know what kind of a mother she was? Living like that, exposing Skyler to ... to God knows what. How do we know it didn't happen the way they said it did?"

"Oh, Will." Kate suddenly realized that what she'd thought of, all these years, was Will's deep-seated aversion to a painful subject, was in reality something far more serious. *He hasn't just swept it under the rug. He's made believe it didn't happen.*

In her mind's eye, she was seeing Grady Singleton, in his monogrammed French cuffs, silver-haired and looking more like an actor in a television drama than the kind of lawyer who would be involved in something illegal.

She saw Grady lean toward them across his Italianate desk. "Your father and I go way back, Will ... we were classmates at Yale." His smile was warm, confidential. "There's an unwritten rule among us Yalies that we look after our own. That's why, when Ward mentioned to me that you were looking to adopt, I did something I technically shouldn't have— I held out on a waiting list of clients who'd be at my throat if they knew. I told Ward I'd put you right at the top ... if you're interested, that is." His voice dropped to a confidential whisper. "You see, there's this baby. . . ."

A baby you conveniently neglected to mention was stolen, you smooth bastard. Well, it worked, we let ourselves get suckered ... in exchange for a fee hefty enough to help you build a house on Sanibel, where I hear you're a tough one to beat at golf.

"There's no proof of anything, Kate, so let's just drop it." Will spoke in the deep, authoritative tone he used on employees when dressing them down.

Yet at the same time he was looking at her in a new and disturbing way, almost as if pleading with her. And suddenly, her strong and resourceful husband of twenty-five years—the man she'd always looked up to and thought she could lean on—became someone she wasn't altogether certain she could look straight in the eye.

Kate felt . . . abandoned. The most momentous thing in their lives, and they couldn't even talk about it. But there was nothing new in that. Had Will *ever* acknowledged the terrible burden she alone had been forced to carry all these years? Now she was left to cope with Skyler's pregnancy as well; to find the delicate balance between her own wishes and those of their daughter. For there would be no leaning on Will's shoulder, not unless she teamed up with him and agreed to fight Skyler's decision every inch of the way.

Anger rose in her, as righteous as it was frightening.

"Not talking about it isn't going to make it go away! If you had any idea ... the nights I lie awake, thinking about it." She brought her hands to cheeks that felt scalded.

"Whatever really happened, it's over with, Kate," Will pointed out reasonably. "This business with Skyler is something entirely separate."

She dropped her hands, and looked at him. "We played God once already. I won't do it again. I won't interfere in her decision."

"Skyler is just a child herself. She doesn't know what she's doing!"

"She's twenty-two, old enough to make up her own mind." Kate remained firm despite the shakiness she could feel spreading through her like some sort of dreadful palsy.

"That's it, then? You're going to just sit back and do nothing?" She had never heard such scorn in Will's voice before, at least not directed at her.

Kate began to shiver uncontrollably, and she drew the tatted coverlet to her chest. All her old bearings, the compass that had kept her on course all these years, seemed to be gone, and she was left with only her own possibly unreliable sense of direction.

Only one thought stood clear in her mind, like a full moon showing her a path: *Will is right about one thing—what happened all those years ago can't be undone. We did a terrible thing that nothing we do now can ever make up for ... but we can learn from it, can't we? We can try to be, if not better for it, then wiser at least.*

"Nothing? No, Will, what I'm proposing isn't *nothing,*" she said quietly. "We're just fighting for different things, is all."

Suddenly, she felt so tired ... too tired to cope with whatever else Will might be keeping to himself. What were money worries next to the well-being of their only child—and now their grandchild, as well? Still, something was prodding her, forcing her to strike now, before the door that stood open a crack was slammed shut again.

Careful to look directly at him—her dear, misguided husband in his striped pajama bottoms, standing there with his arms folded over his bare chest—she said gently, "Will ... you've been a good husband to me all these years, *too* good in some ways. Often, you've tried to protect me with your silence when coming out with the truth would have been the better way. But it's time to stop playing these games. We're both too old for it." She gathered what was left of her resolve, and said, "I know about the firm. I know it's in worse trouble than you've been letting on. And I want to help."

He gaped at her in astonishment, as if she'd just offered to balance the national budget. Then, with a sigh, he sank down beside her on the bed.

"Kate, this isn't something you need to be involved in right now," he told her wearily. "I won't deny things are a little rough right now, but . . . I'm managing."

"I'll be sure to inscribe it on your tombstone," she replied tartly. " 'Here lies William Tyler Sutton. He managed.' "

"Kate, for God's sake—"

"No!" she cried. "For once, Will, make it for *our* sakes. *Tell* me what's going on, even if all I can do is listen. I'm good at listening. I might even have a suggestion that's worthwhile."

She watched his jaw tighten as he studied the lovely old carpet at his feet. Finally, drawing in a sharp breath, he admitted, "All right, you asked for it. The truth is I'm not even sure we're going to be able to meet next month's payroll."

Kate felt his words sink home with an impact that was almost physical. Oh, dear God, that bad? It was *that* bad? But she resisted the urge to burst out with a thousand anxious questions. Instead, she said simply: "I want to help."

"I don't see how you can," he told her. But his tone was respectful, and he was eyeing her with a new, considering look.

"How much would it take to tide you over?"

"Several hundred thousand, at least. And that's just

payroll and operating costs, enough to keep us from going belly-up. It wouldn't cover any of the bank loans that are due."

"But if you could keep going until . . . until things got straightened out?"

"This Braithwaite deal I'm killing myself over—if it goes through it'll net several million. But with a limited partnership on property this valuable, you're talking big players, high stakes, lots of variables." With his fingers steepled against his forehead, he rubbed his thumbs over the puffy skin under his eyes. Frowning thoughtfully, he added, "I'll need another month, maybe. Two at the most."

She sat up, and leaned forward, bringing her palm to rest against the crease of his pajamas where it flattened over his kneecap. Something had just occurred to her—something so daring, and yet so simple, she could hardly believe she hadn't thought of it before.

"Will, we could take out a loan on Orchard Hill."

"Kate." His frown deepened to a scowl. "I couldn't ask that of you."

"You're not asking me to do anything. *I'm* the one suggesting it. Will, think about it." The mortgage on Orchard Hill had been satisfied back in her parents' day, so they didn't owe a dime. And as recently as two years ago, the house and land had been assessed at close to four million.

"I *have* thought about it," he told her, some of the sternness going out of his voice. "But have *you*? Kate, think what might happen if the firm does go under . . . if we're not able to meet the payments."

Kate was flooded with panic at the thought, and had to fight to keep it from spilling over. She tried to imagine what it would be like, not living here—not being able to sit out on the porch with her coffee on mild mornings and watch the sun rise over the trees; or stroll down to the orchard to harvest a basket of tree-ripened peaches for pies; or sit by the fire in the parlor in the winter, watching the old windowpanes grow milky with snow. Not to have the scent of the honeysuckle that trailed over the porch in summer, or the cidery tang of windfall apples that filled the air in the autumn? To lose the nuthatches and finches swooping in and out of the eaves as they built their nests; the delicate herringbone patterns of animal tracks on virgin snow?

Even the vague prospect of having to give all that up was like a knife twisting in her heart. And how could she ask Skyler to entrust her baby to them with so much in jeopardy? Their daughter's final decision couldn't help but be influenced by all the bounty her beloved Orchard Hill had to offer a child. Without that . . .

Feeling her panic begin to spill over, Kate quickly set herself straight. What was more important—a house, or the people in it? Besides, she wouldn't let it come to that. If this plan didn't work out—well, then, they would simply have to think of something else. She knew that Will had long since sold off most of their securities, but there was still the principal on her trust, which, though she'd been raised to hold sacred the rule that the principal must never be touched, could be dipped into if necessary.

Emboldened by that thought, she said quietly, "Let's do it, Will."

Will was staring at her openly now, with a new regard that bordered on admiration. She'd always known he loved her—in a kind of distracted, diffuse way, as if she were a light source whose usefulness he didn't have to think about much—but this was different. Now he was actually *listening* to her.

"It's an idea," he said slowly. "But why don't we sleep on it, okay?"

"Fair enough." Kate watched him get up and head for the adjoining bathroom. She waited until he was finished and had returned to bed, pajama top buttoned on, before switching off the light by the bed.

They were lying side by side in the dark, not touching, embraced only by their thoughts and fears, when Will broke the silence. "You never cease to amaze me, Kate."

She felt a flush of pleasure that seemed to warm the pillow on which she lay, staring up at the lacy tree shadows on the ceiling. "Is that so?"

"Take it from me."

He put his arms around her then, and she gratefully inhaled his warm, familiar smell, burying her face in the curve of his neck. "We'll get through this," she murmured. "We'll be a family again."

She was thinking of Skyler at that moment, and knew that Will was too. But neither of them mentioned her name.

Even so, in the fragmented instant before she drifted off to sleep, Kate found herself wondering once again about the unknown man who'd fathered her grandchild.

Who was he? And what did he mean to Skyler?

And, most important of all, was he someone who loved her daughter?

CHAPTER 8

Troop B was the most centrally located of the Mounted Unit's five troops—on Forty-second Street, a block east of the West Side Highway— but as Tony got of the squad car that had dropped him off in front of the two-story building, painted NYPD-issue blue, he might as well have been in downtown Beirut, for all he would have noticed. He'd just come back from making the rounds of the other troops— "scratching a log," as it was commonly known in the Unit, was one of his responsibilities as sergeant—and he was beat. Oddly, a tour of duty away from the saddle wiped him out more than a hard day's ride. Besides, it had to be a hundred fucking degrees. September? What a joke. He felt as if he was stepping into a steam bath.

But that wasn't the main reason Tony was feeling so lousy. What was bugging him was the same thing that had been bugging him yesterday and the day before, and would no doubt be served up on tomorrow's plate as well.

Skyler. She was three months along, and starting to show. More beautiful than ever, too. And more desirable, if such a thing was possible. How did he know?

Because he'd made it his business to know—coming up with every excuse he could think of over the past weeks to swing by and see her. Luckily for him (or unluckily, depending on how you looked at it) her cabin at Gipsy Trail wasn't more than a fifteen-minute drive from his place in Brewster, so it wasn't really out of his way. She didn't have to know he'd have driven all the way to Albany to be with her even for an hour. She also didn't need to know that *not* seeing her drove him even crazier than seeing her. And that was why he was so uptight at the moment: he'd promised to stop by tomorrow afternoon, no big deal, but already, with still a day and a night to go, Skyler was all he could think about.

And then there was the kid. *His* kid. The more he thought about Skyler giving it up, the more it stuck in his craw. Bad enough, he thought, that she'd shut him out of her decision, but was he supposed to just stand by and let his son or daughter get shipped off to Christ-knows-where? Who knew what kind of parents he or she would get? His kid could end up with a father like Pop.

That thought was more than Tony could handle right now. He shoved the whole mess under a mental rug and told himself he'd check up on it in a day or two to see if it had materialized into anything he could even approach dealing with.

As he neared the barn, the first thing that caught Tony's eye was the big black gelding standing on the sidewalk, tethered to the street-entrance gate. He recognized it at once as the new horse that in a short period of time had become the terror of Troop B. Another kind of mess, he thought, but one he could handle. Rockefeller, so named because he'd been donated by the Rockefeller Foundation, had, in his first week off Remount, thrown one of the officers, Vicky De Witt, and put Officer Rob Petrowski in the hospi-

tal with a shattered kneecap. And furthermore, Rocky
had shown no sign of repenting his evil ways.

Tony stopped to eye the big brute on his way in.
"You got any ideas about throwing *me,* buster, you
got another think comin'," he advised Rocky, who
stared back at him blandly, unaware that he'd met his
match. Tony had plans for this horse. Instead of
Scotty, he was going to take Rocky out on patrol tomorrow. Yeah, he and old Rock were going to have
a come-to-Jesus meeting, all right. And at the end of
tomorrow's detail, if the big black devil wasn't converted, one of them was sure to be dead.

It was just what he needed to take his mind off
Skyler. The thing Tony *wasn't* looking forward to was
dealing with the can of departmental worms that had
somehow been opened by this whole business.

A week ago, the C.O., Deputy Inspector Fuller, had
wanted to assign Rocky to one of the new guys, but
Tony had objected. The four rookies fresh from Remount needed a few months on the Unit before they
were up to handling a horse as edgy as this one, he'd
argued. Fuller had merely nodded and made note of
it. Too late, Tony realized he'd been set up. Fuller, it
turned out, had just gotten the command from on high
to cut back on personnel, and had been looking for
any excuse, however flimsy, to ax a couple of the new
guys—veteran patrol officers themselves who'd just
graduated from Remount after three months of intensive schooling. And what made it so shitty was that
there was deadwood right under Fuller's nose, guys
like Lou Crawley and Bif Hendricks, who were always
looking for ways to stay indoors or in a squad car,
especially in bad weather—desk detail, chauffeuring
the deputy inspector, making hay runs, whatever.

In Tony's opinion, which was shared by the majority
of the twenty-five officers under his command—men
and women who were both hardworking and fear-
less—the situation stank. He'd seen the look on Pete

Anson's freckled face when he was given the bad news; poor guy had looked like he was about to cry. Being in the Mounted had been a lifelong dream of his, he'd told Tony. And tough, tattooed Larry Pardoe—there *had* been tears in his eyes, which he'd knuckled away before the others could see.

No, it wasn't fair ... and Tony wasn't going to just sit back and do nothing. True, he couldn't go head to head with Fuller on this, but it might not be impossible to pull some moves on the side. If nothing else, he would keep a close eye on that fat-assed Crawley, who, unlike Hendricks, didn't have the excuse of being a year away from retirement; he'd record all of Crawley's fuckups and diddly-squat excuses—and then, he hoped, Fuller would see the light. Transfer Crawley out of the unit, and replace him with Anson or Pardoe. Tony would see what he could do. . . .

But when Tony asked around the stable for Crawley, where the four-to-twelve shift was tacking up in preparation to ride out, nobody had seen him. Furthermore, nobody seemed very surprised.

Tony climbed up to the second-floor offices, the pungent smell of the stable following him to the metal door. He pushed it open and stepped into the large room that housed Mounted headquarters, where he was met by more of the same stale, ammonia-laced air, courtesy of the NYPD, where state-of-the-art air-conditioning consisted of a rotary fan propped on a sill in front of an open window.

He stopped at the Wheel, where he was greeted at the desk by Bill Devlin. "Hey, Salvatore ... you missed all the fun."

"What came down?" Tony asked.

Devlin, a twenty-three-year veteran whose beer gut disguised a build as solid as a John Deere tractor, shook his head. "Fuller's on the warpath again. City Hall must be breathing down his neck, 'cause all of a sudden he's gunning for us. We're sloppy, we cut cor-

ners, we act like our shit don't stink. He told us he's
cutting way back on our overtime. Tell me, how'm
I supposed to support a wife and two kids on my
regular pay?"

"Join a rodeo," Tony joked. But that reminded him
of Crawley. He asked, "You seen Lou? He's supposed
to be working the four-to-midnight, but nobody downstairs has any idea where he might be."

"That's 'cause he called in sick about an hour ago,"
Devlin told him, shaking his head in disgust. "That
piece of shit has taken so much sick leave they'll either
have to can him or call it a national holiday every
time he moans about a hangnail." The phone on the
desk rang, and Devlin picked it up. "Mounted Unit,
Sergeant Devlin speaking. Oh, yeah, hey, Sally. You
·got them? Sure, don't mention it. Listen, I can't talk
now. I'll give you a call when I get off. Catch you
later." He hung up, and grinned sheepishly at Tony.
"Women. You send 'em flowers for their birthday, and
they think it's some kinda big fucking deal. Lucky
you're off the hook far as that goes—for now, at
least." He winked broadly.

"Damn straight," Tony agreed cheerfully. But an
image of Skyler rose in his mind, filling his chest with
dark, jagged longing.

How could he be in love with a woman he hardly
knew, a woman he'd slept with on only one occasion—
however memorable—and whom he had about as much
chance of going the distance with as he had of winning
the lottery?

A woman who planned on giving his kid away to
strangers.

That was the part that really got to him. And, just
like he wasn't going to let go of Anson and Pardoe
so easily, Tony decided he wasn't going to sit back
and let Skyler call all the shots.

It occurred to him suddenly that maybe he didn't
have to sit back and do nothing. What if he could find

a couple—people he knew and could trust—to adopt the baby. Would Skyler accuse him of butting in? Probably. But that didn't have to stop him from at least *trying*. He'd *make* her listen somehow. And think what it would mean, being able to see in his mind the faces his kid would look up into every day, the eyes that would crinkle with amusement at each cute thing he or she said.

As he was signing out, Tony glanced over the duty roster for tomorrow's seven-to-four. There was a detail scheduled for City Hall, where an AIDS demonstration was expected to take place. And Central Park would require at least six officers on account of some jazz festival. If Crawley, who was on the seven-to-four starting tomorrow, pulled another bogus sick day, even Fuller might get fed up enough to do something about it.

Tony himself was more than just fed up, he was *pissed*. There were guys out there who were *really* sick. Guys like Jimmy Dolan who would give everything they owned to be healthy, to be able to put in a good day's work. . . .

"I'm outta here," he told Devlin, heading for the locker room.

"What's your hurry?" Devlin wanted to know. "Stick around, have a bite to eat with me. Sally packed me enough food for six."

"You *eat* enough for six," Tony ribbed him. "But thanks anyway. I'd take you up on it, but I'm visiting a friend in the hospital." Dolan had checked into NYU Medical Center yesterday, where he was being treated for yet another lung infection. Dolan had joked that he spent so much time in the hospital these days, he was going to have new stationery printed with that address. But Tony knew it was no joking matter.

Not ten minutes later, showered and dressed, he was breezing through the stable's gateway when he passed Joyce Hubbard. Joyce, he couldn't help noticing, looked exceptionally foxy in her breeches, with her silky chestnut hair loose around her shoulders. Out of the corner of his eye, he watched her slow down as if hoping he would stop to chat, but he only smiled and lifted a hand in her direction as he walked by.

Joyce was a knockout, all right, he thought as he crossed the street to where his car was parked. Trouble was, these days he couldn't seem to focus on her or on any woman other than Skyler. He woke up every morning as horny as a teenager, wanting only Skyler. He even dreamed about her at night. It was like some kind of freaking sickness, one he could only hope would go away on its own.

Yeah, sure, and maybe a miracle cure for AIDS will come along, and Dolan will be dancing the Nutcracker Suite *come Christmas.*

When Tony walked into Dolan's hospital room a quarter of an hour later, he discovered that his buddy wasn't alone. Dolan's therapist, Dr. Nightingale, was seated in a chair next to his bed. She rose to greet Tony as he walked in.

"Jimmy told me he was expecting you." She smiled warmly and clasped his hand in both of hers.

She was an attractive woman of forty, with forthright features and an unflinching gaze; today, in jeans and a sporty blouse, her fair hair caught up with combs, she looked much younger. More down to earth. In fact, she reminded him of someone he knew, only he couldn't think who.

He eyed the chair she'd been sitting on. There was a book lying face down on it. She must have been reading aloud to Dolan, whose eyesight was beginning to fail, though he didn't like to admit it.

Tony, warmed by her thoughtfulness, found himself remembering something she'd said to him the last time they'd run into each other, two months ago when Dolan had been in the hospital with pneumonia. At one point, after having been banished briefly from the room by Dolan's internist, he and Dr. Nightingale had shared a Snickers bar from the vending machine in the solarium. After a few minutes of low-key conversation, she had surprised Tony by remarking, "It's too bad about Jimmy's parents."

Tony had just shrugged, not wanting to get into what he thought of Dolan's folks—which couldn't be expressed in any way that was fit for her to hear.

Out of the blue, in a wistful voice not at all like the smooth professional one she used around Dolan, she had confided, "My husband and I have been trying to adopt a child for years. Maybe that's why it's so hard for me to understand how a mother could turn her back on her own son."

Watching her now, as she helped Dolan adjust the pillow at his back, Tony replayed those remembered words in his mind. *"My husband and I have been trying to adopt for years."* Were they still trying? Two months wasn't so long ago, so he had to assume they were. But they could have found a baby by now.

Except maybe they hadn't.

An idea was forming in Tony's mind, one he kept turning over and over like a lucky penny picked up off the sidewalk.

Would she . . . ?

Would *Skyler*?

Only one way to find out, he thought. Ask her. Find some excuse to get her alone, and feel her out about it.

He didn't know her all that well, true. But according to Dolan, she all but walked on water. It was a long shot maybe, because even if Dr. Nightingale *was* interested, Skyler might not be. Still, it was worth a try.

His cop's instinct for sizing people up was almost foolproof, and right now something was telling him that this woman was the genuine article. That she would make one hell of a mother.

Suddenly, it struck him who Dr. Nightingale reminded him of: Skyler. Their coloring was the same, even their build. Maybe that was what made him think of her adopting his and Skyler's child ...

"Listen, Doc, you could do a great business here. Like a traveling salesman, only instead of door to door, you'd go bed to bed. Think of it, a regular gold mine of angst." Jimmy, propped up on a raft of pillows, made Ellie think of a child's stick-figure drawing—his head too large for his wasted body, and his sunny smile etched in place. "Except when they're poking needles in your gut and tubes up your rear, then you don't really give a shit anymore if your mother loved Bobby best or your father spanked you for playing with dolls when you were five."

Ellie retrieved the book of poetry she'd been reading aloud and placed it on the table beside the bed. "I have enough to keep me busy as it is, but I'll keep it in mind." She cast a wry, sidelong glance at Tony before dropping her eyes to her wristwatch. "Speaking of which, I should get going. I have a group at six-thirty, and if I don't get something to eat before then I'll be a wreck."

"Sure you don't want to stick around for the floor show?" Jimmy's blue eyes sparkled. "After dinner is when things really start to jump. Evening rounds, man, it wouldn't play in Peoria, but it sure packs 'em in around here."

"Save me front-row seats for next time," she told him.

"Dolan, don't you ever quit?" Tony was grinning. He caught Ellie's eye and said, "You know what this guy says to me the other day? He says, 'You don't know what you're missing, Tony, twenty-four-hour room service with a river view and Bob Barker to keep you company.' Me?" he added. "I'll take a suite at the Plaza any day."

Ellie looked at the two men, so different from one

another, yet so utterly companionable. Tony, in faded, snug jeans and T-shirt, was bursting with health, and unabashedly masculine. Jimmy, reduced to little more than a pair of cobalt eyes that burned ever hotter and brighter as the rest of him wasted away, could die tomorrow. But neither seemed to mind the disparity. Tony had his hand on Jimmy's shoulder, and was kneading it lightly. And Jimmy, without realizing it, had angled his torso slightly so that he was leaning in Tony's direction, like a pale seedling turned toward the sun.

Ellie hardly knew Tony, but she had a pretty good idea he was far more complex than he appeared. He seldom talked about himself. On the few occasions they'd had an opportunity to chat, he'd seemed more interested in her than in trying to wrangle free therapy—he'd asked her about her practice, and what it was like working primarily with AIDS patients; he'd made a point, too, of telling her how highly Jimmy had spoken of her.

Nowadays, more than ever before, Ellie found herself appreciating the company of an honest, straightforward adult. Because the truth was that no matter how busy her practice kept her, or how often she got together with Georgina and her other friends, she was lonely.

There was a time Ellie would have thought she couldn't have lasted six days without Paul, and it had been six whole months. *How can this be?* she asked herself each morning, convinced she wouldn't be able to get through the day without him. She saw herself as stumbling across an open plain, with no landmarks to help her find her bearings, simply putting one foot in front of the other. But somehow she managed to keep going.

She and Paul talked regularly on the phone, and saw each other on occasion. They'd even gone a few times to a colleague of hers who specialized in couples therapy. But when Ellie had a bad day, or when a member of her AIDS group took a turn for the worse, or when she was just plain heartsick, the simple fact of the matter was that Paul wasn't around. He wasn't there to hold her, or rub her shoulders, or make her a cup of tea. And when she reached for him in bed, there was only Paul's side of the mattress, smooth, vacant, cool to the touch.

Even at this moment, with her husband in another part of town, tending to very different sorts of patients than the one before her now, she found herself longing for the feel of his arms around her. Her heart ached terribly, as if bruised somehow. It even hurt to take too deep a breath.

She watched Jimmy pick up the book of poetry on the bedside table, his hand trembling visibly. "One more for the road, Doc?"

Ellie, not trusting herself to speak, simply nodded. She took the book from him, and opened it to one of her favorite poems. Haltingly, she began to read.

Halfway through, she looked up from the page and saw that Jimmy's eyes had drifted shut. Closing the book, she caught Tony's gaze and gave a little nod in the direction of the door. Gathering up her belongings, she followed him out into the corridor, but when she started to tell him it was time for her to go, he stopped her by placing a hand on her arm.

"Buy you dinner?" he asked. "I'm sticking around until Jimmy wakes up, so I can't offer anything better than the cafeteria, but you'd be doing me a favor, keeping me from eating alone." On second thought, he added, "Unless you have to get home ..."

"I have an hour or so until group," she said, flashing him a smile that was too bright. "I'd love to have dinner with you ... and the cafeteria is fine. My four years at St. Vincent's, I practically lived off cafeteria food."

"Yeah? Lucky you survived."

"What can I tell you? I'm a tough lady."

It wasn't until she was seated at a table in the cafeteria, with a tray bearing a plate of some unrecognizable meat smothered in marinara sauce, that Ellie realized how hungry she was. Meals without Paul had been reduced to nibbles snatched here and there when her growling stomach became an embarrassment, or when she quite simply ran out of steam. It was nice to sit across a table from a man, she thought, even if the table was Formica, and the man little more than an acquaintance.

Perhaps what drew her to Tony also was that steadfast quality of his. He gave off the quiet air of someone who could be counted on under any circumstance, someone who wouldn't walk away when the going got rough. And she could use a little of that right now.

"You've been a good friend to Jimmy," she told him. "I wish everyone in the group had someone like you."

Tony smiled the rueful smile of a man who didn't accept compliments easily. "Except for the fact that I'm in 'major denial,' right?" He forked up a bite of what Ellie recognized now as meat loaf. "Since he and I sort of avoid the subject, I figure Jimmy must've talked to you about it."

"We talk about a lot of things," she told him, careful to maintain confidentiality.

"Look, the way I see it, Dr. Nightingale—"

"Please, call me Ellie," she interrupted.

"Ellie, then. Okay, Ellie, let me tell you something." He leaned forward on his elbows, wearing an expression of such fierce intensity she had to fight to keep from inching back in her chair. "I'm probably the only one in Dolan's life who's got the full picture, in Technicolor, of what he's going through. And it ain't pretty, believe me. If we don't talk much about it, that's just fine. Hey, the guy *knows* he's dying. Why

waste valuable time we could spend on things that
might give him a reason to want to go on living?"

Ellie smiled at him. "Your mother raised a smart
son."

"My mother?" Tony gave a snort of laughter. "You
want to talk about smart, she wrote the book. Never
finished high school, but the old lady could spot a liar
or a cheat a block away. Anyone who tried to put one
past Loretta Salvatore was lucky to get away with his
eardrums intact and his hair parted in the same place."

"Does she live around here?" Ellie asked.

"Rego Park," he told her. "Two years ago, Ma
moved in with my sister and her husband, so she could
help out with Gina's kids. Don't ask if she's happy,
though. Ma had that beat out of her when my father
was alive."

"Sounds like you had it pretty rough growing up."

Tony shrugged and looked away. The cafeteria was
bustling this time of day, but Ellie hardly noticed. She
was too busy concentrating on Tony ... and on the
feeling she was getting from him; the sense that he
was holding back, and not just about his childhood.
All at once, Ellie felt sure that Tony's offer to buy
her dinner hadn't been so spontaneous after all. There
was a reason he'd wanted to be alone with her. Was
it something to do with Jimmy, or a personal problem
he needed professional advice about—a wife or girlfriend he was having trouble with?

She realized she didn't even know if he was married
or not. A glance at the third finger on his left hand
told her he wasn't, but a barely visible tan line just
below his knuckle showed that he'd worn a ring until
not too long ago. Divorced? Had he walked out on
his wife, or had she asked him to leave? Did he love
her still? Did she love him?

Suddenly, Ellie was seeing Paul in her mind's eye,
seated across from her as Tony was now. Those first
few years after they were married, during her extern-

ship at Langdon, how many cafeteria meals had they shared? And how often had it been just an excuse to be together in the middle of the day, to hold hands, to talk in whispers of the delicious things they would do to each other when they got home?

She could almost feel Paul's hand wrapped about hers, the warmth of it, the patches of roughness where it was chapped from being scrubbed. In her mind, she saw him wave hello to one of the nurses, a pretty girl with a yellow cardigan draped over her shoulders ... pretty enough to have warranted a second glance. But Paul never looked at anyone but *her*. He'd made her feel, just in the way his gaze lingered on her mouth as she talked, that she was the only woman in the world he wanted to make love to.

The sense of loss that cut through Ellie at that moment was so sharp she had to brace her elbows against the table to keep from doubling over. Immediately, it was followed by anger—bright, hot, galvanizing.

Why, why *does it have to be this way? Yes, I see Paul's side of it. Of course I do. But if he truly loved me, he would come back. He would understand.*

She couldn't stop wanting a child any more than she could have voluntarily stopped breathing.

Tony must have sensed the shift in her mood, because at once he was leaning toward her solicitously, asking, "Hey, Ellie ... you feeling okay?"

"I'm fine," she replied briskly. "I guess I wasn't as hungry as I thought." She pushed her untouched tray aside. "I'm sorry, Tony, but I really should get going. Unless," she added with studied casualness, "there was something you wanted to talk to me about."

Tony appeared to hesitate; then he put down his fork and said, "Actually, there is. The thing is, I was wondering ... " He cleared his throat. "You mentioned a couple of months ago something about you and your husband wanting to adopt a kid. I wanted to know if you're still interested."

Ellie felt a cog slip deep inside her chest, causing her heart to wobble dangerously before righting itself. She forced herself to remain very still, the kind of stillness that came instinctively when she felt threatened. But there was nothing to fear in the man whose dark eyes were studying her so intently across the table, she told herself. What frightened her was the hope spinning itself around her heart like delicate blown glass—a hope that could so easily be shattered, as it had been, again and again.

"Why do you ask?" she answered cautiously.

Tony looked away, his handsome face, with its strong chin and Roman nose, darkening. "See, there's a girl I know," he said. "She's pregnant—a little over three months."

Ellie was swamped by all the familiar symptoms— shortness of breath, icy coldness in her hands and feet, a prickling of the small hairs on the back of her neck. "A friend of yours?" inquired a voice she couldn't believe was hers; it was far too calm.

"You could say that."

"I see."

"No. You *don't*." Tony raked a hand through the thick curls above his temple. His posture was so tense she could almost feel the hum of muscles and tendons stretched taut as the steel cables of a suspension bridge. Then, with a visible effort, he forced himself to sit back. "Sorry," he said, "it's just that this thing has gotten me so uptight I can hardly see straight anymore. Truth? She's more than a friend ... and less than one, if that makes any sense. We were only together this one time."

Ellie remained silent. There was a faint buzzing in her ears, and her hands felt suddenly clammy. *Don't get excited,* she warned herself. *It's too soon. You don't know anything about this girl.*

"This friend—does she know you're talking to me about this?" Ellie asked softly.

Tony gave a short, hard laugh. "Not a chance. She'd bite my head off for not running it by her first. She's ... well ... she does things her own way."

His eyes, which had deepened to a shade beyond black—the color of a back road on a moonless night— told Ellie something more: there were levels of emotion beyond any he had revealed to her.

But he was being honest with her, at least; laying the cards, such as they were, on the table. Ellie thought hard for a minute. Was this something she wanted to get involved in? A girl she hadn't even met, who might not even want to meet *her*? Did she dare risk getting her hopes up all over again for what was so clearly a long shot?

The answer, when it came to her, was so obviously the right one that Ellie didn't hesitate. "I'm interested."

Tony nodded slowly, his eyes never leaving her face. This time, she had the distinct feeling of being sized up, not by an expectant father, but by a cop whose business it was to take careful measure of anyone he allowed in close.

"I'll be honest with you, though," she went on, fists clenched in her lap. "My husband and I are separated." Better for him to know up front. If he backed off now, she'd save herself days, possibly weeks, of stomach-wrenching anxiety.

She thought of Paul then, and wondered what his reaction would be. Naturally he'd be skeptical. But if, by some miracle, the promise of this baby actually became a reality, he'd come around, wouldn't he? He loved her; she didn't doubt that. The only thing that remained to be seen was whether or not he loved her enough to take one more shot at their being a family. . . .

Tony frowned, letting her know that this clearly wasn't part of the program. He asked, "And you still want a baby? Even if you'd be raising it on your own?"

"More than anything in the world."

Tony must have sensed it, the raw power of her longing, for he was looking at her now with an understanding that went beyond words. Seated before her, she guessed, was a man who was no stranger himself to deep longings.

Ellie was trembling as she reached for her purse. Her hand, she noted on some distant plane of awareness, seemed to be acting all on its own, riffling like a pickpocket's among wallet, keys, lipstick, pen. At last she found what she was looking for, the flat leather case stocked with her business cards. She slid one out, scribbling her home number on the back before handing it to Tony.

"Any time," she told him, breathless in spite of herself. "She can call me any time, day or night. If I'm not at home, she can leave a message on my machine. Tell your friend I'll be waiting to hear from her."

At six-forty-five the following morning, Sergeant Tony Salvatore was seated behind the desk in the Troop B roster room, flipping through the pages on his clipboard as he prepared for roll call. His mind, though, was miles away. He wasn't seeing the cluster of schoolroom desks before him, with their sleepy-eyed occupants—those on the seven-to-four shooting the shit with one another while waiting for the day's assignments. He was thinking about seeing Skyler later in the day . . . and wondering how he was going to tell her about his conversation with Ellie Nightingale.

Skyler wouldn't like it that he'd talked to Ellie without discussing it with her first. She'd like it even less, Ellie not having a husband. But, dammit, she owed it to him to at least *see* the lady, give her a chance. It was his kid, too.

"Hey, Sarge, you got anything on that Forty-second Street stabbing? The guy pull through or what?"

Tony glanced up to find Gary Maroni perched on a

corner of his desk. Maroni had transferred over from the Tenth around the same time he had, but seemed not to mind that Tony had been promoted to sergeant over him. Maroni was munching on a doughnut while absently brushing powdered sugar off the front of his uniform. It was truly amazing, Tony thought, taking in the skinny frame and hollowed cheeks of the guy everyone in the barn called Bony Maroni. He could out-eat his horse and still manage to look like a starving preacher in search of a Sunday supper.

"D.O.A.," Tony replied shortly. Yesterday, he and Maroni had been among the first to respond. Ugly as hell—the victim had had his throat slashed with a piece of broken bottle. Gang-related, probably. Tony didn't know, because he hadn't made the collar on the perp who allegedly did it. He'd had enough on his hands just holding back the jackals pushing in for a closer look.

"Jesus, yeah, all that blood."

"Cut right through his jugular," Tony said.

"I wouldna touched him if I thought there was a chance of saving him. Lowlife like that, he probably had AIDS."

Even though it was S.O.P these days to wear gloves while handling anyone with an open wound, Tony found himself bristling at Maroni's suggestion that the disease was somehow the exclusive domain of drug addicts and lowlifes—"fags" belonging, of course, in the latter category. But he held his tongue. Maroni was too dumb to have meant anything by it.

"You heard about Joyce Hubbard?" Maroni, perhaps reading his mood, was quick to change the subject.

"What about her?"

"She got engaged to a guy from Troop A. Kirk Rooney. Hear they're planning some kind of master-blaster weddin'. Surprised she didn't say nothing to you."

Tony wasn't surprised, but he couldn't help feeling a touch of guilt. Since meeting Skyler at the beginning of the summer, he'd hardly given Joyce the time of day. The truth was, he scarcely noticed her. Now here it was September and she'd somehow gotten engaged without his knowing it.

When Joyce showed up a few minutes before roll call, Tony went out of his way to congratulate her. She flushed to the roots of her chestnut hair—pulled back today in a French braid—and cut her eyes away at once.

"Thanks," she muttered. "I guess it must seem sort of sudden, but Kirk and I, we've known each other a while."

She really did have nice eyes, Tony thought when she finally risked a glance in his direction. Green with little flecks of gold in them. Nice legs, too. The kind you really notice even when they're not wrapped around a horse. In her blue breeches, custom-made black boots, uniform shirt pressed to knife-edge crispness, she could have posed for a recruiting poster.

"Set a date yet?" Tony asked.

"Not yet. His mother, she wants to make it next spring so she can invite half of Brooklyn." She rolled her eyes. "Kirk and I—we'd just as soon not wait. We'd kind of like to get started on a family."

Joyce was thirty-one, he knew from her stats. It made sense, her wanting a family, marrying a fellow cop, somebody she'd have everything in common with. A hell of a lot more sense than his screwy nonrelationship with Skyler Sutton.

"Well, you tell him from me he's a lucky guy," Tony said, feeling suddenly tender toward Joyce, almost wistful.

Joyce's blush deepened alarmingly, and she looked as if she might be on the verge of tears. She met his gaze then, fully and frankly, and what he saw behind the shimmer in her eyes was enough to make him wish he'd kept his mouth shut. It also made him wish he'd been smart enough to fall for Joyce, a woman his own age, an equal, someone he could bitch to at the end of a week of four-to-midnight tours ... someone who would understand.

There was something else in the look Joyce was giving him, something that made him distinctly uncomfortable. Her eyes were telling him, *Just say the word ...*

He dropped his gaze, scanning the post sheet in front of him. Joyce got the hint, and something dark and hard glinted under the forced lightness of her voice when she said, "You can tell him yourself. You'll be at the wedding, right?"

"Sure thing." Tony glanced at the clock on the wall, and did a head count of the officers gathered in front of him—twelve in all, some still tucking their shirts into their breeches and buckling their holsters. He spotted Crawley, built like a fire hydrant, his graying crewcut still sparkling with moisture from the shower he'd waited until the last minute to take. Crawley looked amazingly bright-eyed for someone who'd supposedly been sick in bed all day yesterday. Tony felt a small stab of disappointment. *Too bad he didn't stay in bed today; then I'd really have had something to nail him with.*

Tony barked, "Douglas! Post Twenty-one, lunch at eleven hundred hours.... Tamborelli, you're on Twenty-two, break at eleven-thirty.... Smith, I need you and Doherty to run some hay down from Troop D ..." He went down the rest of the list, finishing with the usual: "You know the score. No discounted meals. No freebies ... unless I'm in on it."

His grin was greeted by a chorus of good-natured groans. Another day, another tour, another load of shit waiting to be shoveled. And at the end of it, Tony thought, he was going to be kicked in the gut, not by a horse, but by the woman he'd had the bad luck to fall for.

He and Maroni took Posts 16 and 17, which covered Times Square. Maroni was on Prince, a spirited bay with a dark patch around one eye that gave him the look of a pirate. But Prince had nothing on Tony's substitute mount. As he rode east on Forty-second Street astride Rocky, Tony could feel the big black horse fighting him, skittering sideways at every car horn, rolling a baleful eye back at him with every squeeze of Tony's viselike thighs.

But Tony wasn't giving him any quarter. Maintaining a light hold on the reins, he dug in with his seat and legs instead, forcing Rocky to grudgingly obey. When they reached the intersection, and the black horse started to buck, Tony nailed him with his spurs and threw his weight back to anchor the beast in place.

Horses were easy, he thought. Even bruisers like Rocky. It was women he didn't seem to know how to handle. Look at how he'd fucked up with Paula, marrying someone he'd had almost nothing in common with. And now here he was making the same mistake all over again ... falling in love with a woman he'd gotten pregnant even before the high had worn off from the beers they'd drunk on their first date. The only difference was that he and Skyler weren't getting married. Now the only thing left for him to do was make sure their kid was going to be looked after properly, and given the love every kid deserved.

Face it, Salvatore, you're just trying to make up for what Pop never gave you.

But this was an entirely different situation. His son or daughter might never even know who he was. He or she would most likely grow up thinking he hadn't cared enough to phone or even drop a line.

Tony felt his gut wrench, and he was glad for the reflector glasses that hid his eyes from view.

As he patrolled Times Square, with its endless array of flesh joints and fast-food restaurants, Tony tried not to think about all the ways he was letting his kid down, and all the things he wanted to say to Skyler about what it was like growing up hating your own father. At the corner of Broadway and Forty-fifth, he lifted his stick in greeting to another veteran of the streets. Maxie, in hot-pink spandex and a sequined tube top, waved back. A skinny little thing with a mouthful of bad teeth and a soft spot for horses, she made him thankful he wasn't on Vice. Busting victims wasn't his idea of a good time.

At twelve, he and Maroni met for lunch. Sammy, who managed the underground parking garage where they routinely tied up their horses, had a carrot apiece for Rocky and Prince. Smart guy, he knew who to butter up—in Mounted, it was the rare cop who put his own needs before his horse's. Tony thanked Sammy and made a mental note to remember him with a big tip come Christmas.

"What happened with your ex-wife?" asked Maroni while they were waiting at the deli counter for their sandwiches—turkey on rye for Tony, a monster sub for Maroni. "You forkin' over for alimony, or what?"

Tony hadn't thought of Paula in weeks; it was an effort even to conjure up her image in his mind. "There's nothing she'd like better, believe me," he told Maroni, surprised to hear in his voice none of the bitterness that had dogged him for so long. "But her lawyer talked her into settling for a lump sum."

"Ouch. That must've hurt."

Tony shrugged. "I've got too many other things to worry about."

"Yeah, I've noticed." He slid a knowing glance Tony's way. "She anybody I know?"

"I kind of doubt it," Tony said, adding with a laugh, "In fact, I'd say the chances of you knowing her are about even with your making a collar any time in the next decade."

"Keepin' her all to yourself, huh?" Maroni took a huge bite of his sandwich, his eyes dancing merrily as he chewed.

"Ain't nothing to keep," Tony said.

"Yeah, sure, I get it." Maroni nodded sagely. "It's the same old story with you, Salvatore—always holding your cards close to your vest. Only guy on the force don't know what a locker room is for. T and A, that's what. Good old tits and ass—half the fun is shooting the shit about it afterward."

Tony never knew just how seriously to take Maroni, so as usual he just ignored him. They managed to get through the rest of the detail without making an arrest or either of them breaking their necks, and as they were heading back to the barn at the end of their shift, Tony noticed that even the heavy humidity that had sat crouched over the city all week like an over- turned bucket had lifted.

Forty-five minutes later, as he was driving north along the Henry Hudson, being treated to the first signs of fall in the splashes of red and gold among the dense greenery that lined the parkway, it occurred to Tony that maybe this day wasn't going to turn out so badly after all. He was edgy about seeing Skyler, sure, but there was nothing new about that. And if he had business with her, it didn't mean they couldn't enjoy each other's company.

Which reminded him: his brother Dominic was or- ganizing some kind of family get-together, and he'd been bugging Tony to bring this woman he was being so close-mouthed about. Tony hadn't told Dom and Carla that Skyler was pregnant with his baby. The only thing his brother and sister-in-law cared about was making sure Skyler wasn't anything like Paula, whom they'd despised.

Skyler wasn't like Paula, Tony thought. But would

she be able to hack his family? Brothers, sisters, in-laws, nieces and nephews? They were a rowdy bunch. They swore; Dom drank too much; Carla screamed at her kids—but any one of them would have given the shirt off their backs for a member of the tribe. Tony would never apologize for them—not to Skyler, not to the friggin' Queen of England.

And even if Skyler was okay about his family, would he feel so kindly toward *hers*? He'd seen enough of the set she moved in to know that even from the sidewalk, looking up at him on his horse, they somehow managed to look down on him. Like that woman not too long ago, outside Bergdorf Good-man's, who'd imperiously asked him to hail her a cab. And that Mounted fund-raiser he'd once attended at Tavern on the Green—the ladies in their designer gowns and the men in tuxedos had clustered around Tony during the cocktail hour, but once their curiosity had been satisfied, they'd pretty much left him alone. They hadn't really wanted to know anything about *him*.

No, he couldn't picture it, him with Skyler. Any more than he could see himself living on a mountain in Tibet or taking a shot at the moon in a space cap-sule. The problem was getting that message from his head to his heart, which for some reason wasn't pick-ing up on the signals.

Tony turned off 84 onto Route 312, where the blacktop gave way to tree-shaded country roads dot-ted with pastures and storybook frame houses. On the other side of town, just north of the reservoir, the road grew steeper as it wound through Fahnstock State Park. He drove slowly, keeping his eye out for deer amid the tangled undergrowth where the grassy berm gave way to deep woods.

At the top of the hill, he turned onto a narrow road and parked in front of a two-story split-log clubhouse that faced onto an open green. There were no signs advertising the Gipsy Trail Club—the rationale being, he supposed, that if you didn't already know its whereabouts, you didn't have any business being here.

But despite feeling somewhat out of place, Tony couldn't help being charmed. The pond where swans glided atop mirror images of themselves; the bridle paths that meandered through the club's seventeen hundred acres; and the houses—some truly palatial, though quaintly called cabins—tucked among the trees.

He found Skyler down at the stable at the other side of the trout pond, taking her horse around the ring at an easy canter. The animal was a nice-looking chestnut gelding, around sixteen hands, with a gait as smooth as butter on toast. Skyler, in leather chaps and a baggy cotton sweater that hung over the top of her jeans, looked flushed and pretty, but it was the easy way she sat on her horse that took his breath away. As he watched her elegant, almost airborne grace and the way her pale hair caught the light of the setting sun in glints of red and gold, it was once more brought home to Tony—who rode the way cowboys ride, hard and interested only in getting the job done—how vast the gulf between them was.

He stood at the fence, watching her in silence, until Skyler spotted him and trotted her horse over to him. "Why didn't you let me know you were here?" she scolded lightly.

"Too busy watching you," he told her, adding gruffly, "Hey, you sure it's okay? I mean, with the baby and all."

Skyler swung to the ground with a grunt of annoyance. "This isn't the nineteenth century, Tony. Pregnant women aren't confined to their beds unless there's some medical reason for it. Besides, I'm taking it easy."

"No jumping?"

She started to bristle, then seemed to think better

of it. "My last show, I almost got thrown," she admitted. "After that, I decided I'd better lay off until
after . . . until it's safe." She threw him a lopsided
grin that didn't quite hide the glimmer of anguish behind it. "My trainer threw a fit when I told him why.
I don't know whether it's because Duncan is an old
prude, or because he's mad at me for screwing up
what he thinks could be a great career in show jumping. Anyway, I'm boarding Chancellor here for the
winter." She patted the gelding's neck. "At least *he's*
not complaining."

"Scotty would think he'd died and gone to heaven,"
Tony told her.

"Listen, why don't we go for a trail ride before it gets
dark? John can saddle up one of the horses for you."
Skyler gestured in the direction of the Adirondack-style
stable, a smaller version of the clubhouse, with a moss-
encrusted shake roof. A pair of barn cats were sunning
themselves in the patch of fading light outside the
open double doors that faced the ring.

Tony wanted to remind her he'd been on horseback
most of the day; he made his *living* that way, and in
his off-duty hours he wasn't exactly in the mood to
play country squire. But, oh, what the hell. With a
brief nod, he headed toward the stable.

John, who looked more like a silver-haired former
movie star than a stablemaster, gave him an Appaloosa mare, in surprisingly good shape for a hack
horse. Even so, as Tony tacked up, he couldn't help
smiling at the contrast between Penny and the horse
he'd been riding earlier in the day. That was one of
the things he loved most about his job: the Mounted
Unit's horses might not be anything special to look at,
but they were used to being ridden by pros, and it
showed. Put Rocky in a place like this, with a bunch
of recreational riders, he thought, and he'd turn into
a gold mine for liability suits.

"There's a nice trail up behind my cabin . . . it's

really pretty up there this time of year," Skyler told
him when he rode out to meet her. She flashed him a
bright smile before turning to lead the way down the
dirt road that curved past the duck pond under a can-
opy of maples and elms.

Tony thought: *Something's wrong with this picture.*
Beautiful day, beautiful trail—it was like a magazine
spread, too good to be true. Where he came from, a
girl you'd knocked up wouldn't be placidly remarking
on the scenery. She'd be a wreck, probably, but she'd
be an *honest* wreck, at least.

Tony, not convinced it was safe for Skyler to be
riding, kept a sharp eye out for potholes and low-
hanging branches. In silence, they wound their way
through the woods, coming at last to an open, marshy
area, where the only sound was the sucking of hooves
in hock-deep mud. A flurry of pheasants burst from
the tall reeds with shrill cries, startling the horses. Automatically Tony brought his mare around, using her
to block the path ahead of Skyler's horse, which was
dancing about nervously, looking ready to bolt.

"Good work." Her voice carried an edge of irony
he didn't much care for.

But Tony said nothing. How was it possible, he
wondered, to feel so irritated with a woman and at
the same time want nothing more than to pull her
down from her saddle and take her, right there, on
the ground, amid the leaves and grass and trampled
wildflowers?

Where the trail branched off at the top of the hill,
Skyler took the path that circled back down to the
main road. By the time they got back to the stable, it
was nearly dark, and there was a discernible chill in
the air.

Tony was silent as they tacked down and turned the
horses into their stalls. The barn was deserted; John
must have gone home. There was only the contented

sound of horses munching their feed, and the swish of tails against plank siding.

He was soaping his hands at the deep, rust-stained sink off the tack room when he noticed Skyler staring at him. He smiled, and said, "You're looking at me like you suddenly don't know me."

"I'm not sure I do." She pointed at his middle. "Is that what I think it is?"

Tony, looking down, saw that his sweatshirt had ridden up and was caught on the butt of his off-duty revolver, a Smith & Wesson .38, tucked snugly into the waistband of his jeans. He shrugged. "You never know."

"I never noticed it before."

"Maybe you never looked."

"Why on earth would you need to be armed in a place like this?" She spread her arms out in a gesture that took in the stable's tongue-and-groove siding, its rows of whitewashed stalls.

"Like I said, you never know." Tony wiped his hands on a rough scrap of towel hung on a rusty nail over the sink.

"Armed and dangerous. Wow."

She was laughing now, and the sudden sour taste in the back of Tony's throat told him it wasn't because she found him so amusing. He turned slowly to face her. Caught in the glare of the overhead bulb, her eyes puddled in shadow, she made him think of a perp being interrogated—cocky, defiant, but underneath it all more than a little scared.

With a swift movement, Tony stepped forward and grabbed hold of her upper arms. He felt her jerk in startled response. When he was certain he had her full attention, he addressed her in a low, steady voice that carried no hint of the dark cocktail brewing in him—a mixture of anger and desire, with just a touch of bitter.

"There's two things a cop has to remember. One, *they* can see us, but we can't always see them. Two, you're never really off duty." He dropped his hands, leaving smudges of dampness on her sweater. "Listen, let's get something straight between us—I don't like playing head games. You got a problem with me coming around, you lay it on me, no bullshit."

She stood there, staring at him as if he were a complete stranger who'd accosted her out of the blue. Tony felt his anger start to drain away, and he wanted to grab it, hold on to it, because what was underneath was a whole lot worse.

"I don't know what you're talking about," she said slowly.

"Yeah, you do." He deliberately kept his voice hard. "I'm like the hangover after a night of knocking back vodka tonics ... something that won't let you forget that every wild party has its price. Only this is one hangover that isn't going away so fast." His gaze dropped to her belly, its rounded outline barely visible under her sweater.

She threw her head back, her eyes blazing. "Who asked you to get involved? You don't even *know* me."

"Even when something happens that you didn't ask for—something you didn't even *want*—it's not always so easy to just walk away."

"Tell me about it." Skyler put a hand to her belly with a hollow laugh.

Tony searched her face, but despite the color spreading up into her pale cheeks, it remained closed to him. "What I'm trying to say is if you changed your mind and decided to keep the baby, I'd be there," he told her softly. "I'd make sure you and the kid were looked after."

"Tony—"

"Wait. Hear me out. I'm not talking about anything stupid like us getting married or anything, so just relax. This isn't about you and me." A lie ... but a small one, he told himself.

"Just what did you have in mind?" she wanted to know.

"You're looking at me like I've got something hidden up my sleeve." A corner of his mouth twisted up. "Listen, Skyler, I'm just a regular guy ... what you see is what you get. If I make a promise, you can bank on it. And what I'm promising here is that if you decide to keep it, our kid will *know* who his father is."

There was a brief silence punctuated by the thud of a hoof against a loose box. Then Skyler, with a defiance matched by the blazing fury in her eyes, told him, "I'm not changing my mind."

"Sometimes a mind has a way of changing on its own," he responded mildly, taking it no further than that.

Skyler said nothing. She only stared at him, that odd, misplaced fury draining from her eyes, leaving her with an expression he could only have described as woebegone.

At last, she declared wearily, "Tony, I'm handling it, okay?"

Tony wasn't so sure about that, but all he said was: "If you say so." He waited a beat before asking, "You talked to anyone yet ... about adopting?"

"There's still plenty of time," she said, her mouth tightening.

"I was just wondering if you had anybody in mind."

"Why? Do *you*?"

Tony cursed himself for putting her on the defensive. Taking a breath, he replied calmly, "There's this lady—remember I told you about my friend, Dolan? Well, she's his shrink. And she's been trying forever to adopt a baby. I had a talk with her the other day ... about us ... about our kid. She's interested. She'd like to meet you."

That hard glint had returned to Skyler's eyes. "What do you know about her other than that she's your friend's shrink?"

"I know she's good people."

"So is the lady who cuts my hair."

Tony fought to remain calm, and to keep his voice steady. "All I'm asking is that you meet with her. You wouldn't be committing to anything more than a cup of coffee." He paused. "There *is* one thing, though." It would come out sooner or later; better spill it now.

"What?" Her eyes narrowed.

With a tightening of his jaw, he told her, "She and her husband ... they aren't exactly together at the moment."

Skyler crossed her arms over her chest. "Forget it then."

"Don't you want to at least talk to her?"

"What for?"

Tony lost it then. The dark brew that had been building in him burst through the flimsy walls of his control. "Because I'm *asking* you, that's why." His harsh voice hammered at her. "Isn't that enough of a reason? For chrissakes, Skyler, whether you like it or not, this is my kid, too."

A ragged hole was opening in his gut, wide enough for him to have put his fist through. Why didn't she say something? Why was she just standing there, looking at him like he was way out of line?

But then he could see that Skyler was relenting. "I suppose it wouldn't hurt to meet her," she said at last.

Tony rocked back on the worn heels of his cowboy boots. He'd won—the first round, anyway. But what did it prove? Nothing. Except that Skyler cared enough about the baby to take a chance on someone who just might end up being what she was looking for after all. Her feelings about him—if she had any—were as carefully concealed as the gun tucked into the waistband of his jeans.

Skyler kept her head down as she walked to the tack room, fearing that if Tony could see her face he'd know what she was thinking.

But what was so terrible about being in love?

Everything ... everything under the sun, she thought miserably.

They wouldn't feel comfortable around each other's friends. His family would probably think she was a snob just because she was rich. And *her* family would bend over so far backward to make him feel included that their efforts would have exactly the opposite effect. There would be weddings and christenings and graduations at which one or the other would feel out of place. In restaurants, there would inevitably be that awkward moment when he reached for the check and she insisted on paying simply because she had more money. She and Tony didn't even like the same kind of music—he listened to rock and country-western, and all he knew about operas was they were over when the fat lady sang.

No, it would never work. Besides, she didn't really love him; she only *imagined* she did.

Hormones. She could chalk this whole craziness up to her pregnant hormones. After the baby came, her life would go back to normal. She'd written to the University of New Hampshire's veterinary school, and they'd agreed to let her enroll next September instead. Even her parents, as bewildered and upset as they were, would eventually come around. And Tony? He'd stop playing bodyguard and go back to just being a cop. He'd forget her in no time.

Keep at it. Maybe you'll convince yourself.

The unpleasant truth, she thought despairingly, was that the hormones appeared to be a package deal. Not only was she getting ideas about Tony, but she was becoming all gooey about the baby. These days, anything was capable of setting her off—an AT&T commercial with a little girl phoning to wish her grandma a happy birthday, a Gap Kids window display of overalls and tiny denim sneakers, the cherubic babies in her obstetrician's waiting room magazines.

Skyler had to keep reminding herself over and over that she was doing the right thing. She wasn't running away. She wasn't abandoning her child. This baby was going to have everything it deserved. And mostly what it deserved was loving parents who were in a position to raise a child.

Why, then, she wondered, had she agreed to see Tony's friend? Without a husband, what made this woman any more capable of raising a baby than *she* was?

That's not why you gave in, and you know it. You're doing this because he asked.

A hand dropped onto her shoulder, and Skyler spun around. Tony stood there, studying her with an expression so grave it made her think of every movie she'd ever seen in which a cop appears on someone's doorstep with news of a tragic accident.

"If you want, I'll go with you," he offered.

"Go where?" For a moment, hypnotized by his black eyes—the kind of black you could fall into and never touch bottom—Skyler was too dazed to think.

"Her name's Ellie," he said. "Ellie Nightingale."

Skyler shook her head to clear it. "Thanks, but I'd rather meet her alone." For one thing, it was hard for her to think straight when Tony was around. All he had to do was look at her, as he was now, and her knees turned to water.

He was standing so close she could feel his breath, warm against her faintly chilled skin. She saw the chain glinting at his neck, and before she knew what she was doing, Skyler hooked her index finger through it and drew it out from under his sweatshirt. She examined the raised image on its medal—the Archangel Michael with wings spread wide. On the reverse side was etched: "Keep my husband safe."

"My ex-wife gave it to me when we were first married," he explained.

"It must have worked." Skyler didn't dare look up,

for he might see the longing in her face, a longing so acute it was like an illness. She was wound so tight she felt slightly sick to her stomach being this near to him.

Tony gave a short, dry laugh and said, "I'm not so easy to get rid of. You probably noticed that, huh?"

"Tony . . ." She lifted her head, and sighed. "I know you feel responsible, and you want to do the right thing. I appreciate it. I do. But, honestly, I wouldn't think you were bad if you stopped coming around." .

"Is *that* what you think this is all about?" His voice had a low, dangerous tone that raised the hairs on the back of her neck.

This was no time to be coy or evasive, Skyler realized. Besides, what would be the point? They wouldn't be in this mess if they'd felt nothing for each other.

"I don't suppose it would do any good to deny there's chemistry between us," she confessed. Chemistry? That was the understatement of the century. This felt more like the disastrous results of a mad scientist's experimenting.

"No, it wouldn't," he agreed, his mouth shaping itself into a crooked smile.

"But that doesn't mean we have to do anything about it," Skyler hastened to make clear.

"Not unless we wanted to." There was nothing suggestive in the way he said it. "In the meantime, I don't see anything wrong with us being friends, do you?"

Skyler saw a lot wrong with it, but she didn't object. Instead, she blurted, "Friends *do* things together . . . like . . . like going to concerts. And the opera. Do you like opera? I love opera. I love everything about it. My favorite is *La Traviata,* did I ever tell you that?" She realized she was babbling, but couldn't seem to stop herself.

Tony at the opera . . . are you insane? *He'd probably hate it . . . and you'd only end up feeling annoyed at him.* But maybe that was what she wanted . . . to *prove* to herself just how unsuitable a match they were. It was childish and wrongheaded, she knew, but at the moment she felt just desperate enough to try anything that might break the stranglehold he seemed to have on her emotions.

"I've never been to the opera. But I'd be willing to give it a fair shot," Tony replied with a gravity she found oddly endearing.

"Fair enough," she said, wondering if maybe she'd been wrong about him that way.

"My brother Dominic is planning a big family dinner—sometime in the next few weeks," he told her. "I'd like you to come with me." He flashed her a grin. "As a friend."

"Deal," she told him, suddenly shy . . . far more shy than she'd felt that day, on the sofa in her father's pied-á-terre, when they'd made love for the first time.

Skyler was suddenly remembering how he'd looked naked, dark and matted with hair, the feel of his body pressed against her, the heat that had baked off him. His mouth . . . bold, insistent.

A faint tremor sneaked into her legs, forcing her to lean back against the wall to the right of the open door to the tack room. She thought of the gun tucked into his waistband, and, against every one of her sacred liberal beliefs, felt a small, tingling thrill. *I must be losing my mind,* she thought.

Yet instead of dropping the medal, she was using it to draw him to her. She watched him sway to meet her, his eyelids heavy. She felt his arms go around her, and then his tight, muscled body—the body she'd dreamed about more times than she cared to count—was pinning her against the stall. His breath hot against her mouth. The outline of his gun pressing into the fullness of her belly.

"Skyler . . ."

Suddenly, she was imagining the gun going off. A

bright flash, then searing pain. *The baby.* Skyler dropped the medal and abruptly turned away.

Ducking into the tack room, she removed her chaps and stowed them in her trunk. On the other side of the open doorway, she could hear Tony walking about, putting things away, his boot heels making a hollow clacking sound against the concrete floor. She felt awful, the pain in her chest as real as if the gun *had* gone off. She wanted to say something, anything, to break this awkward silence.

But she said nothing.

As they were leaving, Tony dug into his back pocket and pulled out a tooled leather wallet polished with age and shaped to the curve of his hip. From it he slipped a slightly bent business card.

The way he handed it to her was equally business-like. "You pick the time and place," he said. "She'll be there."

Skyler nodded, suddenly weary. The question wasn't where, but *why*.

Because there was absolutely no way on earth, she thought, that she was letting this woman adopt her baby.

CHAPTER 9

Ellie had been the one to suggest this place. On a weekday afternoon, between lunchtime and rush hour, the upstairs coffee bar at Barnes & Noble on Twenty-first and Sixth was seldom very crowded, and many of the patrons had their noses buried in books. No one was paying much attention to the handsome fortyish woman in a white turtleneck and navy blazer who sat at a table by the cast-iron railing; a woman who kept glancing anxiously toward the stairs, as if she half expected the person she was waiting for to disappoint her.

Ellie thought: *Five more minutes. If she doesn't show, I'll call. Maybe she got the time wrong, or mixed up the date. Maybe she forgot.*

Struggling to appear calm, she gazed down at the browsers strolling among the shelves and relaxing with books on deep-cushioned love seats and sofas. The superstore, with its cozy groupings of tables and chairs, covered more than an acre of floor space, but had the look of a library in an English manor house, all polished brass and gleaming dark wood. The music of Erik Satie drifted toward her, hypnotic, soothing. But Ellie wasn't soothed. The back of her neck was

dewed with sweat, and the napkin that had come with
her herbal tea lay in a mangled knot before her. She
glanced at her watch. The meeting had been set for
three, and it was now a quarter past.

*What if she doesn't show up at all? Dear Lord,
please let her come. I don't think I could take another
disappointment.*

The young woman had sounded so sincere over the
phone. Confident. Well-spoken. Not like the skittish
teenagers Ellie was used to dealing with, most of
whom had gone from Barbie dolls to making babies
with little else between. Ellie had found Skyler Sutton
refreshing ... but their conversation had also left her
puzzled, and more than a little dubious.

Sutton. The name had sounded distantly familiar,
like something half-remembered from a newspaper's
society column ... or a list of patrons in the back of
an opera program. Skyler Sutton's short list would no
doubt be chock-full of Mensa members who were active in their churches and community affairs, happily
married, and physically fit. They would be animal lovers and experienced with children. What would Skyler
Sutton want with an overworked psychologist whose
marriage might be on the rocks?

Ellie ticked off points in her own favor. She was
educated. People-oriented. Not so old. In pretty good
shape, though she could use a little work in the thigh
department. Most important of all, she desperately
wanted this. More than success, money, or adulation—
and, apparently, even more than a husband—she wanted
a baby.

Would it be *this* baby? Reason told her no ... but
instinct was pulling her in a different direction.

*Remember, you didn't go looking for this; it came
to you. Maybe there's some significance to that.*

Destiny? Ellie smiled to herself, thinking of what
Georgina's reaction would be. They'd spoken about

it, of course ... and her dear old friend had warned
her against investing too much in signs and symbols.

"It's rather like walking around a ladder rather than
under it ... or believing you can only get lucky during
certain phases of the moon," Georgina had observed
recently over one of their leisurely dinners, this one
in an elegant Upper East Side bistro. "Superstition,
my dear, I very much fear, is a good part of why
you haven't succeeded in your quest. Deep down, you
believe there is only *one* child who is fated to be
yours."

At the time, Ellie had passed this off as nonsense,
but now she was gripped with uneasiness. Suppose
Georgina was right? Had she perhaps held on to the
subconscious belief that Bethanne, in some form,
would be restored to her? And could this hidden
agenda somehow have altered events that had
seemed random?

"Dr. Nightingale?"

Ellie was startled into looking up.

Her first impression of the young woman standing
before her was how astonishingly pretty she was. Slim
in an athletic, rangy way, with eyes as blue and clear
as a mountain lake, and a spill of satiny blond hair
that fell to just past her shoulders. She wore no
makeup and was dressed in jeans and T-shirt, with a
loose suede jacket. A canvas backpack was hooked
over one shoulder. She would have blended in perfectly on any Ivy League campus, except that something about her suggested a maturity far beyond her
years. Something in the way she held herself—head
high, arms folded over her chest, and a nobody-tells-
me-what-to-do-look that Ellie recognized well.

Ellie was instantly engulfed by a glassy wave of
panic. With a graceless lurch, she rose to her feet, and
extended her hand. "Skyler? I'm so glad you could
make it."

"Sorry I'm late," the girl apologized. "I was stuck

in traffic." Her voice, in person, was even more Ivy
League than it had sounded over the phone, a blend
of smooth tones that went down as easily as the sweet-
ened tea Ellie had been sipping.

"The important thing is you're here now." Ellie
smiled, not wanting to appear too eager. "Please, sit
down."

The young woman remained standing. Ellie became
aware that Skyler was studying her in a not unfriendly
way. Even so, she felt like a specimen butterfly pinned
to corkboard. A line from "The Love Song of J. Al-
fred Prufrock" popped into her head: "The eyes that
fix you in a formulated phrase." Did she fit the picture? Did she measure up? She squirmed, while
around her the babble of voices, the hiss of the cappu-
ccino maker, the muted clatter of cups and dishes, all
faded into a blur of white noise.

But all Skyler said was, "You look younger than
I expected."

Ellie felt some of the tension drain from her. "When
you get to be my age, you'll find that forty really isn't
so ancient," she said with a smile, then wished she
hadn't. Had she sounded condescending?

But Skyler was acting as if she'd barely heard. Finally, she said, "It's weird ... but I feel like I know
you from somewhere."

"It's possible," Ellie replied thoughtfully. "I speak at
colleges now and then. Where did you go to school?"

"Princeton—but that's not it." Skyler blinked and
shook her head, as if clearing it. "Oh, well, maybe
you just remind me of someone. It doesn't matter."
She stowed her backpack under the table and sank
into the chair opposite Ellie's.

"Would you like something to eat?" Ellie asked.
"They have soup and sandwiches, if you're hungry."

Skyler rolled her eyes. "No thanks. These days, if I
can keep a handful of saltines down, I'm lucky. I can

hardly remember the last time I actually *enjoyed* a
meal. A cup of tea would be nice, though."

Ellie got up and went to the counter, returning minutes later with a steaming glass mug. She placed it in
front of Skyler, feeling oddly solicitous toward her, as
if she ought to be blowing on the tea to cool it, or
insisting that Skyler try and eat *something*. But that
was silly. She didn't know this girl at all.

"I remember the first three months I was pregnant,"
Ellie said. "Sick as a dog. I couldn't keep anything
down. Even the glue on the back of postage stamps
made me run for the toilet." She gave a little laugh,
then wondered if a sense of humor ranked among this
young woman's list of requirements. She hoped so.

But Skyler wasn't even smiling. She was staring at
Ellie, this time in a way that made Ellie feel certain
she'd said something wrong. Was she making too light
of what had to be a sore subject?

"But I thought . . . I mean, Tony didn't say anything
about . . ." Skyler stopped, color rising in her cheeks.

Ellie understood at once, and was flooded with mis-
giving. Why hadn't she kept her mouth shut?

"I had a daughter," she explained, realizing with a
pang that she'd spoken in the past tense. She settled
back in her chair and sighed. Where to begin? How
much to tell? How to fit a bucketful into a thimble?
Ellie glanced over at a stocky older woman whose
Barnes & Noble name tag read "Bea Golden," and
in that instant felt an insane urge to trade places with
her. Bea Golden, with her permed gray hair and her
access to so many books, might have an answer. Elea-
nor Porter Nightingale did not.

"Look, we don't have to talk about this if you don't
want to." Skyler twisted a hank of hair about her
index finger, looking almost as uncomfortable as Ellie
felt. At the same time, Ellie knew that if she didn't
grab hold of this opportunity, and grab hold of it *now*,
it would be lost to her forever.

"Her name was Bethanne," Ellie said simply. "She was kidnapped."

Skyler was silent for a long, weighted moment. Ellie watched the color drain from her cheeks, and when she finally was able to speak, her voice was little more than a whisper. "Did she . . . was she . . . ?"

"They never found her."

"Oh, God. That's . . . " She bit her lip and stared down at her lap. "That's about the worst thing that could happen to anyone."

"It was."

"I'm sorry."

"It was a long time ago."

"Some things you don't get over. Ever."

Skyler lifted her head, her eyes blazing, and in that instant Ellie was struck again by the odd feeling of their being connected somehow. And she wasn't alone; Skyler had sensed it, too. A light chill stole over her.

Almost before she knew it, Ellie found herself asking softly, "Skyler . . . are you sure this is what you want? Are you really prepared to give up this baby?"

Any cordiality they'd established vanished in that instant. Skyler's expression hardened, and in a cool voice she said, "I have my reasons."

"Fair enough," Ellie said, but she remained troubled.

Skyler, though, was looking contrite. "Tony said you were nice," she offered, her voice softening.

"I hope that's true." Ellie smiled halfheartedly. The music from downstairs had switched from Satie to Scarlatti, and it seemed to carry her, helpless, a leaf borne by a rippling current.

"What did he tell you about *me*? Let me guess. That I'm neurotic and stuck-up, and generally a pain in the ass, right?"

The gawky, adolescent pose Skyler struck at that moment—slumped forward on her elbows with her

chin propped in the cup of her palms, her cheeks pink
with whatever emotion she was desperately trying to
keep under wraps—was so at odds with the confidence
she'd radiated earlier that Ellie was instantly
disarmed.

Gently, she said, "I think he wanted me to form my
own opinion."

"Oh, well ... sure." Skyler glanced away with a
small frown.

The time had come to take the plunge she'd been
dreading, Ellie decided. Her heart grew heavy at the
prospect, but she could see no way around it. The
truth would come out eventually, and wouldn't it be
better to know now where she stood? Save herself
weeks, possibly months of anguished wondering?

Bracing herself, she said, "To be honest, I was surprised that you called. Tony must have told you that
my husband and I are separated." Ellie waited, feeling
like a fragile pane of glass that might shatter if
breathed on too hard.

"As a matter of fact, he did," Skyler confessed.

"And that didn't scare you off?" Ellie maintained
a light tone, but her heart was thudding.

"Truth? I wouldn't be here if Tony hadn't insisted,"
Skyler said, not unkindly.

"I see." Ellie tried not to feel too disheartened.
After all, she'd known it was a long shot. What was
there to be upset about? What was one more thorn
in a heart already so badly rent?

"Look, it's nothing against *you*. I just happen to
believe a child is better off with a mother *and* a
father."

"Ideally, yes." Ellie paused, uncertain of where to
go from here. Carefully, she said, "Paul and I ... we
still love each other very much. I'm hoping we can
work things out."

"I wouldn't want to count on that," Skyler told her.
"I'm sure you understand."

Ellie's hands clenched into fists, and she quickly jerked them onto her lap so Skyler wouldn't see. The humiliation! Every time, feeling as if she had to beg, sell herself as if she were a set of encyclopedias. She wouldn't, not anymore. If this wasn't meant to be, well, okay. She wouldn't force the issue.

"I understand you want what's best for your baby," she said evenly.

"Who wouldn't?" Skyler cried, then slumped back in her chair, cupping a hand over her eyes and muttering, "Look, I'm sorry . . . I never should have agreed to this. Coming here was a mistake."

The area around her grew still, so still that all Ellie seemed to hear was the rustling of pages being turned by patrons hunched over their coffee, book in hand. Countless pages filled with countless words, none of which held any significance for her.

In a crisp, professional voice, Ellie said, "In that case, I don't suppose there's any point in us continuing this conversation."

Inside, though, she was seething. She suddenly wanted to shake this girl, berate her for having the nerve to drag her here, get her hopes up, then tell her it was all a mistake. She felt feverish, and a band of sweat had formed under each arm. The aroma of coffee that had filled the loftlike space so enticingly now brought a bitterness to the back of her tongue. Before she could say something she'd regret, Ellie shoved her chair back and started to get up.

Skyler's hand closed over her wrist, stopping her. "I'm sorry," she repeated.

"No need to be."

"This is really hard for me." She dropped her hand, adding, "Honestly? I don't know what I'm looking for exactly. I just hope I'll know when I find it."

"You will," Ellie told her, compassion getting the better of her.

"You see, I'm adopted. My parents are the greatest,

but ... I've always wondered about *her*. My real
mother. Why she ... she decided not to keep me. Why
she—" Skyler broke off, her expression guarded. "I
guess what I'm saying is that I want my child to at
least know I cared enough to find the best possible
home."

"How do your parents feel about all this?" Ellie
couldn't resist asking.

"My mom's not happy, but she's trying to be understanding. My dad is the one who can't get used to the
idea. His grandchild. Well, you'd have to know Daddy."
Skyler sighed, and sipped her tea.

"I can understand their position." Ellie felt a corner
of her mouth turn up in an ironic smile. She asked,
"Am I your first?"

"My first what?"

"Interview."

"Oh, that." Skyler shifted in her chair, looking uncomfortable. "I talked to one couple, but I didn't like
the husband. He kept calling me honey, like I was his
daughter or something. It was a real turnoff."

"I would have excused myself and walked away. I
don't suffer fools gladly, I'm afraid."

Skyler flashed her a smile of such ingenuousness
that Ellie was warmed in spite of herself. "What I did
was even more of a put-down in a way. When the
check for our lunch came, I snatched it out of his hand
and paid it."

Again, Ellie felt the tug of some connection ... it
was almost palpable. *Had* they met before?

"You're nothing like the young women *I've* talked
to," Ellie told her candidly. "In fact, I'm having a
tough time believing you couldn't handle being a
mother on your own, even at your age." So what if
Skyler took it to heart? What did she have to lose?

But this time, Skyler didn't look offended. "Actually, I don't see it as a question of what *I* can handle.
It's the baby I'm thinking of," she said quietly.

Ellie kept her mouth shut after that. For the next few minutes, the two sipped their tea in what might have passed for a companionable silence to anyone who happened to be watching them. What those observers had no way of seeing was the awful blight of memories crowding in on Ellie.

When they grew too dense, she found herself musing aloud, "I was seventeen, and for the longest time I couldn't believe I was actually pregnant. The idea of a baby, well, it was just so... so overwhelming. In the beginning, when I found out, I wanted to die." She'd never confessed that to anyone, not Paul, or even Georgina. In fact, she'd managed to block it out of her own mind until this very moment.

When Ellie looked up, she saw that Skyler's eyes were bright with tears. "I know I'm doing the right thing ... but I didn't know I would *feel* this way," she choked.

"You can always keep the baby. It's not too late to change your mind."

"Everybody keeps telling me that. But I'm not going to."

"Well, then. I wish you the best of luck." Ellie couldn't think of what else to say. Her disappointment was so keen she could almost taste it, like some dry, bitter herb she'd swallowed. Rising to her feet, the movement seemed to go on and on forever, as if she were elasticized somehow. In a constricted voice, she said, "May I give you one piece of advice, though? Don't make a decision based on what your head tells you. Go with your heart. It won't steer you wrong."

Skyler gave a slow, considering nod before answering. "When I was a baby, the one person who was supposed to care about me more than anyone in the world let me down. I won't do that to my own child."

A tear slipped down her cheek, and Ellie felt an absurd longing to wipe it away, a longing so intense she was left shaken by it. What was this young woman

to her? Why did she care so much in the face of
Skyler's obvious rejection?

"I'm sure you won't," Ellie told her, and meant it.

She was halfway to the stairs when she felt a hand
on her elbow. She turned, and there was Skyler, her
pretty face stripped of all its earlier guardedness. "Dr.
Nightingale, wait. I was wondering if—if you'd consider . . . I mean, if I don't find a couple I like . . . if
you'd be interested in talking again."

Ellie felt a surge of mindless joy. She didn't care if
the hope being offered to her was slim, if this should
end up being yet another mirage in the desert she'd
been wandering in for so long. Or that it could be
weeks, months, before Skyler came to a decision.
What mattered was that Skyler Sutton, not she, had
tossed the ball. All she had to do was catch it.

Struggling against the tears that threatened to overwhelm her, she said, "You know where to reach me."

The moment she got back to her office, Ellie phoned
Paul. She didn't dare report to him what had happened today. What would she have said? That she'd
been offered a slim chance, nothing more? That she
had the strangest feeling of being somehow connected
to this girl? No. All that would have to wait. Her
reason for wanting to talk to him was much more
basic: she simply needed to hear his voice.

"Ellie! You'll never believe this, but I was just about to
phone *you.*" Paul sounded genuine enough, but she
wasn't sure she *did* believe him. "I spent the weekend
out in Sag Harbor with my parents, and they never
stopped asking after you. I decided I'd better give you
a call and see how you were." There was a flatness to
his cheerful tone that sent a faint chill through her.

"Actually, I was hoping we could get together for
dinner tonight," she suggested, not realizing she was
holding her shoulders tightly bunched until she felt a

nerve jump in her neck. Softly, she added, "You're right. We haven't talked in a while."

They agreed to meet for dinner at the Union Square Café. Nevertheless, Ellie hung up feeling more bereft than before she'd spoken to him. She might have been talking to an old friend—someone she hadn't seen in ages and probably wouldn't see again for quite some time.

Had there been a beat of hesitation in his voice when she'd asked if he was free for dinner? Was he seeing someone? She shivered at the thought. No, he would have told her if he was dating. Besides, he still loved her. Didn't he?

The moment she walked into the restaurant and spotted him at the long mahogany bar, her heart did an anxious little double take. He looked a little thinner than the last time she'd seen him, several weeks ago. And there was something guarded in the way he sat, leaning forward on his elbows, his back straight, a tumbler of Scotch cupped lightly between his palms. Like a burdened traveler who knows that if he were to stop, even for a moment, he wouldn't be able to make it to the end of his journey.

Sidling up alongside him, she touched his elbow. "Paul."

He turned, giving her a smile as cautious as his posture. "Hi," he said. "Table's not ready yet. They'll call us." He eyed her more closely. "You look good. Lost weight?"

"I could say the same for you. Obviously, the cafeteria at Langdon hasn't improved since the last time I ate there." She slid onto the stool next to his, and ordered a gin and tonic.

Ellie looked around her. Huge sprays of fresh flowers sat at either end of the polished surface against which she leaned. Conversation hummed all around her, punctuated by the occasional whirr of the bartender's blender.

"Remember the last time we were here?" Paul asked lightly. "There were no tables, so we ate right here at the bar. Just like it was the Empire Diner, not something we were shelling out forty dollars apiece for."

She smiled. "I remember us getting drunk on margaritas." He was wearing the tweed blazer she'd helped him pick out at Paul Stuart, she noted. Gray, interwoven with soft shades of blue, the color of his eyes. Her heart constricted. "How's it going? Any interesting new cases?"

"One—an achondroplastic dwarf," he told her. "Father has achondroplasia, mother's normal."

"What do you mean by 'normal'? Who's *normal*?" Ellie sipped her drink, screwing up her face at the sharpness of the gin. "Sorry. I'm just nervous. I never know how to act around you anymore."

She felt a spiraling lightheadedness, followed by a familiar prickling in her sinuses. She reached into her purse, and pulled out a handkerchief. The last time she'd been with Paul, she'd managed to hold her tears back until she was in the taxi on her way back to the apartment; then she'd wept so hard the poor cabbie probably hadn't known whether to take her home or to Payne Whitney.

Paul took his glasses off and wiped them carefully on his napkin before putting them back on again. He wasn't exactly a rock, either, she was perversely pleased to note. But when he looked at her, his slate-colored eyes were steady.

"We're in the dark, aren't we?" he said softly. "Still feeling our way."

"When do I get to yell, 'Somebody turn on the lights'?"

"Ellie—"

"I know, I know. I promised myself we wouldn't get into it." She gulped enough of her drink for a mild buzz to kick in. "It's hard, though. I look at you and . . . oh, God, there I go again. No, I'm *not* going to start. We're going to talk about something other than our marriage for a change. Let's pretend this is our first date.''

A slow, bittersweet smile touched his lips. "Our first date? Considering that you passed out on me, I'm not sure that's such a good idea."

"Don't worry," she said sharply. "I'm a lot tougher now than I was then."

Next to her, a woman rose from her stool, jostling Ellie into nearly spilling her drink. A tinkle of flirty female laughter was followed by the deep rumble of a man's voice. Ellie used her napkin to mop up the small puddle around her glass, glad for any distraction that kept her burning eyes from Paul's.

Paul gently laid a hand on the back of her wrist. "Wasn't it our second date, the night we saw Stanley Turrentine at the Vanguard?"

"I'll never forget. He played the saxophone like I've never heard it played before. We stayed for both sets, remember?"

"We closed the joint down at two in the morning, then couldn't find a cab."

"It was Easter Sunday, that's why. We were so caught up, we forgot."

Paul sat there smiling, lost in thought as he finished his Scotch and soda. When the glass was empty, he ordered a second. Then, as if slipping out of one jacket into another, more casual one, he asked, "What's up with you? Did that couple I referred ever call?"

"You mean the Spencers?" She nodded. "I saw them last week. I'm sure you already know they're not in the best shape."

"Who would be? Their third preemie. This one lived longer than the others, which I'm not sure was a blessing." He paused, then said, "They were really beating themselves up about it, so I told them they should see someone. Liz Spencer, especially. She felt that God was punishing her somehow.''

Ellie knew all that—she'd spent the hour listening and handing tissues to Liz, who'd wept uncontrollably while her husband stared stonily into the distance. Ellie wished Paul hadn't reminded her of the Spencers and their terrible loss. She suddenly wanted to fling her glass at the mirror behind the bar, to shatter the image of the two of them, seated side by side so stiffly.

As if sensing her mood, Paul switched to another subject. "Guess who called me the other day? Jerry Berger. My roommate from Berkeley . . . I think you met him once. Well, he's in town. Some sort of conference. He's on the Fulbright committee.''

"Short, bald guy? The one who came on to me at Fletcher and Louisa's Christmas party?''

"You're thinking of the unfortunately named Alan Tower." He cocked his head, one eye squinted at her in amused skepticism. "He really came on to you?''

"I didn't know whether to laugh or drop the shrimp dip on his head.''

"The bastard.''

"Is this a case of retroactive jealousy?'' she teased.

"If I got jealous over every man who came on to you, I'd be in worse shape than I already am.''

She wanted to reassure him that she wasn't seeing other men; not even close. At the same time, part of her wanted to punish him, make him squirm. She decided to say nothing.

They were rescued by the maître d', who led them to their table, in the cozy step-down area behind the bar. She glanced around at the other tables. The other diners all appeared to be couples. Next to her, a middle-aged man and woman were holding hands across the table, their faces lit with the glow of the candle flickering between them. Ellie felt an envy so profound she wanted to snatch back the past six months, pretend they hadn't happened and she and Paul were as happy as they.

Just then, their waiter appeared to take their wine order. He was a tall, thin-lipped man with slicked-back hair who made Ellie think of Jeremy Irons as Claus von Bülow in *Reversal of Fortune.* She nudged Paul, who immediately saw the resemblance, winked at her. Just like old times, she thought, warmed in spite of herself.

They'd finished eating before Ellie remembered to ask, "By the way, how's your miracle baby these days?"

Paul grinned and signaled to their waiter, who was busy doing his Claus von Bülow imitation at a table on the other side of the room. "Theo? He went home a few weeks ago, all six pounds of him. There's some damage to his lungs from all that time on the vent, but considering what he went through, he's in damn good shape."

"His mother must be thrilled." Ellie felt a tug in her chest, like a fishhook that if pulled too hard would rip away the soft tissue it was buried in.

"Serena's over the moon. All the years of trying, and she's finally got something to show for it." He shot her a cautious glance, then added softly, "This feels a little like we're trying to ignore the proverbial elephant." He combed his hair back from his forehead with a quick, nervous thrust of his hand.

"Talking about it won't necessarily make it go away," she reminded him. "We tried that, remember?"

"I miss you," he said, his voice catching.

Paul's face, so dear, so unhappy, dissolved in a blur. But when Ellie spoke, her voice was oddly firm. "Paul, I want us to be together. I can't just sit here pretending we're not married. I want you home. In our bed. In our *life,* dammit."

"Ellie, I want that more than anything, but—"

"Only if you can have it *your* way," she finished for him. "Paul, we've been over and over this. You're asking me to give up something I just can't." She blinked, and he swam into clear focus.

"All right, okay. I shouldn't have brought it up." Their check arrived, and without even glancing at it, he tossed his credit card down.

Ellie took a deep breath. "I saw a young woman today. She came to me through one of my patients. Paul, *she* came to me. It was like ... like fate was stepping in." The words came spilling out of her; she couldn't have stopped them if she'd tried.

Paul cut his eyes away with a pained grimace. "Ellie, don't. I can't."

But it was too late. "Oh, Paul, I felt as if we had this *connection*. It was like ... like all those other times I'd been simply stumbling around in the dark— and now, suddenly, I could see. Whatever comes of it, I know that this was meant to be. This girl was brought into our lives for a reason." She lowered her voice, aware that her excitement was threatening to boil over. "Paul, please ... give it one more shot. If you love me at all, help me do this."

Her heart was pounding, and despite all the wine she'd drunk, she couldn't stop shivering. Paul, though, looked flushed and angry.

"So that's why you wanted to see me tonight," he said in a low, hard voice. "Why didn't you just say so up front?"

He was right to feel tricked, she realized. Deep down, she must have known all along that she wouldn't be able to keep this to herself. But it was more than that. She missed him. And she loved him ... despite the fact that right now she was so furious she could have hit him.

"Maybe I would have, if you didn't make it so damn hard." Ellie felt on the verge of losing her temper, but she didn't want to make a scene, not here, not surrounded by all these people, some of whom she could see, out of the corner of her eye, glancing at them curiously. Lowering her voice, she pleaded, "Paul, will you at least think it over? Is that too much to ask?"

"I've been doing nothing *but* thinking it over. For the past ten years, as a matter of fact," he shot back. "And, frankly, yes, it *is* too much to ask. Even if I decided to go along with this, where would it lead? What guarantee do we have?"

"What guarantee did Serena Blankenship have that she'd walk out of the hospital with a baby in her arms?"

"The difference," Paul said slowly, "is that Theo's her son."

Ellie reeled as if he'd struck her. "How can you say that?" she cried, no longer caring if the couple at the next table could hear them. "After what happened to me—"

"That's right," he cut her off. "To you, Ellie. To *you.* I never had a child, so I guess I don't know what it's like to suffer." The bitterness in his voice cut through her like a jagged saw blade.

Ellie rose so abruptly that she was left feeling as if she'd been plucked off her feet and held dangling in midair. From this new height, which commanded a view of her husband as she had never before seen him—sad, lost, defiant—she decided to take a gamble, risk everything. She took a deep breath.

"If I promise this will be the last time ... would you do it?"

The anger went out of his face, but after a moment, he shook his head sadly. "I wish I could believe you, Ellie. But even if you do mean it, I won't, *can't,* put myself through that again. I won't go through another day with that particular sword of Damocles over my head."

"It won't be forever," she argued, vehement. "For

God's sake, Paul, what do you have to lose? We're already living apart, so tell me, *what do you have to lose?*"

His face twisted with an emotion she'd never seen in him until now, a pain that sent a shaft of recognition through her. For the first time, she saw in Paul's suffering a reflection of the deep, abiding grief that had sustained her through her seemingly endless search to fill the gap left in her by the child she'd lost.

"Right now, I still love you," he said in a soft, wrenched voice. "What I'm most afraid of is that I'll lose even that."

Silence fell over them, broken only by the clatter of silverware against china, the sound of voices mingling in a harmony of romance both celebrated and recaptured. Only she and Paul seemed to have been set adrift, a pair of wanderers who had lost their bearings.

"Then I guess there's nothing more to say."

Ellie thought, *I have to get out of here.* If she didn't leave, this instant, she'd burst into tears in front of everyone.

But as she was turning away, something made her glance back.

Paul hadn't moved. He just sat there, staring at her, the agonized look on his face making her think of those old movies where the hero arrives, breathless, just as his lover's train is pulling out of the station.

Except in the movies, Ellie thought, *the hero always runs after the train.*

CHAPTER 10

By the time Tony and Skyler arrived at his brother's house in Massapequa, they had spent almost an hour and a half on the Long Island Expressway, crawling in near-stalled traffic. It was the last week in October, and the weather had cooled considerably. But Tony had neglected to get the broken heater in his Explorer fixed, and Skyler developed a chill that had settled into her fingers and toes. As he pulled into the driveway of the medium-sized Cape Cod where Tony's brother and sister-in-law lived with their three kids, she was shivering despite her slacks, undershirt, T-shirt, and sweater. A stitch formed in her stomach, and Skyler thought: *I'm not going to fit in. They're going to wonder why I'm here ... what Tony's doing with a pregnant woman who isn't even his girlfriend? Why did I agree to come?*

What she said was: "Why would anyone have a barbecue this time of year?"

"That's my crazy brother for you, he's always late with everything," Tony laughed, not taking offense. He noticed that she was shivering, and looped an arm around her shoulders as they were walking away from the car. "Don't worry, we're not eating outside. Even Dom's not *that* crazy."

The house itself lifted her spirits a little; it reminded her of an illustration in a first-grade reader. Shaded by huge elms and maples that had scattered a carpet of yellow and red leaves over the lawn below, it stood nestled at the far end of a cul-de-sac aptly named Elm Drive. Following Tony on the side path to the back-yard, Skyler saw a wisp of smoke curling above the high board fence and caught a whiff of grilled meat. A Halloween skeleton, already beginning to curl at the edges, was pasted in one of the windows, and clay pots of fluffy yellow and white mums were lined up along the porch railing like rabbits in a carnival shooting gallery.

Skyler felt the stitch in her stomach pull tight. Was meeting Tony's family simply her way of proving she could get away with it, that she could break bread with anyone?

Or your way of proving to yourself once and for all how wrong Tony is for you? a nasty voice insinuated.

Tony, who must have picked up on her mood, tight-ened his arm about her shoulders and said, "Relax. Nobody's gonna give you a hard time. All they know is you're a friend of mine."

"What did you tell them about the baby?" she whispered.

"Nothing. Yet. It's your call."

He smiled encouragingly, and she couldn't help thinking he must have gone out of his way to look especially handsome today: broken-in jeans and a flannel shirt, with a crewneck pullover that didn't quite hide the bulge of his gun. She both wanted and hated him. Why did he have to go around looking so damn sexy?

She thought of how he'd looked the week before last, when he'd gone with her to the Met (spurred by the same misguided sense of challenge, no doubt) to see *The Marriage of Figaro*. Seated beside her like a boy in church trying his best not to fidget, Tony had been the picture of discomfort in a suit that was an inch too short in the sleeves. During the intermissions, he'd read the program, and afterward asked intelligent questions. But Skyler would never forget stealing a glance at him as the curtain went up on the second act: a glazed look had come over him, like that of someone hearing a story told by his spouse for the hundredth time. Once, he brought a fist to his mouth, and she could see he was struggling not to yawn. Another time, she caught him with his eyes shut.

Skyler had wanted to kick him; then she'd wanted to kick herself. What could she have been thinking, dragging him to the opera? What had she expected? That he would become instantly enraptured by the music she'd been listening to since she was a child? That in a three paragraph synopsis, he would gain an appreciation for a libretto she knew practically by heart?

Now the tables were turned, and she was the one who had to fit in. Not only that, she had to either make up a story about the baby, or admit the truth. God, what would his family think if she told them it was Tony's baby she was carrying, and she planned on giving it away?

The thought of Ellie Nightingale surfaced in her mind, and Skyler was once again left to wonder how a brief meeting that had taken place several weeks ago could have had such an effect on her. Since then, she'd interviewed four more couples, but for one reason or another none had seemed right. There hadn't been that sense of connectedness she'd felt with Ellie. At odd times, when she was brushing her teeth, or at the clinic holding down a shivering puppy while Dr. Novick administered its shots, Skyler would find herself imagining Ellie Nightingale cradling a baby, *her* baby, keeping it safe from harm. She couldn't seem to shake the feeling that this woman, husbandless or not, would love her child like no other.

Yet she hadn't called Ellie. She wasn't ready to trust her instincts—suppose they were wrong? For some reason, Skyler thought of her father, of his methodical approach to everything, the firm hand with which he gripped life's helm. His saying to her once, quite sincerely, when she was fourteen and bereft over Cam Linfoot's lack of interest in her: "If you think it would help, I'd be happy to speak to the young man."

No, much as she adored him, she didn't want to be like Daddy, who was so invested in doing the obvious, rational thing that he often missed the whole point. On the other hand . . .

"Tony! Hey! Get your butt over here! I need you to try my potato salad! Dom says I didn't put in enough salt!" belted a husky voice loud enough to call a play at Yankee Stadium.

As they stepped through the gate, the first thing Skyler noticed was a petite, brown-haired woman who didn't look as if she could possibly belong to that umpire's bellow. The woman was waving to Tony from the doorway to the covered porch. She wore leggings and a loose striped top. Her hair, cut short in front, was pulled into a ponytail that bounced girlishly as she raced down the porch steps to kiss Tony on both cheeks.

Tony kissed her back and waved to the burly man in jeans and a Knicks sweatshirt who was tending the grill. He was a heavier version of Tony, with a receding hairline and the beginning of a gut. "Hey, Dom! You're the only guy I know who gives out barbecued ribs on Halloween," he joked.

"How else can I have the family over without my wife bitchin' that it's taking over the whole kitchen?" Dom yelled back from the Weber grill. It was parked in the far corner of a brick patio bordered in juniper and leggy impatiens.

"Jeez, will you listen to him? You'd think I haven't been in there slaving all day." Tony's sister-in-law rolled her eyes. Turning to Skyler, she stuck out her hand, "Hi, I'm Carla. We've all been dying to meet you. Not that Tony's told us anything much—which is why we're so curious." Her eyes dropped to the barely noticeable swell of Skyler's belly, her round, lightly freckled face registering mild surprise.

Skyler felt a slow heat crawl up her neck. She darted a panicked glance at Tony, who rescued her by lightly cuffing his sister-in-law on the shoulder, and saying, "Hey, don't give me that. I told you about Skyler. She's a friend of mine. I'm sort of lookin' out for her until the baby comes."

Putting it like that, without elaborating or lying, Tony managed to skate by with only a narrow, speculative look from Carla as they trooped past her into the house.

In the big, airy kitchen, every inch of counter and stove space was crammed with pots and pans and bowls. Carla dug a fork into a mammoth tub of potato salad and offered it to Tony, who pronounced it just right. Then she insisted that Skyler sample it. Skyler thought it could use a touch more salt, but she told Carla it was delicious.

Through the kitchen door to her right was a long table set with more places than Skyler would have thought it could possibly accommodate. She felt the stitch in her stomach give another tug. Just how big *was* Tony's family, anyway?

She followed him into a darkish living room arranged in an uninspired way with furniture that looked as if it had just come off a showroom floor. A glance into the den next to it, with its frayed sofa piled with little kids watching TV, explained why. The den was where the family hung out; the living room was for company. Skyler wondered if she had ever truly appreciated until now her mother's touch, how Mom had managed to make every room in their big old house feel cozy and welcoming.

As Skyler made the rounds with Tony, shaking hands with his assorted family members, she felt as stiff as the brocaded sofa and chairs from which they rose to greet her. Tony's brothers and sisters and in-laws were friendly, but it was as if a switch had been flipped. All spontaneity went out of their conversation, and even their gestures became stiff, unnatural. They sensed she was different; it wasn't something anyone could have put a finger on. The gulf was just there, undeniable, unbreachable.

Tony's mother was the only one who didn't disguise how she felt. As Mrs. Salvatore stood up and walked toward her, Skyler immediately sensed an amber caution light blinking on.

"It's nice to finally meet you. I've heard so much about you from Tony," Skyler greeted her, shaking a dry wisp of a hand.

Loretta Salvatore was a petite woman, with wavy dark hair shot with iron, and the careworn face of a woman well acquainted with life's miseries. Her small dark eyes, ringed in brownish pigment that made them appear sunken, moved over Skyler with the weary acuity of an undertaker sizing her for a coffin, coming at last to rest on her belly.

"My Tony? The big talker?" Mrs. Salvatore snorted. "You must be somebody special, him telling you his whole life's story. With us, it's like pulling teeth just to get a word out."

"I'm a good listener," Skyler told her.

"Patient, huh? That's good, 'cause you gonna need all the patience you can get when that baby comes," the older woman observed drily. Her thin mouth slanted up in a knowing smile. "Tony didn't mention you were expecting."

"I'm due the end of March," Skyler told her, too flustered to think of anything else to say.

Loretta Salvatore snatched up Skyler's left hand, and pointedly examined the ringless third finger of her left hand. "A shame . . . nice girl like you, with no husband," she clucked. "No wonder my Tony is lookin' out for you. He's a good boy." With a casualness that didn't quite hide the sly edge in her voice, she asked, "You two known each other long?"

Before Skyler could embarrass herself, Tony's youngest brother jumped up from the sofa. "Will you give her a break, Ma? She's gonna think we're the FBI or something." Eddie, with his sandy hair and deep-set eyes, didn't look anything like Tony, but he clearly had his brother's knack for putting people at ease. Eddie smiled at Skyler and asked, "Can I get you a Coke or something?"

"Water would be nice." Skyler heard the prim note in her voice, and flushed. She glanced around wildly, but Tony had disappeared. A child's squeal of delight drew her attention to the den, where she could see him romping with his nieces and nephews. Good old Uncle Tony. Didn't he realize she was floundering?

Before Eddie could make a move, his wife—Vicky? Nicky?—got up and went into the kitchen, returning a moment later with a tumbler of ice water. She wordlessly handed it to Skyler, who thanked her while secretly thinking *She'd look so much prettier without all that hair around her face. Someone should tell her.*

Immediately, Skyler felt ashamed of her thoughts. What business was it of hers if Tony's sister-in-law needed a new hairstyle?

The next half-hour passed with excruciating slowness. The men drifted into the next room, where a football game was in progress on TV. Skyler was left alone with Tony's mother and sisters, who kept getting up and running into the kitchen to help Carla. When Skyler offered to help, they all looked at her like she'd said something cute, but no one took her up on it.

Finally, Tony's sister Gina took pity on her and gave her the job of folding napkins.

"Boy or a girl?" asked Gina, with only a glance at Skyler's belly. The prettiest of Tony's three sisters, she wore her curly black hair short and played up her looks with big hoop earrings and a blouse that showed off her naturally brown shoulders. "Me? I never wanted to know. It kinda spoils the fun of it, don't you think? I mean, what does it matter, long as it's got ten fingers and ten toes, right?"

Skyler remembered how she'd kept her face averted while Dr. Firebaugh was doing the sonogram. She'd lain on the examining room table, wanting nothing so much as to bury her head in the folds of her obstetrician's crisp white jacket and cry her eyes out. In her mind, she had seen her baby curled up inside her like a sleeping kitten. She didn't need to know whether it was a boy or a girl. She didn't need to add any more to the sense of loss that was growing keener with each passing day.

"How old are your children?" Skyler asked, sidestepping onto a safer topic.

They were standing in the dining room, between the florid Mediterranean-style table and its matching buffet, where a pair of Currier & Ives souvenir plates stood on either side of a cut-glass bowl of silk carnations. From her vantage point, Skyler could see into the kitchen, where Tony's mother was overseeing the unmolding of a Jell-O salad, and Carla was holding open the back door for Dom as he sidled in, loaded down with a tray of barbecued ribs.

"Three and five," Gina told her. "And don't you believe if it anyone tells you two are as easy as one. Every morning when I'm scraping Play-Doh off the kitchen floor, I swear I'm gonna get my tubes tied." She took Skyler's arm and pulled her off to one side, where they were partially hidden by a china closet that lovingly displayed Carla's collection of Hummel figurines. In a low, friendly voice, Gina said, "Listen, you can tell me it's none of my beeswax, but what's with you and Tony? I see the way he looks at you, so don't give me that crap about you two being just buddies."

It was clear to Skyler that there would be no point in lying to sharp-eyed Gina. She had a feeling Tony's sister had already guessed how she felt about him. Gina looked as if she also had a good idea about whose baby it was she was carrying. Skyler took a deep breath, and glanced over her shoulder to make sure Mrs. Salvatore wasn't within earshot. From the kitchen drifted the rise and fall of voices mingled with the banging of drawers, and the clatter of bowls and pots. A wild chorus of man-sized whoops from the den signaled that the favored team had scored a point.

"It's complicated," she sighed.

Gina cocked her head. "Why?"

"I'm not keeping the baby."

Gina's dark eyes narrowed, but she didn't comment. All she said was, "Does Tony know how you feel about him?"

Skyler, aware that she was blushing, looked down at the napkin she'd been folding. "It doesn't matter, really. What we feel for each other is beside the point," she said softly.

She would most likely never see Tony's sister again, so what was the harm in setting the record straight? Even if Gina ran and told Tony everything she'd said, nothing would change, really.

"It's funny," Gina said slowly, "but before Johnny and I got married we fought all the time. His dad, you know, never much liked me ... and his mother, well, you don't score with Mama Catalano unless you go to church every Sunday and first Friday. Johnny, he was all the time after me to cover up my cleavage and stop wearing such bright lipstick ... and could I please, if I felt a four-letter word coming on, just keep it to myself?" She made an in-your-face gesture. "You know what I told him? 'You keep your fucking parents to yourself ... and you can keep on fucking me.' " She grinned. "And look at us, ten years later."

Gina reminded her so much of Tony just then that Skyler let out a delighted laugh. Then, lowering her voice, she confided, "I don't think your mother likes me."

"Oh, don't mind her. She's just looking out for Tony. She hated Paula like sin ... but you're nothing like Paula." She studied Skyler for a moment, then said, "Though I have to admit, I wouldn't have figured you for his type." Her eyes dropped and in a voice that was almost a whisper she said, "It's Tony's baby, isn't it?"

Skyler nodded. "It was sort of an accident." Her face felt scorched.

Gina sighed. "Aren't they all?"

A minute later, everyone was called to the table. Skyler, surrounded by Salvatores and their in-laws and offspring, all of them jabbering at once, felt herself melt into obscurity. No one was paying much attention to her, except occasionally to ask if she'd like another helping of ribs, or coleslaw, or potato salad. The children squealed and made silly faces at one another while the adults absently wiped barbecue sauce off chins and mopped up spilled milk. Tony held court at one end of the table, with his mother at his right elbow, hanging on every word. On his left, Gina and Carla were huddled in whispered conversation, and for a panicky instant Skyler was sure they were gossiping about her. Then Gina looked over at Skyler, and winked, using her fingertip to draw an invisible zipper across her mouth.

Tony's sister-in-law Laura had made Mississippi mud pie for dessert, and though Skyler was full, she forced herself to take a few bites of the almost sickeningly sweet confection. Tony left most of his, too, which did not go unnoticed. Plump, round-faced Laura scolded him as she was clearing away the plates, but made no sign of disapproval when she got around to taking Skyler's.

When it was finally time to go, Skyler felt exhausted. She hadn't done much of anything; she'd barely spoken two words to anyone other than Gina. She hadn't even eaten that much. The effort of trying to fit in where she didn't belong was what had tired her, she concluded as she was saying her good-byes. As she and Tony walked through the gathering dusk to his car, her face felt as if it would crack in two from all the smiling she'd done.

Even as they were driving away, her childhood schooling in good manners wouldn't let her off the hook. A mile or so down the road, she turned to Tony and said brightly, "I had a good time."

"Bullshit. You hated every second of it." Tony cast her an amused glance, but behind his hooded black eyes she thought she saw a glimmer of disappointment.

"Not *every* second," she admitted.

"What was it? Gina giving you the third degree?"

"I liked your sister. It wasn't her ..."

His mouth tightened, and he kept his eyes trained on the road. The last of the sunset's sepia light had faded, and purple twilight had set in. Headlights began to appear, blooming mistily in the dusk like whispered promises. Here, a mile or so beyond where his brother lived, the houses were larger and set farther back from the road. Tony found a wide shoulder between two lots, and pulled over. Switching off the engine, he turned to her.

"They're a good bunch—a little rough around the edges maybe, but that's not what's bothering you, is it?" In the growing darkness, deepened by the overgrown maples under which they were parked, his face

was all bold planes and angles. The only sound was
the ticking of the car's engine as it cooled.

"No," she said, fighting back tears. "Tony, I don't
know what you hoped would come out of this, but it's
not happening. I don't fit in."

"Who asked you to?"

She stared at him. "I just thought—"

"Listen, and listen good." His voice grew hard, and
in the shifting shadows he leaned toward her, his good
smell—clean sweat, leather, and flannel washed many
times—engulfing her in a tide of longing. "I love my
family. They're not perfect. A lot of the time, they
can be a pain in the ass. But the bottom line is nobody
tells me what to do, or who to see. I don't give a
flying fuck if they don't like you, or if you don't like
them. They'll come around eventually. And even if
they don't, that's not what'll stand between us."

Us? When had they turned into *us?* A chill crept
over her. She hugged herself, shivering in the cold that
signaled the end of their long, glorious Indian summer.
Tony's presence, so close, yet so removed, was making
her a little crazy. She wanted him so badly the thought
of their not touching was almost unendurable. She felt
swollen and tender all over, and damp between her
legs.

"Tony—" she started to say, but he interrupted her
by pressing a warm, callused finger to her lips. The
shock of his flesh against hers tipped Skyler over the
edge into spiraling dizziness.

Then he was kissing her, and oh, my God, she
wanted it to go on and on forever. The sweet pressure
of his lips, the gentle flick of his tongue. She threaded
her fingers through his hair, growing weak at the soft
springy feel of it against her palms. Tony groaned and
drew her in as tight as their separate seats would
allow, enclosing her in the hot, tense circle of his arms.
She could feel a muscle jumping in his throat, and the

bands of muscle in his chest flexing where it was pressed to hers.

He cupped her breast, and despite three layers of clothing, she suddenly felt naked. His heat, that incredible natural heat of his, was burning her. Her nipples, grown almost excruciating sensitive with pregnancy, responded at once, sending small electrical pulses throughout the rest of her body. God, oh God . . . did he have any idea what he was doing to her? Did he know how much she wanted him . . . enough to have him mount her right now, right here in this car, as if they were a pair of sixteen-year-olds?

How could she not give in to this? How could she live without this man, without his touch, his mouth, his whispered words in her ear?

At the same time, a voice in the back of her head cautioned, *You feel that way now . . . but what's it going to be like in a few years, when the thrill has worn off? What then? Will you smile when you eat his sister-in-law's mud pie as if it's not too sweet? Will you look the other way when he falls asleep in the middle of Tosca? And while we're on the subject, just how long do you think you'll be able to pretend it doesn't matter that he risks his life on the street every day for only a fraction of the money you get for doing absolutely nothing?*

She thought of the Suttons' table in the Terraces at the National Horse Show, which their whole family would be attending next week. It had crossed her mind that she might invite Tony one of those nights, but now she knew how ridiculous a notion that was. He wouldn't fit in with her family any more than she had with his. No, better to stop this silly game of pretending they could somehow make a square peg fit into a round hole.

Skyler pulled back, feeling almost a tearing sensation as she did so. Holding a trembling hand to Tony's cheek, she whispered, "If I'd known . . . oh, God, if I'd known . . ."

"Known what?" he asked, his voice a low growl in the cloaked stillness.

"That it would be like this. That we—" Her voice choked off. "Tony, I can't. Things are too crazy for me right now. The baby. *My* family. This would just . . . well, it would just muddy the waters."

Now it was Tony drawing back, only a little, but to Skyler they suddenly seemed miles apart. A car sped past and the slash of its headlights momentarily lit his face. In that instant, Skyler saw that he wanted her deeply, in more depth and in more ways than she could have imagined. More than she even felt comfortable knowing about. It was almost frightening, the intensity of emotion that blazed from his rugged Da Vinci face with its heavy-lidded eyes.

"You got it," he said in a voice as cooly remote as the wind blowing through the canyon that stretched between them. "There's just one thing. And it's got nothing to do with us, or either of our families. It's this adoption thing. Before you decide on anybody, I want to meet them first. I want to know what kind of people will be raising my kid. Will you give me that much?" His jaw was working, and she caught a bright gleam in the corner of one eye.

Skyler nodded. She owed it to him. From the beginning, Tony hadn't asked much of her; he'd always just *been* there somehow. He hadn't nagged her about Dr. Nightingale, either. He was letting her make up her own mind.

Tony didn't need to know that she was on the fence about Ellie, that she'd thought about her many times. It might give him ideas, and she was far from making anything even approaching a final decision.

"Done," she said, keeping silent only about what was in her heart.

I love you.

I want you.
This is killing me.

The Meadowlands' Brendan Byrne Arena had always seemed to Skyler like the Emerald City at the end of the Yellow Brick Road. Her whole life, she'd dreamed of someday competing in the National Horse Show. Ever since she could remember, she'd imagined herself soaring over those glorious jumps astride a horse so beautiful it would make your eyes water. As teenagers, she and Mickey had avidly followed every show, collecting newspaper and magazine clippings, discussing in endless detail the various strategies with which they would attack each course. The amateur events, even the prestigious ones, were merely warmups for the Big One.

Seated at her family's table in the Patrons' Terraces, high above the tiered stands, Skyler gazed down at the arena, where a latticed arch threaded with silk roses marked the beginning of a jump course almost too pretty to be real: gleaming red and white verticals and spreads banked in yellow and white chrysanthemums, a faux brick wall festooned in ivy, a staircase framed by mock stone pillars. In the middle was the course's Waterloo—two fences set so close to each other that the horses would have no more than half a stride to recover in between. That was where they'd see most of the knock-downs and refusals, Skyler guessed. She felt an involuntary tightening of her leg muscles, as if *she* were facing those jumps.

The thought nearly brought her to tears.

This year, for the first time, she *would* have had a real shot at qualifying, if she weren't . . .

Pregnant.

The word struck in her mind like a dissonant note hammered out on a piano.

I'm pregnant.

Now that it was becoming obvious, her condition

haunted her everywhere she went, and in everything she did. The people she worked with at the veterinary clinic were already asking her if she was sure she minded being on her feet all day long. Mothers beamed at her in the supermarket, eager to discuss the benefits of Lamaze over Bradley, breast over bottle. She'd even started receiving literature in the mail, flyers advertising infantwear, an invitation to subscribe to *Parents* magazine, life insurance pitches.

But Skyler had vowed to put it out of her head, for tonight at least. Because tonight was special; it was the Grand Prix, and her friend Mickey was competing in it. Second best only to being down in that arena herself, Skyler thought, would be seeing Mickey fulfill the dream they'd both shared for so long.

And for her friend, she knew, it was more than just a dream come true. This was Mickey's first season riding for Mrs. Endicott, and if she blew this show she'd be jeopardizing her chances at competing in next season's big open classes. On her own, she couldn't afford the exorbitant entry fees, the expensive upkeep and transport of her own horse. As Mickey had said with typical cornball humor, she sure had "a lot riding on this."

From where she sat, Skyler could see the ramp that led behind the scenes to the exhibitor's area. Her friend's familiar figure, astride a handsome black horse—Mrs. Endicott's prize new Dutch Warmblood—flitted into view, and Skyler found herself craning for a better look.

"She's going to eat that second jump unless she takes it slow," she fretted aloud. "Toledo's no good with spreads until he settles down and hits his stride."

"If anyone can handle him, Mickey can," said Kate, seated beside her.

Skyler, leaning forward in her chair at the long table from which their dinner dishes were being cleared, ached to be alongside Mickey right now. In her mind, she saw herself amid the steamy press of horseflesh, Chancellor dancing beneath her, while other riders cut around her in tight circles. She could almost smell the air backstage: dense, gamey—a brew of cigarettes, manure, hoof oil, lather, and human sweat. She saw herself sailing over the jumps, experiencing the adrenaline rush of a perfect landing. . . .

But then, out of the blue, she imagined her horse stumbling, saw herself pitch forward out of the saddle.

Instinctively, Skyler clasped her hands over her belly. Tears stung her eyes.

Oh, baby, what's going to happen to you? Who's going to take care of you?

Ellie Nightingale once again surfaced in her mind. Skyler had seriously considered seeing her again, mainly to find out if the weird connection she'd felt the first time was still there . . . but it didn't seem fair somehow. She would only get Ellie's hopes up. *And what if I end up choosing someone else?*

She found her thoughts turning uneasily to the two couples she'd interviewed just this week, meetings set up by a lawyer friend of Mickey's. The portfolio manager and his aerobics-instructor wife had seemed ideal, both of them friendly and upbeat without seeming as if they were trying too hard to impress her. Marcia had been a DES baby and couldn't have children of her own. They wanted a big family, she'd explained, and were also considering older kids, even those with handicaps. Marcia's husband had looked away then, and Skyler had seen his lips thin. He clearly wasn't thrilled with the idea of some kid in leg braces spoiling *his* rosy family portrait. Skyler had been left wondering: *What if* my *baby isn't perfect?*

The second couple had been older, in their late forties, with a house in Scarsdale and a profitable software firm. The wife, plump, gray-haired, could have been the spokeswoman for Betty Crocker. Their only son had been killed several years ago in a motorcycle accident, and they were desperate for another chance at parenthood, but Diane had already been through menopause.

Skyler hadn't needed time to think that one over. She didn't want her baby growing up in the shadow of a dead boy.

John Morton, Mickey's lawyer-friend, said not to worry—the supply was short, and the demand endless. He'd set up as many interviews as it took. And she had months yet before she had to make a decision.

Skyler felt a heaviness in her chest, accompanied by a shortness of breath, as if she'd suddenly found herself at a dizzying altitude. Resolutely, she pushed the whole question out of her mind. Morton was right— there was no rush. She would deal with it later. Right now, she was fine. Absolutely fine.

What a load of horseshit, Skyler admitted to herself. She felt so anxious about what Tony had called "the adoption thing," she could hardly stand it. A good night's sleep was a thing of the past. She couldn't even sit through a TV show or finish a magazine article without jumping up at intervals to pace the floor.

Frowning, she concentrated on the arena. Stewards dashed about readying it for the next big event, the Fault and Out, where one knockdown meant you were eliminated. The stands were about three-quarters full, she noted, but every head was turned toward the gleaming chestnut stallion now trotting through the in-gate.

Skyler watched its female rider, in a fitted navy hunt coat and cream-colored breeches, circle once around the arena, her horse prancing and bucking. The klaxon sounded, and a perfectly modulated male voice announced, "Number eighteen is Sultan of Suffolk. The eleven-year-old Hanoverian is ridden by Casey Stevens. . . ."

Sultan rushed the first jump, a vertical fence, then nearly ground to a halt before popping over it in a jackrabbit leap. The crowd let out a collective "ahhhhh." Now the spread, then the staircase, and the tricky pair of verticals separated by only half a stride. Casey, like a novice, was rushing it a bit, wanting it to be over while she was on a roll, rather than playing it safe. Not setting up her jumps as well as she could have. Skyler could hear Duncan intoning, "There's no such thing as a bad horse, only a bad rider . . ."

"Oh, dear, she's not going to make that last one."

Skyler turned to find her mother frowning in consternation. Kate looked the picture of elegance in loose black trousers and vest, with a white silk blouse and Hermès scarf artfully knotted about her throat. Her cane was discreetly propped in the corner of the wall at her back.

Just as Kate had predicted, Sultan's left hind foot sent the top pole rolling from its cups. While a pair of stewards rushed in to replace it, Casey Stevens, trying her best not to look crushed, circled her horse back around to the in-gate. The applause that trailed her out of the ring was polite and short-lived.

Next in was a gray that looked too small for the tall man on its back.

"That's Henri Prudent . . ." Kate's voice was a reverential whisper. "*Now* we'll see some riding. I believe his wife is competing, too. I wonder what will happen if the two of them wind up in a jump-off."

"If he's any kind of a gentleman, he'll let her win," Daddy teased. He never pretended to be anything but bored by these events. The only fun he got out of them was in needling Mom from time to time.

"Not if he doesn't want to wind up in divorce court," Kate said with a laugh. "She'd never forgive him. Besides, her chances are every bit as good as his."

Skyler glanced from one to the other, marveling at how her parents managed to pull it off. She knew what a strain they'd been under, not just about her baby, but with some kind of business crisis as well. They were tight-lipped about it around her, but she'd seen the worry in their faces during unguarded moments. Yet here, among their friends and family, they sparkled as if not a thing in the world could be wrong.

Skyler's fists curled in frustration. If only they'd tell *her*.

"Either way, they'll share the purse," observed Reggie Linfoot, using a stubby finger to stir the melting ice cubes at the bottom of his whiskey tumbler. Good old Reggie—Skyler had adored their neighbor since she was eight, when Reggie, a renowned author of children's books, had climbed with her to the top of the huge pear tree in his backyard. Half drunk (as usual), he'd cackled his way to the top and perched alongside her on a high branch like some aging, pot-bellied Puck.

"Oh, Ian Millar will take it," said Aunt Vera in the authoritative tone that seldom failed to elevate her opinion to the status of fact. "That new Thoroughbred of his is quite something." Vera was Daddy's sister and Skyler's least favorite relative. Aunt Vera's great tragedy in life, according to Mom, was that she'd suffered no great setbacks or disappointments (if you didn't include her divorces, which didn't count because she hadn't been that attached to her husbands to begin with); therefore she couldn't begin to empathize with those who were less fortunate.

Skyler privately thought Aunt Vera had suffered more than Mom realized. Just looking at that pinched, horsey face in the mirror every morning would be enough to make anyone feel like jumping off a bridge.

She turned her attention back to Henri Prudent, wincing as he was eliminated for a refusal. Ian Millar, out next, sailed over the course without a hitch. He'd be a hard one to beat if it came to a jump-off, she thought. And that new mare of his was spectacular—her neck was as long as a baby giraffe's, and look how she tucked her feet going over the jumps. Just imagine what she'd be like in a year or two, after cutting her teeth on the circuit.

"Skyler, dear, it's a shame we're not seeing *you* out there."

Skyler glanced over to find mannequin-thin Miranda Harkness, her mother's dear friend and right-hand person at the shop, eyeing her with enough compassion to stage a telethon. She cringed, knowing Miranda meant well, but wishing her mother's friend hadn't drawn attention to what Grandmother had referred to as her "condition." More and more, she was beginning to feel like a child sent home from school with some infectious illness.

"I would have loved to try out, but there wasn't anything in the rule book covering a rider and a half," she quipped, aware of the edge in her voice.

Out of the corner of her eye, Skyler saw her mother redden. Mom had been understanding to a fault, but to her this was no joke. *I should have remembered that,* Skyler thought, feeling chastened.

"Skyler can start training again as soon as . . ." Kate cleared her throat, then said brightly, "Though I imagine she'll have her hands full, with school and all."

"School?" piped Reggie, blinking as he peered at her through his alcoholic haze.

"I've been accepted into the veterinary program at the University of New Hampshire," Skyler explained, noting that his elbow was a hairsbreadth from slipping off the table. She gave it a discreet tap, and watched as he anchored himself more firmly.

"What about the baby . . . who will look after it while you're in school?" crackled a voice like a phonograph needle on an old, scratched record.

All along the table, stricken faces turned to the ancient lady seated at the far end—Great-aunt Beatrice, who remembered when Society had dressed in black tie for the National, long before it had moved from

Madison Square Garden to the Meadowlands. She was wearing a jet-beaded gown that smelled of camphor, diamond ear clips, and real tortoiseshell combs in her mist of blue hair. A pair of watery blue eyes fixed on Skyler expectantly.

Skyler squirmed in her seat. God, hadn't Aunt Beatrice been *told*?

Mom, bless her, maintained her level gaze and the posture perfected decades ago at Miss Creighton's School for Girls. In a clear, unashamed voice, she replied, "Skyler won't be keeping the baby, Aunt Beatrice. She wants it raised by people who can't have children of their own, just as *she* was." Mom's voice was bright with emphasis on the last words.

Out of the corner of her eye, Skyler caught a glimpse of her father scowling into the program that lay open on his lap. Poor Daddy. She wished there were something she could say to make him feel better. He didn't understand why she was doing this, even though she'd explained it to him, over and over. But that was Daddy for you; he only saw what he wanted to see.

Aunt Vera ended the awkward silence that followed Mom's pronouncement. "More champagne, anyone?" She lifted the bottle from its bucket and held it, dripping, over Skyler's glass.

"Not for me ... pregnant women aren't supposed to drink, remember?" Skyler said.

Her aunt's long, horsey face, with its nostrils that always seemed flared, turned a bright, unbecoming pink. In a low voice, she sniffed, "Honestly, I don't see how you can be so ... so *flip* about it. If you were *my* daughter, I'd—"

"Vera, that's enough," cut in Will sharply. He glowered at her, his salt-and-pepper mustache giving his frown even more authority. His sister's eyes narrowed, but she kept her thin lips tightly clamped.

Skyler sank back in her chair, feeling miserable and

even somewhat sheepish. She'd try and be good for the rest of the evening, she really would. For her parents' sake if not for her own.

All you have to do is just hang on until you can be alone with Mickey.

Mickey was the last in the Fault and Out, going up against four riders who'd jumped clear rounds. If she made the final cut, she'd be in the timed jump-off against the likes of Ian Millar and Michael Matz. The prospect of her friend achieving such a pinnacle lifted Skyler's spirits.

As Mickey rode out and circled near the in-gate, Skyler felt a surge of pride. Mickey looked absolutely glorious in black breeches and a scarlet jacket, her curls caught up in a net under her hunt cap. Unlike her poker-faced rivals, she wore a huge grin that at once had everyone applauding and whistling. Mickey knew how to play an audience, always had.

Her horse, Holy Toledo, was Priscilla Endicott's current favorite, black as the velvet collar of a hunt coat. As Mickey brought him around to the latticed arch, he danced sideways, giving a playful little buck to let her know he could take anything she dished out.

But now it was time to get serious. Mickey brought him around to the first jump, the mock-brick wall topped by two vertical poles.

"Take it slow," Skyler muttered under her breath. "You don't have to make the best time, just make it clear."

Toledo soared over the wall like a summer breeze. Mickey, on the other hand, with her cocked elbows and her legs sticking out at nearly right angles, was the picture in every riding instruction book of how *not* to sit on a horse. Good thing form wasn't what counted in this sport; the only thing that mattered was clearing the jump.

Now the oxer, and the triple ... *God, look at Toledo go*. He made some of the other horses look like

Clydesdales, the way he seemed to float up and hang for a split second in midair over each jump. And Mickey—she was eating it up, the applause, the thrill of it all. All she needed now was to make it through with a clear round—after that, if she made it to the finals, she would have to come in with the fastest time in order to beat out the other finalists.

Skyler clapped until her palms stung, and cheered until she was hoarse.

Two more rounds followed, with the finalists narrowed down to a field of three: Katie Prudent, Ian Millar . . . and Mickey. To be with two such greats— it was like being part of the Holy Trinity, Skyler thought in awe. Even if Mickey didn't take the blue ribbon, she could die happy. As she watched Mickey take her Warmblood around the course one last time, Skyler was filled with pride. When her friend nearly missed the tricky middle fences, Skyler experienced all the sensations she imagined Mickey to be feeling— the lurch in her heart, the loosening of her gut, the high singing of blood in her ears.

Her friend soared over the final jump with a clear round, coming in second, after Ian Millar. Priscilla Endicott would be over the moon, Skyler thought. After this, Mickey would be able to write her own ticket. But what mattered most was that Mickey had achieved what she and Skyler had both dreamed of since they were little: she'd made it to the jump-off at the National.

When Mickey appeared in their box, following the presentation of trophies, looking flushed and damp, Skyler stood up and gave her a fierce hug.

"You were wonderful," she said, close to tears. "I was so proud."

"Wasn't he incredible?" Mickey gushed, all her pride centered on Holy Toledo. "God, it's like a dream, jumping an animal like that. You saw what he can do—and he's capable of much more. We don't want him to take on too much all at once; after Toronto we're turning him out until next summer—" She stopped, eyeing Skyler closely. In a low voice she asked, "Are you all right? You look kind of pale."

"I'm fine," Skyler told her. They were standing off to one side, away from the others, who were still seated at the table. "Just a little stir-crazy, I guess."

"Who wouldn't be? Christ, you're too young to be settling down with the *Horse and Hound* set. Let's split. I'll buy you a beer."

"Make it a Pepsi, and you're on."

Skyler and Mickey headed downstairs, where they found a table in the Winner's Circle bar, which mercifully wasn't too crowded. Skyler settled into her chair with a deep sigh, feeling as if she'd narrowly escaped a lynch mob. The moment their waitress hurried away to fill their drink orders, they looked at each other and broke into identical grins.

"I could die right this very moment, and not feel I missed a damn thing." Mickey laughed.

"All except the Blessed Event," Skyler replied with more than a touch of irony.

Mickey grimaced. "Oh, God, I'm such an insensitive jerk. I never even asked how you've been holding up. And we haven't talked in *ages*."

"You've been busy," Skyler excused her. "Anyway, I'm doing okay."

"Really?"

Skyler told her about the last couple she'd interviewed, the Dobsons, and was rewarded by the face Mickey pulled—one that reinforced her own instincts. Not that Mickey approved of her giving up the baby. A while back, she'd even offered, in a typical burst of scatterbrained generosity, to take care of it herself until Skyler was out of school.

"What would you do with a baby on the circuit?" Skyler had challenged her.

"I'd carry it everywhere on my back like a papoose," Mickey had shot back confidently.

They'd both known it was ridiculous, and Mickey had wisely dropped the subject.

"What about that lady you saw a while back?" Mickey wanted to know now. "The psychologist Tony wanted you to meet? I liked the sound of her." She took a long pull on her Heineken.

Skyler felt herself grow tense. She'd purposely played down her meeting with Ellie Nightingale, not sure that even Mickey would understand the weird feeling she'd walked away with that day. She shrugged and said, "She might be getting divorced. It wouldn't make any sense."

"None of this makes any sense," Mickey was quick to point out. "Jeez, back when we were kids, could we have even *imagined* where we'd end up?"

"You ended up exactly where you wanted," Skyler said softly, a lump lodging in her throat.

"And *you* are going to be the best damn show-jumping veterinarian there is," Mickey was quick to reply. She added gently, "Once this is all over with, I mean."

Skyler, though touched, felt as if she might explode with frustration. "Sometimes it feels like it'll *never* be over. Look at my parents, for God's sake. Daddy is practically a basket case. He'll never forgive me for giving away his grandchild."

"Oh, Skyler." Mickey seized her hand. "You've been trying to go by the rules all your life, even when you're bucking them. So, okay, you made up your mind to do this thing. Go all the way with it. Do what feels *right,* not necessarily what makes sense."

"I don't have to make a decision right away."

"Fine. Shop around. See as many couples as you like ... but don't drive yourself crazy. You're not exactly run-of-the-mill, my friend, so what makes you think any kid of yours would be better off with run-of-the-mill parents?"

Skyler was opening her mouth to ask why she

should take advice from someone who'd considered a papoose perfectly sensible when she felt the baby kick. She sat up suddenly, her mouth dropping open and her hands scooting downward. She laced her fingers over her stomach. "God, I can feel it kicking. Not just butterflies this time. It's so . . ." The words evaporated, too flimsy to describe the enormity of what she was feeling—something so bright and magical, it was as if she were enchanted somehow.

"Maybe it's a sign," Mickey said soberly. "He's trying to tell you something."

"I hope so." Skyler sighed, the magic moment passing like a rainbow glimpsed all too briefly from the window of a speeding car. It was followed by a deep, thunderous misery. "Because this is one decision I'd give anything not to have to make on my own."

"You're not listening," Georgina scolded.

Ellie looked away from the second-story window of Georgina's townhouse, where she'd been gazing out at the snow . . . snow that in the early darkness of the winter's evening seemed to funnel down from the streetlamps along Central Park South. She smiled at her friend, who was seated in a wing chair by the fireplace, where a fire was timidly attempting to establish itself. Georgina wore an exasperated expression she was trying her best to hide.

"Sorry," Ellie said. "You were telling me about the conference in Madrid, something about a study on sleep deprivation among pilots. Are you saying I should stop flying, or are you just making small talk to get my mind off other things?"

"*Is* there something else you'd rather talk about?" Georgina, her legs curled up under a voluminous yellow chenille sweater, made Ellie think of an old tabby lolling about but ready to spring into action at a moment's notice.

Georgina's knack for appearing so relaxed, Ellie

was convinced, was a large part of her success with
the private patients she saw in addition to running the
outpatient psychiatric clinic at St. Vincent's. There was
also this wonderful office, a parlor of her East Seventies townhouse, with a sliding pocket door that sealed
it off from the rest of the floor. Cluttered with what
Georgina called her junktiques—brass floor lamps
with tattered silk shades, knickknacks collected from
all over the world, couches and chairs clustered like
fat old men in front of a fireplace that was forever
shooting sparks onto a threadbare Oriental carpet—
the room always gave Ellie the feeling, when she first
walked in, of coming home.

Except that right now there was no place on earth
where she would have felt entirely comfortable.
"Home is where the heart is." She could see the apho-
rism in her mind, as if it were stitched on a sampler.
But if that was true, then she had no home. Because
where her heart wanted to be was with Paul, whose
door remained closed—and with a baby she longed
for, but could lay no claim to.

Ellie felt her hands curl into fists. *Why* hadn't Skyler
Sutton called? It had been four months, and still no
word. Ellie told herself it was ridiculous to continue
holding out hope. The girl had long since chosen
someone else . . . a nice, loving couple who would give
her baby everything it needed. Still . . .

Ellie hadn't forgotten the almost physical sensation
of their being linked somehow, as if destiny itself had
carefully selected them as players in this drama. Even
now, with Thanksgiving long past and Christmas just
around the corner, she hadn't succeeded in shaking
off the aftereffects of the astonishing impact Skyler
Sutton had made on her.

This evening, Christmas Eve, Ellie had come to
toast the season with Georgina, as she had every De-
cember 24 for the past eight years. What was different
about this Christmas was that it would be the first

Ellie had spent on her own. She thought of the Christmases she'd envisioned—she and Paul beaming beside the tree as their baby tore clumsily at paper and ribbon—and the sadness she felt was so great she understood, as she had those first few winters after Bethanne's disappearance, why so many depressed people commit suicide around the holidays.

Ellie prayed that Georgina would be able to provide some comfort, some guiding light to help her through the blizzard of emotion she was floundering in. She knew that there was no magic cure, that the answers she sought had to come from within—she was a therapist, after all, and a damn good one. But sometimes, she thought, gulping against the lump forming in her throat, sometimes when what you want is answers, all you *need* is a warm shoulder on which to lay your weary head, and a kind voice to soothe your ache.

"What's the point in talking about it?" she told her friend, a bitter edge creeping into her voice. "There's nothing anyone can do."

Georgina tucked a stray silver wisp back up into the untidy braided coil atop her head. With a sigh, she conceded, "Maybe not ... but it never hurts to try. My dear, I truly hate seeing you so unhappy."

Ellie, struggling to keep from sounding gloomy, answered lightly, "There's nothing wrong with me that a husband and a baby wouldn't fix." She reached over to retrieve her cardigan from the back of the sofa.

Georgina, her sharp old eyes trained on Ellie, brought the tips of her fingers together under her chin. "Half is sometimes better than none."

"Are you suggesting I give up trying to adopt?" Ellie shot back, irritated.

"Why must it be perceived as a surrender?" Georgina responded, without missing a beat. "Ellie, have you considered the possibility that you've been so hellbent on one goal for so long that you've overlooked the possibility of other sorts of rewards?"

If this was comfort Georgina was providing, Ellie wanted no part of it. Bristling, she said, "If being on a never-ending honeymoon where nothing exists apart from you and your husband is what it's supposed to be all about ... then I *am* overlooking something."

"My dear, you can't honestly believe that Paul is interested only in preserving some kind of marital Shangri-la. You know better ... and you do yourself a disservice in not confronting what it is you've put so much effort into avoiding."

"And what, pray tell, is that?" Ellie snapped.

"The possibility that you could find happiness even *without* a child."

Georgina's quietly spoken words settled over Ellie like a chill, causing her to shiver. "Why would I want to avoid that?"

"Running from happiness can often be a form of punishment."

Ellie thought for a moment, then said slowly, "You think I'm punishing myself? That I still haven't forgiven myself for what happened to Bethanne?" She smiled a smile as thin as the layer of snow that had collected outside the window sill. "Maybe so. But if that's the case, then there's no cure for it."

"Not even another child?" A crafty gleam came into Georgina's eyes, but it was tempered with such affection and concern that Ellie found her own eyes welling.

Would another child allow her finally, after all these years, to forgive herself?

"I don't know," Ellie answered honestly. "What I *do* know is that I'll never stop trying to find out."

"Well then ... so be it." Georgina, never one to belabor a point, smiled to let Ellie know the subject was closed. Heaving to her feet, she padded over to the tall cabinet where she kept decanters of claret and port, and, this time of year, tins of cookies and cakes given to her by patients. "Now, you must take a nibble of my neighbor's fruitcake with your claret. It's really quite good, only don't let the word get out. Letitia so relishes the look on people's faces when they bite into something they expect to be dreadful.''

Ellie accepted a paper napkin with a slice of cake on it. "If your goal is to fatten me up," she said, "it won't work. I've already tried. Nothing I eat seems to stick."

"Perhaps because you aren't eating enough," Georgina observed scoldingly. "While we're on the subject, what are your plans for dinner tomorrow night? I won't hear of your spending Christmas alone."

"The Brodskys invited me, but I think it's only because Gloria wants me to meet her widowed brother-in-law," Ellie told her with a sigh. "I said I had other plans. I'm not up to explaining about Paul. No one believes any more that this is just a trial separation. There seems to be some kind of statute of limitations on that excuse—after nine months, you either patch it up with your husband, or tell everyone you're desperate to meet other men."

"Well, that settles it then." Georgina poured each of them a slender stemmed glass of claret. "You're coming here. If I knew any single men I'd be saving them for myself, so you're safe on that score. And you haven't seen my daughter in—oh, how long has it been?—ages and ages. Besides, I'm a rotten cook and could use a hand in the kitchen. I won't take no for an answer."

Ellie knew better than to argue. Georgina was right. Being alone on Christmas was just too depressing. Besides, Paul would be spending the holiday with his parents in Sag Harbor. Her heart sank at the thought. Poor John and Susan! They'd been so upset by all this; it would be almost as terrible for them as for her that they wouldn't all be together. The first moment she'd met Paul's parents—on a fiercely windy day in January, when she'd arrived at their house half frozen, then was ushered in with a warm arm about her shoulders and shown to a doggy sofa by a blazing fire, where Paul's father rubbed her hands warm between his wide leathery palms—Ellie had felt as if a great cosmic error had finally been corrected. She'd recognized John and Susan at once as the parents she'd been intended to have all along.

And now even they were being taken from her.

Placing her half-eaten cake on the glass-covered steamer trunk that served as a coffee table, Ellie stood up and went back over to the window. More than four inches of snow had been predicted, and it looked as if more would fall before the night was over. In the milky winter darkness interspersed by glowing street lamps, she watched a man bundled in several layers carefully pick his way along the path that had been trodden in the snow along Seventy-second Street. Ellie was struck by a memory of another Christmas Eve, a night when she'd stood outside St. John the Divine, brought to a standstill by a floodlit manger scene from which the life-sized statue of baby Jesus had apparently been stolen, her breath coming in cloudy bursts, and tears searing her frozen cheeks.

She took a deep breath and turned back to Georgina. "I'd love to come for Christmas dinner. But only if you promise to let me bring my cranberry-pecan pie. It's my mother's recipe, and about the only thing worth salvaging from my childhood." She didn't add that it was Paul's favorite, and that she would get some satisfaction in knowing he'd be deprived of it.

"It sounds wicked and fattening, and I'm sure I'll absolutely adore it," Georgina said. "Now, stop pacing and fill me in on what's been happening. We haven't had a chance to sit down and have a proper talk about all this since you came flying in here nearly on fire about that girl you'd seen, the one you had such a strong feeling about." A troubled look deepened the fine webbing of lines about her eyes and mouth. "I hope you don't in any way think my questioning your motives is a sign of disapproval. I only want what's best for you, my dear."

"I haven't heard from her," Ellie answered, careful to avoid adding what was on the tip of her tongue: *Yet.*

"I gathered as much," Georgina said, taking a slow sip of her claret. "If you *had* heard from her, I'd surely know about it by now. I'm just wondering if you're still holding out hope."

Ellie gave a short, dry laugh. "In other words, do I believe in miracles?"

"Mary was informed of her impending motherhood by the Archangel Gabriel," Georgina reminded her gently. "I know crusty old behaviorists aren't supposed to say this, but miracles *do* happen."

It wasn't at all what Ellie had expected to hear from practical-minded Georgina, and she found herself on the verge of tears. At this moment she wanted nothing more than to rest her head on Georgina's shoulder and simply close her eyes.

"I suppose so." *Miracle? At this point, I'd settle for a late-breaking bulletin.*

Georgina mused on this briefly, then asked, "And that young man from your AIDS group that you're so fond of . . . the dancer?"

Ellie smiled, her first truly genuine smile of the evening. "Jimmy Dolan? It's amazing, the way he keeps pulling back from the brink . . . though a lot of credit, I think, goes to his friend Tony." She didn't remind Georgina that Tony had led her to Skyler Sutton. "Speaking of Jimmy, though, I promised I'd drop by and see him on my way home." She glanced at the carriage clock on the mantel. "I should go; it's getting late."

It was precisely ten minutes to six, and both she and Georgina, realizing this at the same moment, laughed. A fifty-minute therapist's hour. Georgina walked her out into the center parlor, then down a flight of curving stairs to the narrow, tiled foyer. When Ellie had finished buttoning her coat at the door, Georgina, smelling strongly of the jasmine perfume she favored, gave her a hug and kissed her on both cheeks.

"Tomorrow," she reminded Ellie. "I'll expect you at four, with bells on."

Surprisingly, Ellie had no trouble finding a cab. With all the last-minute shoppers thronging the sidewalks on Christmas Eve, she'd been steeling herself for a slog through ankle-deep snow to the nearest subway station. Maybe miracles were possible after all, she thought. Even with its caved-in seat and faulty heating system, the taxi seemed heaven-sent.

Jimmy Dolan, when she arrived at his Hudson Street studio, made her believe in miracles all over again: he seemed to have gained a few pounds since his last hospital stay. And since he'd missed the last few group sessions, the improvement was more noticeable than it might have been otherwise. He let her in with an almost jaunty flourish, grinning as if she were all three of the Magi rolled into one. In keeping with the season, or maybe just the fact that he was alive to celebrate it, he was wearing a red turtleneck and green suspenders. They were as practical as decorative, she guessed from the way his trousers hung on him.

"Merry Christmas." She kissed his cheek, then fished a package from her oversized shoulder bag and handed it to him.

Jimmy looked both pleased and mildly embarrassed. "I don't have anything for you," he said sheepishly.

"Yes, you do, and you've just given it to me. I can't tell you how wonderful it is to see you looking so well."

Jimmy, beaming, ushered her into the large ell that served as living room, kitchen, and bedroom. As she settled on the futon sofa, Ellie's gaze was drawn, as

always, to the ballet posters crowding the walls. Her
favorite was a blowup of Jimmy in midleap, his bare
torso polished with sweat and his arms flung over
his head.

"Open it," she told him, smiling at the awkward
way he stood there with the package in his hands,
looking for all the world like a big kid who still wants
to believe in Santa Claus.

As he plucked feebly at the ribbon, she saw that his
hands were trembling, and not just from excitement.
Jimmy sank into a chair, frowning in frustration and
making Ellie wish she hadn't wrapped the package
quite so well. Finally, though, he managed to get it
open.

"They're from Hammacher Schlemmer ... electric
socks," she explained as he held up a pair of woolly
stockings threaded with wires and topped with plastic
pouches into which batteries had been inserted. Jimmy
had complained that he could no longer keep his feet
warm, no matter how heavy his socks or how many
blankets he piled on.

He grinned and shucked off his moccasins, tugging
the socks on over knobby feet so pale with cold they
were almost blue. "Thanks, Doc. They're great. If I
get hungry while I'm stuck in bed, I can toast marsh-
mallows with my toes."

"Wear them in good health," she said, allowing herself a touch of the gallows humor Jimmy seemed to
thrive on.

"Health is no longer the issue," he said, flinging one
scarecrow arm over the back of the chair he was
perched on. "These days, I settle for making it from
the bed to the bathroom on my own."

"How are you doing ... really?" she asked.

"A little better than I was a few weeks ago, but still
lousy," he admitted, sobering. "But it's Christmas, and
I have only one wish for Santa. I want to see the New
Year in. No paper hats, no champagne, no all-night

partying. Watching the ball drop in Times Square on TV will do. Maybe I'll even catch Tony, out with the rest of the Mounties, preserving peace, justice, and the American way. Mostly, I just want to raise my glass to another year of surviving." He broke into a slow, sweet smile that brought a radiance to his ravaged face. "What about you, Doc—what are *you* gonna celebrate?"

"Hope," she said quietly, feeling more grateful to Jimmy than she could say. She had entered this cold night praying for some sort of relief from her woes, and had found it in the presence of a dying man.

"Hope. Yes, well, that calls for a toast." Jimmy dragged himself to his feet. "I'm fresh out of eggnog and wassail, but I think I can scrounge up some wine."

"Another time," she told him. "I was just at a friend's, and had my requisite Christmas drink."

Instead, she spent the next hour looking through his scrapbook with him while he reminisced about his days onstage. There were programs; there was clipping after clipping of glowing reviews; there were photos like the ones blown up on the wall. Admiring them, Ellie was once again struck by all that Jimmy's parents were missing. She would have been proud to have him as a son.

At last, she stood. "I'd better be going. It's getting late."

She embraced him, gingerly, the way she might have handled an armload of delicate machinery that might fall apart if jostled too hard. He hugged her back, and she felt his chest hitch as if he were trying to catch a breath or hold back a sob. But he was dry-eyed as he showed her to the door. She knew it meant a lot to him that she'd stopped by, and she was glad she had.

When she arrived home, she checked her answering machine. No message from Paul . . . or from anyone, for that matter. Despair once again came crashing in on her.

Call someone, she advised herself briskly. She thought about her old college friend Grazia, in Seattle, and how nice it would be to curl up in a bathrobe and have a long chat with her over a steaming mug of tea. But it was three hours earlier in Seattle, and Grazia, who always put off everything until the very last minute, was probably frantically scurrying around for eleventh-hour presents.

Instead, Ellie found herself a heartbeat away from picking up the phone and calling Paul. She'd sworn she wouldn't. She'd *sworn.* What would be the use? she asked herself. He'd be polite, friendly; he'd even sound glad to hear from her, as he'd been when she called on Thanksgiving. They'd chat about their work. She'd ask after his parents. He'd say they were fine, and put them on. John and Susan would each heartily wish her a wonderful holiday ... and by the time she finally hung up she'd feel like killing herself. Then she'd climb into bed and cry her eyes out.

I can't do that to myself, she thought. Still wearing her coat, its lapels dotted with snow that was melting into dark patches of wetness, Ellie crossed the room and sank down on the sofa. She closed her eyes and allowed her head to fall back, letting the tears she'd been holding in all evening slip out from under her eyelids.

In the apartment next door, someone was playing Christmas carols, badly, on an out-of-tune piano. "Silent Night, Holy Night" ended, and then "Jingle Bells" began. Ellie's head throbbed in rhythm to the pounding of keys. She felt so awful, she even thought about calling her parents and wishing them a merry Christmas. But as she invariably did on the infrequent occasions when Ellie phoned, her mother would say something like, "Isn't it nice, the cheap rates those folks at AT&T give away at Christmastime? Gets people calling home that wouldn't have thought to otherwise."

The phone rang just then, causing Ellie to nearly jump out of her skin.

Paul?

No, not Paul; without knowing why, she felt sure it wasn't Paul.

Yet as she rose clumsily to answer it, her heart was pounding, and her knee went crashing into the glass coffee table. A hot spear of pain shot through her leg as she hobbled toward the phone on the Japanese cabinet against the wall. She was trembling. She told herself it was probably just Georgina, phoning to change the time for tomorrow's dinner . . .

Yet something held her in the grip of a tension so great she would have snapped from it had the phone stopped ringing before she could get to it.

As Ellie answered with a breathless "Hello?" she knew who the caller would be, just as she had known that there truly *was* such a thing as fate, or providence, or whatever you wanted to call it. So she wasn't terribly surprised by the voice at the other end of the line, whose tone was three parts bravado to one part abject fear.

"It's Skyler Sutton . . . remember me?" A quick breath, and she rushed ahead: "I know it's been a while, but I wanted to wish you a merry Christmas . . . and to tell you I'd like to see you again. About the baby. Are you still interested?"

CHAPTER 11

"It's a Belter," Kate said to the woman inspecting the delicate rococo revival chair, upholstered in faded bottle-green velvet, that occupied a prominent spot in the front of the shop.

"Yes, I know." The woman, a sixtyish matron with silver hair and the tweedy look of the North Salem hunt set, straightened and looked around. Her blue eyes, caught in nets of fine wrinkles, sparkled. "Eighteen-sixties, I believe. A fine piece . . . where did you get it?"

"Sotheby's in New York." Kate pulled the chair away from the wall to better display the backrest with its unique design, a patented technique developed by Belter involving laminated layers of wood twisted into a scalloped pattern. "I have the documentation, of course, if you'd like to see it."

"That won't be necessary. It's my daughter I was thinking of, as a matter of fact. She collects Belter, and she's driving down from Boston later in the week. Would it be possible to put it on hold?"

"Certainly. Until Friday?" Kate's mind raced ahead. She'd promised to speak at the Northfield Historical Society's annual tea on Thursday, and the society's

president, Carolyn Atwater, had her eye on the Belter.
It wouldn't hurt to drop a hint that someone else was
interested. In any event, with January firmly under
way and Christmas quickly fading into memory, chances
of a sale were good. People were once more concentrating on home decorating as opposed to gift-buying.
And it really *was* an extraordinary piece.

"Oh, would you?" The woman clapped her hands
together.

Kate smiled. "I'd be happy to." She wrote down
her name and her daughter's—Mrs. Dora Keyes and
Mrs. Linda Shaffer.

As soon as Dora Keyes had left, with a merry tinkle
of the brass bell over the door, Kate lowered herself
onto the ottoman of a Georgian wing chair, part of a
display, grouped under subtly positioned track lights,
that mimicked the library of a British estate. She released the sigh that had been backed up in her lungs.

Kate thought: *She'll go home and call her daughter,
and one of her grandchildren will answer the phone.
She'll ask, "How was school today?" And the grandchild will say, "Grandma, when are you coming to
visit? I miss you."*

Kate shook her head to clear it. *What if she is a
grandmother ... it has nothing to do with me.* She
knew what was bothering her, though: Skyler. Her
daughter was determined to go through with this ...
this unnatural thing. Though she hadn't yet decided
on a couple to adopt her baby, Skyler had informed
Kate last night over the phone that she had someone
in mind.

Who *are* these people? Kate had wanted to demand.
But, in the end, did it really matter? She was sure
they were nice. That wasn't the point.

Kate's head ached, and in one temple there seemed
to be a miniature construction crew at work, hammering and drilling and sawing. Worse, she had no
one to talk to. Miranda was sympathetic, as always,

but she so strongly disapproved of Skyler's decision that it was hard for Kate not to feel as if she were somehow being disloyal to Skyler in discussing it with her friend. She couldn't go to Will, either. Mostly, he pretended it wasn't happening, and these days, what with all the grueling hours he'd been putting in at the office, he was like a steel rigging on the verge of collapse. So now it was up to her, Kate, to put on a brave face and hold everything together.

But, oh, dear Lord, what she would have given for a stronger pair of shoulders. Why was it always up to her to deal with family crises? Why the fabled green willow that bent with the wind, and not the mighty oak? Perhaps if she were more like Will, if she'd been less flexible with Skyler when she was growing up, this never would have happened.

Yet, perversely, it seemed that the more understanding Kate attempted to be, the more her daughter pulled away from her. Kate had tried not to be hurt. She'd told herself that Skyler was merely attempting to spare her and Will painful details about prospective couples. But, at the same time, Kate was resentful. How dare Skyler shut them out! Not even introducing them to the baby's father! All Kate knew was his name, Tony, and that he was a mounted policeman, of all things.

But confronting Skyler would only drive her further away. Better to move cautiously, wait for an opportunity, a weak moment when her daughter would need her and seek her advice. Kate was patient. She'd had to be.

In an hour, she was meeting Skyler at the Wormsley estate just north of Mahopac, where an auction would take place tomorrow. In *Art and Antiques Weekly*, Kate had seen a writing desk she thought would be perfect to take the place of the too-small one at Skyler's cabin. What Kate hadn't told Skyler was that there was also an enchanting spindle-sided cradle that

would be just right if she should happen to change
her mind about the baby.

Of course, she wouldn't do anything as obvious as
bring the cradle to Skyler's attention. But tomorrow,
at the auction, she would bid on it ... and if she got
it, store it in the back room until after the baby was
born ...

... just in case.

Driving east along I-84 in her maroon Volvo station
wagon, past snowy fields and farmhouses stilettoed
with ice, Kate felt tension building in her chest. It was
like the feeling she sometimes got as she was entering
the Lincoln Tunnel, just knowing she was about to be
trapped beneath a body of water exerting hundreds of
tons of pressure—water that might burst through the
concrete ceiling at any moment. Her foreboding was
one that any engineer would tell her was ridiculous,
and yet she believed it could come true. She believed
it all the way through the tunnel, until she emerged
into the light, where she could laugh at her silly fears.

There would be no light at the end of *this* tunnel,
though. The feeling she had was of something truly
terrible coming her way. She couldn't put her finger
on what it was, specifically, that she was dreading.
After all, hadn't the worst already happened? What
could be more terrible than her own grandchild being
given away to strangers?

Still, the thought lingered in the back of her mind:
*All these years, you've been waiting for the other shoe
to drop. And maybe this is it ... a kind of divine retri-
bution. You robbed Skyler's real mother, and now
you're being robbed of Skyler's child.*

Yes, perhaps that was what she was most afraid of:
having to face her own responsibility in all this. For
you couldn't cheat the gods without it catching up with
you one day. She had tampered with fate, and now
she would pay the price.

Kate forcibly shut her mind against those thoughts.

She turned off the highway, following the county road
that led to Wormsley. The estate sat at the end of a
long gravel drive, amid four acres of overgrown lawn
and flower beds gone to seed—a great heap of Victorian excess, complete with mildewed gables and peeling turrets, which had the look of a grand dame on
her last legs.

Kate parked the Volvo in front and picked her way
with the help of her cane over the icy ruts left by the
cars that had already arrived. Minutes later, she was
standing in the cavernous, tiled entry hall, thumbing
through the catalogue, when someone dropped a cool
kiss on her cheek. She looked up to find a red-cheeked
Skyler, in a short wool jacket and handknit blue scarf,
under which she wore thick black leggings and an
oversized Aran sweater. Kate suppressed an urge to
put her hand on the swell of her daughter's belly.

My grandchild, she thought with an ache so sharp
it made her wince. Skyler, now nearly seven months
along, often complained that the baby kept her up at
night with its kicking. How could she feel that, and
not want to keep it? The idea so mystified Kate that
she could not seem to put it out of her mind.

"I almost took the wrong turn at that last intersection," Skyler told her with a laugh, pulling off her
knitted cap with a breathless little shake of her head
that sent her hair crackling in a white-gold storm over
her shoulders. "God, can you believe it? I've driven
these roads a thousand times, and suddenly there I
was at the light not remembering which way to turn.

"It's not so strange," Kate said mildly. "You have
a lot on your mind."

Skyler frowned slightly, as if suspecting a hidden
meaning in that remark, then said, "I guess so."

Kate wanted to pull her daughter into her arms,
hold her tight until they were both starved for breath
and Skyler understood, in a way that words simply
could not convey, just how deeply and unconditionally

she was loved. Instead, she calmly helped Skyler off
with her coat, and hung it beside her own on the metal
coatrack at the door.

Leaning more heavily on her cane than when she'd
walked in, Kate slipped her free arm through Skyler's.
"Let's have a look at that desk, shall we? I've brought
along my tape measure so we can see if it'll fit against
the wall in the ... the study."

"Mom, it's *not* the study ... it's the extra bedroom,"
Skyler corrected her. "Just because I'm not planning
on turning it into a nursery doesn't mean we have to
act as if someone died or something."

Kate felt the blood leave her face. Before she could
stop herself, she snapped, "What an awful thing to
say!" Seeing several browsers glance her way, she immediately lowered her voice. Quietly, she added, "I
only meant that you'll be using it as a study when
you're in school."

"Mom, I'll be in New Hampshire."

"Well, you'll still come back to the cabin on weekends and holidays." Kate was careful not to reveal
what she was secretly hoping—that Skyler would
spend school holidays at Orchard Hill after the baby
was born. There would be more than enough room
for two, if she should change her mind.

They strolled around the once-grand parlor, with its
peeling wallpaper and crumbling ceiling molding. The
old parquet floors were hopelessly scuffed, and the
carved cherubim flanking the marble fireplace seemed
to remonstrate silently with the scarred wainscoting
and tattered drapes. Everywhere, tagged furniture was
clumped about haphazardly. Old Mrs. Wormsley had
died childless, and her estate, along with its contents,
was being auctioned off to pay the overdue taxes on it.

It came as a surprise to Kate when she discovered
that despite the mansion's state of disrepair, its fur-
nishings, for the most part, had been well cared for.
Mrs. Wormsley might not have had money for house

repairs, she thought, but the old lady or whoever had cleaned for her apparently had not lacked for elbow grease.

In the photocopied catalogue she carried rolled up under her arm, Kate marked off the number for a lovely burled-walnut corner cabinet before moving on to the desk she'd come to look at—a late Victorian oak rolltop, with only a few nicks and bruises. Nothing special, but it was practical and would certainly go with the rest of the furniture in the cabin.

"How much?" Skyler asked.

"Twelve to fifteen hundred," Kate said, peering at the estimate, in fine print below a brief description of the desk. "But I can probably get it for eight or nine. It'll be mostly dealers bidding, and since we won't have to factor in any markup we'll be in a better position to bargain."

"I don't know," Skyler said, running a finger along its dusty surface and bending to peer into a pigeon-hole. "It's a lot of money."

Kate considered offering to buy it for her ... then thought better of the idea. No, Skyler would never accept it. On the other hand, there was Skyler's trust, established by Kate's mother when Skyler was adopted. The principal was off-limits to Skyler until she turned twenty-five in two and a half more years, but as executor Kate could okay any purchase or withdrawal above and beyond the interest checks Skyler lived on.

"I'd be happy to talk to Ralph Brinker at the bank, if you like," she told Skyler.

Skyler shot her a puzzled look, and said, "What for?" Then, "Oh, *that.*" As if a five-hundred-thousand-dollar portfolio was hardly worth remembering. "Mom, I appreciate the offer ... but it really isn't necessary. The desk I have is just fine."

Kate sighed. Skyler had never asked for anything; she'd always been frighteningly independent, but Kate found herself hoping that in time those sharp corners

of her daughter's would become rounded. Skyler had
yet to learn that there was a kind of generosity in
receiving as well as in giving.

Out of the corner of her eye, Kate caught sight of
the cradle, a really exquisite example of the Eastlake
period, with hand-turned spindles and gold-detailed
inset carving. It was odd, she thought. The Wormsleys
had had no children, as far as anyone knew. Could
there once have been a baby that hadn't lived?

Kate felt her heart quicken. She stared at her
daughter, willing Skyler, who'd wandered off in the
other direction, to turn around and look at the cradle,
to *see* what it could mean to her.

*We don't always get a second chance, my darling.
When something good comes along, even if it's at a
bad time, you have to take it ... or it might never
come again.*

*And sometimes you have to do more than just take
it,* she thought darkly.

But Kate could only watch helplessly as Skyler
drifted off without a glance at the cradle, heading instead for a dark painting of a gondola gliding along a
Venetian canal. Kate, feeling absurdly disappointed,
merely circled the cradle's number in the catalogue.
She didn't care how high the bidding went, she was
determined to get it. For her, it was more than a po-
tential gift to her grandchild; it was a sign of hope
that Skyler would change her mind.

They poked around some more, but other than a
silver epergne that just needed polishing to be stun-
ning, Kate didn't see anything of particular interest.
After a while, her hip began to ache, and she saw that
Skyler was looking restless.

"Hungry?" Kate asked. "We could get a bite at the
café in town you like so much. Or," she added, "we
could go back to the house."

"The Cat's Cradle? I could eat half a dozen of their
blueberry muffins right now." Skyler, ignoring Kate's

mention of the house, gave a rueful laugh. "God, I feel like I haven't stopped eating since I got over having morning sickness. I've gained fifteen pounds so far, and I still have almost two months to go."

Kate felt the muscles in her face freeze, and quickly looked away so Skyler wouldn't see. In a voice of practiced lightness, she asked, "What did Dr. Firebaugh have to say when you went for your last appointment?"

"According to her, I'm healthy as a horse. She wants me to start Lamaze class next week." Skyler paused, then said, "I've asked Mickey to be my coach."

"What about—?" Kate started to ask about Tony, then thought better of it. What did she know about the man other than that he and Skyler had remained friendly? What if he didn't want to be involved beyond that? She forced a smile, and said, "Mickey can handle just about anything, I'd imagine."

"The worst part will be having her stay with me the week before I'm due. We'll probably be on each other's nerves the whole time."

"Better that than be stranded in the middle of nowhere with nobody to look after you if something should go wrong," Kate reminded her sharply.

Skyler said nothing.

This was one discussion that had had most of the tread worn off it already; Kate and Will insisting that Skyler move back in with them the week before Skyler's due date ... and Skyler being equally insistent on doing it her way, which would mean a twenty-minute drive from Gipsy Trail to Northfield Community Hospital.

Kate was still on edge when they reached the café, where they were tucked into a sunny corner beneath a pair of alphabet samplers. Skyler had yet to broach the subject of adoptive couples. And, truthfully, Kate had been avoiding it, too. However wonderful and car-

ing they might be, she didn't want to know about the
couple Skyler had chosen to be the parents of her
child. She couldn't bear the thought of their having
actual names and identities, of Skyler's decision becoming a reality as opposed to a mere threat.

When their waitress came, she ordered hot tea and
a grilled chicken sandwich. Skyler, despite all her talk
of a huge appetite, wanted only soup and a glass of
milk. Kate eyed her, full of concern. Skyler could jok-
ingly complain all she wanted about gaining weight,
but the bald fact was she looked pale and drawn.

*She might be adamant about her decision ... but
she's not happy about it.* Kate recognized the signs—
the way Skyler's gaze flickered around the room, taking in everything and everyone but Kate; the restless
way she folded and refolded her gingham napkin, and
the high color she wore on her milk-pale cheeks.

Kate waited until they'd finished their lunch before
saying anything. Patting her mouth with her napkin,
she carefully reapplied her lipstick. It seemed she was
able to speak her mind best when wearing lipstick.

"I ran into Duncan this morning. He sends his
best," she said, snapping her purse shut. "He asked if
you'd made up your mind yet, about the couples
you've seen. I told him you had, but frankly, Skyler,
I felt really awful admitting I hadn't a clue as to
which one."

Skyler looked down at her empty soup bowl. "I
wasn't sure you'd approve."

Kate felt a mild jolt of alarm. Approve? She hadn't
approved of *any* of this.

It wasn't just Skyler; it was the financial strain she
and Will had been under, too. Though they'd managed
to stave off bankruptcy by mortgaging Orchard Hill,
the firm was still a long way from being in the black.
Will was scrambling to buy them more time, but
meanwhile they had the proverbial sword dangling
over their heads. She thought of how she'd felt signing

the bank papers on her beloved Orchard Hill—as if she'd been signing away her life.

And now she might have something even worse to contend with.

"I can't imagine you'd choose anyone we wouldn't like." Kate forced her frozen mouth to smile. She felt as if she were chewing ice.

"It's not that you wouldn't like her," Skyler said, scooping her hair away from her face and holding it back with one hand—a nervous gesture that made Kate even more tense and alert. "It's just that . . . Ellie and her husband are separated."

Ellie?

A part of Kate's brain registered alarm, the way it would at a siren's distant wail, but she quickly convinced herself she was being paranoid. Even so, she found herself asking, "Does this woman have a last name?"

"Actually, it's *Dr.* Nightingale, but she told me to call her Ellie."

The alarm Kate had been staving off sank its sharp teeth into her gut. She didn't need to summon up the memory of the young psychologist in training whom fate had seen fit to throw in her path on that terrifying night, fourteen years ago, when Skyler had hovered near death. The incident stood clear in Kate's mind . . . as clear as the handwriting that was now on the wall.

Kate was aware of a roaring in her ears, like ocean surf. In a sea of blue gingham and knotty pine, she floated, weightless, while others—waitresses and customers, a man delivering a huge bottle of water—drifted slowly past.

"Ellie Nightingale." Kate, suspended in her dreamy state, repeated the name as slowly and carefully as a password muttered outside a door she feared walking through.

"You can't forget a name like that." Skyler's lips

moved, but there seemed to be a split-second delay before the words reached Kate's ears.

"No." She felt blood rising in her cheeks.

"I know this is going to sound weird, Mom, but it's almost like I've known her all my life ... like this was meant to be. I can't explain it, it's just something I *feel.*" Anxiously, she searched Kate's face. "Have you ever felt that way about anyone?"

Kate remained stupidly still, unable to speak.

Below the table, she was gripping her hands together so tightly her knuckles felt as if they might pop right through her skin. The floating sensation of a moment ago had been replaced by a prickly numbness, as if the part of her that had gone to sleep was slowly crawling back to life. A thought kept repeating itself over and over in her mind, like a continuous digital readout scrolling across the lower half of a TV screen, warning of an impending storm front.

I must not let her know. I must not let her know. . . .

But Skyler could see that something was wrong, because she was leaning across the table, her forehead creased with concern. "Mom, are you okay?"

"Yes ... yes ... I'm fine." Kate mustered every shred of self-control she possessed. "It's just ... I know we talked about it ... but it's a shock, now that there's an actual person who'll be taking my grandchild away from me.

Skyler winced and said, "I wish you wouldn't see it that way."

"How else *can* I?" Kate was glad for the anger she felt—it helped her to focus. "Skyler, I understand why you're doing this. I told you I would support you no matter what—but you can't expect me to be happy about it. And now you're telling me this woman isn't even married."

"I know what you're thinking," Skyler said. "I came up with all the same arguments. But the thing is, I trust her. If I let Ellie adopt my baby, I know it'll be okay." She stopped, her eyes filling with tears. "Mom, don't you see? I need to be *sure*."

Kate wanted to shout at her daughter that there was no such thing as being sure. Certainty, she had learned, was quickest to elude those who sought most desperately to achieve it. Each birthday that Skyler had celebrated growing up had been like a milestone on a road that stretched in a straight line as far as Kate could see. But now she realized that all this time she'd merely being going in one great circle.

Yes, but what if it's a chance to redeem yourself?

The thought rang in her head.

Kate saw the two options that diverged before her, like Robert Frost's roads in a yellow wood. She could fight this; she could come up with arguments that would make Ellie sound like the *worst* choice. It wouldn't be hard. A single woman? What could Skyler be *thinking?* Kate had every reason to object!

At the same time, a persistent voice in the back of her head, like an ever-dutiful sentry, whispered, *Beware. If you take the wrong step now, there will be no turning back.*

Suddenly, Kate knew which road to choose. She must go along with this bizarre turn of fate which maybe wasn't so bizarre.

Through her silence she could help right a terrible wrong.

Kate took a shaky breath, unfastening her fingers stiffly, one by one, feeling bright pinpoints of pain shoot out from her joints. *Will, forgive me,* she thought.

In a steady voice that in no way reflected the emotions rising in her like black floodwater—fear, anguish, remorse, awe, and, yes, hope—Kate answered, "Tell me. . . . I want to understand."

It was the harshest winter Kate could remember. One snowstorm followed another, each more fierce and crippling than the last. Roads closed, reopened, and were closed again. Mail and packages were delivered late, or not at all. There had been a run on rock salt at Duffy's Hardware, and the only snow shovels to be had were the ones that could be borrowed or stolen. Glynden Pond, for the first time in more than a decade, was frozen solid—but too packed with snow for anyone to skate on. At the shop, and all along Main Street, for that matter, customers dwindled to a hardy few. Even the nuthatches and chickadees that normally flocked around Kate's bird feeders seemed to have fled.

Even so, there were moments—when she was standing at the picture window that overlooked the front yard, watching a new snowfall erase the pocked and muddy remains of the last—when a wonderful sense of calm descended on Kate. The snow, she felt, was a kind of baptism, a washing away of old sins. As if God, with one great celestial sweep of His hand, was giving the world—and her—a second chance.

The trouble was, the feeling never lasted. Before long, the old grayness would creep over her once again. Her leg and hip would start to ache, and she would start counting the hours until her next Advil. No matter how busy she kept herself—and lord knew there was plenty to do both at Orchard Hill and at the shop—Kate couldn't shake the sluggishness that seemed to have settled into her bones like lead sinkers on a fishing line.

Even Will, who rarely noticed her moods, went out of his way to be solicitous. When he was home, which wasn't often, he carefully avoided talking about Skyler. He occasionally brought Kate a mug of hot tea even when she hadn't asked for it, and on Sundays he pulled out her favorite sections of the *Times* and gave them to her to read first.

And yet Kate had never felt so distant from her husband. Upon learning that the woman who would be adopting Skyler's baby was none other than Ellie, he'd simply clammed up and refused to discuss the issue. Kate longed to be able to talk to him about this strange, almost religious conviction she had that they were being given a chance to realign the scales of justice. It was no accident that Ellie had come back into their lives. Even Skyler had a sixth sense about Ellie . . . and she didn't know the half of it.

But Will, damn it, refused even to see that there *was* a wrong in need of righting. And Kate couldn't have explained why she was determined not to let this remarkable opportunity pass her by.

In some ways, she felt guilty for harboring sour feelings toward her husband. He was fighting a different kind of war, one she had not yet felt the full brunt of. Even the not-so-small risk of their losing Orchard Hill didn't seem real to her. Not to be here? Not look out her window and spy a raccoon sitting up on its haunches sniffing up at the suet ball hung out for the cardinals? Not to see the sun slanting in through the icicles on the eaves, making them sparkle like diamonds? Unimaginable. Yet she had shared none of those feelings with Will; she kept her own counsel.

Miranda had been Kate's sole comfort. More and more, she was taking charge at the shop, relieving Kate of the mundane while freeing her to do what she liked best—buying and restoring. Miranda also instinctively knew when Kate needed small talk to distract her from her own thoughts . . . and when to listen without offering advice. She refrained from talking about her own adorable grandchild, and Kate knew without a doubt that nothing she told Miranda in confidence would be repeated. And not once had she asked about the cradle stored under a canvas dropcloth in the back room.

If Miranda *had* asked, Kate might have told her how she ached with the knowledge that she most likely would never hold her grandchild in her arms;

that she wouldn't have snapshots like the ones taped over Miranda's file cabinet. She would have told her friend how she sometimes cried into her pillow at night, thinking of all the birthdays she would celebrate only in her heart, all the candles that would never be wished on. Even her own daughter seemed to be slipping away; Skyler hardly visited, and never seemed very glad to hear from her when Kate called.

It was toward the end of March, early one sunstruck morning when the world lay dreaming under a blanket of new snow, that Kate received the phone call she'd been both anxiously awaiting and dreading.

"I'm on my way to the hospital," Skyler informed Kate with maddening calm. "Don't worry, Mom, please . . . there's still loads of time. I'm only in the first stage. And Mickey promises to drive carefully for a change."

"I'll meet you there," Kate told her, swinging out of bed even as she spoke. "Just let me throw on some clothes. I'll call Daddy from the car phone—he's in the city."

She was in a state of near frenzy as she showered, then pulled on slacks and a black cashmere turtleneck. Minutes later, she was backing her Volvo out of the garage, praying that she wouldn't hit any icy patches or run into any snowdrifts. She forced herself to take the road slowly, even while her heart pounded, and her hands gripped the wheel so tightly that after a few minutes they were numb. A sixties poster slogan (a particularly smarmy one, she'd always thought) popped into her head: "Today is the first day of the rest of your life."

Wound up as if from the coffee she'd been in too much of a hurry to brew, Kate had to remind herself over and over that first labors generally fell into the category of hurry-up-and-wait. But all she could think was *I have to get there in time.*

In time to at least see—and maybe hold—her grand-child, before it was too late.

At Northfield Community Hospital, a nurse directed her to the maternity wing on the fifth floor. Walking into Skyler's private room, Kate, who'd been expecting something stark and sterile, was pleasantly surprised to find it carpeted, with a rocking chair in one corner and bright yellow walls hung with Renoir prints.

Skyler, dressed only in an oversized T-shirt, lay curled on her side on the bed while Mickey rubbed the small of her back with competent circular strokes. With her hair caught back in a ponytail, and a pair of fuzzy pink socks on her feet, Skyler looked like a little girl—far too young to be having a baby. Kate, her heart climbing up into her throat, had to fight the urge to feel her daughter's forehead as she had when Skyler was small.

"Mom." Skyler cocked an eyebrow at her and smiled.

"I'm here, sweetie. Can I get you anything?" Kate smoothed a stray wisp from her daughter's forehead, which did in fact feel hot and clammy.

Skyler shook her head. "Mickey thought of everything. She even remembered my Walkman, though I don't think even Bruce Springsteen could get me through—ooohhh, here comes another one." She scrunched her arms and legs in tightly around her huge stomach, her face flushing an alarmingly bright red.

Mickey glanced up at Kate, her usual devil-may-care grin looking a bit frayed around the edges. "I keep telling her this is good practice for when she's tending foaling mares."

"*God.*" As abruptly as a sailor's knot jerked loose, Skyler collapsed, panting, onto her back. "That's exactly what it feels like—as if I'm giving birth to a

Percheron." A fine mist of sweat shone on her fore-head and upper lip.

Kate smiled as she dabbed at her daughter's fore-head with a damp washcloth. But she could see from the pinched tautness around Skyler's mouth, and the bruised circles under her eyes, that she was scared of more than just giving birth.

She doesn't know yet what she's giving up....

Kate put the washcloth back in its basin and sank into the chair beside the bed. "Daddy should be here soon," she told Skyler. "I had trouble reaching him, but he's on his way."

"That's good." Skyler's eyes fluttered closed. "I was just thinking . . ."

"What?" Kate leaned closer.

"Tony should be here," she murmured thickly, al-most as if talking in her sleep. "He wanted me to call him . . . and I promised I would. But, oh, I don't know."

Kate felt a fist form in her stomach. Though she'd never laid eyes on him, she thought she knew how Tony must feel. To be shut out of his own child's birth! Just as she herself had been shut out of Skyler's pregnancy. No matter what his feelings toward Skyler, he should know she was in labor.

Then it struck Kate: however casual his relationship with Skyler, Tony might actually want this baby. If he were here, he might be able to persuade Skyler to change her mind. There was still time.

Then it would be out of your hands. You wouldn't be responsible.

"Would you like me to call him?" Kate asked softly.

Skyler rolled her head back on the pillow. "Yes . . . no . . . oh, God, I—Oh!" Her face clenched in a frozen grimace of pain.

Mickey caught Kate's eye, and mouthed the words "I'll do it." But all she said was, "Mind filling in for a few minutes while I take a break?"

Skyler's obstetrician walked into the room just as

Mickey was stepping out. Dr. Firebaugh was a young black woman who, in Kate's eyes, didn't look old enough to have her bachelor's degree, much less her M.D. Her voice was gentle and soothing as she examined Skyler.

"Six centimeters—you're farther along than I would have expected for a first baby," she said in her clipped West Indian accent. "But you're doing just fine. Baby's heartbeat is nice and strong. Don't you worry about a thing."

Not worry? Didn't she *know*? Kate thought.

Will arrived as the doctor was leaving, looking pale and anxious.

"It's going to be okay, Daddy," Skyler, pale and shaken-looking, was quick to reassure him even as she pulled the sheet up around her. "It's not so terrible. Not yet anyway. I can handle it."

" I'm not sure *I* can," he joked, but there was nothing funny in the strained whiteness about his mouth and the way his eyes kept darting in the direction of the door, as if to make sure his exit hadn't been sealed off.

"Mom, get him out of here," Skyler implored with a weak laugh. "Find him an extra bed or something." She winced as another contraction began to take hold.

Just then, Mickey returned, wearing a closed, secretive look.

"She'll be fine without us for a few minutes," Kate told Will, her smile pinned in place as she took his arm. "Why don't we get a cup of coffee?"

Will nodded and followed her out of the room. In the solarium at the end of the corridor, they sat and sipped bad coffee while Will pretended to read *The Wall Street Journal* and she made believe they were just another middle-aged couple excitedly awaiting the birth of their grandchild. They didn't talk. There was nothing to discuss. Everything had already been decided upon. In a strange way, he even seemed resigned to Ellie's being the adoptive mother; either that, or he simply hadn't acknowledged the cosmic irony of it . . . even to himself.

Kate found a curious sympathy for her husband welling up in her. She'd been angry with him for letting her down—for making *her* responsible for what they were both guilty of. But looking at Will now, with his head bowed over the paper, his eyes absently tracking events and negotiations happening half a world away, Kate understood at last that it was better to be burdened than to be blind. Somehow, she would gain strength from this. Will, when the time of reckoning came, wouldn't even see it coming.

Kate waited until she was sure she couldn't bear waiting a minute more: then she forced herself to sit still another fifteen minutes. Finally she got up, and placed a hand on Will's shoulder. "You wait here while I look in on her." She was surprised at how firm and authoritative she sounded, and Will must have been, too, for he blinked before nodding and going back to his newspaper.

As soon as she walked back into their daughter's room, Kate felt the baling wire holding her together suddenly snap loose.

A familiar woman sat in the chair by the bed, holding the washcloth to Skyler's forehead. A woman she hadn't seen in nearly a decade and a half—but whose face had haunted her, both sleeping and awake, nearly every day since.

Ellie hadn't changed much, Kate noted in some detached part of her mind. She was still slender, but there were a few more lines around the eyes and mouth. And a sadness in her eyes that the smile she wore hadn't quite dispelled.

Kate suppressed a hysterical laugh at the sheer *drama* of the scene—even down to the hospital backdrop. A sane voice sternly brought her up short: *It's*

*really happening. Your worst nightmare, and you can
do nothing to stop it.*

As if in a cruel mirror image of Kate's own ministrations, Ellie held Skyler's hand while gently patting her face with the wet cloth. Mother and child. The thought came at Kate like a blow to the side of her head, so that she reeled and nearly lost her balance. She reached out, grabbing hold of the iron rail at the foot of the bed as her cane toppled to the floor.

"Where's Mickey?" she asked in a high, thready voice that sounded only vaguely like her own. It was the only thing that popped into her head.

"She'll be back in a minute." Ellie eased her hand from Skyler's and stood up. She looked puzzled as she searched Kate's face, but her gaze was direct and unflinching. "Hello. I'm Ellie Nightingale."

An awkward silence stretched between them as Ellie put out her hand.

In a cracked whisper, Kate managed, "Yes, I know . . . we've met." She'd be a fool not to acknowledge it, she thought. Ellie wouldn't have recognized Skyler, after all these years, as the little girl she'd once brought comfort to in the hospital. But sooner or later, Ellie was bound to recognize *her.*

Ellie, clearly taken aback, said, "You *do* look familiar."

"It's been a long time." Kate's mouth felt dry and numb, as if she'd just been to the dentist's. "We met at Langdon in 1980. You were working there, and my daughter was brought in for emergency surgery."

Ellie blanched, and took a step backward. "God. I'd forgotten. But now that you . . . oh, yes, I *do* remember it now. It was so long ago . . . and there were so many patients. But your little girl—" She cast a glance at Skyler, as if seeing her for the first time. At once, the blood drained from her face. In a low, shaky voice, she said, "It . . . it all makes sense now. The feeling that we'd known each other from somewhere else. We both felt it . . . right from the start."

Her words sent a chill up Kate's spine.

How can you look at Skyler and not know? screamed a voice in her head.

Then reason took hold. True, if you saw them side by side you would notice a faint resemblance, Kate thought, but only if you really looked for it. Skyler's eyes were a lighter blue, her features fine where Ellie's were more pronounced. Ellie's mouth was fuller, and her hair several shades darker. Only Skyler's hands gave her away—they were carbon copies of her mother's: large, almost man-sized, with broad flat nails at the end of tapering fingers.

Kate tried not to stare, but she couldn't seem to help it. Paralyzed, she stood transfixed by the small mole on Ellie's right thumb.

It was Skyler who broke the spell. "Mom, I asked her to come." Her voice carried a note of apology. "I wanted her to be here when the baby—*her* baby—is born."

"Would you like me to wait outside?" Ellie asked, looking directly at Kate. She was wearing a deep purple sweater that made her pale skin look oddly bleached, but otherwise she appeared strong and composed.

Next to her, Kate felt small and mean and powerless.

"No . . . no, of course not," she murmured weakly.

Ellie, to Kate's horror, looked as if she were about to cry. "I know how hard this must be for you," she said in a low voice fraught with compassion. "Believe me, I do. But I want you to know that this baby will be loved more than you can possibly imagine."

Kate didn't know what to say. She felt stricken by the brightness in Ellie's eyes, and by the wave of heat that seized her like a hot flash. She wanted to slap Ellie, slap her right out of the room. At the same time, she wanted to kneel down and beg her forgiveness. And while she was on her knees, she would plead with God for mercy ... this God of hers, who appeared to have not only an infinite capacity for inflicting pain, but a terrible, maniacal sense of humor as well.

"I'm sorry," she blurted. Then, realizing she'd spoken her thoughts aloud, Kate quickly added, "I wish I could think of something to say ... but there just doesn't seem to be any way of making this any less awkward. I can't offer you my congratulations. I wish things had turned out differently, that we weren't having this conversation. But ... I—I've made peace with my daughter's decision."

Ellie did not answer.

Kate opened her mouth to say something innocuous, but was stopped by a low, keening moan that built until it was nearly a scream.

Skyler, she saw as she rushed to her daughter's side, was convulsed in agony, her spine arched as she forced her words through clenched teeth. "I feel like I have to push."

Kate was dimly aware of her own pain, like knives slicing up her leg.

As if from a great distance, she heard Ellie say, "I'll get the doctor."

Skyler had never experienced anything like this—pain worse than any fall off a horse. Her whole body was on fire, and her pelvis was on the verge of cracking apart like a dry wishbone. Good God Almighty, how did anyone *live* through this?

She needed to push this thing *out*—

But now the urge was fading.

As the invisible ropes lashed about her belly began to loosen a bit, she became aware of her mother holding her, and felt an overwhelming sense of being a little girl again, safe in the circle of her mother's arms.

Skyler felt the whisper of Mom's breath in her hair, and the calm strength that flowed from her.

She caught a blurred glimpse of Dr. Firebaugh, hovering at the foot of the bed. She was aware of Mickey, too, instructing her to breathe, for chrissakes, *breathe*.

But something was wrong. Something—no, *someone*—was missing.

Tony should be here, she thought, wanting to weep at his absence.

But hadn't he gone through enough already? If she couldn't spare *herself* the awfulness of all this, and of giving up their baby, then at least she could spare him.

Skyler could feel another contraction coming on—tighter, more painful than before. And this time she *did* have to push. She bore down, and heard something pop in her ears, followed by a high, rushing noise like a thousand angels singing.

The truth came to her in that moment . . . what her heart had known but her mind could not accept: *My baby. Our baby. Tony's and mine. God help me, I didn't know what I'd be giving up.*

Like someone drowning, she clung to her mother, feeling the love that had shone down on her all her life, never wavering, never more than a heartbeat or a hand's reach away. And she wanted that for her baby, too—a mother whose devotion owed nothing to blood, only to a generosity of spirit, and an infinite capacity for giving. She wanted it enough to make what she could already feel was going to be a much greater sacrifice than she had bargained for. . . .

Kate supported her daughter's shoulders while Skyler heaved and panted. "It's going to be okay," she soothed. "You'll do just fine. You're so brave, darling."

She wished she could say the same of herself. She felt lightheaded, and more than a little unsteady. The room shimmered around her, giving her a queer feeling as if she were submerged in some vast aquarium.

Kate remembered how it had been in her day—the fearful isolation her friends had described: wives quarantined from their husbands, gurneys wheeled at a breakneck pace from labor ward to delivery room, babies pried from drugged mothers with forceps. She marveled at the messy spectacle of birth in the modern age. When you got right down to it, wasn't it just a throwback to the days of village midwives?

Now, like generations of women before her, Kate held her daughter braced against her, supporting her as Skyler strained and heaved.

Then Skyler's water broke with a sound like a rubber band snapping, soaking the sterile pad that had been placed under her.

Mickey went on barking out instructions on how to breathe.

The pretty West Indian doctor, wearing a mask and surgical gloves, was bent over, peering between Skyler's raised knees.

"Oh ... *God* ... I can't take it!" Skyler screamed, her face convulsing.

"Yes, you can. Bear down. *Now,*" the doctor urged calmly.

"I have to ... oh God ... no ... I can't ... *It hurts too much—*" Her next words were swallowed by a raw, savage grunt that ended in a mighty push.

Kate, feeling as if she might faint, smoothed away the wet strands stuck to Skyler's forehead. She caught a glimpse of Ellie out of the corner of her eye, poised at the foot of the bed, wearing an expression of reverent wonder. Though she stood a good distance away, it seemed as if Ellie and Skyler were connected somehow, linked by some ghostly thread that only Kate could see.

"The head—I can see the head!" yelled Mickey,

who looked as if *she* were the one about to give birth, her curly dark hair damp and matted, her face flushed.

"You can relax a bit now, stop pushing," the doctor ordered. "I need to turn the head. There. Give me just one more big one, Skyler. Let's see what we've got here. . . ."

Skyler bore down with an animal cry that raised the hair on the back of Kate's neck.

"A girl!" a voice cried—a voice that sounded very much like Ellie's—as something small and wet and dark slithered out between Skyler's thighs.

The baby let out a gargled yelp.

Skyler began to weep. She held out her arms as her newborn daughter was placed on her chest, still attached to its pulsing turquoise cord. Gently, she cupped a hand about the tiny wet head at her breast.

Kate gaped at the miniature girl with her great thatch of black hair, feeling as if she were in a tunnel moving rapidly toward a distant glimmer of light. She'd heard death described this way, but now she was struck by a kind of dazed epiphany: that dying and being born were really the same, both a matter of letting go.

And that was what she must do now.

Kate sat perfectly still, hardly daring to breathe, as Ellie approached the bed, her awestruck gaze fastened on the baby, now in the arms of the doctor, wrapped in a white cotton blanket.

If Ellie had plunged a dagger into Kate's heart, they would have been even—but this . . . this was even worse. Kate watched as Ellie drew near, her arms tentatively, hopefully outstretched, her high, sculpted cheeks wet with tears. She forced herself to watch, knowing that Will wouldn't have, and also feeling a sense of duty. She had to see this through. She didn't know exactly why, or for whom, just that it was so.

But as Ellie, with a muffled gasp, took the small white-wrapped bundle in her arms, Kate couldn't look.

She closed her eyes. It was right ... it was fair ... but it *hurt.*

The only thing left to cling to—the thought that kept her from jumping up and wresting the baby from Ellie's arms—was the reason she had been placed in this unendurable position.

I still have Skyler. I'll always have her.

And Skyler would never have to know of the terrible price Kate had paid.

All Skyler knew was that she felt empty. Hollowed out, lighter than air. As if she'd been measured out in spoonfuls, and now there was nothing left of her. Long after everyone had tiptoed away to let her sleep, she lay on her back in the bed, with only her dismal thoughts for company.

Tears leaked from the corners of her eyes and slid down her temples into her matted hair. *Baby ... I'm sorry ... sorrier than you'll ever know ... but don't you see? It had to be this way. It would have been selfish of me to keep you ... as selfish in its way as my own mother's walking out on me.*

What Skyler hadn't told anyone was that in the last month before her baby's birth, she'd somehow known it was going to be a girl, and had secretly named her: Anna. Simple, yet solid, a name that would not go out of fashion. A name that would last through the decades.

Anna, I love you. I'll always be your mother in my heart.

Skyler, choking back a sob, squeezed her eyes shut. When she opened them, she saw a familiar face hovering over her, and for a moment thought she'd somehow drifted asleep and was dreaming. Then a large warm hand settled over hers, folding her fingers inside his like the petals of a flower that hasn't yet bloomed.

"Tony." The name caught in Skyler's throat like the sob she hadn't dared let go of.

He was standing with his back to the soft light that glowed from the small table by her bed, his solid frame throwing a shadow that angled up the wall, his strong face looking down on her with such tenderness she could hardly bear it.

A callused finger traced a tear as it creased her temple. Eyes as black as midnight glimmered with sympathy, and maybe with more ... with shared loss. For Tony had lost something precious as well: the chance to know his tiny daughter. He had not even had the fleeting joy of seeing her.

"I got here as soon as I could," he told her in an odd, thick voice. "We were out on an all-hands detail in Brooklyn, and I didn't get Mickey's message until I got back to the barn." He managed a brave grin. "She left two, as a matter of fact."

"Oh, Tony—" Skyler gripped his hand, kneading it convulsively as she fought back tears. "She—It was a girl, did they tell you? She's so beautiful. You should have seen her. All that black hair. She looks a lot like you."

"Skyler ... Jesus ..." Tony sank down on the mattress, and gathered her in his arms as she began to weep. He was crying, too; she could tell from the way his body shook, not trembled, but actually *shook,* as if some powerful, invisible force beyond his control had him in its teeth. And she knew that if he lived to be a hundred, he would not put this night behind him. He would not forget the daughter they had conceived in senseless passion ... or the love that had miraculously sprung up between them like a blade of grass forcing its way through a sidewalk.

Skyler threaded her fingers through his hair, and held his head tightly to her breast. "I'm sorry," she breathed. "I had to, Tony. I had to ... for *her.* Please don't hate me."

"Skyler, I don't hate you." With a deep breath, he drew back, and she saw at once what the mighty effort to compose himself had cost him—the deep furrows in his cheeks that hadn't been there a moment ago, the eyes that stared out at her like spent bullet shells. "Jesus, this is hard. I just wish—Christ, I wish it could have been different."

"So do I," she murmured. "Oh, God, so do I."

He touched her hair, stroking it lightly. "I love you."

In a broken voice, she answered, "Don't say that unless you mean it."

"I love you," he repeated stubbornly.

"It won't work," she told him. "We can't ... After today, how can we ever look at each other again and not feel ... *this*?" She knuckled a tear from her cheek with an angry gesture.

"Even being all ripped up inside," he told her, "is better than pretending it never happened." He drew the back of his fingers down the side of her face, leaving a light trail of goosebumps. "Tell me about her," he said softly. "Tell me everything you can remember."

And Skyler did. As she lay there, hollowed-out, afloat like a raft on a sea of self-loathing and unfulfilled love, she told him about the baby girl she'd secretly named Anna.

CHAPTER 12

S hortly before noon on a bright, meat-locker-cold
Monday morning, Tony sat astride his horse at
the intersection of Thirty-fourth Street and
Eighth Avenue, waiting for the light to change. He
and Grabinsky, the officer assigned to the post adjoining his, were about to break for lunch when a silver
Jaguar, going much too fast, made a squealing, illegal
turn against the light onto Eighth, nearly clipping
Scotty's hind end. Tony felt the horse give a startled
jump, and he squeezed the bay tightly to keep him
from bolting. Out of the corner of his eye, he caught
a flash of silver as the Jag caromed up Eighth.

"Asshole." Tony's exhaled breath spiked the frozen
air like an exclamation point. A minute ago, he'd been
shivering with the unseasonable chill that had descended this last week in April like winter's last laugh.
Now he felt a coal of anger igniting in his gut, its low
blue flame spreading through him.

With a short nod at Grabinsky, he hooked Scotty
in the ribs with his blunt-edged brass spurs. The bay
broke into a canter and rounded the corner onto
Eighth. One block north, at Thirty-fifth Street, the

traffic light blinked from yellow to red, and the Jag slowed. *Now I've got you,* Tony thought.

But the Jag didn't stop—it swerved around a braking taxi and shot through the intersection. *Shit.* Tony urged his horse into a gallop. He tried to make out the Jag's license plate as it headed toward Thirty-sixth, but it was too far away. He pushed Scotty on, staying clear of the traffic while effortlessly cutting around the double-parked cars and vans on his right. The jolting rhythm of Scotty's borium-studded shoes had a galvanizing effect on him. It was as if he'd tapped into a current of electricity that lay below the surface of the streets he knew so well.

Fingers of hard, cold light poked between buildings and flashed off hoods and windshields grimy from last week's rainstorm. Tony, thankful for his helmet's visor, kept his eyes trained on the glittering bumper a block ahead. If the light changed, and the asshole didn't run it again, he just might be able to catch him.

His breath came in hard-packed, steamy gusts. He thought of the truncheon tucked into a loop on his McClellan saddle, and the .38 Smith & Wesson on his Sam Browne belt. He wouldn't use them against this guy—unless the creep decided to get cute—but it was good to know they were at his disposal.

He lost sight of the Jag, then picked it up again a moment later as it made a left on Thirty-seventh. Christ, it was getting away.

Tony was damned if he was going to let that happen. He imagined the driver to be a high-level corporate executive, or a surgeon maybe . . . the kind of guy who'd become so used to giving orders and having people suck up to him, he no longer believed that rules applied to him. He'd look down his nose at any man his daughter brought home if the poor slob didn't pull down a six-figure income and boast a 212 area code, with a zip code on the Upper East Side.

In a burst of frustration, Tony pulled sharply on his

right rein, and in the same instant leaned heavily to that side, sending Scotty hurtling up over the curb and onto the sidewalk. The bay cut across the corner between a startled-looking hot pretzel vendor and a woman who cowered against a newsstand as if under mortar attack. As Scotty clattered back onto the street, Tony picked up a gleam of silver half a block ahead. The Jag braked as it swerved around a double-parked truck, and Tony finally got a glimpse of its vanity plate: NO 1 BOSS.

Yeah? We'll see about that, he thought.

The driver must have spotted him in the rearview mirror just then, because he did the stupidest thing imaginable for a guy smart enough to have earned the bucks for such a car—he made an abrupt left turn into a parking garage, maybe hoping to blend in with the other cars. Yeah, like silver Jags with vanity plates were a dime a dozen in this part of town.

Tony slowed his horse to a trot as he headed down the concrete ramp. Scotty was heaving, and Tony leaned over to pat his steaming neck. He was smiling as he dismounted. And judging by the scared-shitless look on the face of the man climbing sheepishly out of the Jag idling in front of the attendant's booth, it wasn't the type of smile designed to win friends. Tony sauntered up to the driver—a middle-aged executive type in a pinstriped suit. His carefully styled hair exactly matched the Jag's finish.

"You got a problem, friend," Tony began in a voice that was as hard as it was even. "In fact, you got *several.* One"—he held up his index finger—"making an illegal turn. Two"—up went his second finger—"running a red light. Three"—up went his ring finger—"attempting to elude an officer of the law." Looping the reins over Scotty's neck, he stepped in closer. "Lucky for you it's no crime being an asshole," he added. "But let me tell you something, mister: if you'd so much as touched a hair on my horse, I'd have had you cuffed so fast you wouldn't know what hit you."

"Listen, do you know who you're talking to?" The man warbled in indignation. "You can't talk to me that way. This ... this is police brutality." He made an attempt to puff himself up, but it was as futile as pumping air into a leaky tire.

Tony's smile stretched into a grin that caused the guy to take a step backward. Out of the corner of his eye, he caught a glimpse of the Latino attendant hovering just outside his glass booth, as if trying to decide whether or not to run for cover. Almost on cue, Scotty neighed loudly and brought a hoof down against the concrete floor with a flinty *klonk*.

"You don't even want to know about it." Tony spoke quietly, but with an undercurrent of something that made the man's eyes widen and his mouth snap shut.

Tony pulled out his book, and with quick hard strokes wrote out the summons. The prick wouldn't go to jail, but he'd swallow a fine that would make those designer glasses of his fog up.

Minutes later, trotting down Eighth in search of Grabinsky, Tony found himself mulling over the whole incident. Scotty had come through like a champ. And he, Sergeant Salvatore, had done his job—and even managed to let off some steam in the process. So why did he still feel lousy? And what was it about that Jag that had pissed him off more than if it'd been a Toyota with a student parking sticker, or a Korean delivery van?

You were mad because it's a symbol of what stands between you and Skyler. And it's not just the money— it's everything that goes with the money. The nice restaurants, shopping on Madison Avenue, trips to Europe ... and, yeah, the kind of car that costs more than twice what you make in a year.

Something else was eating at him, too—something

that made his heart ache. The baby. His little girl. Except for one glimpse of her through the hospital nursery's viewing window, he hadn't even gotten to see her. He'd been told that his daughter was healthy, that she weighed eight pounds three ounces and was eighteen inches long.

That was a month ago; now the baby was with Ellie and apparently thriving. What he didn't know was if, up close, she looked more like him or like Skyler. She had his dark curls, but did she have Skyler's eyes?

A question hammered at Tony: *How long can I go on pretending I'm not involved? Pretending she's not part of me, and I'm not part of her?*

By the time Tony hit the shower at the end of his tour, his temples were throbbing, and a dull ache at the back of his throat made him wonder uneasily if he might be coming down with something. Even after he'd toweled himself dry and thrown on jeans and a sweatshirt, his mood was so foul that even Joyce Hubbard, when he passed her on the stairs, brushed by with just a mumbled "Hiya."

Only fat-assed Lou Crawley, standing outside the front gate chomping on a garlic bagel slathered with cream cheese, seemed oblivious to the dark cloud hanging over Tony. "Hey, Sarge," he called. "You heard what came down over at Troop F? Two of the female officers got into a catfight. Fuller had to go over there and read 'em the riot act. Wish I'd been there to see that—the deputy inspector cracking the whip over those two pussies."

Abruptly, Tony felt the lid come off what was left of his control. Stepping in close, he grabbed hold of Crawley by the front of his crumb-sprinkled shirt, disgusted by the smear of cream cheese in the corner of Crawley's blubbery mouth. "Listen, you fat fuck," he growled. "Any more remarks like that, and you're outta here. I'll make it my personal mission in life to run your hide off these premises for good."

Crawley gaped at him, a hectic flush seeping into his jowly cheeks. "Jesus. What the fuck's got into *you*? What did I say?"

"Just watch your mouth, that's all. You want some asshole talkin' about your sister that way? Or Joyce?" He leaned in closer, and caught a whiff of Crawley's garlicky breath. "And another thing, I catch you taking any more bogus sick time when there are guys here who'd go out in below-zero weather running a temp of a hundred and two, I'll find a way to bust you. Big-time. So you better be watchin' your ass."

As he strode off, leaving Crawley to stare after him open-mouthed, Tony felt a little guilty. Crawley had deserved a dressing-down, all right ... and if it got Crawley to clean up his act, fine. The thing was, Tony knew perfectly well that Crawley wasn't the only burr under his saddle.

He couldn't help feeling that he'd been cheated somehow. He had a brand-new daughter, and he wanted to shout it from the rooftops. Instead, like some farm team's second-string shortstop, he'd been relegated to the bench. Fuck this. No *way* was he going to walk off without even a glance over his shoulder. What if, one day, his daughter asked about her real dad? No matter how heroic Ellie made him out to be, his little girl probably wouldn't buy it. She'd grow up believing he hadn't cared enough to even leave her his phone number. Christ.

He'd memorized Ellie's address from the adoption papers he and Skyler had signed. He also knew that she was working out of her apartment for the time being, to be with the baby. She probably wouldn't appreciate him dropping by unannounced ... but she wouldn't turn him away. He'd sized her up early on as the kind of woman who honored her debts. And, like it or not, she owed him.

Fifteen minutes later, Tony was pulling into an illegal parking space half a block from Ellie's brownstone on West Twenty-second. On the dash of his Explorer, he propped a square of cardboard with his shield number Magic-Markered in bold black letters, so he wouldn't get ticketed.

Mounting the steps of 236 and shouldering his way through the heavy front door, he thumbed the buzzer labeled "Nightingale" ... and waited. No answer. Damn. He waited a minute and buzzed again. Just as he was about to walk away, a woman's voice crackled over the intercom. "Yes?"

"It's me, Tony Salvatore. Okay if I come in?"

It took a good fifteen seconds before she responded, during which Tony thought, *She's gotta be nervous as hell, wondering what I'm here for.* After all, the adoption wouldn't be final for another five months, and she had to be well aware of the fact that either he or Skyler could renege at any moment.

Yet when he walked through the door of Ellie's apartment, his first impression was one of welcoming calm. He could imagine a kid, any kid—not just his— being happy here. His gaze took in the friendly clutter of books and magazines, the Indian rugs scattered among couches and chairs that looked like they were meant to be sat on, and even jumped on by little feet. Table and floor lamps gave the living room a friendly glow. There was a fireplace, with a pile of ashes letting you know it wasn't just for show.

Ellie looked tired, he thought. But even in jeans and a baggy sweater, her hair pulled back with an elastic band, she seemed to glow with happiness. Not only that, she appeared years younger than when he'd seen her last. Again, he was struck by her resemblance to Skyler.

"Excuse the mess ... I wasn't expecting company." Her greeting was guarded, but the hand she put out was warmly welcoming. Up close, she smelled faintly of baby powder ... a smell that triggered in Tony an unexpected pang of loss.

He gave her a reassuring smile that did nothing to alleviate the awkwardness he felt. "Baby must keep you pretty busy," he said.

"It's not the kind of busy I mind." Her face lit up, melting the last of her reserve. "Tony, she's so good! You have no idea—" She caught herself, darting him a stricken look.

No, he agreed silently. *But not because I don't want to.*

He shifted from one foot to the other, suddenly unsure of where his hands should go, or what to say next. Finally, he cleared his throat and asked, "She sleeping now?"

"Yes." He saw the hesitation in her eyes, and she seemed to struggle with herself before asking softly, "Would you like to see her?"

Tony felt touched ... and resentful, too. Nobody had twisted his arm into signing that release, but when all was said and done, that little girl in there was *his,* and it left a bitter taste in his mouth, having to ask permission just to take a peek at her. "I'm in no rush," he said, not wanting to appear too eager. "If I'm not keeping you or anything, can we sit and talk a minute? I wouldn't say no to a cup of coffee."

"Oh, well, of course. . . . Please, sit down," she said much too quickly, as if relieved that he wasn't dashing in to snatch the baby from her crib. She gestured toward the sofa with its jumble of mismatched cushions. "I put her down a couple of hours ago, so she should be waking up pretty soon. She's like clockwork usually. Not even six weeks old, and she already sleeps through the night." Ellie beamed, as if this were some truly amazing accomplishment.

"You planning on going back to work soon?" he asked.

"I've started seeing a few patients here," she told him. "And I hired a nanny, but she won't start until next month. By then, I hope I'll be ready to let Alisa

out of my sight for more than five minutes at a time."
She gave a rueful laugh.

"Alisa." Tony spoke his daughter's name aloud for
the first time. "I can live with it," he said with a
lightness that masked the thunderhead gathering on
his mind's horizon. *He* should have been the one to
choose his daughter's name, he and Skyler.

Ellie seemed to pick up on his mood, and she
jumped up from the sofa as if she couldn't get away
from him soon enough. "Hang on a minute, I'll get
us some coffee."

She disappeared into the next room, returning a
short while later with a tray holding two steaming cups
and a plate of what looked like homemade cookies.
He felt a little embarrassed that she'd gone to so much
trouble, but looking into her face, he saw that she'd
needed those minutes alone to compose herself. Even
so, her hands were trembling, making the coffee cups
chink softly against their saucers as she crossed the
room.

Tony took the tray from her and set it down on the
coffee table. He laid a hand lightly on her shoulder
and drew her back down beside him on the sofa.

"Listen," he said. "I'm not here to stir up trouble.
I just want to see her. One time, that's all. So you can
tell her someday that her old man cares." He cleared
his throat, which suddenly felt tight.

"I *know* you care, Tony." She sounded a little
angry, more at herself than at him. "You have to understand . . . I'm just—You see, I waited so long for
this, it feels as if she's been in my life forever. You
can't imagine . . ." She stopped, her hands twisting in
her lap, her eyes shiny with tears. "You've given me
the most wonderful gift. There are no words that could
ever convey the gratitude I feel toward you. *Please*
know that."

He nodded, unable to speak for a moment. Then
he said, "I do . . . but it's tough. Like I'm sitting here

wondering what it's gonna be like for her, growing up without a father."

Ellie looked away. "I'm hoping that won't always be the case."

"Your husband, you mean? Pardon me for sticking my nose in, but if he's so hopped up about being a dad, how come he's not here now?" Anger crept into Tony's voice.

The smile dropped from her lovely, strong face, in which he could see a battle being waged between her instinct to protect her child . . . and her sense of obligation toward Tony.

Ellie looked back at him squarely, her clear blue eyes grave and thoughtful. "You know that old saying—once burned, twice shy. Paul just needs time to get used to the idea that Alisa is here to stay." She sighed as she picked up her coffee mug. "I'm not saying we don't have some rough sailing ahead of us. We've been apart for so long, a baby isn't going to magically heal everything. But we're working on it."

Tony didn't know what to say. He found himself thinking how difficult it was even under the best of circumstances, when the scales are perfectly balanced, for couples to stick together.

As if she'd read his mind, Ellie asked tentatively, "Have you spoken to Skyler lately?"

"She's been kind of lying low," Tony answered truthfully, though there was more to it than that. The fact was, she hadn't been returning his phone calls. "It can't be easy getting back on your feet after having a baby." He kept his voice steady, but he was more worried than he would admit.

"Believe me, it isn't." Ellie looked off into the distance as she sipped her coffee, holding the mug with both hands. Then, as if eager to change the subject, she said, "Speaking of health, I'm concerned about Jimmy's. He claims he's feeling fine, that his T-cell count is up. But every time I invite him to drop by and see the baby, he has some excuse."

Tony felt something inside him shift and rise to the surface of his mind, dripping and rank, like a swamp creature out of one of those cheap late-night monster flicks that used to scare the living daylights out of Dolan and him when they were kids. It was all he could do not to cover his face now . . . to hide his eyes both from Ellie's probing gaze, and from the future he couldn't bear to face.

"Dolan?" Tony shrugged. "I twisted his arm into letting his cleaning lady put in a few extra hours a week looking after him—she's a real nice woman, raised six kids on her own, and thinks the sun rises and sets on Dolan. He's doing okay." Ellie didn't have to know how bad off Dolan was, not if Dolan didn't want her to.

"At least he hasn't taken a turn for the worse," she said, looking troubled.

"He's a lot tougher than he looks."

She gave him a pointed glance. "What about you—how are *you* holding up?"

"I'm managing." Outwardly, at least, that was true. Following another awkward silence, Tony glanced at his watch. "Jeez, will you look at the time? Listen, I oughta get going. Why don't I just look in on the baby, and be on my way?"

His chest ached, and a dryness had settled in behind his eyes like a long arid spell before a storm. It was almost more than he could take—his tiny daughter in the next room, but a world away as far as he was concerned.

Ellie stood up beside him and led the way down the hall to a small bedroom awash in the day's fading sunlight. It wasn't fussy like his nieces' rooms, with everything pink and ruffled. He took in the walls stenciled with clouds and stars, framed movie poster from *The Wizard of Oz,* a lone teddy bear perched atop a white-enameled bookcase lined with all the books Ellie would one day read to his daughter. As Tony stepped soundlessly over to the crib, his hands squeezed into fists.

His daughter lay under a soft pink blanket, her small cheek as round and fat as the stenciled moon on the wall over her crib, her mouth pressed open slightly as if blowing him a kiss. *Jesus . . . oh, Jesus Christ.* Tony, gazing down at her, felt the floor shift beneath him, and his knees started to give way. For a fleeting moment, the room turned as gray as the New Jersey skyline.

She had his hair, all right. A great black tuft that rose to a feathery peak atop her crown. Her eyes were closed, so he couldn't see what color they were, but the shape of her nose, the determined way she held her fist to her chin made him think of his sister Gina. Tony felt his breath catch.

He kept his head bowed, not wanting Ellie to see the tears in his eyes. But when he finally darted a glance in her direction, he saw that she was no longer standing in the doorway. He felt a surge of gratitude, knowing how much it must have cost her to give him even these few minutes alone with his daughter.

Tony brought his forefinger to the baby's cheek, brushing it so softly that he was surprised to see her twitch in response, her face scrunching and her bottom waggling from side to side like that of a burrowing hamster. He gently lifted the blanket, grinning at her long legs—legs custom made for horseback riding.

He drew the blanket back up around her shoulders and turned away, closing his eyes for a moment. He shouldn't have come. He should have taken Skyler's advice way back in the very beginning and gotten the hell out of Dodge.

Tony somehow made it to the door and out into the hallway, where he found Ellie leaning against the wall with her arms folded over her chest. She straightened, glancing at him, then discreetly looking away.

Before he knew what he was doing, Tony was reaching under the collar of his sweatshirt and hooking a finger about the chain of his St. Michael medal. He pulled it out and lifted it over his head, the overhead light glancing off the archangel's outstretched wings, which for an instant looked on the verge of taking flight. He held it for a moment in his fist, memorizing its shape, thinking of all the bullets from which St. Michael had shielded him. The Big Guy had only let him down once. Even if the medal's power lay in pure superstition, it was worth more to him than anything he owned.

A lump formed in his throat, roughly the size of the medal he was now dropping into Ellie's hand. "For her," he said in a voice made gruff with tenderness. "For my daughter."

All the way home, Tony couldn't stop thinking about Skyler. Christ, what she had to be going through. It had been hard for him, walking away from their baby. For Skyler, who'd carried their daughter inside her for nine months, it had to have been murder.

She shouldn't be alone, he thought with a certainty as clear as the sign up ahead marking the exit to Interstate 84. *She should be with someone who knows just how she feels.*

Taking the exit, Tony stopped at a Sunoco station, where he found a pay phone. He dialed Skyler's number, and as it was ringing prayed that this time she would pick up, that he wouldn't get her damn answering machine.

"Hello?" Skyler answered brightly, surprising him into nearly dropping the receiver. The tone of her voice was ... well ... almost *cheerful.* As if nothing on earth could possibly be the matter.

Tony felt more than a little stupid. What the hell

had he been expecting—a damsel in distress? A woman on the verge of suicide? That wasn't Skyler, not by a long shot. That night in the hospital, when she'd cried in his arms, she hadn't been herself. She'd just given birth, for chrissakes. By now, though, she probably had it all worked out in her head. She'd only resent him for stirring it all up again.

"It's me, Tony." He spoke in an even, friendly voice, hoping she wouldn't guess his heart was clocking a hundred miles a minute. "I was just calling to see how you're doing."

"I'm doing okay."

"So how come you never answered my other calls?" He tried to hide it, but the accusation was there, buried like a rusty nail in soft earth.

There was a pause; then, with a touch of frost, she replied, "I've been busy."

"Too busy to return a fucking phone call?" he wanted to snap. But all he said was "Yeah... well, you probably wouldn't have gotten me anyway. Last week and the week before, I worked double shifts. Big detail up in Harlem."

"Harlem?" It wasn't an expression of interest, merely a vague echo.

He cleared his throat. "Look, the reason I'm calling is, I was wondering if maybe you felt like some company. That is, if you're not too busy," he couldn't resist adding.

She was silent for so long he began to wonder if she was still there. He felt the seed of resentment that was never far from the surface start to crack open. Like it or not, they were in this together—did she think he wasn't hurting, too?

Finally, with a reluctance that cut him to the quick, she said, "I'm not doing anything special right now."

"I'll be there in fifteen minutes," he told her, hanging up before she could protest.

On the drive up, Tony felt his anxiety building. Was

she really as okay as she'd sounded? Could the cheerful woman he'd just spoken with be the same one who'd cried so bitterly in his arms the night she'd given birth? Maybe ... but his cop's instinct for trouble was flashing its hazard lights. A minute ago, Skyler had made him think of the time he'd had to inform a Brownsville woman that her son had been the victim of a gang war shooting. The woman had received the news calmly, had even invited him in for a cup of coffee. Days later, he'd learned that afterward she'd collapsed and been taken off to Bellevue for psychiatric observation.

Tony pressed his foot down harder on the gas pedal.

Minutes later, he was winding his way up a steep driveway dense with trees on either side. Then Skyler's cedar-sided A-frame came into view. Smoke curled from the fieldstone chimney, and he noticed as he was pulling in that the woodpile stacked alongside the porch was getting low. He'd come back and split some of the deadfall he'd seen on his way up, first free day he got. That is, assuming she wanted him to.

As he was climbing the porch steps, Tony caught a flash of movement in the sliding glass door to his right. He couldn't see her—only a hazy outline—but he could feel Skyler watching him. The small hairs on the back of his neck stiffened. When she opened the door at last, it took all his cop's training to keep from doing a double take.

She was so thin her jeans and oversized shirt hung on her pathetically. Jesus. And those purple hollows under her eyes ... Tony felt as if he were watching the curtain go up on one of those tragic operas Skyler so adored. Because anyone who looked like *that,* and who'd sounded the way she had over the phone, had to be either a very good actress, or on the verge of a nervous breakdown.

"Tony ... hi. Come on in."

Skyler's smile of welcome, like the fleeting hug she

gave him, did nothing to alleviate his concern. Observing her closely, the way she drifted ahead of him into the large, open-beamed living room, and the fact that she was barefoot despite a slate floor that had to be cold as ice, he realized that what he'd mistaken for calmness was in reality something else. She was simply . . . disconnected.

Reaching the fireplace, in which only a few embers glowed amid a pile of ashes, she turned and said, "I was just going to heat up a can of soup. Would you like some?"

Soup? Lady, you look like you could use a transfusion.

But Tony was careful to keep his alarm hidden from her. In a relaxed voice, he said, "How about I treat you to dinner instead?"

"The nearest restaurant is half an hour from here," she argued listlessly. "Besides, I'm not really in the mood."

The soup apparently forgotten, she sagged onto the scuffed leather ottoman belonging to a chair that looked like it had been dragged over twenty miles of dirt road. That was one thing Tony hadn't been able to figure out—why, if her family had so much money, didn't Skyler just replace all this old, beat-up stuff?

Not only that, she seemed oblivious to it being cold as the South Pole in here.

Not stopping to ask permission, Tony strode over to the hearth and hefted a couple of logs from the woodbox, tossing them onto the ashes. Sparks rose in a swirling cone, and then came the slow lick of flames. The sweet smell of woodsmoke drifted toward him, and he felt himself relax as warmth began to percolate into the room.

He turned around to find Skyler staring into the fire with a vacant, glassy expression that was even scarier than the bruised hollows under her eyes. The time for game-playing was over, Tony realized with a jolt.

"You look terrible," he told her. "When was the last time you ate?"

She snapped out of her trance with a scowl, and opened her mouth as if to tell him off. Then, with a deep sigh, she shook her head.

"I haven't had much of an appetite lately," she said.

"That much is obvious. The question is, what're we gonna do about it?" This time, he couldn't keep the anger from his voice.

"We?" This time she managed to muster up a faint indignation. "Since when is it *your* business to take care of me?"

"Since you stopped doing the job yourself."

Jesus, did she think he didn't care what happened to her? These past few weeks of ignoring the messages he'd left on her answering machine, had she stopped for one minute to consider that he might have been worried?

I love you, dammit! he wanted to shout. *Is that more than you can handle too?*

Before he could say something he'd regret, Tony went into the kitchen, where he found a nearly empty refrigerator and mostly bare cupboards. He scrounged up some saltines, and a can of mushroom soup he heated up with the little bit of milk left in the fridge. Arranging the food on a tray, he thought of the countless times he'd done this for Ma, when she was so tired and heartsick she couldn't even crawl out of bed. He'd fix dinner for his brothers and sisters, then bring Ma a bowl of soup and watch her spoon it up with measured slowness, as if she were eating only as a favor to him.

Watching Skyler do the same now, Tony made up his mind that he wasn't leaving until he was sure she could take care of herself. And knowing how stubborn she could be, he didn't expect the job to be easy.

Skyler, though, surprised him with a smile that appeared as genuine as the color that was seeping into her cheeks. Setting her empty soup bowl down on the rickety table next to the sofa, she told him, "Thanks. I *do* feel better. I guess I needed something in my stomach after all."

"You look like you could use something on your bones, too. How much weight have you lost?"

She shrugged. "All I know is, I weighed a lot more the last time I stepped on a scale." She gave a hoarse little laugh. "Amazing, isn't it, how much of a difference it can make when you're not carrying a baby around inside you?"

Tony, watching her smile crumple and her eyes fill with tears, was pierced to the core. He went to her, pulling her up from the ottoman and gently gathering her to him. He felt her head drop onto his shoulder, and her chest heave as she let loose a raggedy sigh.

"It's okay," he murmured into the warm musk of her unwashed hair. "You can let go."

Her arms rose tentatively and he felt the pressure of her palms against his shoulder blades, not so much as if she were holding him, but as if she were bracing herself against whatever was causing her so much pain. He hugged her more tightly, and heard a sound so faint it could have been coming from outside—the wind moaning through the trees.

The moan gathered, becoming louder, finally breaking into a harsh wail.

"Oh, Tony . . . its worse than I thought it would be," she sobbed. "*So* much worse."

"I know . . . I know," he soothed.

She pulled back sharply, her eyes blazing at him like the swollen red suns of an uninhabitable planet. "You *don't* know. You can't. You didn't carry her inside you. You didn't give birth to her. You weren't the one who gave her . . . a-a-away." A fresh sob broke loose in a torrent. When she could get her breath again, she choked, "I—I wander around all day like I'm suh-suh-sleepwalking. I thought I could handle this ... but I don't suh-seem to be able—" She lost control once again, crumpling bonelessly against him. He caught her and felt her snatch a handful of his shirt like someone sliding down the face of a cliff and scrabbling desperately for purchase.

He couldn't think of any words that would comfort her, so he comforted her with his body instead, holding and rocking her, stroking the back of her head. He let her cry, knowing she needed this more than food, more than sleep.

Finally, a muffled voice rose from the sodden patch of sweatshirt against which her face was pressed. "Tony?"

He waited.

"I can't help thinking I've made a terrible mistake." She spoke in a thin whisper. "Maybe I should have ... tried harder to think what would be good for *me*, not just the baby."

He swallowed, at a loss for words. Finally, he said the thing he figured she most needed to hear. "You did the right thing. Don't beat yourself up."

"Did I?" She raised her head, and her hot red eyes seemed to cut through him. "I'm not so sure."

"You feel that way now, but in another month or two—"

"No! It's not like that!" she cried. "In a year, in *ten* years, I'm not going to feel any different. Oh, Tony, what have I done? *What in God's name have I done*?"

With an odd grace, like a flimsy scarf dropped at his feet, she folded down into a kneeling position on the braided rug in front of the fireplace, her head low. Her arms wrapped tightly about her chest, she rocked back and forth against her heels with strange, pulsing little cries.

Tony became aware of a stabbing ache in the back of his throat, and something else ... a feeling so alien he almost didn't recognize it at first. Helplessness. He felt so goddamn helpless.

"Skyler?" He crouched in front of her on the scorch-marked rug, cupping his hand over the pale, exposed stem of her neck.

Abruptly her head jerked up, and she was looking straight at him, her lips parted and trembling. Without a sound, her eyes open and knowing, she tipped her face up to be kissed. He brought his mouth to hers and felt the sudden, sharp intake of her breath nearly suck the air from him. He shuddered, and he felt something that had been sealed away for far too long finally let loose. He sank down as she pressed her hips forward, clinging to him and kissing him, biting his lower lip as if wanting—no, *needing*—to burrow into his flesh, lose herself completely.

Tony knew he should stop. Wrong time, wrong reason. But at the same time he also knew that trying to stop himself, or her, would be as useless as calling back the bullet of a gun that's been fired. Heat kicked through him in a series of tiny explosions. Then suddenly *he* was the one frantically kissing *her*—her cheeks, her throat, the pulsing hollow of her throat. He captured one of her hands and brought it to his mouth, running his tongue slowly across her palm. She started, and he felt a shiver travel through her.

Tony tore at the buttons on her shirt, gasping at the feel of her bare skin under his fingers, the play of her ribs, the downy undersides of her breasts against his thumbs. She moaned and spread her knees, and he thought of that first time, of how wet she'd been, and how he'd felt it right through the seam of her shorts.

He shoved a hand down the front of her jeans, and found her as wet as he'd remembered, and this time she was actually *pushing* against his hand, rocking with a wild, almost desperate rhythm. Jesus.

Driven by a need that was more powerful than any he'd ever known, Tony pushed her gently onto her back, where she lay with the firelight dancing over her pale breasts. He noted their fullness, the veins visible

just below the skin; these were not the breasts of a
girl, but of a woman who has recently given birth. He
felt sorrow well up in him ... but it only made him
want her more.

He watched her wriggle out of her jeans, growing
nearly faint with excitement at the sight of her long
pale legs scissoring free and spreading open before
him. He quickly pulled off his own jeans, then his
sweatshirt, and lowered himself on to her.

"Not ... not inside me," she gasped. As if he *would*,
after what had happened the last time they'd made
love.

"Don't worry," he whispered against her temple as
he slid along the damp curve of her belly. He was so
hard, he felt as if he could come with the lightest of
strokes; it took every ounce of his control to hold
back.

She rocked against him, and he felt how her girlish
tautness had become soft and rounded. He slipped a
hand between her legs, cupping her wet mound, both
of them moving in tandem. It was strange, but it felt
right somehow. The two of them dipping, thrusting,
their breath coming in shortening gasps. He could feel
his control slip away as she arched and stiffened, letting out a sharp cry. He moaned, gripping her, past the
point of caring, or even noticing, if he was hurting her.

In that moment, as if his climax had been torn from
his loins, he felt himself spill onto her belly. He
strained against her, yelling, "Skyler, oh God, Skyler!"

With a convulsive shudder, she wrapped her arms
and legs around him, burying her face in the crook of
his neck. She started to cry again. He could feel the
wetness of her cheek, and his seed, hot and sticky
between their bellies, sealing them somehow.

"I want her back," she whispered fiercely. "Tony,
if I can't have her, I'll die. I don't care what it takes.
I made a terrible mistake. Please. Help me get her
back."

Tony thought of Ellie, of how she'd smiled at him when he'd pressed his St. Michael's medal into her hand. It was the smile of a mother tiger who needed no flimsy scrap of medal to protect her child from harm.

Jesus. Did Skyler have any *idea*?

Relax, he told himself. *She's not thinking straight.*

But something told Tony this was every bit as serious as it sounded. Skyler might regret tonight, might regret *him,* but she wouldn't change her mind about wanting their baby back.

He experienced a low, burning sensation that spread upward . . . an odd, hot-cold feeling that was just south of dread and maybe a little bit north of hope.

He'd thought the worst was behind them, but it looked as if the hard part had just begun.

CHAPTER 13

It rained off and on for the remainder of that gray-skyed week; the spectrum of weather ranged from drizzle to downpour and showed no signs of letting up until late Friday afternoon. At four-thirty, Ellie was seeing a patient to the door of her apartment—Adam Burchard, one of the men from her AIDS group—when she noticed how quiet it had gotten all of a sudden. The clock-steady ticking of rain against the windowpanes had finally wound down. And not a peep from Alisa, asleep in her crib down the hall, oblivious to the vagaries of the weather ... to everything, in fact, but the arms that picked her up when she cried, the warm breast she snuggled against while taking her bottle. Her sweet, sweet Alisa, who made even a rainy day cause for celebration.

Ellie was putting the kettle on to boil for a cup of tea when it occurred to her that she was happy. Standing in her tiny kitchen, she looked out over a tangle of ivy-walled garden in back, where a watery streak of sunlight had pried its way through a chink in the cloud cover to illuminate the daffodils. She leaned into the wall, hung with copper skillets and vintage advertisements for food companies long gone out of business, and smiled to herself. It had been such a long time since she'd experienced anything close to happiness that she hardly recognized the feeling—as if all the years beforehand she'd been struggling to keep time to an unfamiliar beat, and now the music came effortlessly.

If only Paul were here to share it with me. If he were back home, living here instead of just dropping by once or twice a week . . .

If only, when Paul looked at Alisa, she could have seen in his face the undisguised tenderness she'd seen in Tony's. Paul had put up so many walls she wasn't sure even he was capable of pulling them down. Tuesday evening, she'd watched him when he picked Alisa up to examine a rash on her arm that Ellie had been worrying about. What had struck her then was the contrast between the gentleness of his hands and the distant troubled expression he wore.

The moment of dumbstruck happiness she'd felt a moment ago faded as abruptly as the brief glimmer of sunshine, being swallowed up once more by the clouds. With Alisa to measure the days for her now, Ellie felt each precious passing moment as acutely as a theft. Whenever Paul headed for the door, she wanted to grab him by the lapels and shout into his face that what he was missing could never, ever be recaptured.

Not to mention how much *she* missed him. It had been over a year, and still not a day passed when she didn't yearn for him. Only yesterday, she'd heard their favorite Stan Getz solo on the radio, and had started to call out to Paul in the next room before remembering he wasn't there. And last Thursday, she'd run into an old friend of theirs, Betsy Wiggins, in D'Agostino's; Betsy had been surprised to learn that she and Paul were separated . . . and even more surprised when Ellie burst into tears in the middle of the frozen-food section. She knew that if Paul walked in through that door tonight, she'd make sure that this time it was for good.

Why? she asked. *Why one cup that runneth over ... and another that's run dry?*

The phone rang as she was dropping a teabag into a mug of steaming water.

Ellie hurried to answer it, not waiting for her machine to pick up. She was afraid the ringing would wake Alisa from her nap, and lord knew she could use these few extra minutes in which to put up her feet and savor her tea. But as she reached for the phone on the wall over the counter, her second thought was of Paul.

Please let it be him. Let him say he's thought it over, that he needs me too much to ever again let anything stand between us—even a baby we might stand to lose ...

But when Ellie picked up the phone, the voice on the other end of the line wasn't Paul's. There was a rush of exhaled breath followed by a whisper as alarming as a child's cry for help.

"Ellie ... it's me—Skyler."

Ellie felt a sudden thudding heaviness in the pit of her stomach. "Skyler, what's wrong?"

Silence, punctuated only by the desperate, labored sound of Skyler's breathing.

Groping behind her, Ellie found the padded seat of the bar stool nearest her, and hoisted herself onto it. Her heart was slamming against her rib cage, but she forced herself to speak calmly. "Skyler, are you sick? Do you need a doctor?"

A sharp intake of breath, then: "No ... that's not it," before the words poured out in a strangled rush. "I—I'm just—well, I'm a mess. I can't eat. I sleep all the time, but I never wake up rested. I didn't know it would be this way. I had no idea ..."

Ellie's first panicked thought was *This can't be happening, not again, not to me.* Then she recalled what it had been like for her just after she'd given birth, the wild mood swings, the crying jags that would follow fits of euphoria. Skyler had to be going through the same hell, she told herself. Only in her case it was worse, because she had nothing to show for it.

If I handle this properly, she'll calm down, Ellie told herself, struggling to retain her own composure.

"I know some of what you're going through," Ellie told her gently. "After my daughter ... after she was taken from me, I didn't think I could go on living."

"Alisa wasn't taken from me. I *gave* her away."

"For all the right reasons."

"No. I was *wrong.*" The firm certainty in Skyler's voice sent a chill zigzagging up Ellie's spine.

Only years of practice at keeping her emotions in check saved Ellie from screaming into the phone, "It's too late, do you hear me? Too late! She's mine now. *She's mine.*" Instead, she wrapped the phone cord about her knuckles tightly enough to cut off the supply of blood to her fingers.

"I understand your feeling this way, and I can't honestly say it will go away ... but it *does* get easier with time." She forced herself to speak evenly, as she had minutes before to Adam Burchard, who'd sat in her living room and wept for fifty minutes over the inescapable fact that he was dying. "Skyler, I really think it would be a good idea for you to see someone. I know a woman, a friend of mine, who—"

"I don't need a shrink!" Skyler's voice rose, cracking on a shrill note before falling to a pleading whisper. "Ellie, I know you love her. And you'll probably hate me for this, but ... but I was wrong to give her up. I—I want her back."

Ellie stared down at her hand, which had turned ghastly white below its bracelet of tightly wrapped coils. She felt a prickling in her fingers, a sensation that made her think of sparklers on the Fourth of July. But there was no fire in her. She felt only cold.

"I'm afraid it's too late for that." The flat, faintly nasal voice that rose out of the deep well of cold in her wasn't anything like her own—it belonged to Ellie Porter from Euphrates, Minnesota, who had left the last of her innocence buried somewhere in the dusty tracks of the Trailways bus that had brought her to New York ... a girl who, in the space of a single winter's night, had learned what it was to lose a child.

She would never let that happen again. Not if she could help it.

"You made this decision all on your own," Ellie went on, anger taking the place of sympathy. "I didn't seek you out. *You* came to me. And I never begged. I never interfered. I was honest about my circumstances. But she is mine now. She's my baby."

"I gave birth to her!" Skyler shrieked. "I carried her inside me for nine months. Do you think any piece of paper could ever change that?"

Ellie immediately knew she'd been wrong to put Skyler on the defensive. "Can we talk about this when you're not so upset? You pick the time and place, I'll be there." Ellie, though her voice was shaking, spoke as she would have to a peer, one of her own colleagues.

"I don't see what the point would be," Skyler said stiffly. "My mind's made up."

"If that's true, then seeing me won't change it. What do you have to lose?"

"Stop it!" Skyler cried, sounding close to hysteria. "I know what you're trying to do ... but it won't work. Do you hear me? It won't!"

"Skyler, listen to me—"

"NO! I will NOT listen!"

A fit of trembling gripped Ellie, so profound she could feel the muscles in her calves cramping and twitching, and she had to press the receiver tightly against her ear to keep it from jerking away. In a low, hoarse whisper, she asked, "What do you want from me?"

There was a pause, then, "Oh, Ellie ... I'm sorry. It's all my fault. God, I'm so sorry—" Skyler broke off, her voice dissolving into desperate sobs.

Ellie waited until the awful gasping sounds on the other end had abated. When she finally began to speak, it was with the grave, deadly calm of an undertaker.

"Sorry? You don't know what sorry is. Unlike you, I never had the luxury of knowing what had happened to my little girl ... if she was safe or even alive ... if she had gone to decent people who would love her." Tears stung her eyes, but she held them back. "Not a day goes by when I don't think of her, and hope she's well and happy. At least you know Alisa will be loved. You know—"

Ellie was interrupted by a piercing wail from the nursery down the hall. Alisa had woken from her nap.

Ellie was swept with terror. She wanted to clap a hand over the receiver's mouthpiece to keep Skyler from hearing her baby's cries, but she felt too weak to even move.

"Please," she begged, beyond attempting to be reasonable, beyond dignity even. "Don't do this. Give it some time, a few days at least. Think it over—"

"Believe me, I've thought of nothing else for the past four and a half weeks." Skyler's voice trembled. "It's no good. I go around feeling sick to my stomach all the time. I feel ... cheated. Worse, I feel like I'm cheating her. I know, I know what you're going to say—that my reasons for giving her up in the first place are still valid. But it's like I was a different person when I made that decision. Everything's changed now. I'm a mother. I can't help that any more than I can help how I feel." She took a deep breath, then came the words Ellie had been dreading most of all. "If you fight me, you'll only make it worse for all of us."

Down the hall, Alisa began to wail in earnest.

"I have to go now," Ellie said, and hung up.

For a full minute, she sat frozen on her stool. Even while she ached to respond to her baby's cries, she couldn't remember the order in which her arms and legs were supposed to move; the code was all scrambled in her head. A single, clear image stood out in her mind: an empty wicker basket stranded in the corner of a tenement living room.

Slowly, Ellie stood up, feeling her head start to throb, and the muscles in her legs pulse to life with stabbing little aches. Yet as she headed in the direction of her baby's cries, she felt oddly weightless, as if she were being transported along a shallow, moving walkway made of air. An almost manically cheerful voice she hardly recognized as her own called out brightly, "Mommy's coming! Oh, listen to you . . . carrying on like the world's coming to an end."

In the nursery, she scooped Alisa from her crib and brought the squirming baby to her shoulder, kissing the spot where her dark hair was plastered in damp whorls to the side of her head. Ellie felt the tension go out of the baby's body, and her tiny fists stop flailing. "Hush now. I'm here. There . . . that's better, isn't it? Everything's going to be okay—"

Something in Ellie snapped, unleashing a cry of such anguish she was nearly doubled over by it. She staggered backward to catch her balance, and felt the baby jerk in surprise, her hiccupping whimpers rising again to full-blown shrieks.

Clasping Alisa tightly against her chest as she swayed from side to side, Ellie vowed that this time, whoever tried to take her baby away would have to kill her to do so.

But she couldn't fight this alone. And there was only one person capable of giving her the help she needed.

When Alisa had cried herself back to sleep, Ellie gently laid her back down in her crib and tiptoed out of the nursery. This time, as she walked into the living room and lifted the receiver, her hand was steady.

"Neonatal," answered a girlish voice at the other end. Ellie recognized it at once as belonging to Martha Healey.

"Martha, it's Ellie." She tried to sound natural, as if she weren't on the verge of a nervous breakdown. "Is Paul around?"

"Evening rounds," Martha said distractedly, and Ellie could see in her mind the diminutive head nurse, who for some reason always made her think of Judy Garland in those old movies with Mickey Rooney. "I'll give him the message, though. Hey"—her voice changed, became more focused—"I forgot to congratulate you, but you know how crazy it gets around here. How's it going? Baby okay?"

"She's . . . she's beautiful." Incredibly, Ellie found herself smiling.

"Well, just count your blessings she's got ten fingers and ten toes and is healthy." There was an awkward silence, and Ellie could almost hear Martha thinking what she knew had to be a subject of water-cooler gossip on Deacon: *Too bad about you and Paul, though.*

Ellie sipped a shallow breath—she didn't dare take in too much air all at once, or dizziness would overwhelm her—and said, "Thanks. Just tell him I called, okay?"

Evening rounds at Deacon was not unlike operating a triage unit in a war zone. Paul led half a dozen harried, sleep-deprived residents through the maze of isolettes, oximeters, monitors, med cabinets, and the electrical cables necessary to run it all. In the midst of it all, twenty-some fragile lives hung in constant jeopardy, attended to by the four nurses who scurried to and fro. Never—not for a single instant—did any of those present forget that a patient could die at any moment. Death was the enemy on Deacon, the front line they were forever attempting to advance, even if only in increments and even when it seemed a losing battle.

"Dorfmeyer, why don't you do the present on the Ortiz baby?" Paul was perched on one of the six desks, all jammed together, which served as the nurses' station. He glanced over at the pimply, fair-haired young man who stood poised at his elbow, scowling in furious concentration at the stat sheet clipped to the manila folder in his hands.

There was a splotch of blue ink, like an untidy boutonnière, decorating the front pocket of Cal Dorfmeyer's lab coat where he'd absently stuck an uncapped pen. But the other five residents, busy studying the contents of their own stat sheets, wouldn't have noticed or cared if he'd been wearing a gorilla suit. Ability, and the speed with which it was applied, were the only things that counted here.

The boy glanced up, his acne-scarred face reddening as if he'd been caught off-guard, which Paul knew was far from the case. This was one seriously smart kid. Before being recruited by Cornell, Cal Dorfmeyer— affectionately known as "Doogie Howser"—had graduated summa cum laude from Harvard at the ripe old age of eighteen.

With a clearing of his throat, Dorfmeyer at last found his voice. "Day seventeen . . . weight nine hundred grams . . . blood gases seven-point-four pH and forty p102," he recited from memory as he stood before the Plexiglas warmer in which a twenty-seven-weeker lay basking under a heat lamp, attached to a battery of wires and tubes. "Meds? Let me think." The resident scratched idly at a pimple on his chin. "Ampicillin—forty milligrams every twelve hours. Cefotaxime, same dosage. Over the past two days, he's had several bradycardias, but a subsequent head ultrasound ruled out intraventricular hemorrhage."

"Would you recommend continuing this course of treatment?" Paul quizzed.

Dorfmeyer didn't hesitate. "I'd order another head ultra. Just to be on the safe side. And I think we ought to increase his feedings. I'd push him up another cc on the Similac. If that doesn't—"

Before he could continue, a commotion that had begun in the hallway outside suddenly burst through the double doors of the unit in the form of a scrappy, sallow-skinned teenaged girl with the huge limpid eyes of a Keane painting and the stance of a fighting cock.

"Fuckin' assholes say I can't see my baby! I gotta right to see my kid!" the girl bellowed in the raspy voice of someone too zonked out on drugs to even notice she was shouting.

"Uh-oh ... Ortiz's mom. Here we go," Paul heard Ken Silver mutter. Even Silver, at one eighty, all of it solid muscle packed onto a six-foot frame, looked nervous.

Paul had had his share of dealing with druggie moms over the years, but none as difficult as Concepción "Cherry" Ortiz. Ever since the morning two weeks ago when her barely breathing infant had been rushed to Langdon, eight weeks premature as a result of her crack habit, Cherry Ortiz had done everything under the sun to make their existence on Deacon a living hell. The focus of her rage was a court order barring her from seeing her son, to which she paid no more attention than if it had been a parking ticket. In her battle to get past the nurses, she'd employed every tactic from screaming fits of hysteria to wheedling tears. Once, she'd even tried to bribe her way onto the unit by offering to have sex with one of the residents.

Out of the corner of his eye, Paul caught sight of Martha Healey marching over with her hands on her hips, wearing the grim look of a general leading her troops into battle. Martha was wonderful in a crisis ... but tact was not her strong suit.

He stood up and walked quickly over to where the scrawny teenager stood ready to face off the female cannonball in cranberry scrubs headed her way. A fraction of a second before Martha could descend on her, Paul stepped in front of the girl.

"Miss Ortiz, I'm afraid you'll have to wait outside," he told her with a polite calm that masked a vein of steel in him as thin and sharp as a surgical scalpel.

"Who d'you think you are, tellin' me what to do? Bigshot doctor, think you're such hot shit! That's my kid in there!" Cherry's head, with its corkscrewed hair, bobbed forward in quick, banty thrusts, and her hands gestured wildly in midair.

"You should have thought of that when you were pregnant and doing drugs," snapped Martha, darting around Paul to snatch hold of the girl's arm.

Martha's effort to steer Cherry outside, however, was rewarded by having her own arm nearly torn out its socket. Shaking off the head nurse, who reeled backward and against the stainless scrub sink, Cherry came whirling at Paul like an evil genie unleashed from a bottle.

Her eyes, the whites showing all around the irises, were frantic. Her hands were curled into claws, fingernails bared. Paul had a good six inches on her, but even so, he barely managed to pin her down. Grabbing hold of her by both her wrists, he squeezed until she winced.

"Miss Ortiz, you'll have to wait outside," he repeated with the same steely calm. The only difference now was the pressure he was applying to her wrists . . . wrists with bones that felt as thin and brittle as sticks. Gravely, he added, "Your son is very sick. He could arrest at any minute. Do you understand what that means?"

He felt her wrists slacken in his grasp. "You're sayin' he could die?"

"That's exactly what I'm saying. And I know you wouldn't want that."

"No," she rasped, licking lips that were white and chapped.

"We know you love your son, but your constant disruptions are only making it worse for him. If you really want to help him, you'll let us get on with our work."

Tears rose in the girl's limpid eyes. She whined, "I just wanna see him. That's all. I'm his mother."

Paul was struck by a sudden inspiration.

"Martha," he called, "do we still have that Polaroid camera around here somewhere?"

He turned to the diminutive nurse, who stood several feet away by the sink, wearing a look of heavy disapproval. Nothing this scrap of a teenager could throw at him could be worse than the wrath of Martha Healey, R.N. But after glaring at him a few seconds longer, she stalked off, returning a few minutes later holding the camera at arm's length like a canister of toxic waste.

Paul took it from her and walked over to the Ortiz isolette, where he snapped a Polaroid of the tiny creature, hardly recognizable as a baby. The image that surfaced on the square of stiff cardboard looked more like an anesthetized squirrel than anything human. But when he handed it to her, Cherry Ortiz gazed at it as if it were a Raphael cherub.

Paul watched Martha steer the newly docile young woman out through the double doors with a sardonic smile. He couldn't help admiring Cherry Ortiz in a way. At least she'd had the guts to fight for what was hers.

What if he were to do the same for his marriage? Fight for it instead of analyzing it to death? Everything was different now that the baby (he still had trouble calling her by her name) had entered into the equation. They could finally be a family, just as they'd always planned. So what was stopping him?

Paul wasn't sure. Maybe he was just too damn cynical, too weary. He wasn't ready to trust that Alisa was really here to stay. And even if the adoption went through without a hitch, a piece of paper wasn't magically going to wipe away all the time he and Ellie had spent apart. This wasn't—though he often wished it could be—an ABC Movie of the Week, at the end of which the couple fell into each other's arms and there was a slow dissolve.

No? Well, that's your head talking, buddy. How about tuning in to your heart for a change? While you're hanging back, too scared to take a risk, you might be missing out on the greatest thing that ever happened to you.

Paul, shutting his mind against these thoughts, completed his rounds, then went into the next room with Brad Elcock, Langdon's pediatric ortho man, to review the X rays of a full-term baby born with a displaced hip. By the time he finished with Brad, it was nearly nine o'clock, and he realized he hadn't eaten since the bagel he'd consumed on the run around lunchtime.

He was just about to go get a bite in the cafeteria when Martha came running after him, looking sheepish.

"Paul, I forgot to tell you ... your wife called a couple of hours ago," she informed him. "With all the commotion, it slipped my mind."

Instantly, he was tense. "Did she say what she wanted?"

"She just left a message for you to call her back."

Martha's look bristled with unasked questions. Speculation about his marriage ran high on Deacon, he knew. But Martha, married herself, with two kids in elementary school, was far too circumspect to pry.

A year, he thought. It had been more than a year

since he'd walked out on Ellie. A year in which to stockpile resentment and accusations—and, yes, carve out separate paths. Time in which the proverbial grass had done more than grow under their feet, it had damn near engulfed them.

And yet, more often than he would have cared to admit, Paul awoke in the middle of the night in the bedroom of his furnished sublet on Thirty-second and First, missing her so badly still it was all he could do to keep from throwing a raincoat over his skivvies and running downstairs to jump in a cab.

He missed the scent of her on the pillow next to his. He missed the smoky nights of gin and tonics and jazz at the Vanguard and Blue Note. He missed the way she greeted him in the morning, rolling over in bed and hooking a bare leg over his ... and the way she threw her head back in throaty laughter whenever he said something that amused her. He even missed her pantyhose drying on the shower-stall door, and the empty tea mugs she was forever leaving around.

Most of all, he missed knowing that at the end of the day she would be there, in that quiet place of love called home.

"Thanks," he told Martha, more curtly than he'd intended.

But before Paul could reach for the phone nearest him, he spotted a familiar figure shouldering her way through the swinging doors to the unit—a slender woman with smooth honey-colored hair and a smile as bright as the overhead fluorescents. Cradled in her arms was a bundle wrapped in a crocheted blanket, from which poked a tuft of gingery hair. Paul immediately felt himself grow lighter, freer, as if he were in the bucket of a Ferris wheel being lifted off the ground.

"Serena!" he called.

He hurried over to her, feeling a surge of the swash-buckling optimism he'd been steeped in as a young resident, before disenchantment had set in. It had been some time since Serena Blankenship's last visit, several months at least. But whenever he saw her with Theo, Paul was reminded of what he frequently forgot around here: that God's will wasn't necessarily immutable.

Serena beamed at him, and folded the blanket back from a sleeping baby the size of a six-month-old. "We celebrated his first birthday yesterday." She spoke softly to keep from waking Theo. "He wouldn't be here if it hadn't been for you." She dipped her free hand into the oversized bag slung over her shoulder, fishing out a foil-wrapped packet, which she handed to him. "I know it's not much, but the least I could do was bring you a piece of his cake."

Paul, his throat tightening, stroked Theo's plump cheek, as soft as a rose petal. The baby stirred, and a pair of blue eyes popped open, searching Paul's face with bright interest. Paul grinned. "Come on, you two, let's find somewhere quiet where I can eat my cake in peace. It's not every day I get to celebrate a birthday none of us thought we'd ever see."

In the once-streamlined lounge, with its hodgepodge of stored files and the medical equipment shoved up against the walls, Paul helped Serena arrange Theo on the sofa, where he promptly fell back asleep. Paul couldn't help noting the irony of the scene. How many times had he found Serena, cramped and sound asleep, on this very sofa?

Their eyes met, and she gave him another welcome dose of her radiant smile.

"You look good," he told her. In fact, he could hardly believe how good she looked, her blue eyes sparkling, her once-pallid cheeks pink with color.

"Thanks... so do you," she answered too quickly, dropping her eyes.

Paul knew it wasn't true. Just last week, venturing into his neighborhood Gap, he'd found himself easily fitting into the same size jeans he'd worn in high school. And back then he'd been the original ninety-pound weakling.

"What about Theo's checkups? Everything look fairly normal?" Paul asked.

"Pretty much ... except for the asthma, which you already know about." A faintly troubled look flitted across her face.

"What about crawling—he doing that yet?"

"Dr. Weiss says he's on the low end of the developmental curve for his age . . . but it's nothing to worry about."

He patted her arm. "He's right. Give it time. A slow start doesn't mean he won't catch up eventually."

Serena rewarded him with a smile. "Catch up? You should see him ... the way he flirts with every sales-clerk and supermarket checker. In the charm department, he's already miles ahead of most grown men."

"What about his dad—where does he figure into all this?" Paul asked, then immediately wished he'd kept his mouth shut. What business was it of his?

Serena lowered her gaze and fingered a corner of blue blanket that had fallen over the knee of one exceptionally shapely leg. "The divorce was final last month," she replied. "To tell you the truth, it was a big relief. Dan was never really that interested in having children. In some ways, it'll be easier raising Theo on my own than it would've been with Dan around." She glanced up with a tentative smile. "Don't worry, we'll be just fine."

"You never know—you could meet someone who'd make a terrific stepdad," Paul said a touch too heartily.

Serena blushed crimson. Then, as if needing something to distract her, she seized the foil-wrapped packet from his hands—he'd forgotten it was there—and briskly unwrapped it. "It's carrot cake," she told him. "I made it myself. Theo ended up with more of it in his hair than in his mouth, but overall I think it was a hit."

Paul broke off a chunk with his fingers, finding that he was much hungrier than he'd realized. "My favorite kind . . . how did you know?"

She smiled. "Lucky guess."

In his mind, Paul was seeing the snapshots that had been taped to Theo's isolette. The house with its riotous garden; the great moose of a golden retriever lolling on the front path in an oblong of sunlight; the dignified older couple, Serena's parents, standing with their arms around each other, toasting with champagne what he'd been told was their fortieth wedding anniversary.

Whenever he pictured Serena in that setting, Paul was reminded of the stories his mother read him when he was a child—tales of princesses in far-off castles, and of enchantments requiring the services of stalwart princes. He thought of how nice it would be to find himself magically transported to a realm far removed from the thorny patch of his marriage—to wake up in a bed that held no memories, bad or good, nestled beside a woman with whom he shared no history other than one in which he'd played dragonslayer.

"Would you have dinner with me?" The words were out before he even realized he'd spoken.

Serena gave him a startled look, and the color in her cheeks deepened.

"I was just on my way down to the cafeteria for a bite to eat, but there are a couple of restaurants nearby where a baby wouldn't be a problem," he rushed ahead, feeling like a man recklessly diving into a pond before he'd tested its depth.

Serena regarded him with a faintly puzzled expression. "Paul, are you asking me out on a date?"

Was he? Well, yes, he guessed he was. Somewhere along the line he'd stopped seeing Serena merely as a patient's mother in need of comforting . . . and had started thinking of her as a woman with comfort to offer him. An undeniably attractive woman.

Now the cat was out of the bag. With a sheepish smile, he confessed, "The last time I felt this nervous asking a woman on a date was back when Nixon was in office."

"I hope you're not drawing any kind of parallel," she joked.

"You're much prettier than Nixon," he told her.

"I'll bet you say that to all the girls."

"Only the ones who feed me cake."

Her smile flashed with a brilliance that was nearly dazzling. Then, just as abruptly, it faded. She regarded him soberly, faint lines forming between her brows and at the corners of her mouth.

"Paul, I'd like nothing better than to have dinner with you, but ... " Her voice trailed off. Finally, she said, "I don't think it would be a good idea. You're married."

"We're separated, actually." Paul felt like a traitor, as if he were stabbing Ellie in the back.

Serena considered this a moment before answering. "Look, I don't know you very well," she said softly. "But there's one thing I do know—you're not someone who gives up easily. If you have something, anything, worth fighting for, you'll hammer it out to the finish." This time, the smile she gave him was weighted at the corners, as if with bittersweet regret. "I wouldn't be here now if you'd been another kind of person, and neither would Theo."

"You're giving me way too much credit," he said lightly, grateful for the opportunity to pull the conversation back to more familiar turf. "Theo's the one you'll have to watch out for. A couple more years and he'll be the terror of the neighborhood."

She rolled her eyes. "Don't I know it! He's already into everything he can reach sitting up. The other day I caught him cramming a cracker into my CD player."

They chatted for a few more minutes before Serena stood up, smoothing her skirt. Theo was still asleep, curled on his side. He had one thumb corked in his mouth, and was sucking contentedly. She gazed down at him in silence for a moment before gently hoisting him onto her shoulder.

Paul helped her with her bag, then walked her to the elevator. She was reaching to thumb the Down button when he took her hand and pressed it between both of his. "Thanks," he said softly.

Looking into her lovely, gentle face, he wondered if he might regret missing the chance to get to know her better . . . but at the same time he felt sure she'd saved him from making what might have been a fatal error.

"Good-bye, Paul." She stood on tiptoe to kiss his cheek and he caught the faint scent of some floral perfume.

Watching her step into the elevator, Paul was filled with sudden resolve. Turning, he headed briskly back down the hall to Deacon, to the phone call he felt a sudden, urgent desire to return.

Ellie had been pacing the floor for half an hour, ever since Paul had called to suggest a late dinner of Chinese takeout. She hadn't told him over the phone about Skyler; she was saving that conversation for when she could look into his face, and know she was only a heartbeat away from being in his arms.

At the same time, she warned herself, Don't act too desperate. . . . *That'll only make him back off.* It would look as if she'd only just now discovered she needed him, when, in fact, she'd needed him all along, and had been too damn stubborn to let him know just how much.

But when the knock came, and she pulled open the door to find Paul standing there in his navy coat, smiling crookedly at her, Ellie remembered not a word of her carefully rehearsed speech. It simply flew out of her head. She just stood there, drinking in the sight of him, tears of gratitude filling her eyes like balm after the ravaging hours of weeping that had followed Skyler's phone call.

"Hi," she said. Despite the cold water she'd splashed on her face, it felt stretched and hot. Would he know she'd been crying?

Greeting her with a kiss on the cheek, he said, "You look tired—are you sure you're up for this? We could do it another night if you'd rather hit the sack early."

"Chinese takeout isn't exactly dining out at the Carlyle." She managed a quick, light laugh. "Come on in, sit down. I'll scrounge up menus ... they're around here somewhere."

"Stay put," he told her. "I know where they are ... at least, last time I looked." He shrugged off his coat and crossed over to the desk by the kitchen doorway, where he began rummaging in the bottom drawer.

Ellie stopped to stare at him, filled with a sense of completeness—of *home*—at the sight of him bent over the drawer, his hair that seemed forever in need of a haircut falling over his forehead, and his steel-rimmed glasses slipping down his too-long nose. He looked tired, too, but his cheeks were ruddy with cold, and he carried with him an air of welcome, wonderful vitality.

"Paul ... " Her voice emerged in a cracked whisper.

"They're here somewhere, right? Unless you threw them out," he muttered without turning around. Then he stopped and straightened, slowly swiveling to face her. "Ellie, what is it? What's wrong?" His expression registered the pain she was feeling at that moment ... pain she could no longer keep hidden.

"Oh, Paul, it's happening again. The baby—" Her words were choked off by the cry that rose in her.

He grasped her meaning at once. Ellie watched him stiffen slightly, and she experienced an instant of panic, fearing he would withdraw, leave her to handle this entirely on her own.

But Paul didn't let her down. He walked over to her, and took her in his arms. She felt his shirt buttons pressing in cool circles along her breastbone. He smelled of damp wool, and soap laced with iodine, and underneath, more faintly, of the indefinable scent that was Paul's alone—the scent she now associated mainly with the jackets and sweaters still hanging in his closet. Ellie felt an almost overwhelming sense of relief, mixed with a longing so acute she thought she might die from it.

"Do you believe in karma?" She spoke with her cheek pressed into a creased lapel.

"Only the good kind," he murmured.

"Maybe you were right . . . maybe it just wasn't in the cards for us. For me." Her hands knotted into fists, which she squeezed against his back as she struggled to keep from dissolving once more into tears. "But, damn it, Paul, we're not talking about some theoretical baby. Alisa is . . . is . . . my child. My baby."

"I know."

Do you? she wondered.

"I'm not giving her up," she stated fiercely. "If I can't convince Skyler to back down, I'll fight her."

Paul's face, she saw as he drew back, was grave, his lenses stamped with half-moons of moisture that partially hid his eyes. Tears? she wondered. Did Paul care more about the baby than he'd let on?

She thought of the last time he'd visited, how tenderly he'd held Alisa, and how he'd grinned when she rewarded him with a smile. Watching him with her, Ellie had imagined the three of them strolling through the park in the not-too-distant future, swinging their daughter between them, a small hand in each of theirs.

A sharp splinter wedged itself into her heart.

Ellie searched Paul's face, her breath lodged in her throat like something solid that might choke her. As a single mother, she would have a hard time convincing a judge that it would be in Alisa's best interests to grant her custody. Her whole life depended on his answer to her question. Their whole future.

"Will you help me?" she asked quietly.

Paul was shaking his head, and the look he gave her filled her with dread. "Ellie," he said, "I know how much you want this, but you have to understand one thing: you don't have a leg to stand on. I've seen it happen—we had a baby this nice churchgoing couple tried to adopt, and the court awarded custody to the teenaged mom, even though she had no means to support her son other than by going on welfare."

This is different! Ellie wanted to scream.

But how was it different? Because she already knew and loved Alisa? The fact was that Skyler, aside from being smart and able, had parents with financial resources a high school dropout on welfare couldn't even begin to dream of.

Ellie knew Paul was right, but at the same time she wanted to hit him. "Are you saying you won't help me?" She took a step back, her eyes narrowing, a thread of icy cold unraveling down her spine.

Paul stared at her for a long, full moment before speaking. Then in a voice breaking with anguish, he said, "Ellie, in spite of everything that's come between us, and all the time we've spent apart, one thing hasn't changed: I love you. I'd probably keep loving you if you went on tilting at windmills forever."

Ellie held back the smile that trembled at the corners of her mouth. She couldn't afford to lose herself to the happiness blooming in the hollow at the base of her throat. Not just yet.

"It's just this one windmill, Paul, and she's not such a big one. All I'm asking is that you move back in ... at least until after the hearing, if there is one. After that—well, after that, we'll see, I guess."

"Even if I did, you know there's no guarantee we'd win."

"*Almost* no chance is better than none," she reminded him. "And maybe Skyler will feel differently once she sees that we're together. A family."

"Do you really think that will happen?" He raised a skeptical brow.

Ellie thought for a moment. "No. If she's anything like me, and I think she is . . ." She shook her head. "No."

"Stubborn, huh?" He gave her his patented crooked smile.

"You ain't seen nothing yet." She hooked an arm through his. "Let's talk about it while we eat. I just put Alisa down for the night."

She found one of the elusive menus under the telephone directory on the kitchen counter and handed it to Paul.

"Sung Lo Ho hasn't been shut down by the health department yet?" he joked.

"Judging from the way it looks on the outside, I don't even want to *know* what goes on in the kitchen. All I care about is that their stuff tastes good." Ellie, busy grabbing plates from the cupboard over the sink, whirled around so suddenly she nearly collided with him. "Oh, Paul," she cried, dropping the plates onto the counter with a clatter and wrapping her arms around him. "Paul, I love you so much."

He buried his face against her neck. She could feel his breath sifting through her hair, and the rim of his glasses against her skin like a slice of something deliciously cool and wonderful. His lanky body pressed to hers, his heartbeat strong and swift, filled her with confidence. *Stay*, she willed him. *Don't leave me this time.*

She felt him shudder, as if the depth of her longing was too much even for him. "I'll do what I can." He sighed. "Not because I think it will help. But because you're my wife, and I love you. God help me for saying this, but if you wanted me to climb Mount Everest for you, I'd probably do it."

A flood of relief washed through her, nearly lifting her off her feet, even as she said cautiously, "You might fall."

"On the other hand, I might not."

She pulled back, giving him a look weighted with equal measures of hope and fear. "What if we make it all the way up?" she asked softly. "What then?"

"Then we'd be on top of the world." He smiled, and shook his head. "But don't count on it, Ellie. Christ Almighty, don't count on it."

CHAPTER 14

As she wound her way up the long drive to Orchard Hill in her Datsun, Skyler was mildly surprised by the explosion of green that had taken place while her back was turned. In the fields rolling past on either side of her, spring grass covered the bald spots left by winter. Hedges and shrubs sported tiaras of paler green, and tree branches were tipped with new growth. It was mid-May, and the mock plum trees lining the one-lane road were almost past their peak, the ground beneath them misted with fallen, bruised petals.

Where had April gone? she wondered. Last month, and the first half of May, seemed to have passed in a kind of dream, the kind you wake from with a head stuffed with goose down. It had been two weeks since she'd spoken to Ellie—a confrontation that had filled her with remorse, but had done nothing to lessen her yearning. No, not a yearning, a *sickness*.

It wasn't the kind of sickness that kept her in bed, or even prevented her from going about her business—making breakfast for herself every morning, exercising Chancellor, even resuming her job at the veterinary clinic.

But there had to be more to life than simply going through the motions. That's why she was here, wasn't it? It had come down to this: she needed help.

Skyler played over in her mind her meeting with Verna Campbell, the no-nonsense family lawyer she'd chosen.

"Nothing is ever watertight, of course," the matronly older woman had warned. "A lot depends on the judge and his particular prejudices. But the precedents are overwhelmingly in your favor. I'd like to file a motion for temporary custody until we know the outcome of the hearing. You're not likely to get it, but we can always try."

Except that Verna Campbell, who was reputed to be among the best, didn't come cheap.

Skyler had done everything in her own power to raise the twenty-thousand-dollar retainer required by her lawyer, but it was no use. Without her mother's permission as executor, she couldn't invade the principal of her trust. Even the cabin at Gipsy Trail wouldn't be hers outright until she was twenty-five.

After all she'd put them through, she hated having to go to her parents. But, on the other hand, what was she asking for, really? Nothing that wouldn't be hers eventually. It wasn't as if she'd be hitting them up for a loan.

So what are you so worried about? When you tell her what you need the money for, she'll be falling all over herself to phone the bank. The only thing that will matter to Mom is having her grandchild back. . . .

But if there was no reason for her to feel anxious, why was her heart racing and her stomach in knots?

She shivered and turned the heat up. No matter what the actual temperature outside, or how warmly she dressed, she was always cold. She thought of an Emily Dickinson line: "And Zero at the Bone."

Zero—what you get when you subtract one from one.

A pang shot through her lower belly, almost a cramp, like the ones she'd had in labor. A memory came to her: a warm, damp weight against her tender stomach, a small dark head rooting blindly at her breast.

Skyler's hands knotted about the steering wheel. *God, oh, God—how did I let it happen? How could I have let her go?*

Skyler was sorry for the pain she was causing Ellie. None of this was Ellie's fault; she, more than anyone Skyler had ever known, deserved to be a mother. But though Skyler had agonized over Ellie's plight, tossing in her bed night after night, no amount of compassion could prevent her from the course she had set upon: reclaiming her baby.

And oddly, the one person who had to know exactly how she felt was Ellie.

I'm sure she knows all too well. That's the problem. After all she went through, do you honestly think she won't pull out every stop to keep it from happening again?

"She can try all she wants, but it won't do any good," Skyler said aloud into the Datsun's humming, overheated silence.

Are you so sure? piped a coldly reasoning voice in her head.

No, she wasn't. Not a hundred percent. No one had held a gun to her head when she'd signed that paper terminating her parental rights, and the judge would surely take that into consideration. And Ellie . . . oh, God, Ellie would fight her tooth and nail. It could get nasty. It could take months. And all the while, it would be Ellie watching Alisa cut her first tooth and learn to pull herself upright. It would be Ellie collecting snapshots for her photo album and proudly showing Alisa off to her friends.

Skyler knew she would have to act swiftly and decisively before Alisa became any more attached to Ellie than she already was.

Until yesterday, it wouldn't have occurred to Skyler that her mother might refuse to help. But when she had called to ask if she could stop by today, Mom had immediately sensed something was up. When had Skyler ever needed permission for that, especially on Sunday?

"Oh, darling . . . of *course*," her mother had gushed. "It's been much too long. And it wouldn't be exaggerating one bit if I were to tell you your father and I have been worried sick about you." She sounded upset, but didn't scold Skyler for not having called or visited sooner. Then she blurted: "What is it, Sky? Can't you tell me what's wrong?"

Skyler, fighting back tears, had taken a deep breath and confessed, "Mom, I made a mistake giving Alisa up. I'm working on getting her back." There was a long silence, in which she could hear her mother breathing. "Mom? Did you hear me?"

"I heard you." But her reaction wasn't at all what Skyler had anticipated. Mom had sounded so strange . . . not delighted, as Skyler would have expected.

Now, driving up to see her mother, Skyler couldn't shake the disappointment she'd felt at Kate's response. Where had it come from—the disapproval she'd sensed in Mom's tone? Was Mom disgusted with her for making a decision that had dragged them all through the fires of hell . . . and now doing exactly the same in reverse?

It didn't seem like her mother; she wasn't a bit judgmental. Nevertheless, as she wound her way up the hillside, Skyler couldn't help feeling anxious and more than a little bewildered.

Wasn't it her mother who'd pleaded with her not to give her baby up in the first place? Not only that, she'd been there, right there in the room, when Alisa

was born . . . and the tears streaming down her face
had not all been tears of joy.

*Something's going on, something she's not telling me.
Trouble between her and Daddy?* Skyler knew that
even happy marriages sometimes fell apart when
money became a problem. Maybe her father's firm
was in far worse trouble than she'd imagined. . . .

The sight of the old stone stable sliding into view
from behind a raft of greenery helped her to relax
a bit.

Skyler remembered her very first pony, and her
mother's hands about her waist, firm and strong, as
she lifted her into its saddle. In her mind's eye, she
could see Mom's face turned up to hers like a daisy
tracking the sun, her smile loving and encouraging.

She won't let me down now, Skyler told herself.

As she crested the hill, the house rose as if to greet
her, white and sparkling in the sunshine, its gables
alive with nesting swallows swooping in and out of
their peaks. The redbud trees flanking the front porch
had lost most of their blossoms, and were beginning
to leaf out. Below them, flower beds jeweled with tu-
lips and hyacinth held out bravely against the encroaching alyssum and sweet william. And purple
clematis spilled from the pair of eighteenth-century
bronze urns—Mom's big "find" that she'd been so excited about—that stood on either side of the flagstone
path leading up to the front door.

As she parked the Datsun and climbed out, Skyler
imagined she was seeing the house through the eyes
of someone visiting here for the first time—a man un-
accustomed to luxury, who might be a bit intimidated
by such obvious wealth. Well, not intimidated exactly;
she couldn't imagine Tony feeling that way around
anyone or anything. Awed, perhaps. The way someone
who was perfectly content with himself would feel
about pulling off to the side of the road to take in

a spectacular view before moving on to wherever he was headed.

Of course, Tony's likes or dislikes wouldn't have concerned her at all if it hadn't been for two unavoidable truths: that he was the father of her child . . . and that she was hopelessly in love with him.

The memory of the night they'd spent together at the cabin rose in her mind like the shadow flames that had danced on the wall as they'd made wild, sweet, life-giving love. She remembered the heat from the fire, and how it had seemed to be coming from inside her, flickering just below her bare, sweat-polished skin. And how, afterward, Tony had gone into the bathroom, returning with a warm wet cloth, which he used to wash away first her tears, then the stickiness from her belly. Then he'd tenderly lifted her up and carried her to bed, where he had lain beside her, holding her, just *holding* her, until she had started to believe that maybe the world wasn't coming to an end after all.

But whatever magic he'd used that night to restore her, she couldn't imagine it being powerful enough to carry them through all the nights and days that lay ahead. It wasn't just their being so different; it was Alisa, too. It was knowing that they wouldn't have been thrown together like this if Skyler hadn't gotten pregnant. Their courtship, if you wanted to call it that, hadn't been one of wine and laughter and valentines . . . but of bitterness and shared pain. What kind of life could be built on that?

Don't think about Tony, she warned herself. *Alisa comes first.* As she made her way up the flagstone path, only the thought of how theatrical it would look to anyone who might be watching her from a window kept Skyler from pressing her palms to her temples, exactly as she'd seen in a hundred movies.

She found her mother in the small room off the kitchen that once upon a time had been the laundry porch, before the washer and drier had been banished to the basement. Now the deep corrugated sink was filled with ailing houseplants, and the tiled work counter was cluttered with pots and cuttings sprouting in mason jars. Kate, wearing a denim butcher's apron over corduroys and a plaid shirt, was bent over a ceramic pot into which she was transplanting a root-bound asparagus fern.

She looked up as Skyler walked in, her frown of concentration dissolving into a happy smile. "Hi, sweetie. Is it lunchtime already? Oh, gosh, look at me, all covered in dirt, and I haven't even given a thought to what we're going to eat.... Skyler, what's the matter? Oh, darling ..."

What Skyler felt right now was ashamed, for standing here like a ten-year-old with her eyes leaking like one of Mom's freshly watered plants. But she couldn't seem to help it. Whenever she was really upset, seeing her mother had this effect on her, as if a button had been pushed, one that brought tears and made her remember Mom's way of always making everything better.

Skyler accepted the paper towel Kate was pressing into her hand, blowing her nose while taking comfort in the smell of potting soil and greenery that she associated so richly with home.

"I swore I wasn't going to do this." Her voice broke, and she shook her head in disgust. "I didn't come here to cry on your shoulder."

"Well, for goodness' sake, why not? Isn't that what mothers are for?" Kate gave a gentle laugh and patted her cheek.

"It's more than that. Mom, I need your help."

Kate set down the pair of shears with which she'd been separating the fern's tangled roots. Washing her hands and drying them on her apron, she turned and slipped an arm about her daughter's shoulders. "Come on, let's sit down and have something to eat. We can talk about it over lunch."

Skyler noted the fine sprays of wrinkles around her mother's eyes; there was a deep line between her eyebrows that she didn't remember from the last time she'd visited, only a few weeks ago. Kate's hair, which had been brown with a little gray mixed in, was now almost all gray. She seemed to be leaning more heavily on her cane, too, as she made her way from the laundry porch into the big, sunny kitchen beyond it.

She doesn't always show it, but this has hit her hard, Skyler thought as she watched her mother unhook a copper pot from the circular rack over the butcher block island. On the heels of that thought came: *It's all my fault.*

Awash with guilt, Skyler sank into a press-back chair at the round oak breakfast table. Vera, it turned out, had made sandwiches, and there was asparagus soup from last night that Mom was now heating up. The table had been set, and a bowl of fresh-cut irises sat in the center of the sprigged tablecloth. Kate appeared at the table a few minutes later, carrying two steaming bowls, which smelled delicious. Skyler, who for weeks had hardly been able to eat, felt suddenly ravenous.

"Nana used to say that everything is always worse on an empty stomach," Kate said with a smile, settling into the chair opposite Skyler's.

"Grandmothers always think food is the answer to everything."

"What about mothers?" Kate arched a brow.

"Mothers are always quoting their mothers."

Suddenly, Skyler was struck by the very real possibility that she might never have the opportunity to know her firstborn child, might never sit with Alisa at the kitchen table as she and her mother sat now. She and Alisa might never joke with each other, and roll their eyes at old family sayings.

Responding at once to her stricken look, Kate reached across the table and covered her hand. "Oh,

my darling—I don't know what to say that will be of
any comfort.... All this must be so confusing for
you."

"I'm not confused anymore," Skyler told her. "Just
plain old miserable."

"Losing a child isn't easy. I know." Her eyes flashed
bright for an instant.

"This isn't about losing Alisa, it's about getting her
back." Skyler took a deep breath and said, "I've seen
a lawyer."

Kate sat back with a dazed look. "A lawyer. My
goodness, isn't that rather ... extreme?"

Skyler felt annoyed by her mother's failure to grasp
the urgency of the situation. "What else can I do?"
she asked. "It's not as if Ellie is going to just hand
her over. I've spoken with her, and we ... well, it went
pretty much the way I expected." Surprising herself as
much as Kate, she added staunchly, "And you know
something? I don't blame her. I'd do exactly the same
in her place."

Kate was quiet as she stared out the window, where
a nuthatch flitted in and out of the bird feeder over
the sill. Finally, she turned to Skyler, and in an odd,
flat voice said, "I don't blame her, either."

Skyler stared at her mother. Mom was simply agreeing with her ... but for some reason Skyler couldn't
help feeling slightly irritated. Why wasn't Mom rushing to say how eager she was to have her granddaughter back?

Maybe she's afraid of getting her hopes up, a voice
in Skyler's mind reasoned. *Maybe she doesn't trust you
not to back down. You have to show her that you mean
business* ...

"Mom, I need your help," she said.

"What kind of help?" Kate stiffened ever so
slightly.

"It's not what you think ... I'm not planning on
dragging you and Daddy into anything messy," Skyler

hastened to explain. "I—I know you two have your own stuff to deal with." It was the closest she'd come to admitting she knew how worried they were about their finances.

Kate cast her a pained look. "Oh, honey ... I'd *never* get so caught up in my own problems that I wouldn't be there for you."

Skyler took a deep breath. "All I need right now is enough money to pay my lawyer a retainer. Twenty-five thousand dollars." Quickly, before Kate could respond, she added, "I'm not asking for a loan—just a letter from you okaying the withdrawal from my trust account."

Kate blinked at her as if she'd just been asked to serve up a slice of green cheese from the moon. Softly, she asked, "Isn't this awfully sudden? We only spoke about it the other day."

Skyler felt as if all the blood in her veins had been replaced with ice water. Why was her mother acting this way?

In a voice numbed with shock, Skyler observed dully, "I thought you'd be thrilled."

"Under any other circumstances, I *would* be," Kate said defensively. "But— Oh, dear, it's all gotten so complicated. Darling, are you sure you know what you'll be getting into?"

"You mean unlike when I stupidly let myself get pregnant?" Skyler snapped.

The injured look that came over her mother's face immediately made her regret her outburst. At the same time, Skyler had the awful, unsettling sense that her mother was stalling. Why? What could Mom possibly hope to gain by putting her off?

"That's isn't fair, and you know it!" Kate cried. "Didn't your father and I do everything under the sun to convince you not to give up the baby? And when you wouldn't listen to us, didn't we respect your wishes? So don't you dare sit there now and look at me as if I've let you down. If anyone's been let down, it's your father and me."

Kate's anger had been directed at her so rarely, Skyler almost didn't recognize it. Now, seeing the pinched white flesh around Kate's mouth and the stiff way she was holding herself, Skyler felt herself flinch.

Knowing her mother was right only made matters worse. More than merely contrite, Skyler felt ashamed of how she'd behaved. With a sigh, she said, "Mom, I know I should have listened to you. I was trying to be so rational, trying to think of what would be best for the baby. I didn't think I had what it took to give a child everything it deserved. But who does? Look at all the sacrifices you made for me."

Kate's eyes filled with tears, and the stiffness left her as abruptly as if an invisible thread had been pulled. "Oh, darling, I never regretted a minute of it. I would have done anything for you. If you only knew ..." She bit her lip, and a single tear slipped down her cheek and dropped off her chin to form a dark smudge on the woven green placemat.

"I *do* know," Skyler said. "And that's why I'd never ask for your help now if it involved your making any kind of sacrifice. I'll even write the letter myself, if you like. All I need is your signature."

Mom was gripping the edge of the table, wearing an odd, faraway look. "It's too late," she said in a small, choked voice.

"Too late?" Skyler echoed, unable to believe she'd heard correctly.

With a deeply troubled sigh, Kate brought her fingertips to rest under her chin. "I'm sorry." This time her answer left no room for doubt; Skyler felt it in her gut, as sharply as the knife point tracing its way up her spine. In that same soft but implacable tone, Kate said, "I wish I could help you, but it wouldn't be right. It wouldn't be fair to—to her."

Skyler sat back, too stunned at first to react. Finally,

she gasped, "Ellie? This is all about *Ellie?* You don't even know her!"

"I know what she must be feeling," Kate said. "You're young. You'll have other children. But this is her last chance to be a mother."

Skyler felt the blood leave her face as she stared at the woman seated across from her . . . the mother she'd loved and counted on, who had been replaced by a complete stranger.

Kate held perfectly still. She imagined that if she made the tiniest movement, even so much as a twitch of her finger, she would shatter like very old, very fine crystal. It was all she could do to steady herself against the tide of emotion crashing through her.

Her anguish was only deepened by the look on Skyler's shocked white face.

Did I really say that?

The words, they'd just . . . slipped out. She hadn't planned them, and would have been stunned had anyone suggested that she might react this way.

It had nearly broken her heart that day in the hospital, seeing Skyler's newborn daughter cradled in Ellie's arms. And not a day had passed since then when she didn't feel a throb of loss at the thought of her granddaughter. She would be puttering about the house or doing something mundane at the shop, and it would hit her. Then she would have to stop and catch her breath, one hand fluttering to her throat, another to her stomach as if to ward off a blow.

She would have moved heaven and earth to help Skyler win back her daughter. She would have sold Orchard Hill to give Skyler the money out of her own pocket. There was only one thing she wouldn't sacrifice: her conscience.

She'd been given a second chance, and she must not throw it away. She no longer even believed it was mere fate that had brought her and Ellie together.

Perhaps if she had been more religious, she would
have said it was God's will. And maybe it was. All
she knew for certain was what she must do—it was
clear as a finger pointing out the path she must take
in order to redeem herself.

An eye for an eye, a tooth for a tooth . . .

A child for a child.

With a supreme effort, Kate forced herself to speak.
She had to try and help her daughter understand, even
if Skyler couldn't know the whole story.

"Darling . . . if you'd asked for my help even three
months ago, I would have stood by you in the face of
an invading army," she said in a frayed voice. "But
now it's too late. Alisa is her child. I can't just—" She
swallowed hard, adding softly, "It'd be like . . . like
killing the woman."

Skyler was shaking her head, a strand of her pale
hair catching on the corner of her mouth where it was
wet. The eyes she fixed on Kate were those of a mar-
tyr in a Renaissance painting—they seemed to give off
an odd, translucent light. But it was more than just
suffering that Kate was witnessing. The look on her
daughter's face was one of profound betrayal.

"What about your own daughter?" Skyler spoke in
a whisper. "This is killing *me*. Don't you even care?"

Kate wanted to cover her eyes, to shield them from
that tortured light in her daughter's eyes. *Oh, my darling, if you only, knew!*

Under normal circumstances, she would have
moved heaven and earth to help Skyler in any way
possible. Refusing her plea was like a stake in Kate's
heart—an agony as great, surely, as that which Skyler
was suffering now. But she couldn't do this . . . she
simply *couldn't*.

There would be Will to deal with later as well, she
realized. He'd be furious when he learned that she'd
refused to help Skyler. Doubly so, because he was in

no position to simply make out a check, as he normally would have.

"I'm sorry," she told Skyler, squeezing her eyes shut and pressing her palms together so tightly she could feel the muscles in her arms begin to quiver. "I would do anything you asked of me ... anything except this. No matter how much I might want to, I can't. I don't expect you to understand. Just don't forget that I love you. I've loved you from the first moment I held you in my arms. If anyone had tried to take you away from me then, I..." She opened her eyes and looked directly at Skyler. "I would have died."

"I know the feeling." Skyler's voice was flat and cold.

"Darling, I know this is hard, and I won't presume to suggest that you'll get over it someday. There are some things we never get over. But I can promise you this: life *will* go on."

Skyler looked back at her bleakly. "That's what I'm afraid of."

"It *will* get better," Kate told her, feeling like a cheat, a snake-oil salesman, for making such a promise.

"You're right about that much," Skyler said bitterly, "but not because I plan on sitting back and licking my wounds. I'll get the money somewhere. No matter what I have to do."

Kate brought a hand to her mouth. "I wish you wouldn't talk that way," she said.

"What did you expect? That just because you wouldn't help me, I was going to give up?"

"No ... I suppose not." Kate gave a slow nod of acknowledgment. That much she had to admit: no one could ever have accused her daughter of being a quitter. "I just wish ... I wish you didn't always have to rush headlong into things without thinking them through."

"How long did it take you and Daddy to decide to adopt me?" Skyler challenged.

Even as Kate smiled and said, "Less than a second," she was remembering as well her anguish upon discovering the truth about her baby.

And now the terrible debt she owed had come due.

"If you love me so much, why won't you help me?" Skyler brought her fists up, anchoring them on either side of the bowl of soup going cold on the table: "This isn't some moral principle we're talking about. It's my baby. Your granddaughter." Her voice rose and cracked. "You can't just turn your back on me— *you're my mother!*"

"And I always will be," Kate reminded her quietly.

"No." Skyler was quivering, her wounded expression like a bolt shot through Kate's heart. "I don't know who my mother is . . . but you're not her."

Kate watched wretchedly as her daughter pushed herself to her feet, pausing a moment as if to steady herself before she turned and began walking away. Kate wanted to snatch back her words, and Skyler's; she wanted to say or do something, *anything*, that would close the terrible gap that had opened between them. All Skyler's life, she'd been afraid of losing her . . . and now it was finally happening.

And this time Kate could do nothing to stop it.

Driving away from Orchard Hill, Skyler was oblivious to where she was headed until she found herself turning down the road that led to Stony Creek Farm. Minutes later, she was parking in the graveled lot below the stable and climbing out of her Datsun on legs that wobbled as they hadn't since the days she'd first started riding. It was late in the afternoon, and the sun had sent long shadows rippling out from under the paddock fences. Here spring rains coupled with the hooves of grazing horses had left the fields churned into hock-deep mud. But the outdoor schooling ring, she noticed, had been spread with a fresh layer of tanbark; Duncan had seen to that. Off in the distance, she spotted his lean, imposing figure in front of the hay shed that serviced the paddocks along Stony Creek's far north quadrant, playing traffic director to a flatbed truck loaded with hay.

But it wasn't Duncan she needed right now, Skyler realized. It was Mickey. Her friend was training Mrs. Endicott's new horse, Victory Lap, for the Hartsdale Classic in West Palm Beach next month, and was here at least four hours a day, every day, working him on the flat and taking him over jumps.

When Skyler walked through the stable and under the wide arch that led to the attached indoor exercise ring, Mickey, astride a handsome chestnut Thoroughbred, immediately trotted over to the fence. Taking a good look at Skyler's tear-swollen face, she swung down from the saddle.

"Jesus ... who died?" Mickey palmed open the gate latch.

"I think it might have been me," Skyler told her.

"This is the part where I'm either supposed to slap you or give you a shot of whiskey and say, 'It's for your own good'—I can't remember which." Mickey gave a throaty laugh that only partly disguised her concern.

"You don't know the half of it."

Mickey shrugged. "I'm sure you'll get around to telling me when you're ready."

Skyler thanked Mickey silently for not pressuring her. As Skyler took in her friend's sweat-stained, open-collared shirt and muddy breeches, the length of grimy adhesive tape wound around the butt of her crop, she knew she'd come to the right person—one who wouldn't smother her with sympathy. What Skyler needed more than a shoulder to cry on was a good dose of common sense and some hardheaded advice.

"Come on, help me get this brute tacked down, and you can tell me about it." They had reached the grooming area just inside the entrance to the stable, where several pairs of cross-ties were bolted to the walls on either side. Mickey unhooked the curb chain under Victory's bit and slipped off his bridle, snapping a cross-tie chain onto each of its cheek rings.

After rubbing the Thoroughbred down with an old towel, she picked his hooves, then brushed his underbelly. Minutes later, a bridle slung over one shoulder, a saddle tucked under her arm, she headed for the tack room while Skyler led Victory Lap to his stall. As she breathed in the familiar smells of hay, sawdust, and manure and listened to the horses knock about in their loose boxes, she felt her pain ease a bit. She could hear Duncan shouting outside, in one of the lower paddocks. One of the stablehands, a dark-haired kid she didn't remember seeing before, cast her a shy smile as he wheeled past a barrow full of sweepings. She managed a wan smile in return.

Skyler found Mickey by the double doors that opened onto Stony Creek's east-facing exposure, beyond which lay the outdoor exercise ring. She stood looking out, her elbows crossed languidly over her right knee, her heel resting on the wooden bench where countless times the two of them had sat struggling to tug on their boots. Outside, a cloudburst that seemed to have come out of nowhere was letting loose a torrent of rain that ran off the eaves in tattered sheets.

Skyler slumped onto the bench and watched Mickey light a cigarette. Mickey didn't say anything, just stood there smoking and staring out at the rain. The stable cat hopped onto Skyler's lap and began purring as she stroked him.

Mickey offered her a cigarette from the crumpled pack stuffed in the front pocket of her shirt. Skyler took one, even though she didn't smoke. For old times' sake, she thought.

"Tough, huh?" Mickey said at last. "I told you being a mother was no joke."

"A lot you would know about it." Skyler shot her a mock disdainful look, then went back to studying the smoke curling up from the glowing tip of her cigarette.

"Yeah, you're right, I'd be a washout, probably," Mickey agreed. "You're going to do it, aren't you? You're really going to fight this." Skyler had confided in her as soon as she realized what she had to do ... but even Mickey didn't know just *how* determined she was.

"I have to."

"Jesus." Mickey's expression bordered on awe. "Skyler, let me say one thing: you sure know how to fuck up. I mean, big time. But I've got to hand it to you on one score: when you want something, you really go for it."

Mickey would know, Skyler thought. Then she said: "According to my mother, it's both a curse and a blessing." She took a drag off her cigarette that tasted like dried manure.

"Do I take that to mean you talked to her about the money?"

"I just came from the house."

"And?"

Skyler took a deep breath. "She won't do it. She won't write the damn letter to the bank."

"I don't believe it." Not much could have shocked Mickey, but the idea that Kate, whom Mickey idolized, could do such a thing was staggering. "Are you sure? I mean, could you maybe have misinterpreted her?"

"I'm sure." Yet even for Skyler, it hadn't yet sunk in all the way. She kept turning the scene over and over in her mind, hoping that she'd been mistaken, that her mother hadn't really refused to help her. But, no, Mom had been utterly clear. There was no way Skyler could have misunderstood.

The reality of the situation slammed home, and Skyler slid onto her tailbone, her back braced against the wall, hugging the cat to her chest. Her heart ached, and there was a hole in her stomach that nothing could have filled. She felt as if she'd lost not only her baby, but her mother as well.

Suddenly, she was swept with longing for Tony—for the solid feel of his arms about her, the strong beat of his heart against hers . . . for his very ordinariness, which she could use a dose of right now, in the midst of her own extraordinarily fucked-up life.

"It wasn't just my mom. I—I said some things I shouldn't have," Skyler admitted, the memory of her angry words like some poison she'd swallowed that she was just now beginning to feel the effects of. "But I felt so . . . betrayed. Mickey, how could she?"

"She must have given you some kind of explanation."

"I think it's all tied up somehow with her adopting me. She identifies with Ellie. Still, I just don't get it." She dropped her cigarette onto the concrete, worn to a shallow depression by countless hooves. "Besides that, I don't know what I'm going to do. I need that money."

"What about your father? He'll give it to you, won't he?"

"Sure, he would. In a minute." She stopped, not sure how much she wanted Mickey to know about her father's financial difficulties, though God knew Mickey's family had plenty of their own. "But I don't want any handouts from them. I want to do this myself, with my own money."

"I wish I weren't so strapped. I'd lend it to you."

"I know you would." Skyler sighed.

Mickey shot her a sly glance. "You could ask Tony. I'll bet he'd find a way to get the money."

"Forget it," Skyler snapped. This was one subject she definitely did not want to pursue, especially with Mickey, who couldn't understand why, if she was so crazy about the guy, she wasn't sleeping with him.

"All right, scratch that," Mickey said with a shrug. "Any other ideas?"

"I could rob a bank."

"Too risky. Plus I don't think they award custody to convicted felons." She paused, taking a last drag on her cigarette before grinding it out against her boot heel in a minor fizzle of sparks. "Listen, I have a better idea. You could go to West Palm Beach with me. Hartsdale is four weeks away. There's still time to train if you really knuckle down."

Skyler stared at her, aghast. "You've got to be out of your mind. Mickey, it's been months since I've taken Chance over a jump. He's been turned out most of the winter—he'd be nowhere near ready by then."

"The Grand Prix carries a thirty-thousand-dollar purse." Mickey let the words hang there.

"It could be a million. I still wouldn't stand a chance of winning it."

Mickey shrugged. "Well, if that's the attitude you're going to take, then you're probably right."

"I *know* I'm right."

"In that case, forget I mentioned it."

"Duncan would throw a fit. I don't even have the entry fee. I—"

"I thought the subject was closed." Mickey slanted her a crafty look.

"It is." Skyler, realizing how close she'd come to falling into Mickey's trap, clamped her mouth shut.

"Want another cigarette?" Mickey offered her the pack.

"No thanks." Skyler fell silent, her heart beginning to race at the thought of what it would take to get in shape for a world-class competition like Hartsdale. More than grueling dawn-to-dark days; more than

Duncan shouting at her, telling her to do it over, over, over; more than maybe even Chancellor, at his best, could deliver. It would take the one thing that had been absent from her performance until now: a desire to win that came from a place much deeper than mere competitiveness.

"Duncan would have to agree to it," Skyler told her. "I couldn't pull it off without him."

"Oh, sure, but you know Dunc. He loves nothing better than a challenge."

"Chancellor would have to be built up. His leg muscles aren't nearly what they were a year ago."

"He'll get back into the groove in no time. He's a champ."

"And look at me—I'm in the lousiest shape I've ever been in. It's crazy to even think I could do this. By summer maybe I'd be ready, but, Mickey, a *month?*"

"How soon do you need the money?" Mickey asked.

"Yesterday."

"Well?"

"We're not even talking about me taking the purse, it'd be a miracle if I even qualify."

"So what's stopping you from at least trying?"

Skyler thought it over for a moment, then asked, "Can I bunk with you in West Palm? After I scrounge up the entry fee, and pay for shipping Chance, I'll be pretty broke."

Mickey's tea-brown eyes narrowed. "You didn't need me to talk you into this, did you? You knew the minute I brought it up that you were going to go for it."

"Do I have a choice?" Skyler watched the stable cat uncoil and leap off her lap, darting off into the shadows. A phone was ringing in the office. The rain had nearly stopped.

For the first time in days, weeks even, she felt free

of the helplessness that had swamped her each morning upon rising and had clung to her like a mist until she fell into bed at night.

. . . and the cow jumped over the moon.

The line from the nursery rhyme popped into her mind, and despite the shallow, scared racing of her heart, Skyler found herself smiling. *Could* she pull it off? God knew she had something worthwhile to fight for this time. For Alisa, she'd jump over the moon on the back of a cow . . . or she'd fall off trying.

Mickey had been right about one thing: Duncan was up for it.

However cranky, contentious, and demanding he was; however he bitched and protested, he nonetheless couldn't resist the call to arms of pummeling into shape leg muscles turned to jelly, and sharpening a sense of timing gone to seed. Day after day, often for eight hours at a stretch, Skyler worked with him in the ring. In fair weather, they trained outdoors. When it rained, they used the indoor schooling ring. Through it all Duncan was relentless.

"Head up! How many times have I told you to keep your chin up!" he'd bark, as he hadn't since she was ten years old. "And smile, goddammit, you're supposed to make it look like you're having fun. Like going over a six-foot jump is a bloody piece of cake!"

Skyler had taken a month off from the clinic to devote herself to training full-time, and she dragged home every night exhausted. The bridge of her nose burned, then peeled, then burned again. Freckles appeared on cheeks that had been pale as frost. Often, she would wake from a deep, drugged-seeming sleep to find her calves twitching and her fingers curled, thumbs up, as if around a pair of reins.

After two weeks, she began to notice a difference. The parts of her body that had been soft were becoming lean and hard again. Duncan's yells of disgust gradually gave way to brisk orders peppered with an occasional stiff-necked nod when she got it right. The jumps he constructed got higher and more difficult. And she no longer dropped out of the saddle at the end of each day on legs of foam rubber.

Unruly as a child that's been left unsupervised for too long, Chancellor had rebelled at first, bucking to show his displeasure when she disciplined him, and refusing to take jumps he'd have sailed over effortlessly a year ago. But after a prickly start, he settled down and even seemed to enjoy himself. Mickey had been right about that, too—Chancellor was a champion. And champion horses liked nothing more than the opportunity to show off.

At the end of the third week, Chance developed a mild case of lameness, and Skyler spent several fretful days at the barn applying cold packs and poultices. When Dr. Novick ruled out a bowed tendon, she relaxed a bit. Still, he couldn't be ridden for several days . . . and that was a source of panic in itself. What if he was still showing signs of lameness by the time they had to leave for Hartsdale? She wouldn't be able to enter him. All her hard work would have been for nothing.

Fortunately, though, Chancellor's leg was sound by the following Monday. Breathing a huge sigh of relief, Skyler nonetheless babied him until it became obvious to her—and to Duncan—that she was going to get nowhere this way.

On the vet's advice, she began dividing her training sessions between Chancellor and a five-year-old German Warmblood named Silver Trophy that Duncan had high hopes for. Silver Trophy wasn't as attuned to her every movement as Chancellor, but he was willing and strong. And he proved himself to be more than a substitute: he kept Skyler from becoming too settled into one groove. He kept her always on edge, looking for subtle ways to correct his performance.

Throughout the whole grueling month, what had at first seemed a curse turned out to be a blessing: working her butt off, and being so tired at the end of each day that she could hardly see straight, kept Skyler from thinking too much about her mother. She even had an excuse for not returning Kate's calls: she was almost never home.

What Skyler *did* think about was her baby. Each muscle she packed in ice, each new saddle sore on her rear end brought her another step closer to her goal. She didn't mind the long hours in the ring. She gladly put up with Duncan's bullying and Chancellor's balking. Because all of it was making her stronger, more ready to meet not only the challenge that lay just ahead, but the one beyond that: getting Alisa back.

She allowed herself to focus only on that. She refused even to let Tony visit. Oh, yes, more times than she could count, especially at the end of a blistering round with Duncan, Skyler wanted nothing more than Tony's easy presence ... his callused hand resting on her shoulder ... his straightforward approach to everything, coupled with that sardonic little smile that always seemed to be creeping in at the edges of his mouth. But every time she picked up the phone to call him, she forced herself to put it down. His presence would only distract her. As much as she longed to see him, she had to remain firm until after Hartsdale.

Hartsdale. Suddenly, what had been in the near distance was just around the bend. The two days before she was to fly down to West Palm Beach, Skyler spent haggling with the driver of the horse van that was to transport Chancellor, then putting herself even deeper into debt with MasterCard and Visa in order to scrounge up the two-thousand-dollar entry fee. By the time she boarded her flight on Thursday morning, her stomach was in knots.

It wasn't until the plane touched down in West Palm

Beach two and a half hours later that Skyler felt her strung-out tenseness begin to transform itself into genuine excitement.

She still doubted that she stood much of a chance of placing. A snowball in hell? Try a glacier. Even with all her brutal training, she wasn't in nearly as good shape as riders like Mickey, who competed all year round. But, dammit, she wasn't going to let anything or anyone stop her now. It wasn't just about the money anymore.

Win or lose, she needed to ace that competition—if only to prove to herself that she was no quitter. For if she didn't give it her all, how would she be able to make it over the hurdles that lay beyond Hartsdale's?

CHAPTER 15

The great white heron wheeled overhead; then, with a graceful swoop that seemed to carry the newly risen sun on the tip of one wing, it dropped down to land at the edge of the hibiscus-flanked water jump forming the centerpiece of the Hartsdale Grand Prix course.

Skyler, walking the course with Mickey, stopped short a dozen yards or so of the bird, which regarded her with haughty suspicion, as if to say, *"Don't get any big ideas about placing in this event. You don't have a prayer."* Good advice, she thought. It was Sunday, and the Grand Prix was less than two hours away. Far from feeling confident due to the fact that she'd placed high enough in the preliminaries to qualify, Skyler was certain she would wash out. In her opinion, the past two days of events had been nothing more than a run of spectacular luck.

Skyler looked around at the almost unbearably bucolic setting. A cloudless sky as blue as a postcard's made her forget how sticky and humid the climate was. Stretching out for acres on all sides of the stadium, with its open-air arena, the freshly sprinkled Floritam grass sparkled like some fabled city—one

populated with egrets and herons, and ringed with
huge hibiscus bushes. To the north, built on a slight
rise less than a quarter of a mile from the arena, the
sprawling, New England-style Hartsdale stables
formed the outside perimeter of the tent city—makeshift stables jockeying for space with Winnebagos and
horse trailers and Portosans—that had sprung up between it and the exhibition grounds. A thin trail of
smoke rose from the blacksmith's portable furnace.

Watching it evaporate into the implacable blue sky,
Skyler couldn't help feeling that her chances of success
were no more solid than that smoke. In the high preliminaries, she'd barely squeaked through in ninth
place, well behind Mickey in fifth, though ahead of
many who were far more seasoned. Earlier in the
week, in the Six Bars, she'd jumped clean, only to be
eliminated in the Fault and Out when Chancellor refused the last double oxer. This morning's Grand Prix,
however, would be the real test. She'd be competing
against the best of the best, and even luck might not
be enough to carry her through.

In an effort to cover every base, she had joined
Mickey and the dozen or so riders and trainers ab-
sorbed in mapping out the course. It was spread out
over half an acre—oxers and verticals and triples
painted in shades of turquoise and white; mock brick
walls constructed of balsawood blocks and flanked
with miniature orange trees; the water jump with its
sky-reflecting rectangle where the heron stood guard.

Walking slowly over the sand and shredded rubber
footing, she and Mickey carefully measured how many
strides their horses would need before each jump.
They rattled the poles in their cups, squinted like pool-
hall sharks as they paced around double and triple
spreads, gauging the best angle of approach. Kneeling
to test the give of the rubberized padding at either
end of the water jump, Skyler felt her stomach lurch.
She hadn't eaten breakfast yet, and now she wondered

in a panic if she was going to be able to keep anything down.

She had never felt this nervous before an event—heart palpitations, dry mouth, sweaty palms, the whole nine yards. But then again, she'd never had so much at stake.

"No pun intended, but there's your Waterloo," Mickey said, pointing at the glistening nine-by-three rectangle of water with its two-foot fence at the take-off. "Unless Chancellor took Red Cross swimming lessons that I don't know about."

"He won't refuse it. I'll make sure of that," Skyler answered in a hard voice she barely recognized as her own. Straightening, she adjusted the brim of the baseball cap under which she'd crammed her hair to keep it off her sweat-sticky neck. A wave of dizziness spiraled up through the top of her skull, and she held very still as she waited for it to pass.

Mickey, in a red polo shirt and cream-colored breeches with a grass stain on one knee, turned to face Skyler, one hand cupped over her eyes to shade them from the brilliant sun. "Well, look, you've made it this far. There's a good chance—"

"—I won't make it to the jump-off. I'll fall flat on my ass. Chance will pull a muscle or a tendon." Skyler reeled off the casualties that were commonplace at competitions with courses as difficult as Hartsdale's. What she didn't say aloud, because it was too appalling even to *think* about, was this: *And if I don't win that prize, there's only one way I'll be able to raise the kind of cash I need in a hurry: by selling Chancellor.* The idea had crossed her mind several weeks ago, when she'd first started training with Duncan. Her horse was worth at least fifty thousand, maybe more, if she could find an eager buyer on short notice. And as much as she loved Chancellor, if she couldn't find the money any other way, she'd be forced to do the unthinkable.

It pained her, though, like a blade with dull, rusty teeth sawing at her gut. She'd lost so much in such a short space of time. She couldn't bear the thought of losing Chancellor as well.

A loud barking distracted Skyler from her thoughts. Streaking toward her from the far end of the fair-grounds was a border collie she recognized as belonging to Beezie Patton's groom. The dog's ears were pricked, his eyes on the heron, which seemed in no particular hurry to decamp. Not until the collie was nearly on it did the bird unfold its wings with a desultory flap and take flight.

The collie slowed and trotted over to Skyler, who crouched down to scrub his ears. "Never mind, Ralphie," she consoled him. "Remember, every dog has its day." Satisfied, he licked her hand and loped off to sniff one of the potted orange trees.

"Nice to see you haven't lost your touch," Mickey said, cocking her head as she looked down at Skyler, her full mouth denting inward in a wry smile. "You heard back from UNH yet about deferring until next year?"

"Not yet, but I worked really hard to persuade them. I think they'll agree."

"I guess you've got bigger problems at the moment."

"You got that right." She kept her tone light, not wanting her friend to know just how panicky she felt.

"Do you mind me asking where Tony figures into all this?" Mickey asked cautiously.

Even since that long-ago afternoon when Tony had taken her niece and nephew under his wing and shown them around the barn, the man could do no wrong in Mickey's book.

"I don't know yet," Skyler answered truthfully. "He . . . he's in a tough spot. After all, it was his idea in the first place, putting me together with Ellie. And one thing I've learned about Tony—once he's made a promise he doesn't go back on his word."

"That could be a good thing, if you two were living together," Mickey observed.

Skyler stopped, tipping back the bill of her baseball cap to glare at her friend. "That's not funny," she said.

"It wasn't meant to be."

"Oh, right—that's all I need right now. A live-in boyfriend, on top of everything else."

"I'm not saying it would solve your problems. You're perfectly capable of solving your own. But it might do something about the lousy temper you've been in lately." She cast Skyler a sidelong glance.

"You *know* the reason for that." Missing her baby so much did more than put her in a bad mood; some days she felt as if she would simply go crazy.

The two of them finished walking the course, then headed out past the stadium toward the gypsy-like camp that occupied several square acres of flattened Floritam. The bare-chested farrier, in flame-proof chaps, had set up shop with a propane forge near his Range Rover and was bent over his anvil, hammering at a shoe. Over the hum of generators, Skyler could hear riders and grooms calling out to one another, swapping good-natured insults and last-minute advice. Men and women in short-sleeved shirts sat perched on tack boxes and tailgates, lovingly cleaning bridles and boots. The morning sunlight sparkled off bits and bridoons, stirrup irons and girth buckles, and the air smelled of saddle soap and warm leather and the sweat of high stakes.

Skyler and Mickey, though bunking at a motel down the road, were using Mrs. Endicott's camper, which was palatial enough to have accommodated a country-western star and her entire backup band. But at the moment, Skyler wasn't thinking about the refrigerator stocked with champagne and soda. All she wanted was

a shower, and a drink of water to wash away the dryness in her throat.

Then she would think about the Grand Prix, less
than an hour away. But not about losing—only about
what it would mean if she were to win.

"You go on ... I want to check up on Victory,"
Mickey told her as they were approaching the camper.
Yesterday, after the Six Bars, the Thoroughbred had
been limping, and though the vet had said it was nothing serious, Mickey wasn't taking anything for granted.
In a low voice, in case the old lady happened to be
within earshot, she added, "If the swelling hasn't gone
down, I'm not going to ride him, no matter what she
says."

As their eyes met, the irony of the situation brought
a faint smile to Skyler's lips. She touched Mickey's
sleeve, knowing that for the first—and maybe last—
time the tables between them had been turned. She
said: "You can afford not to."

Mickey smiled back, then trotted off with an up-
lifted arm.

The door of the camper was slightly ajar, and Skyler
could hear someone moving about inside. Mrs. Endicott? Or one of her hangers-on? The old lady—a
widow whose husband had made a killing in the inter-
national diamond trade—was rumored to be almost as
rich as Queen Elizabeth, with possibly as many syco-
phants and courtiers. She cautiously poked her head
inside before entering.

But the solidly built man in faded jeans and scuffed
cowboy boots seated on the built-in leather sofa
wasn't some wannabe in search of a sponsor.

"Tony!" she cried as she stepped inside, startled
into letting the aluminum-and-glass door whack shut
behind her.

As he rose, he seemed to fill up the whole cabin.
What was he doing here? More to the point, how had
he *gotten* here?

Then it struck her: Tony must have flown down just to see her.

Skyler felt a queer, guilty joy steal through her. These past four weeks she'd missed him more than she would have thought possible. Even while tallying up all the reasons they didn't belong together, all the obstacles they would face, she couldn't help remembering the feel of his arms about her... the soft nap of shirts washed and buttoned by the same hand—the hand lifted to her now in a gesture that was halfway between hello and a shrug—the sharp little intake of breath that always preceded the first of his kisses.

"I was in the neighborhood," he said, a corner of his mouth twisting up.

"Like hell." But Skyler couldn't stop the laugh that spilled out of her.

"Okay, I had vacation time coming."

"Some vacation you picked." She stepped inside, and flopped into the armchair opposite him, peeling off her muddy boots. "You could have warned me, you know."

"What for? You'd have told me not to come."

"You're right, I would have."

"Yeah? Well, old Sergeant Salvatore here is more used to giving orders than taking them. Anyway, here I am. One of the grooms told me I might find you here. A nice old lady told me it'd be okay for me to wait inside."

"Mrs. Endicott ... this is her trailer," Skyler explained. "Mickey's riding one of her horses in the Grand Prix."

Tony shrugged. "I guess she didn't think I looked the type who'd rob her."

"You're a cop."

"That I am." He gave her a challenging look.

"I need to take a shower," Skyler announced abruptly, standing up. Her tank top was soaked with sweat, and even in shorts she felt hot and sticky.

"I'll wait."

"I'll be pretty tied up after that," she told him. "The event kicks off in an hour."

"I know. I bought a ticket." He sank back down onto the sofa, propping his boots on the low table in front of him. "You go ahead ... I'll still be around when it's all over."

Skyler could feel his heat making the cabin too close, his eyes asking questions she'd rather not answer. She fought the urge to bolt into the next room.

"Tony, I don't need anyone's company right now. I even asked my parents not to come. This is a bad time."

"You could have told me," he said, his voice hard and his eyes riveted on her face. "The least you could have done was *told* me you needed money."

The sudden shift in his mood had the effect of a cloud passing over the sun, darkening his olive skin and throwing a shadow over his black eyes that made Skyler think of peering into the barrel of a gun that might go off at any moment.

"Who told you?" she demanded.

"Mickey. But don't blame her—I practically twisted her arm."

She felt a brief stab of anger at Mickey nonetheless. "Okay, what if I *had* told you? What could you have done about it? Assuming you even wanted to help, where would you have gotten that kind of money?"

"The point is, you didn't ask." He brought his heels down on the carpet with a hard thunk that seemed to rattle the trailer's metal underside. "You just figured me for the kind of guy who lives from one payday to the next. You didn't even give me the benefit of the doubt."

"Tony, I really don't need this right now." Her voice caught, and she pressed the heel of her hand to her temple, which had started to throb.

At once, his expression softened, and he rose, step-

ping around the coffee table to place a hand on her
shoulder. She could feel his hard palm, the rough
edges of its calluses pricking her where the sleeve of
her tank top didn't cover her shoulder. She wanted to
pull back ... but at the same time she wanted him to
take her in his arms. Her heart thudded in her chest,
weighted with longing.

"Hey, listen, I'm sorry," he said. "I didn't come all
the way down here to give you a hard time. Honest."

"What *did* you come for?" She looked at him
squarely, taking in the whole of him, poised before
her—a man who'd made it his job to look after her
whether she damn well liked it or not.

"For you," he said softly. "I came for you."

He folded his arms around her then, holding her
head pressed to his hard shoulder. As she buried her
face in the warm creases of his shirt, and felt his belt
buckle, cool and sharp through the thin fabric of her
top, Skyler was aware only of her need for him, and
the ache of knowing they'd gotten it all backward
somehow ... conceiving a child before they could even
conceive of loving one another, losing Alisa before
they could even imagine being a family.

But even as she ached for what they'd missed, and
what they would mostly likely never have, she felt
closer to Tony than ever before. And if he could make
no promises, nor in any way protect her from the battle with Ellie that lay ahead, then at least she would
have had this: a pair of strong arms to comfort her,
and a heart beating sure and strong against hers.

First, there were the legends.

Beezie Patton, a granddaughter of General George
Patton. Michael Matz. Ian Millar. Katie Monahan Prudent, and her husband, Henri. Names that, for Skyler,
were like the faces chiseled on Mount Rushmore. If
that wasn't intimidating enough, there was a handful
of new talent as well, the rising stars of show jump-

ing—like Mickey, who was rumored to be a sure thing
for next year's U.S. Olympic team, and Bettina Ler-
ner, an eighteen-year-old from Roanoke, who'd practically stolen the cup at California's La Quinta Classic
last year.

They numbered eleven in all, eleven out of a field
of thirty-two—those who'd made it to the Grand Prix
jump-off following three harrowing rounds marked by
knockdowns, refusals, and falls. Skyler, seated astride
her horse just outside the warm-up ring, could hardly
believe she'd made it into the pantheon, and now the
dreamlike state that had carried her through the first
rounds was wearing off. She was as nervous as Chancellor, whose flanks she could feel quivering under
her.

The clearing in which she stood, along with half a
dozen other riders poised at a standstill or walking
their horses in tight circles, was situated just fifty feet
from the stadium. Bordered on one side by yuccas
and low-growing palms, it had the advantage of being
halfway between the warm-up ring and the gated entrance to the arena. From here, Skyler could hear the
low roar of applause, punctuated by the muted blare
of the klaxon and the announcer's amplified voice. She
was struck with anxiety so keen it bordered on
paralysis.

It's all a mistake, Skyler thought. *Any minute someone's going to come up to me and tell me the wrong
score was announced and I didn't make the jump-off
after all.*

Her heart pounding, she closed her eyes and sum-
moned up her lucky talisman: an image of Alisa's
small, scrunched face, and the way her tiny hand had
flippered in the air before closing over Skyler's forefinger like a miniature starfish.

She felt her loss in one long, clean swipe up the
middle, like a scalpel slicing through her. *I can do this.
I have to do this.*

Mickey strode over, leading Victory Lap by the reins, and began struggling with the Thoroughbred's girth strap. "He's blowing out, the bastard." She smacked his side with the flat of her hand and darted a furious glance over her shoulder. "Where *is* that fucking groom?"

Skyler wasn't surprised that he was nowhere to be found. Mickey, keyed up before a big event, was like a downed power line—nobody in his right mind dared get near her.

"I think I see him over there." Skyler pointed toward the small group clustered around Diamond Exchange, Lisa MacTiernan's jittery Hanoverian. The big gray was attempting to rear, and several grooms struggled to hold him down while Lisa swore and sawed on the reins.

Business as usual, Skyler thought, feeling herself relax a little. She wasn't the only one around here who was a nervous wreck. They were all a little frayed around the edges.

Skyler turned her attention back to Mickey, who succeeded in tightening the girth on her own, then swung up into the saddle in a single liquid motion. The deep line between her dark, unplucked eyebrows had disappeared, and she was wearing her usual cocky grin as she leaned forward to pat the Thoroughbred's neck.

"At least he's not limping," Mickey observed. "The vet says his leg is fine. He just needs to rest it. After this, he'll have the north forty for the next three months, if I have anything to say about it."

"You're not taking him to Toronto?" Skyler asked.

Mickey's sleepy lids lowered in a look that was almost coy. In another woman, Skyler would have thought it had something to do with a man—but with Mickey it could mean only one thing.

"Priscilla is training a new gelding, a Westphalian. Oh, God, Skyler, wait until you see him. He's so gor-

geous! White as snow, a dead ringer for Milton,"
Mickey added in a hushed tone, invoking the legend-
ary British jumper that had earned a million pounds
in purses.

Skyler wondered if Mickey would ever fall in love.
Probably not. She was married to show jumping.

The riders were lining up outside the stadium now,
their grooms making minute, last-second adjustments
to tack. Neal Hatcher, the slight, ponytailed groom
who had accompanied Chancellor on the ride down
in his horse trailer, appeared at Skyler's side to check
her girth one more time. As Neal yanked at the straps,
she caught a glimpse into the arena through the covered passageway that led to the in-gate. A partial view
of the stands showed folded rectangles of blue fluttering like petals in a breeze as thousands of spectators fanned themselves with their programs. In the
patrons' box, sunlight reflected off the lenses of cameras and binoculars.

Skyler thought about Tony, out there somewhere,
and her heartbeat scattered into a hundred racing
pulse points. She suddenly felt bolstered by the idea
of him cheering her on, even if she couldn't pinpoint
his exact whereabouts.

As if from a great distance, she heard Mickey say,
"Wish me luck." Her friend was second in line to
jump, and none too happy about the placement.
Mickey liked knowing what she was up against, what
time she had to beat—it was the edge that drove her.

Skyler was struck by the irony of the situation—she
was competing against her best friend for a prize that
would mean the difference between life and death,
figuratively if not literally. Though they'd talked about
how wonderful it would be if Skyler won, no mention
had been made of what would happen if Mickey came
away with the blue ribbon. Their friendship, of course,
would survive. But the question in Skyler's mind was,
would *she*?

Minutes later, the klaxon sounded. In the stadium, Skyler could see heads turning, people straining forward, the heat and lack of breeze forgotten. In the press and judges' boxes, with their yellow and red striped bunting, conversation had stopped and minicams were poised.

Katie Monahan Prudent, on Silver Skates, was up first. Like the seasoned pro that she was, Katie seemed to create barely a ripple in the air as she took the magnificent white horse over the triples, oxers, brush boxes, and verticals. Her pace was steady, even stately; her time just a hair over thirty seconds.

Mickey had a long way to go to beat Katie's elegant style—but it was clear from the high color in her cheeks, and the steely set of her mouth as she rode into the arena that she wasn't thinking about how she looked. The only thing Mickey cared about was speed.

Victory Lap bucked several times, and Mickey gave him his head, letting him work off some of his high spirits while the master of ceremonies made his introduction over the P.A. system.

"Our second rider, Mickey Palladio on Victory Lap, a seven-year-old Thoroughbred owned by Priscilla Endicott of Sunnyhill Farm, had an impressive record last season. . . ."

Skyler tuned out the announcer as she watched her friend streak over the first jump, a patchwork wall flanked by ivy and azalea. She found herself both rooting for Mickey and half wishing she would knock a pole down, miss a stride, anything that would keep her from taking first place.

God, she was fast! The spectators, caught up in the heightened tension, leaned forward in their seats. The sun, directly overhead, sent Mickey's foreshortened shadow rippling like dark creek water over the sandy footing below. The seat of her breeches strained with her ungainly, bottoms-up posture. Scattered applause gathered to a roar . . . but Mickey was oblivious to it all. She was a knight on a charger, riding full tilt into battle.

She was glorious.

For the first time in all the years they'd been friends, Skyler felt keenly jealous of her friend.

Look at her take that double oxer, leaning so far over her horse's neck it was a wonder she didn't pitch forward into the sand. Now the diamond gate . . . and the Michelob fence with its seven-foot beer bottles for wings. Skyler could have sworn she saw steam rising from Victory's withers. Even the water jump that so many horses had balked at didn't faze the Thoroughbred a bit. He practically took flight. One more, a triple, and—

—over they went, horse and rider seeming to hang in the air for an excruciating split second before plunging down the other side in a small sandstorm.

As Mickey took Victory around the arena in triumph, numbers flashed on the scoreboard: 28.7 seconds. The crowd began to cheer, and then people were on their feet, clapping and waving their programs.

Eight more riders followed. Five met with knockdowns and refusals—and none came close to Mickey's time except for Ian Millar on Big Ben, who clocked in at 28.9.

Then it was Skyler's turn.

Please, God, for once let it be me instead of Mickey. . . .

Approaching the first jump, she wheeled Chancellor in a circle. Skyler could feel how charged up he was, ready to cut loose at the whisper of a heel. She tightened her legs about him, feeling her own muscles quiver in response.

The klaxon sounded.

She squeezed Chancellor to a canter . . . and over the patchwork wall, feeling him strain as he pitched himself forward, nicking the top rail with his hind foot.

Pick up your feet, Chance, she commanded silently as they barrelled toward the vertical.

As if he'd read her mind, Chancellor tucked up his feet on the next jump, his knees practically brushing his chest. He sailed over the top rail with inches to spare, and Skyler let out a breath that was more a grunt.

But to jump a clear round wouldn't be enough. She needed to be fast—and then even faster. She needed to beat Mickey's time.

There were seven jumps in all, each more difficult than the last. But Chancellor wasn't slowing down a bit. He flowed from one to the next with none of the tiny breaks and missteps that would have meant he was off his stride. Best of all, he was concentrating. Like precision clockwork, every part of him was moving in perfect synchrony.

The sun, a shimmer of fiery orange skating along the brim of her helmet, was making her eyes water, but she didn't dare blink. She had a split second's image of a rail leaping out before the ground was snatched out from under her. She leaned forward as Chancellor arched over the oxer, and was rewarded an instant later by the thud of his hooves striking down.

As her chestnut soared over the next jump, a balustrade fence flanked by huge sprays of purple bougainvillea, Skyler was conscious of every muscle in her body straining forward, propelling him faster—faster—faster—until he seemed to take flight, like Pegasus, and soar straight up into the sun. She was bent so far forward, she could feel the rough kiss of his mane against her cheek.

Come on . . . just two more . . . you can do it, boy—

The water jump loomed ahead. For an instant, she felt Chancellor tense, his muscles bunching; then he was over the grass-carpeted rolltop, their flattened reflections skimming across the sheet of glittering aqua beneath them.

Skyler felt a sob tear loose from her throat as they were met with a ripple of applause.

Almost there . . . almost home free . . .

One last triple, no more than four and a half feet at its highest. But with only a stride and a half leading to the first element—a fence only slightly lower than the one directly ahead of it—there was hardly room to gather momentum. She could feel Chancellor start to falter, to pull up. *God, no . . . not now . . . we're so close.*

Skyler, her heart in her throat, her whole body humming with adrenaline, jammed her heels into his flanks. *Go. Dammit, Chance, you've* got *to*—

All at once, she became weightless, like a feather floating just above the saddle. And then the earth was once again falling away, the sun plucking her up into its blinding brilliance. A rolling dip, the jarring thud of hooves, and Chancellor was past the second element, and launching himself over the third and last. Skyler was aware of blurred faces skimming past, of flattened, elongated shadows rippling over the churned footing beneath her.

Thonk.

The unmistakable sound of a hoof striking wood snapped Skyler out of her euphoria. In that split second, she felt, rather than saw, the top pole rattle in its cups. Her heart nearly stopped. *Oh, God!*

But the heavy thud of a fallen rail never came; there was only the sound of wild applause, breaking over her like an ocean wave. She caught a glimpse of the scoreboard as she streaked past, before she was blinded by flashbulbs and the glare of the sun on dozens of camera and minicam lenses.

Twenty-eight point six seconds. A tenth of a second faster than Mickey. *She'd won!*

Outside the in-gate, as Skyler slithered from her saddle onto legs that threatned to buckle under her, she didn't have time to worry about whether her friend would be jealous—because suddenly there was Mickey, folding her in a fierce embrace.

"You did it," she whispered into the tangle of hair spilling from under Skyler's hunt cap despite the net meant to anchor it in place. "I knew you could. I just knew it."

Then everyone in the world, it seemed, was thumping Skyler on the back, drowning her in hugs, wanting to snap her picture. Someone handed her a plastic cup of something bitter and fizzy—beer, she realized only after several gulps. Her head swam. She held up the cup for Chance to dip his nose into, and a roar of laughter erupted around her, accompanied by a galaxy of exploding flashbulbs that left her half blinded, her eyes swimming with black dots.

TV news crews muscled their way into the winner's circle, and Skyler tried to sound coherent as a woman with torpedo-proof blond hair fired questions at her. Why hadn't she jumped last season's circuit? Were the rumors true that she'd dropped out to have a baby? Would she be going on to the West Palm Beach Invitational after this?

Skyler, turning so she was facing directly into the lens of the whirring minicam, answered emphatically, "No. This is it. Tomorrow, I'm on my way home."

Just then, she caught sight of Tony, in a faded red tank top with his chambray shirt tied around his waist by its sleeves, pushing his way through the throng around her. He was grinning and holding up something that looked like a bottle of champagne. Her heart grew light ... as light as the pocket of air just under her skull that seemed to be lifting her off the ground like a helium balloon.

"To my baby," she added, so softly that all anyone watching would have seen was her lips moving, as if in prayer.

It was well after midnight when Skyler finally gave up trying to sleep. In the bed next to hers, Mickey snored

away, oblivious both to the wheezing of the ancient
air conditioner and the garish glow of the motel's neon
sign, caught in the gauzy drapes drawn over the window facing the parking lot.

Skyler slipped out from between sheets as limp and
clammy as cold cuts and padded into the bathroom,
where she pulled on jeans and a fresh T-shirt. Stepping
outside, where the temperature hovered just below
that of a lukewarm bath, she felt impossibly wide
awake and bristling with excitement.

A watery moon slid out from behind a caul of cloud,
and she drew in a deep breath, closing her eyes and
offering up silent thanks to the kind and munificent
God she'd prayed to in church when she was
young . . . but who, over the past ten years or so, had
been more or less consigned to a walk-on role. Now,
though, after all she'd gone through, it was clear to
Skyler that to believe you are walking the earth alone
and unguided is only an illusion . . . a misleading one
at times.

*God, I know I haven't always done the right thing.
I've taken what I wanted, without giving much thought
to the consequences. I've rushed in where I should have
tiptoed. Please, God, help me get through this next battle without causing any more harm than is absolutely
necessary—*

"Don't move."

A man's deep voice. Skyler jerked and spun
around.

Tony. He was standing a few feet away. "Mosquito.
There . . . got him." He stepped forward and delivered
a gentle slap to her left arm, just above the elbow.

Skyler stared back at him. He had changed into
lightweight khakis, with an open-necked shirt that
glowed white against the burnt sienna of his skin.

She shivered, but not from cold. What she should
have asked God for was protection against the longing
that engulfed her like a flash fire. Just knowing he was

only an arm's length away from embracing her ...
that they were breathing the same air ... that the
perspiration glistening on his forehead and in the
groove above his upper lip was generated by the same
heat that had sent her stumbling out into the night,
restless and yearning—oh, God, it was enough to drive
her up a mountain to howl at the moon.

Earlier, she'd been tempted to slip away to his
room, but had resisted the urge. Being with Tony was
like being on a ship torn off its path by high seas. As
far as Alisa was concerned, yes, she needed him ...
but what she *didn't* need right now was the fierce desire he stirred in her.

"It's late. What are you doing up?" she asked.

He shrugged. "I could ask you the same thing. I'm
only two doors down—I heard you go out."

"I couldn't sleep," she told him. "Actually, I was
thinking of heading over to the stables. See how Chancellor is holding up after all the excitement."

It sounded exactly like what it was: an excuse to get
away from him. Tony, though, didn't challenge her.
She allowed her eyes to rest on him for a moment,
taking in the muscled forearms below his rolled-up
sleeves—muscles that came from riding a horse eight
hours a day, four days a week. She resisted the urge
to run a finger along the strong clean line of his jaw.
Her heart quickened, and she turned away before he
could see the effect he was having on her.

"I'll drive you," he said.

For once, Skyler didn't argue. Hugging herself to
keep her arm from brushing against his, she walked
with Tony across the parking lot, nearly deserted now
that most of the riders and their entourages had de-
camped. Climbing into his rented Blazer, she wondered if this was such a good idea ... and decided it
wasn't. Definitely not. But somewhere a wheel had
been spun into motion, one she no longer appeared
to have any control over. She could feel it inside her

432   *Eileen Goudge*

... turning ... turning like something disconnected
from the cog that would have enabled its otherwise
useless machinery to run.

He waited until they were on the highway heading
south before he spoke. "You were something out
there today," he told her in a low, even voice full of
admiration. "I know a rider when I see one—but that
was ... it was more than just good riding. That was
fucking awesome."

"Thanks again for the champagne, " she said with
a lopsided grin. "But how did you know? I could just
as easily have lost."

Tony shrugged. "I had a feeling."

She didn't tell him that the unopened bottle was
still in her room; that she'd decided to save it for when
she could celebrate something even more wonderful
than taking first place in the Hartsdale Grand Prix.

"You came a long way for a feeling."

He gave her a sideways glance, then went back to
concentrating on the road. Strip malls and service sta-
tions interspersed with rows of palm trees swept past
on either side. The intersection leading to the road
that would take them to the stables was only a mile
or so ahead, but to Skyler their journey suddenly
seemed as never-ending as the Oregon Trail. Riding
with Tony in a car was too much like the first time,
the afternoon he'd taken her back to her father's
place. Even with the air conditioner going full blast,
Skyler felt warm and nearly breathless.

Ten minutes later, they were turning on to a two-
lane road that bumped over several more miles before
finally leading them to a wide graveled driveway. At
the end of the drive stood a rambling stable capable
of accommodating more than fifty horses; flung out on
either side was a sprawl of outbuildings ranging from
hay barns to the original farmhouse, which had been
converted into offices.

At this hour, there was no one about. Even the

stable hands were asleep; not a single light was on in the windows of their dormitory. The stable, painted barn-red and trimmed in white (as if it were in Vermont, for heaven's sake, not smack in the middle of what had once been a swamp), was deserted, except for the rangy figure who emerged from the shadows alongside the entrance as Skyler and Tony climbed out of the car.

"Hey there, folks ... kind of late for visiting, ain't it?" The white-haired night watchman appeared to be in his late sixties, his seamed, rugged face that of someone who makes his living outdoors. He looked friendly, but Skyler got the feeling that trespassers would most definitely not be invited to share a cold beer. Nearing her, the man screwed up his eyes to peer at her more closely; then a slow, crooked smile of amazement spread across his weathered face. "Well, I'll be damned. You're the girl who won the first-place trophy! Miss, let me shake your hand."

Skyler clasped his dry, leather hand. "I just want to check up on my horse," she explained. The old man pumped her hand once more, then shook Tony's before pushing open the wide double doors of the entrance.

A passageway wide enough to accommodate several horses led to a concrete-floored area the size of a small gymnasium, off which marched double rows of stalls. Set into the knotty-pine wall at her back was the door to the tack room, over which a dim yellow bulb glowed.

In the mellow light, Skyler and Tony found their way to Chancellor's stall. She called his name softly, and his head appeared at once over the white slatted gate, as if he'd been expecting her. He whinnied and stretched forward to nuzzle her.

She looped an arm about his neck, and held her cheek pressed to his until he jerked back in protest. "Yeah, I know, getting pretty full of yourself, aren't

you?" she teased, fishing in the pocket of her jeans
for the lump of sugar she always carried there.

"You'll spoil him," Tony said.

"He's already so spoiled, nothing could make a
difference."

"Scotty's the same way." Tony grinned. "Give him
a lump, and he'll want the whole box."

"Some people are like that, too," she said with a
laugh.

"Know a few myself." He nodded. "On the other
hand, there's the kind who'll turn away from something even when they know it's good for them."

Skyler swiveled slowly around to face him. "Why
do I get the feeling you're talking about me?"

He shrugged. "If the shoe fits . . ."

"Tony—"

"Don't say it," he warned, his expression hardening.
"I've heard it all before, remember? From the beginning, you never wanted me to be a part of this. It was
your way, or the highway. And your way didn't leave
room for a cop with a tattoo and a law school diploma
catching dust in a drawer."

"That isn't fair," she told him, feeling the sudden
hot sting of tears.

"And now I can see you plan on raising our kid the
same way—on your own." She heard the anger buried
in his mild tone, like a diamond wrapped in layers of
black velvet. "That is, if you get her back."

"What do you mean?" she demanded.

"It hasn't been decided in court yet," he reminded
her coolly.

"Of course, I'll get her back," she snapped. "I'm
her *mother.*"

"That simple, huh?" He stepped into the puddled
glare of the overhead fixture directly above him, and
the hard planes of his face leaped into view. "Everything mapped out, all systems go. Like when you
found out you were pregnant. You had it all figured

out then, too, what'd be best for the kid. Now it's all changed, and suddenly I'm not just a loose end. You're thinkin' it'd look good in court if I was on your side, if I showed an interest in our kid. But, dammit, Skyler, did it ever occur to you my interest might be *real*? That I might want to be in Alisa's life— apart from you, apart from your whole friggin high-society trip?"

Skyler, feeling suddenly unsteady, allowed herself to sag against the smooth wooden post at her back. "I can understand how you'd see it that way," she told him stiffly. "I'm sorry."

"Sorry for what? Sorry for not including me in your master plan, or sorry I was the one who knocked you up?" He took a step closer, and she could almost taste his breath, hot and spiced with anger. In a low, tight voice he added, "Yeah, that's it, isn't it? I'd fit into your life about as smooth as trying to cram a penny into a parking meter."

Skyler sucked in a breath, pressing clenched knuckles into the hollow of her solar plexus. Thick, sullen outrage climbed its way up her throat. Damn him. Why did he have to pull this on her now?

"Am I supposed to get down on my knees and beg your forgiveness?" she replied, furious. "Neither of us would even be here, we wouldn't be *having* this conversation, if somebody upstairs hadn't pulled the wrong lever or something. It was an accident, a fluke, me getting pregnant. I just didn't think it fair, messing up two lives instead of one." Suddenly exhausted, she closed her eyes and sighed. "Look, forget it. I'm too tired to argue with you. Let's just go back before one of us says something we'll really regret."

She turned and began making her way along the passageway between the double row of stalls.

"Skyler, wait." She felt Tony grab her arm.

She wrenched her arm free and marched on ahead.

"Goddammit, Skyler, I'm talking to you!" His voice

boomed in the stillness, prompting a chorus of nervous whinnies.

Skyler kept walking until she reached the closed door to the tack room. Then, seeing Tony out of the corner of her eye—the clenched fury in his handsome face as he closed the distance between them in several long strides—she froze. This time he didn't try to grab her. Instead, with a grunt of frustrated rage, he punched the wall.

A framed certificate from the Broward County Health Department flew off its hook—and hit the concrete floor in a starburst of shattered glass. Skyler felt a hot, sharp pain in her left ankle, like a bee stinging her just below the cuff of her jeans. She stared down at the twinkling shards at her feet.

Dimly, she became aware of something warm trickling down the arch of her foot. She reached down and lazily brushed at her ankle. Her fingertips were smeared with blood.

Skyler was too surprised to be upset. Tony had done that to her? *Tony?*

He looked even more shocked than she felt. She caught only a glimpse of his face, gone hard and white as stone, before he sank to his knees to examine the cut.

"Christ Almighty, Skyler, I didn't mean—"

Skyler just stood there, staring down at him dumbly. In the dim light from the yellow bulb over the door, his dense, tightly coiled curls gleamed like some ancient tooled helmet. She could feel him bracing her as he lifted her injured foot—and suddenly she was remembering the day they'd first met, Tony on bent knee before her in the middle of Fifth Avenue, slipping her newly retrieved shoe onto her foot like some latter-day Prince Charming. *A fairy tale,* she thought, *where the princess gets pregnant, and all hell breaks loose.* Skyler felt a hysterical giggle threaten to burst free, and she had to clamp her mouth tightly shut to hold it in.

Tony rose with a grim look, and took her hand. Pushing open the tack room door, he led her inside and slapped at the wall beside it with his free hand. The light came on, illuminating a long, neatly kept room lined with benches and tack trunks, its walls pegged with wooden trees on which were perched rows of gleaming saddles. Hooks clumped with bridles were suspended from the ceiling, and a row of metal lockers stood against the far wall. Tony steered Skyler over to one of the benches, where a stack of freshly laundered saddle blankets sat folded at one end.

"Sit down," he ordered.

Skyler did as she was told. In a daze, she watched Tony kneel and carefully remove her sandal. The cut was deeper than she'd realized—half her foot was covered in blood. But in her trancelike state, she didn't seem to care much at all. Even the pain had dwindled to a kind of distant throbbing.

Without hesitating, Tony shucked off his white shirt and used it to wipe the blood from her foot. She wanted to protest, to tell him he'd never get the stain out, but she found herself unable to speak. She stared mutely down at him, at the polished patches of sweat on his muscular back and shoulders, at the beads of moisture glittering like crushed diamonds in the black hair on his broad chest.

"Does it hurt?" he asked.

"Nothing a Band-Aid won't fix." Watching him rise and begin hunting for a first-aid kit, she said with a shaky laugh, "Look, I'm not some damsel in distress God appointed you to look out for."

He turned toward her, and the dark eyes that fixed on her were no longer sympathetic. "You don't give an inch, do you?" His voice was soft with anger.

"I can't afford to ... especially now." She took a deep breath in an attempt to steady herself. "I don't need to be rescued, Tony. All I want from you is your support."

"Ellie's gonna fight you," he warned. "You two are a lot more alike than you realize."

"God, don't you think I know how alike we are?" she sighed. "That's how it all got started in the first place. The minute we met, I had this feeling we'd known each other from somewhere ... only I ..." She shook her head to clear it of the fogginess that had crept in around the edges.

"You're asking me to choose sides," Tony said, his eyes never leaving her face.

"She's your daughter, too."

"Christ, don't you think I know that?" he snapped. Then he was stepping over to her and pulling her to her feet.

Suddenly he was kissing her, with that sharp, shivery intake of breath that sent a shaft of desire shooting through her lower belly. And she was kissing him back, tasting the inside of his mouth, catching his lower lip lightly between her teeth in greedy little nibbles. She heard him moan, and he pressed her to him, his bare arms tensing, relaxing slightly, then tensing again.

Stop! cried a voice in her head.

But she couldn't stop. She was paralyzed by the warmth that spilled through her like some precious golden liquid ... as helpless as if she were bareback astride a runaway horse.

She ran the tip of her tongue along his throat, which tasted salty and faintly, deliciously tart. She licked his Adam's apple, and felt it quiver against her mouth. The skin under his jaw was gritty with beard. She bit him gently ... there ... and there ...

"Skyler—oh, Jesus ..."

He plucked frantically at her T-shirt; then his palms were skidding stickily up her bare back, his fingertips playing along her spine. She felt the golden heat fill her belly and send trickles of fire down lower ... down her thighs ... into the backs of her knees. In a kind of stupor, she watched him jerk the pile of folded saddle blankets off the bench and spread them over the floor.

As Skyler sank onto the soft, quilted fabric, the blankets' faint horsey smell—a smell that defied every known laundry soap—rose up around her, earthy and comforting. She no longer cared if it was wrong to lead Tony on, wrong to make herself love him even more than she already did. All she knew—the only thought her brain seemed capable of—was that she wanted him, *craved* him ... and that to deny herself would be like turning down food if she were starving, or a drink of water if she were dying of thirst.

"Skyler ... Skyler ... " He murmured her name over and over, drawing out its syllables.

God, those hands. His palms hot and rough, his fingers kneading her, moving in slow circles down her back, up around her rib cage to cup her breasts. Again, that hitching intake of breath as he bent to kiss first one nipple, then the other, drawing it into his mouth, licking, sucking, making her arch back with a moan. Gently, he worked her jeans down over her hips, careful of her cut foot, which had finally stopped bleeding but was still tender.

Tony rolled away from her to unbuckle his belt. When his khakis lay in a crumpled heap beside his discarded cowboy boots, he dug a hand into one of the back pockets and produced a foil-wrapped square.

"This time I came prepared," he said.

"You bastard, you knew." But there was no bite to her words.

"I know how I feel, that's what I know." He looked down at her gravely, his eyes searching hers.

"Put it on, then," she whispered.

"You sure?"

"Sure, I'm sure. Unless you want to get me pregnant again."

"Not a chance ... not until I know what it is to be

a father to the kid we already made," he murmured against her ear.

Skyler flinched. But in the next moment, as he thrust into her, she was aware of nothing but the sudden, blinding rush of pleasure he brought her. She wrapped her legs around him, raising her hips, bringing him into her as far as he could go. The exquisite heat gathered, making her slick with sweat that gave off a soft sucking noise with each lift and sway of their bodies. Her breasts tingled as they had when her milk first began coming in.

Tony picked up her rhythm, and they rocked together in frenzied harmony. He was so deep inside her now she could feel him at the very core of her, each plunging thrust bringing a tiny, delicious little ache.

She clung to him, her legs trembling uncontrollably. And then she felt herself being swept away ... swept by some dark, sweet river to a place where nothing mattered other than this. She came then. She came as she never had before, biting his shoulder to muffle the cry that exploded from her.

Tony, holding himself clenched against her, followed with a hoarse yell of his own that unleashed in her a second climax—less intense than the first, but in an odd way more satisfying.

Afterward, they lay very still. Skyler slowly became aware of her surroundings—and remembered that the night watchman could walk in on them at any minute. She stirred and wriggled out from under Tony, hugging her knees as she sat up.

God. What if they'd been caught? Imagine the story: Skyler Sutton, winner of the Hartsdale Grand Prix, caught fucking on the tack room floor.

They pulled on their clothes in silence, and then Tony rustled up the first-aid kit. Expertly he cleaned and dressed her cut, then he helped her on with her sandal.

Outside, as they crunched their way to the car

across the gravel driveway in the dark, Tony didn't put an arm around her or even try to hold her hand. Skyler felt relieved, and at the same time oddly disappointed.

They had traveled more than a mile down the dark, palm-lined avenue before she spoke.

"Tony," she said softly. Just that, his name . . . like a caress.

"Yeah?" he answered.

She opened her mouth to speak, then thought better of it. "Never mind."

He didn't press her. He didn't even *look* at her, except to glance once in her direction as he scanned the oncoming traffic before making a left turn.

After a while, Skyler ventured, "I don't expect you to decide anything right now. I mean, about . . . about taking sides."

"There's only one side, far as I'm concerned," he told her, still without looking at her. "And that's whatever I decide is best for our daughter."

He fell silent again. The reflections of oncoming headlights slid down the side of his face and neck, where a tendon stood out in sharp relief. Skyler shivered, and found herself wondering if once again she had underestimated Tony.

He keeps his own counsel. The old-fashioned turn of phrase suited him. Tony would not rush to make up his mind about anything.

She would just have to be patient. For if she'd learned anything in all this, it was to curb her impulses. Wasn't it impulse that had gotten her into this mess in the first place?

Maybe. But Skyler couldn't shake the feeling that with Tony, even from the very beginning, there had been a force at work far greater than either of them had bargained for. A force that even now was driving them with a fury beyond their control.

CHAPTER 16

Kate stared at the newspaper article without really reading it. She was seated in her kitchen, steeped in the morning sunlight that slanted in through the open French windows to form a leafy tapestry over the tiled floor and dark cherry cabinets. The June 14 edition of the *Northfield Register* was spread out on the round oak table before her, and a china cup filled with coffee had gone cold at her elbow. She held herself very still, but even so the words swarmed before her eyes like insects. There was the photo of her daughter, posed beside her horse, wearing a grin as wide and bright as the trophy cradled in her arms. "Local Woman Takes First at Hartsdale Classic," the caption read.

A sick, curdled feeling seeped into Kate's stomach. *It's settled, then. She'll have the money to hire that lawyer.*

Yet whatever the consequences, and despite how much it pained her to have been excluded, Kate rejoiced at her daughter's victory. It would be so easy to pick up the phone and tell Skyler how proud she was! And how she'd rooted for her . . . even knowing what it would mean if she won.

At the same time, Kate wanted to snatch Skyler's victory away. Because what appeared to be a triumph would lead only to grief in the end. Tears flooded Kate's eyes, even while she told herself it was too early in the morning to go all weepy, not even eight o'clock yet. She still had the whole rest of the day to get through, and Will to see off to work.

Will. She'd come so close to crying on his shoulder yesterday evening, when she'd first learned—through Duncan—of Skyler's triumph. But she'd held back. Out of pride mostly, she realized now. Pride mixed with envy. For though Skyler had pointedly ignored her phone calls these past weeks, Kate knew their daughter had been in touch with Will, whom she freely called at his office. Hadn't Will told her so, blithely reassuring her, "There now, Kate ... you see? She's not turning away from us."

Us? Didn't he see? Was he as blind about the hurt their daughter was causing her as he was about Ellie?

"Good morning, Kate."

Kate looked up as Will entered the kitchen, looking impossibly crisp and well rested in his light gray summer suit. He'd regained some of the weight he'd lost over the winter, and his face no longer appeared sunken.

He had every reason to look vigorous. The paperwork on the most lucrative of the limited partnerships Will had been sweating over—an office building on East Fifty-ninth—had at last been completed, and now he was simply waiting for the ink to dry. Though far from placing the firm in the black, the deal was a sorely needed boost. And best of all, they'd be able to make the payments on Orchard Hill.

Even so, Will's eyes hadn't quite lost their haunted look, and she could still see those little white tucks of tension around his mouth. What struck her most, though, was his hair: it was as thick as ever, but white, as silver-white as the spoon propped against the saucer of her coffee cup. It gave him the look of a distinguished older man ... but an older man, nonetheless.

The strain he'd been under—both with his business and with Skyler—had left its mark. And knowing Will, knowing his obsessive need to wrest control of every situation that he *could* control, she wasn't the least bit surprised—hurt, yes, but not *surprised*—to find him flicking a cool glance at her. He blamed her for her refusal to help their daughter. But though they'd exchanged tense words about it, he didn't dare unleash his anger on her—the subject was far too loaded. He didn't want to be reminded of what they owed Ellie; deep down, he had to be aware of it already, or why else would he be taking such pains to avoid any mention of her?

"There's coffee in the pot," Kate said. "Would you like me to make you some breakfast?" Under the table, Belinda snuffled softly in her sleep.

"Don't bother; I'll pick up something on my way to the office," he answered, stopping to peer over her shoulder as he headed for the coffeemaker on the marble counter. Behind her, she felt him abruptly grow still ... and knew that he'd spotted the news photo of Skyler.

"It's wonderful, isn't it?" she said, her words ringing with false cheer, like keys plunked on an out-of-tune piano.

She could feel Will's heavy silence at her back as he scanned the article. Finally, in a voice fraught with reproach, he said: "We should have been there, Kate."

Kate felt the flesh on the back of her neck tighten, as if a chill breeze had come wafting in through the French windows that stood open to the sun-drenched garden, where her peony bushes nodded with blossoms the size of small cabbages, and pale green runners of clematis stitched in and around the boxwood hedge.

"She didn't ask us," Kate reminded him gently.

"What did you expect—engraved invitations? You'd

made it clear we weren't behind her. And you know Skyler has never been one to beg."

Kate sighed, turning to look up at him. "Will, we've been over this—"

His eyes flashed. "If you mean that we've discussed it, I won't argue with you there. But if you think for one minute that I'm in any way satisfied with the situation, you're mistaken."

"I'm not satisfied with it, either," she informed him, bristling with an anger that seemed to spring out of nowhere. "If the situation were any different . . . why, I'd sell everything I own to pay her legal fees myself."

Will didn't answer . . . and the reason for his silence made her even angrier. He was backing down, not because he was too polite to argue with her, but because he didn't want to push her into opening a Pandora's box.

With a heavy heart, Kate watched her husband lift the coffeepot off its burner. His shoulders were stiff and unrepentant . . . and how was it possible that in all the years they'd lived under the same roof she'd never before noticed how, when he was furious, his neck seemed to jut out of his collar like a mastiff straining at its leash?

"Coffee's cold," he pronounced.

"I must have switched it off by mistake. Give it thirty seconds in the microwave," she advised listlessly.

"I'll grab a cup at the office," he replied, his voice carefully even.

Normally, she would have offered to brew him a fresh pot, but on this morning she didn't stir from her chair. It was more than just pettiness that kept her nailed to her seat. Oh, why, *why* did it have to be this way? Why couldn't she be like other mothers, mothers who slept the contented sleep of the righteous, who didn't arrive at the breakfast table with a dry mouth and pounding heart, too stiff to walk from one end of their kitchen to the other?

Never mind about you . . . think of what Ellie must be going through right now. Kate could only imagine what the woman must be feeling, knowing her baby could be snatched away from her at any moment.

The way her firstborn daughter had—the child that Kate and Will had kept from her all these years.

Kate knew that it would be months before anything was decided. Motions would have to be filed, depositions collected, a court date set. But when the day came, she prayed that she would be ready for its outcome, whatever that might be.

She prayed for her daughter, too . . . and, yes, for Ellie.

It was Jimmy Dolan's last group session.

Seated in her armchair in the downstairs meeting room at GMHC, Ellie looked across at Jimmy, who had been confined to a wheelchair since August. It was the middle of September now, and he was nearly spent—his eyes set deep in his head, and his parchment skin stretched across his skeletal frame. The one thing he hadn't lost was his spirit. Jimmy had gotten the group off to a lively start by cheerfully announcing that tonight would be his farewell performance.

"No encores, please." He grinned, his face a gaunt shadow of what it had been even two months ago.

"Don't worry, man . . . we'll save the standing ovation for your funeral." Armando Ruiz, bare-chested, in a denim jacket with the sleeves torn off, was as defiantly cocky as ever . . . even toting a portable tank that fed oxygen into his lungs through a pair of nose prongs.

His joke was met with a round of chuckles. In this room, gallows humor was the rule rather than the exception. Most of the men, at one time or another, had confessed their relief at not having to tiptoe about, speaking in whispers. Laughing in the face of death, it seemed, had an oddly revivifying effect.

Ellie looked around at this ragtag crew she'd come to know and care for ... and, in the case of those who were absent, to mourn. Following the eight weeks she'd taken off to be with Alisa—leaving the group in the capable hands of one of her colleagues, Grant Van Doren—she'd resumed leadership in July, the hottest month of the year, when attendance had been at a record low. And here it was autumn already. Outside, the leaves were starting to turn—and in this room, the subject under discussion was endings.

Would tomorrow bring yet another ending? she wondered. The custody hearing was set for nine a.m. sharp at the courthouse on Centre Street. After three months of filings, motions, social worker evaluations, and preliminary hearings, the day had finally arrived. ...

It was like her nightmare, the one she'd been having off and on for the past twenty-three years. The dream was always the same. In it, she was chasing someone down a series of pedestrian-clogged streets ... a man clutching hold of a baby. The only thing that changed from one time to the next was the identity of the baby. Sometimes it was Bethanne ... sometimes no more than a faceless infant. But in recent months, the baby she could see over the shadow man's shoulder was Alisa.

A quiet panic settled over Ellie. Would she ever sit in the audience at a school play, applauding her child's performance? Light sixteen candles on a birthday cake? Watch a grown daughter march down the aisle in her wedding dress?

The realization of all she would miss if Alisa were taken from her drove a sharp, hot spike of pain between her ribs. But nothing had been decided yet, she was quick to remind herself. There was a chance—albeit a slim one—that the judge would rule in her favor. And she had Paul on her side.

Yes, Paul. She thought of how he'd returned, flowing back into her life as seamlessly as if he'd never left. Of course, there had been some initial awkwardness, and the lingering feelings of hurt and betrayal on both sides. But those rough bumps had been smoothed by the gentle, caring hand of their abiding love for each other.

Ellie smiled to herself, remembering his first evening home, when Paul had returned at last to bed. How delicious it had been . . . his arms around her, their bodies moving to rhythms as familiar as an old, beloved melody. Their desire so intense, it had left them breathless and bathed in sweat.

"Paul," she'd whispered afterward, her voice choked. "Oh, Paul."

He'd cradled her head, holding it against his shoulder. "Never again," he'd murmured. "I don't care what happens. I'll never be apart from you again."

Now, in the cold white glare of the meeting room, Ellie fought to hold on to that warm, wonderful sense of security she'd felt in Paul's arms. But it was fading . . . fading like the smile from Jimmy's face. The thought of Alisa invaded her calm with heavy, thudding urgency.

Alisa. Oh, God.

Tomorrow, she quickly reassured herself. *You don't have to think about it until tomorrow.*

"Speaking of my funeral, you're all invited." Jimmy's thready laugh punctured her thoughts. "I'm throwing a big party afterward—got it all planned. Champagne and caviar. Nobody will say Jimmy Dolan didn't go out in style."

No one had to ask when the funeral would be; it was obvious from the way Jimmy looked, and from his labored breathing, that it wouldn't be long. His leaving the group said it all. The good fight he'd fought so hard was nearly over . . . he'd simply run out of strength.

"And who, pray tell, will be hosting this extravaganza?" asked Erik Sandstrom, looking almost a parody of the owlish professor with his side-combed hair and red clip-on tie. "Your friend Tony, I would assume. But champagne and caviar? Won't he find it all rather macabre ... like some kind of celebration?"

"Hey, what's not to celebrate?" Jimmy cracked. "You guys are gonna be the ones left holding the bag, not me. When the curtain goes down on old Jimmy, you can bet your ass that wherever I am I'll be dancing."

"You make kickin' the bucket sound *easy*," groused beer-bellied Daniel Blaylock.

Jimmy, sunk in his wheelchair, broke into a grin that made Ellie think of an aging movie star holding up the tattered remnants of a once-glorious costume. "Piece of cake," he said. "The hard part, my man, is living."

Sure, he was was scared, Ellie thought. But he was dealing with it in his own inimitable style ... just as she would have to deal with whatever happened when she walked into that courtroom tomorrow.

How much did Jimmy know about her situation ... how much had Tony told him? She supposed it didn't matter, really. But it made her wonder about Tony. Where did he stand in all this? Would he be appearing in that courtroom tomorrow as a witness, or a spectator ... or at all? Nobody seemed to know, not even— as far as her lawyer could determine—Skyler herself.

"I'm going to be buried in a vintage Mercedes SL100," said Adam Burchard with a laugh. "On my tombstone, it'll say: 'Cadaver on board.' "

Ellie fixed her gaze on him—Adam, of the two-thousand-dollar suits and gold Rolex, which he armed himself with in the hope that material riches might protect him from what lay ahead.

"What good is laughing," asked Erik dolefully, "if there's no one left to hear it?"

"What about God? I gather He's got a pretty good sense of humor," cracked Nicky.

"I don't know about you guys ... but when *I* go, the only thing I care about is making sure Robert gets half of what's mine. It ain't much, but my old man, who calls me his 'faggot son,' sure as hell don't deserve it." There was a hard gleam in Armando's dark eyes as he folded his arms across his chest.

"That's a good point," Ellie said. "What do you do when your family's wishes aren't in keeping with your partner's?"

"You know the old saying, 'blood is thicker than water,'" said Erik in his most sardonic voice.

Ellie, in the back of her mind, was left wondering darkly if blood was indeed thicker than water. After several more minutes of heated discussion she looked up at the clock and saw it was time to stop. The session had passed quickly ... disturbingly so. Like the men seated around her, she was abruptly, acutely aware of how limited was one's time on earth ... and how cruel the encroaching night.

Tomorrow, she thought. *If I can just hang on until then ...*

She'd half risen from her chair when she happened to look down and seen the angry red marks where her fingernails had bitten into her palms. And it was only with the greatest effort that she was able to hold back the sob gathering in the back of her throat as she bent over and lightly clasped Jimmy Dolan's frail, ravaged body in her arms.

After the grandiose, pillared façade and amphitheater-sized marble lobby through which she'd entered, the shabby courtroom on the fourth floor of 55 Centre Street, with its scuffed wooden floor and flaking plaster, made Ellie think of the time she'd attended a function at the Waldorf-Astoria and had wandered into the wrong meeting room. Everything about this place felt wrong. It was nine o'clock in the morning, and the sun filtering dingily though the tall east-facing windows still seemed like a distant promise. She sat at an oak table that looked as if it hadn't seen a polishing since Eisenhower was in office, her gaze fixed on the chipped and faded WPA mural on the wall above the judge's bench—a neoclassical rendering of the scales of justice, featuring a pair of women in flowing Greek robes poised at either end of a brass scale.

Justice? she thought. *What justice will there be for me?*

Beside her, Paul stirred. She felt his hand on her elbow. "You're shivering," he whispered. "Do you want my jacket?"

"Thanks, I'm not cold . . . just nervous as hell." She reached over, and squeezed his hand with her own slightly sweaty one.

On her right sat her lawyer, Leon Kessler, with his squirrely thatch of reddish-gray hair, wearing a rumpled brown suit and a patterned tie that flowed in waves over his mountainous slope of a belly. He was frowning as he rummaged through his open briefcase.

Ellie allowed herself a quick survey of the double rows of benches behind her, relieved to see that they were occupied by no more than a dozen witnesses. She recognized the social worker, an engaging young black woman who'd visited Paul and her at home, and the court-appointed psychiatrist, a pasty-faced man in whose office she'd spent an unpleasant couple of hours.

She gave a little nod to Georgina, who looked unnaturally respectable in a dowdy beige suit . . . and was pleased to see that Martha Healey, from the NICU, had been able to reschedule her shift to testify as a character witness on Paul's behalf.

Catching sight of Tony, seated in back, sent a mild jolt of alarm through her. In a sport jacket and tie, he looked uncomfortable and out of place . . . but, more than that, he was purposely avoiding her eye. A bad sign? Ellie felt slightly sick to her stomach. If only Tony would decide at the last minute to testify on *her* behalf. . . .

You'll be lucky if he stays out of it altogether, a rational voice weighed in. For if Tony joined forces with Skyler instead, if he got up on that stand and pledged to play a big role in raising his daughter— well, then, the judge would have even less of a reason to award custody to an over-forty professional woman with an off-again-on-again marriage, now wouldn't he?

Ellie gripped her elbows and turned her gaze toward the plaintiff's table, occupied by Skyler and her matronly lawyer. Skyler was the picture of girlish innocence. In her straight blue skirt and unadorned white blouse, her fair hair anchored at the nape of her neck with a wide tortoiseshell clip, she looked exactly like what she was—a well-bred young woman from old money.

Ellie felt a curious rush of affection. *How odd,* she thought. *I should resent the hell out of her . . . but somehow I don't.*

There was something about Skyler Sutton . . . something she couldn't put her finger on that had nothing to do with Alisa . . .

Skyler caught her staring, and glanced over. Her cheeks colored, and she quickly lowered her eyes as if in shame. The firm, almost defiant set of her mouth didn't change, though. Ellie felt herself stiffen as Skyler leaned over to speak to her lawyer, who nodded and scribbled something on the yellow legal pad in front of her.

Verna Campbell, in her severe navy suit, made Ellie think of those brisk middle-aged women who mobilize neighbors into crime-watch committees, spearhead fund-raisers for feminist causes, and save foundering old wrecks of buildings from being demolished. She was stout without being fat, and the streaks of gray in her wiry black hair looked as if they'd been applied with a paintbrush. Verna's one concession to femininity was the string of pearls that swayed from her ample bosom. She looked not only as if she meant business, but as if she, and she alone, were capable of conducting it properly.

On the bench directly behind Verna and Skyler sat a distinguished-looking middle-aged man in an obviously hand-tailored charcoal suit, whom Ellie recognized as Skyler's father. His thick silver hair and neatly trimmed mustache gave him the look of an aging but remarkably well-preserved movie star, and from the way he held himself it was obvious he was accustomed to being in charge. Even as he sat talking to the young woman on his right—Skyler's tomboyish friend, the one who had acted as her labor coach—his eyes kept darting around the courtroom like those of a general plotting his next military maneuver.

But where was his wife? Ellie couldn't imagine what—other than being desperately ill—could have kept Kate from attending today's hearing. Unless ...

... *unless she's not worried, because she knows I don't have a prayer.*

Ellie, holding her elbows tucked in against her rib cage, spoke in a voice low enough so that her lawyer, seated on her other side, wouldn't hear. "Oh, Paul, I'm so scared. I don't know if I can do this."

"Someone I once knew said that tilting at windmills was what she did best." He gave her an encouraging smile. "You're not thinking of taking that back now, are you?"

Ellie didn't answer. She was just so grateful for his presence. That in itself was a kind of triumph, wasn't it?

"All rise ... the Honorable Judge Benson presiding," ordered the bailiff, a stringy man in his sixties with a deflated potbelly that hung over his belt like a sack.

Ellie pulled herself stiffly to her feet. Watching the

black-robed judge step up to the bench, she felt a hard little nip of disappointment. What could this dyspeptic little man, with his two strands of hair pasted over a crown as bald as a newel post, know of a mother's love for her child? He looked like a bank clerk nearing the end of a workday in which nothing had gone right. Wearily, he read aloud the docket before gesturing in the direction of the plaintiff's table.

Verna Campbell thrust up from her chair like a ship plowing into a wave. "Your Honor," she began in a crisp voice that rang with authority. "On behalf of the petitioner, I intend to demonstrate that my client, when she made the decision to give her unborn child up for adoption, was under a great deal of stress. She is young and unmarried, and believed she was acting in the best interests of her baby. I wish to emphasize that she did not think it necessary to be under advice of counsel at the time." The attorney paused to draw in a deep breath that made her nostrils flare dramatically. "My client, who has since had a change of heart, is prepared to take full responsibility for the infant. She receives a monthly income from a family trust, so she's not without means. I believe I can also demonstrate to your satisfaction her absolute sincerity. Your Honor, Skyler Sutton is the natural mother of this child . . . and she deserves to be recognized as such."

Natural mother. The words, chosen precisely for their effect, rang in Ellie's ears. She wanted to scream that she, too, was someone's natural mother . . . but that she loved Alisa no less than she'd loved her own flesh-and-blood child.

Judge Benson wore a sour, impatient look that Ellie didn't find particularly reassuring, even though it was directed at Skyler's lawyer.

"Before we begin, counselor, I'd like to caution you. From the depositions in front of me, it appears there's no shortage of character witnesses . . . on both sides," he added, with a sharp glance in the direction of the respondent's table, where Ellie sat. "I'm sure you two can produce any number of friends and family members to testify as to the sterling character of these two ladies, but I'm warning you in advance—I'm liable to lose patience if it gets out of hand."

"I'll keep that in mind, Your Honor," Verna replied respectfully.

The judge fixed his watery gaze on Leon. "Counsel, do you wish to make an opening statement at this time?"

Leon rose to his feet, a great shambling bear of a man whose untidy appearance made Ellie wince inwardly. But Leon was like a wily country lawyer; she suspected he cultivated his look in order to throw people off. By the time they realized how clever he was, it was too late.

"Your Honor, I'm glad you raised that point. I couldn't agree more." Lacing his hands over his ample belly, Leon beamed with goodwill. "My client's character certainly speaks for itself ... and we have no intention of casting aspersions on the petitioner's. I don't doubt for a moment Miss Sutton's sincerity, or that her initial actions arose out of misguided naïveté rather than malicious intent. Our main concern here is to establish what is in the best interests of the child." He paused, his voice deepening to a rumble. "I'm not blowing anyone's horn here in saying it's pretty clear what my client has to offer. Both she and her husband are professionals, with a more than adequate income between them. They've suffered the trials of Job in their efforts to adopt a child, and this baby coming along when she did ... well ... it was like a miracle from heaven. And don't let us forget it was Miss Sutton who first approached Dr. Nightingale. She was looking for caring, responsible parents to raise her child, and though at the time Dr. Nightingale and her husband were separated, Miss Sutton was willing to overlook that. A mistake?" Somberly, he shook his leonine head. "We believe that Miss Sutton acted entirely appropriately, and that the court should stand by her decision."

Leon, still beaming, settled into his sturdy oak chair with a sigh of satisfaction. Ellie could feel some of the tension go out of her neck. But it would be a mistake to grow too confident. The fun was just beginning. Even now she could see Verna Campbell poking a pair of half-rim reading glasses onto her nose and consulting her notes. "Your Honor, I'd like to call Michaela Palladio to the stand," she said, peering at him over the tops of her glasses.

Skyler's friend rose and stepped to the front of the courtroom. Her mop of dark curls and her heavy-lidded eyes, even the bright red scarf she wore draped over the collar of her blouse, made Ellie think of a Gypsy about to be interrogated by the local constable.

"Call me Mickey ... everybody does," she said in the throaty voice of a much older woman as she settled onto the chair in the oak-paneled witness box.

"Mickey, how would you describe your relationship with Skyler Sutton?" asked Verna, rising from her chair and perching on the edge of the table.

"She's my best friend," Mickey replied matter-of-factly.

"How long have you known each other?"

Mickey smiled. "Since the age of three. We were the only two kids in riding school who still wore training pants."

"Would you say she was reliable and responsible?"

"Oh, absolutely. I mean, you should see the way she takes care of her horse. Skyler ..." Mickey frowned in concentration, as if wanting to choose her words carefully. "She's always had this way with animals. They *trust* her, you know. That's one of the reasons she'll make a good veterinarian."

"Being good with animals is one thing ... but a baby is something else altogether," the lawyer observed, arching an eyebrow. "What makes you think Skyler would be up to the rigors of raising a child?"

"Oh." Mickey sat up straight, as if surprised that there could be any question. "Well, she just *would,* that's all. When she makes up her mind to do something, there's absolutely no way she'll back down." She caught her mistake at once—after all, Ellie thought, hadn't Skyler reneged on the biggest promise of all?— darting a furtive glance at Skyler. Staunchly, she added, "She's the best friend anyone could ever have."

Ellie felt herself wither inside. No memorized speech could have had more of an effect than the heartfelt testimony of this young woman who clearly wasn't given to emotional outbursts. Something else occurred to Ellie just then . . . a dark thought that came winging out of nowhere: *Dear God, what if it's true . . . what if Alisa* does *belong with her real mother?* Skyler had given birth to Alisa. Despite every instinct, Ellie's heart went out to her. She felt herself break out in a light sweat, and glanced anxiously at Leon as he rose to cross-examine Mickey, approaching the bench with his heavy, lumbering gait.

He stopped a few feet from the witness box and cleared his throat. "Miss Palladio, would you say that your friend Skyler has led a *privileged* life?"

"If you mean did she live in a nice house and go to good schools, then yes . . . but if you're implying that she's spoiled, well, she's *not.*" Mickey's eyes flashed with indignation.

"Spoiled?" he echoed, smiling. "I wouldn't have gone so far as to suggest that. I was merely wondering if Miss Sutton, given the comfortable lifestyle you describe, has a clear grasp of the *sacrifices* she'd have to make. As Ms. Campbell so aptly pointed out, a baby is not a horse. You can't just park it with a groom while you go gallivanting about."

"Objection, Your Honor!" Verna barked. "I resent

the implication that my client's heartfelt wishes are some sort of a . . . a *whim*."

Judge Benson leaned forward, scowling. "Mr. Kessler, if you have a point to make, I suggest you get to it."

Leon waved a hand in vague acknowledgment before once more fixing his twinkly brown eyes on Mickey. "So. We've established that Miss Sutton is far from *spoiled*. But would you describe her as sophisticated? Someone who isn't about to be bamboozled by the first snake-oil salesman to come along?"

"I'd say so," Mickey answered warily.

"Would it be fair to say she's a clear-headed young lady, capable of making an intelligent decision?"

"Yes, it would."

"Then you believe her decision in choosing Dr. Nightingale to raise her baby was an intelligent, informed one?"

Mickey hesitated. "I—well . . . yes."

"You don't think maybe she was being a bit . . . what's the word I'm thinking of? *Naïve.*"

"No, I don't."

"Then you would agree she made a good choice?"

"It seemed like it . . . at the time."

"And now?"

"I couldn't comment on that."

"Oh? Has something altered your opinion of Dr. Nightingale?"

"This has nothing to *do* with her."

"Your friend simply changed her mind, is that it?"

"Yes."

"And what about Dr. Nightingale? Was she supposed to just fall in line?"

Ellie could feel her heart thumping thickly in her chest as she watched Mickey drop her eyes. Through the muffled roar of blood in her ears, she heard the young woman say hesitantly, "It . . . it wasn't anything so . . . so calculating. Skyler can't help the way she feels."

"Nor, I'm sure, can Dr. Nightingale," Leon responded quietly. "Thank you, Miss Palladio, that'll be all."

Ellie couldn't help noticing the tiny frown that had appeared between Verna Campbell's brows. *Score one for Leon,* she thought, a small bead of hope rising in her.

She saw Skyler look over her shoulder, and anxiously scan the back of the courtroom until she caught Tony's gaze. She held it for several beats, as if silently signaling him in some way. But Tony merely stared back impassively, his dark eyes as bright and unreadable as the glare of headlights on blacktop.

So far, he'd managed to steer clear of the whole ugly business, refusing to take sides. But what if he decided to join forces with Skyler? He loved his daughter. Ellie knew that very well—she had the St. Michael's medal to prove it. By testifying on Skyler's behalf, he'd have more to gain than by remaining silent. And whether or not she and Tony were living together, if Skyler were awarded custody, he'd have a chance to play an active role in Alisa's upbringing.

What was stopping him? Ellie wondered. Was it loyalty to *her*? Or did he know something about Skyler that no one else did?

Three more character witnesses followed. Skyler's riding master, whose military bearing didn't quite mask his obvious discomfort. A roommate from Princeton. A former teacher. No one, that is, who had anything much to say other than what a wonderful, capable, caring person Skyler was.

But still no sign of Skyler's mother. What was keeping her? And what about Skyler's father? He hadn't been called upon to testify. Was there a reason other than the obvious one—that he'd be far too prejudiced to offer anything close to unbiased opinion?

She caught Leon's attention, and jotted a single word on his yellow legal pad: "Dad?" Her lawyer responded by lifting a shaggy eyebrow and shaking his head.

Did Leon seem worried, or was she just imagining it? Ellie was seized by a powerful urge to dash out of the courtroom and run home to Alisa, whom she'd left with the Jamaican nanny, Mrs. Shaw. Maybe she could run away with Alisa, to a foreign country where no one would find them—

Oh? And what about Paul . . . you'd leave him behind, too? And your practice?

Don't panic, she told herself. In a little while, Leon would call his own witnesses. Georgina would take the stand, and Paul. Then would come the expert witnesses—the social worker and the psychiatrist. By this afternoon, tomorrow morning at the very latest, it would all be over. But even so, it could be days, weeks, before the judge handed down his decision.

Ellie had nearly convinced herself it was safe to breathe when Verna Campbell shot to her feet. "Your Honor, at this time I'd like to call Skyler Sutton to the stand."

Skyler heard her name spoken aloud, but it was a second or two before she felt able to respond. It was as if her true self were locked inside the cool, polished shell she'd presented to the world, like those Russian nesting dolls Gram had given her when she was little—each one fitting into the next until you got down to the last one, no bigger than a child's thumb.

She rose and walked to the stand, conscious of holding her head up and keeping her arms loose at her sides. The air roared softly around her. *It's going to be okay,* she told herself. Hadn't Verna told her, again and again, how the odds were in her favor?

Verna *had* admitted that it might look bad to the judge that Kate wasn't here. In cases where the biological mother was young and single, she'd explained, it helped when the grandparents demonstrated their supportiveness. On the other hand, Skyler wasn't exactly a kid. She'd been living on her own for more than a year, and she had her own income, plus a start on a career.

What Verna hadn't counted on was how Skyler would feel, walking into the courtroom and seeing the empty space beside Daddy where her mother should have been.

It hit Skyler again as she sat down in the witness box and met her father's apologetic eyes. *Why, Mom, why?* It still didn't make any sense to her. If you loved your child you fought for her.

Mickey gave her a thumbs-up, and Skyler felt a rush of gratitude. God, what would she do without Mickey?

Skyler could feel Tony's eyes on her, too, but she steadfastly refused to look back. She was glad he was here ... but in a way, his presence was making her even more nervous. She was acutely aware of her heart, beating too rapidly, and of the pocket of sweat that had formed between her breasts.

"Skyler, do you love your daughter?" Verna cut right to the quick.

Skyler straightened. "With all my heart."

"Bear with me, Skyler, but some of us might have trouble understanding how a mother who claims to love her baby could give her up. Could you enlighten us?"

They'd rehearsed this carefully in Verna's office ... but now that her moment in the spotlight was here, Skyler felt her stomach twist in panic. A hand fluttered to her cheek before she remembered to force it back onto her lap.

"At the time, I thought I was doing the right thing," she said softly.

"The right thing for whom?"

"For my baby."

"Your decision had nothing to do with what would be best for *you*?"

"In a way, yes," she admitted. "I'd planned on going back to school, and I didn't know how I could juggle my studies with taking care of a baby." They'd rehearsed this, too. Verna thought it would look better if she were to acknowledge it herself, rather than have her painted as selfish and unfeeling by Ellie's lawyer.

"And now?"

"I'd still like to go back to school, but it doesn't have to be right away. And when I do, I could take a light class load, in order to be with Alisa as much as possible." Skyler felt Ellie's eyes on her, and she would no more have dared look in her direction than she would have jumped in front of a speeding car.

Forgive me, she pleaded silently. *I never meant to hurt you.*

Verna positioned herself directly in front of the witness box, strategically blocking Ellie from Skyler's view. When she spoke, her tone was gentle but firm, the voice of an indulgent parent.

"Let me see if I've got this straight. For a variety of reasons, you decide to give your baby up for adoption . . . then you do an abrupt one-hundred-and-eighty-degree turnaround and decide you want her back. Skyler, would you mind telling us what brought about this sudden change of heart?" Verna remained stock still, waiting for the answer.

Skyler took in a shallow breath, and said, "Honestly? I didn't know what I'd be giving up." The words might have been rehearsed, but not the emotion that charged them . . . or the tears now filling her eyes. "As soon as I saw her, I knew. Deep down. But I'd had a long labor. . . . I was tired and . . . and the wheels were already in motion. It wasn't until a few weeks later that I knew for sure."

"*What* did you know, Skyler?" Verna took an oddly delicate step forward.

"That I'd die if I couldn't be with her." A single tear slipped down Skyler's cheek and dropped off her chin. It struck her wrist like hot wax from a tipped candle, and the room dissolved before her.

"Thank you, Skyler," Verna said gently. "That will be all."

But it wasn't over, Skyler knew. Now it was Leon Kessler's turn to cross-examine her, and though she'd prepared for this, too—for all the questions and innuendos he was likely to hammer her with—she found herself breaking out in a cold sweat.

Verna had advised her to keep her answers simple and direct, but there was nothing either simple or direct about the big, rumpled man who ambled toward her. His brown eyes sparkled with merriment, and his ruddy cheeks formed two shiny knobs.

"Miss Sutton," he began in his good-humored growl. "Maybe it's just me, but I'm having a little trouble understanding something." He waited a beat before continuing. "You've had this remarkable change of heart ... yet throughout your pregnancy you gave no indication to my client of having second thoughts. How do you explain that?"

"Most of the time, I just blocked out my feelings," she told him. "It was easier to be ... numb."

"Do you often block out your feelings?"

"You're making it sound like ... " She caught a warning glance from Verna, and stopped. "No, I don't think I do. Not as a rule."

"But in this case, you felt nothing. No, excuse me, you felt *numb.*" He tapped his fingertips together over his belly, and pursed his lips. "Miss Sutton, how many couples did you interview before you decided to let my client adopt your baby?"

"Six," she told him.

"And yet you chose Dr. Nightingale, even though she'd confided that she was having marital difficulties at the time?"

"I . . . I had a good feeling about her."

"Even though her situation was less than ideal?"

"Yes."

"What are your feelings about Dr. Nightingale now?"

Skyler hesitated, then said, "I'm sure she'd make a very good mother—but that isn't the point."

"What *is* the point?"

"The point is—" she bit her lip—"*I'm* Alisa's mother. Her real mother."

"I see." He nodded sagely. "And her father? Does he have any role in this?"

"Tony and I . . . we're not . . . well, at the time, we weren't . . . Our relationship, it's not what you think." Skyler's face felt tight and swollen, and she was acutely aware of how she must sound—stupid, flighty, prone to sleeping with men she hardly knew.

"I'm not thinking anything, Miss Sutton," he answered mildly. "Why don't *you* enlighten us about the nature of your relationship with your baby's father? Tony Salvatore, is that correct?"

"We're just . . ." Skyler stopped, her mind spinning. What *was* Tony to her? Lover? Friend? Protector? None of the above? "Friends," she finished, feeling somehow like a traitor.

"What was his reaction when you told him you were pregnant?"

She thought for a moment. "He was concerned . . . he wanted to help."

"When the subject of adoption came up, wasn't it Mr. Salvatore who initially recommended Dr. Nightingale?"

"Yes."

"And didn't Mr. Salvatore arrange for you to meet with my client?"

"Yes."

"Did Mr. Salvatore subsequently agree to terminate his parental rights?"

"Yes."

The attorney moved closer, so close she could see the tufts of hair protruding from his wide nostrils. "Mr. Salvatore appears to take his obligations seriously, then. Could that be why he isn't testifying on your behalf today?"

"Your Honor, my client can't speak for Mr. Salvatore!" protested Verna.

Skyler shot a glance at Tony, who sat stone-faced in the back of the courtroom. Was he angry? By publicly denying their love for one another, had she succeeded in pushing him away for good?

She felt sick at the prospect.

"Fair enough . . . fair enough," Leon acceded affably, rocking back on his heels and clasping his hands behind his back. "One more question, Miss Sutton. Are your parents present today in this courtroom?"

"My father is sitting over there," she said, pointing toward the front row.

"And your mother?"

"She . . . wasn't able to come." Bands of sweat broke out along her back and chest.

"Oh—may I ask why not?"

"I . . ." Skyler wanted to scream that it was none of his business, but that was probably just what he wanted. Instead, she finished weakly, "I'd rather not speak for her."

"I find it odd," the lawyer commented as if ruminating on the mysteries of the universe, "that two people who would seem to have quite a large emotional stake in all this have chosen not to testify on your behalf. Does that strike *you* as odd, Miss Sutton?"

"Your Honor!" cried Verna in a disgusted voice.

The judge started to say something that Skyler couldn't hear; it was as if a glass wall divided him from the rest of the courtroom, a wall through which—even by straining—she was able to catch only about every other word.

"Badgering . . . warned you, Mr. Kessler . . . recess . . ."

Moments later, the heavy double doors in back swung open and a stylish middle-aged woman with silver-streaked brown hair arranged in a smooth page-boy began making her way up the aisle between the rows of benches.

Skyler felt something give way in her chest, like soft earth crumbling after a heavy rain.

Her mother looked paler and drawn in a hounds-tooth-checked Chanel suit, and she seemed to be leaning more heavily on her cane. But despite the obvious pain she was in, her expression was composed.

Relief rushed through Skyler as she whispered under her breath, "Mom."

Kate would have given anything not to be here.

But, in the end, nothing could have kept her away.

She'd tried, of course. She'd told herself that if she could just stay busy, then she wouldn't have to think about what was taking place miles away, in a court-room in New York City. She'd gone to the shop, where a shipment had come in from Kansas City, a Biedermeier bookcase. But no sooner had she pried the first nail from its wooden crate when a clear voice had spoken in her head.

Skyler needs you.

It didn't matter, she'd realized, whether or not her daughter would actually *want* her there. Kate's mind had room for only one thought: *I'm her mother.*

She'd known, of course, that Will would not be able to stay away . . . but the sight of him nevertheless brought a stab of dismay. To the outside world, it would seem (as it always had) that Will was strong, and she was not. People would whisper that she'd had to drag herself here, that it was only for appearance' sake that poor, delicate Kate had forced herself to face the ordeal. But they were wrong. It was *she* who was strong—strong enough to face the truth.

I've made too many compromises over the years, she thought as she sank down beside her husband with barely a glance in his direction.

No more. Whatever came of this, Kate would not remain silent with Will any longer. He could hide from the truth all he wanted . . . but did that mean she had to go along?

Kate fixed her eyes on Skyler, who looked shaken as she stepped down from the witness stand. Her daughter stared back at her, wearing a faintly questioning look, as if waiting for some signal or gesture from her. With a subtle shake of her head, Kate let her know that she wasn't here to testify. Her only motive in coming was to show support for her daughter.

The one person in this courtroom whom Kate could not bring herself to look at was Ellie. As Ellie was called to the witness stand, Kate kept her eyes downcast, fixing them on her cane, propped at an angle against the bench alongside her.

Shame on you, a voice in her head scolded, forcing her to lift her gaze.

As she made her way toward the witness box, Ellie appeared calm. She walked with a purposeful stride, head up, shoulders back, wearing a muted plaid suit with a silver Paloma Picasso pin on its lapel. She had too much at stake to reveal the utter panic she had to be feeling right now, Kate thought.

Of all the emotions this woman had evoked in Kate over the past two decades, none had been stronger than the admiration she felt now, watching Ellie face the courtroom with all the grace and dignity of a queen.

"Dr. Nightingale, do you have any other children?" boomed the big, untidy man who was Ellie's lawyer. He leaned forward, his fingers steepling over his chest.

Ellie shifted in her chair and cleared her throat before speaking. Even so, her voice was thick and slightly hoarse as she replied, "Yes . . . a daughter.

Bethanne. But I have no way of knowing if she's even alive."

A silence settled over the courtroom, thick as frost.

Kate felt a hot pain slice through her chest. Oh, dear Lord, how could she bear to sit here and listen to this? She stole a glance at Will out of the corner of her eye, marveling at his lack of expression. It was as if Ellie were a complete stranger . . . someone not even remotely connected to him. For the first time in their nearly thirty years of marriage, Kate wanted to hit him.

"I know this must be painful for you, Dr. Nightingale, but can you tell us what happened to your daughter?" Ellie's lawyer asked gently.

"She was just four months old . . ." Ellie's mouth trembled. "I was living with my sister. Working nights while Nadine watched Bethanne. One night I came home and"—her eyes squeezed shut for a moment—"she was gone. Kidnapped. My sister's . . . boyfriend. The police looked for him, but there was no trace. . . ."

Her lawyer waited as she struggled to compose herself. Then: "And in all these years, you never learned what happened to her?"

"No."

"Mr. Kessler," interrupted the judge in a peevish tone. "I'm sure I speak for everyone here in saying that Dr. Nightingale deserves our utmost sympathy, but what relevance, if any, does it have to *this* case?"

"Your Honor," began the heavyset attorney, "my client is a woman who clearly knows the grief of losing a child. She did not enter into this situation lightly. She did not wish to adopt Miss Sutton's baby due to some last-minute panic over the ticking of her biological clock. Her motives were pure, and they arose from a lifetime of yearning: being a mother meant everything to her."

It was all Kate could do to stay nailed to her seat.

Her eyes felt hot and dry, and there was a sour ashy taste on the back of her tongue.

The lawyer switched his gaze back to Ellie. "Dr. Nightingale, I understand your marriage has been under somewhat of a strain. Can you tell us about that?"

"I'll try." Ellie's mouth fluttered in a tentative smile. "When Skyler first approached me, my husband and I were separated. We love each other very much . . . but, yes, we *were* under a strain. We'd tried for many years to have a baby of our own, and when that didn't happen, we looked into adoption."

"You did more than look into it, I gather?"

"Oh, yes. We came close a couple of times, but at the last minute, in both cases, the mother changed her mind." She paused. "My husband is director of the neonatal intensive care unit at Langdon Children's Hospital. He deals with life and death every day, with babies for whom there are never any guarantees. It all just . . . became too much for him, I think. We both needed a breather."

Leon Kessler pressed a meaty finger to his upper lip. "And how would you describe your marriage now?"

With a glance at her husband, who sat with his hands tightly clasped on the table before him, Ellie said in a clear voice, "We're very much together."

"Thank you." Kessler nodded to Skyler's lawyer.

Kate found herself tensing as Verna Campbell, in her sensible low-heeled pumps, rose from her chair and approached the bench. The look Verna directed at Ellie made Kate think of the one time in her life when she'd been fired from a job. She'd been all of sixteen, temping in the notions department at Macy's over Christmas vacation, and her boss, a frosty-haired battle-ax who'd dressed Kate down in front of everyone for giving back the wrong change, had been wearing a smile just like Verna's—a smile that could have cut glass.

"I'm delighted to hear that you and your husband are working out your difficulties," she said without emotion. "*When* exactly did you two reconcile?"

"It's been a couple of months," Ellie told her, purposely vague.

"Was this before or after my client informed you she'd had a change of heart?"

Ellie hesitated a beat, then said, "Afterward, I think. I don't recall the exact timing."

A lie, Kate thought. But a justifiable one.

Verna, surprisingly, let this ride. Then, like a wolf circling around her victim for the kill, she asked softly, "Dr. Nightingale . . . how old were you when your infant—Bethanne?—was allegedly kidnapped?"

"Eighteen." Ellie sounded annoyed. "And there was nothing *alleged* about her kidnapping."

"Mmm. You said your sister was taking care of her at the time?"

"Your Honor . . ." Kessler started to object, but was silenced by a sideways chopping motion of the judge's hand.

"Mr. Kessler, *you* opened this line of questioning," he barked. "It's only fair that Ms. Campbell be allowed to continue with it."

Wearing a pained expression, the big man sank back into his seat.

"You were working"—Verna glanced at her notes—"at the Loews State Theatre on Broadway and Forty-fifth Street . . . as a ticket taker?" You had to hand it to her, Kate thought: the woman had clearly done her homework.

"That's correct."

"Was your sister unemployed at the time?"

Ellie hesitated before replying, "Mostly . . . yes."

"Dr. Nightingale, how on earth were the three of you managing on your salary alone?"

"Not easily." She gave a grim smile.

Verna let the silence that followed swell, gather momentum; then, in a deathly quiet voice, she asked, "Were you aware that your sister was—how shall I put it?—selling her favors?"

Ellie blanched, and her eyelids fluttered. Then, pulling herself up even straighter, she replied, "Yes, I was aware that my sister had . . . men. But it wasn't all the time, and she . . . she pretty much kept it to herself."

"You mean even living in this tiny apartment, you weren't *disturbed* by strange men trooping in and out at all hours?"

"It wasn't like that. Anyway, as I explained, I didn't feel I had a choice. I was very young, and my parents had made it clear I wasn't welcome at home."

"Dr. Nightingale, weren't you the least bit concerned about the effect your sister's lifestyle might be having on your baby?"

"Of course," Ellie snapped. "I was saving every penny I could. I planned on getting my own place."

"But in the meantime, you were going off to work every night and leaving your four-month-old baby in the care of a prostitute?"

"She was my sister." Ellie's face had gone chalky, and she was trembling visibly.

"Dr. Nightingale, according to police records, the man you describe as your sister's boyfriend was in reality her pimp. Were you aware of this?"

"I . . . not at first. But, later, yes."

"You told the police at the time that he'd beaten your sister on several occasions."

"Yes."

"So he was violent as well?"

"I . . . never saw it happen. But . . ."

Ellie's voice, so carefully modulated, had taken on the flat cadence of the high plains, and for the first time, Kate glimpsed, through Ellie's hard-won professional demeanor, the terrified teenager she had been.

In her mind, Kate imagined this younger version of
Ellie getting off the bus at the Port Authority, a baby
in her arms, bleary-eyed from a day and night of
travel. The baby would have been fussing; Ellie would
have been trying to soothe her while at the same time
looking about, struggling to get her bearings.

*Ellie is peering at the back of a crumpled envelope.
She knows this is her sister's address, but hasn't the
slightest idea where it is. It's two o'clock in the morning, and she hasn't slept in days. She's scared. Everything about this vast, bustling place intimidates her. She
could take the subway, she knows, but she's heard too
many stories about women getting mugged and raped.
And a taxi is out of the question—way more than she
can afford. Finally, she sees a map on the wall, and
realizes her sister's place isn't far. It's closing in on
winter, and she has both her baby and a heavy suitcase
to carry, but she'll manage. She's gotten this far, hasn't
she? Somehow, she's always managed. . . .*

Kate was snatched from her reverie by a harsh sob.
She watched in horror as Ellie, openly weeping now,
buried her face in her hands.

"No!"

It was a split second before Kate realized the shout
had come from her. Somehow she was standing, though
she had no awareness of having risen. A dull roar
pounded in her ears like distant surf. She watched Ellie
raise a stricken white face to her. Everyone in the
courtroom was looking at her now.

Then an amazing thing happened. It was as if Kate
had finally wrenched open the door she'd kept locked
all these years—but instead of Bluebeard's closet,
she'd found something wonderful: a sense of lightness
and freedom as she hadn't felt since she was a young
girl, riding like the wind on the back of her horse.

In a firm, clear voice she hardly recognized as her
own, she cried: "Ellie didn't do anything wrong. *I'm*
the guilty one. My husband and I. Because, you see,
Skyler isn't really our child. She's Ellie's."

CHAPTER 17

Once, during a visit to California some years back, Ellie had experienced an earthquake. It had seemed like nothing much at first, just a low-grade rumbling that might have been a subway passing underneath—except then she'd remembered there were no subways in Monterey. All at once, the wide bay window of the cottage she and Paul were renting had begun to shiver with a sound like chattering teeth, and when she looked out front she saw something that had sent her stomach plummeting down to her kneecaps: the brick walkway was heaving . . . undulating like the back of an enormous snake half buried in the Bermuda-grass lawn.

She had dropped onto the window seat as abruptly as if a karate chop had been delivered to the back of her knees. The universe had called time out, all rules suspended, leaving her nothing to hang on to, nowhere to turn that was steady or safe.

The earthquake lasted only ten seconds or so, but it had left an indelible impression on her. In that fleeting moment, she'd been taught life's most frightening lesson: there are no givens. For if even solid earth can turn into a writhing dragon before your very eyes, then nothing, absolutely nothing, can ever be taken for granted.

Ellie felt now as she had then ... except the seismic ripple that Kate's words had set off couldn't be seen. Somewhere at her core, a deep humming was gearing up to a rumble. Her head floated miles above her body.

"My God!" she gasped.

The spectators' gallery, with its rows of oak benches peopled with shocked faces, grew gray and fuzzy around the edges, like a scene glimpsed from the rear window of a car as it's heading into a tunnel. For a moment, she thought she might be about to pass out.

Then she was through the tunnel, the room opening wide again ... and the part of her brain that had been disconnected snapped back into place. Ellie gripped the molding that skirted the top of the oak-paneled witness box, using it to propel herself to her feet. She felt her ankle give a painful turn as she stepped down, and experienced a tiny dart of surprise to find that she wasn't suspended in midair after all.

This isn't happening, she thought.

Then why was the judge banging his gavel ... and why did everyone look as if they'd turned to pillars of salt? Even Kate looked shocked as hell, as if she didn't quite believe the words that had come out of her mouth. She stepped around the waist-high railing that separated the gallery from the rest of the courtroom, walking stiffly toward Ellie, her eyes like two holes burned in a sheet of blank white paper.

Was she telling the truth?

No. Impossible. I would have known.

Then, with the force of a descending hammer, it hit her: everything fit. Skyler's age. The fact that she was adopted. And just look at her. Ellie allowed herself to stare at the young woman seated at the petitioner's table, her face drained of color, but even so ... oh, yes, oh, God, there it was ...

How could she not have seen it?

Ellie felt a hand cup her elbow, supporting her as she sank deeper into the floor with each step. She swiveled in dreamy slow motion to find Paul at her side, his slate-colored eyes behind the smudged lenses of his glasses fixed on her in stunned disbelief.

Mouths opened and closed. Leon, his face red as a slab of boiled corned beef. That awful bitch of a lawyer with the electrocuted hair. Voices buzzed and muttered in her ears as if trying to get through on a faulty transatlantic connection.

"Can I speak with you ... alone?" One voice, clear as a note on a wind chime, broke through.

Ellie blinked, and Kate's anguished face shifted into focus—her perfect oval of a face, with its lovely, refined features. Tears stood in her hazel eyes like raindrops after a long, cruel drought.

And somehow Ellie was following in her wake. Kate paused only once, when she reached the chair in which Skyler sat, clutching her throat in stunned confusion. Parking her cane against the oak table, she brought both hands to Skyler's bloodless cheeks, and held them pressed there a moment, as if to say, *I love you and I'll explain everything as soon as you're ready to hear it.*

Skyler tipped her uncomprehending face up to meet her mother's gaze, and Kate murmured something to her, too quietly for Ellie to hear; then she was retrieving her cane, moving toward the center aisle with a disdainful glance at her still-seated husband.

The corridor outside the courtroom reeked of cigarettes from the clusters of smokers huddled like fugitives along one wall, but Ellie hardly noticed as she sank onto a bench next to Kate. There was a moment of awkward silence, then Kate touched the back of Ellie's wrist ... a touch as light and cool as a draft from an open window. Kate's raw, bruised eyes emanated a queer brilliance that was mesmerizing in the

same way an accident on the highway will make mo-
torists rubberneck.

Ellie found her voice at last. "How long have you
known?"

"All along," Kate told her. "Not at the very beginning ... but I put the pieces together soon enough.
There you were, in all the newspapers. And I—I just
knew. God help me, I knew." She paused to press a
finger to her temple, those luminous, bruised eyes
never leaving Ellie's face. "I was too shocked to do
anything at first. I thought about calling the police.
But every time I'd go to pick her up ... my baby—
your baby," she corrected herself with an effort that
clearly cost her, "I'd say to myself, 'Just one more
day. It can wait until tomorrow. Let me have her until
then.' So it went. . . . The days just kept on passing . . .
and I kept on making excuses. Then she started saying
'Mama.' And her first tooth came in. And suddenly
there she was, pulling herself up on anything she could
grab hold of. I ... I don't know when I started admitting to myself that I wasn't ever going to make that call.
I suppose all along a part of me was just waiting for
someone to figure it all out and come get her. But then
one day I realized that wasn't going to happen ..."

"Your husband—did he know?" Ellie choked.

"Oh, yes." Something dark glinted in the depths of
Kate's eyes. "But, you see, it was different with Will.
He was ... is ... incapable of acknowledging anything
he's made up his mind not to accept." She gave a
small, pained smile. "Sometimes, I wish I were more
like him."

Ellie was struggling to put it together in her mind,
but it was too much all at once—like trying to put
together a jigsaw puzzle in the dark. Then the piece
she'd been blindly groping for snapped into place.

Slowly, she asked, "That day in the hospital when
we first met ... you knew who I was?"

Kate closed her eyes and nodded.

"All these years!" Ellie covered her face.

"I know I can't ask you to forgive me." Kate's voice, small and pained, drifted through the darkness behind Ellie's cupped hands. "What I did. What *we* did, Will and I ... was a crime ... it wasn't just unforgivable. It was a terrible sin."

Ellie lifted her head, and marveled softly. "I knew she wasn't dead. I *felt* it somehow. Oh, God, Bethanne. All this time ..." Then it dawned on her. If Skyler was her daughter, then that meant— "I'm Alisa's *grandmother*." She forced the words out, though there seemed to be no air left in her lungs.

Again, Kate nodded.

"You see, don't you, why I couldn't take sides?" Kate sagged back, bringing her tightly clenched hands to her cheeks. "At first, when she told me you were the one who was going to adopt her baby ... well, you can imagine ..." Over the knotted white peaks of her knuckles, Kate's lucent eyes regarded Ellie with something close to awe. In a hoarse whisper, she asked, "Do you believe in fate?"

Ellie thought for a moment, and said, "If I didn't before, I do now."

"Because this couldn't be just a coincidence," Kate went on in a breathless rush. "When I realized that— When I understood that something, some force, call it God if you like, was behind this ... well, then, it was as if I'd been given a second chance, don't you see? I could never give back what I'd taken—but finally here was a chance for you to be given back at least a part of that."

"My own flesh and blood ..." It was sinking in at last.

"When Skyler told me she'd changed her mind ..." Kate swallowed hard. "I wanted to help her—she's my daughter, and this was my granddaughter we were talking about. But I ... I just couldn't. I couldn't oppose her, either. So I decided simply to stay out of it."

"What changed your mind?"

"I'm not sure." Kate sounded puzzled. Then she sat up straight, and said, "All the way here, I told myself I was going to just sit tight and keep my mouth shut. But now I realize that I couldn't have kept silent, no matter what the consequences. I had to tell the truth, because it was killing me not to."

Ellie sat and stared at the woman beside her, letting the earthquake roll and thunder. She remembered the day—months later, or was it merely weeks?—when she'd first realized that her baby might never be found, that she might never see Bethanne again. Never know her sweet milky scent ... or feel that small mouth tugging at her breast. She'd been shaking so hard she'd had to crawl into bed, her knees tucked against her chest under the covers, rocking herself as she moaned and wept.

"All this time ... oh, God." Ellie hugged herself now in a vain effort to stop her shivering. She suddenly felt rage, a great surge of white-hot fury directed at Kate. She cried: "*Do you know what it's like?* No, of course you don't. You had the luxury of merely feeling guilty, while I—" Her throat seized up, and when she could finally trust herself to speak, it was in a voice that was pure Euphrates, her mother's voice— harsh, unforgiving, resonant of tumbledown barbed- wire fences and weed-choked yards marked by aban- doned Chevy pickups. "I was a walking dead woman. I ate and slept. I went to work, then to school. But I wasn't alive. I didn't even feel. It hurt too much to feel. Jesus God. My baby. *She was my baby.*"

Ellie began to weep, noisily, without trying to cover her eyes or wipe her nose, while Kate just sat there looking as if she, too, wanted to weep, but didn't dare. She didn't deserve to take comfort even in tears.

In a hollow, broken voice, Kate said, "I realize there's nothing I can say that will change what hap- pened. But now that Skyler has been told the truth, I don't imagine she'll ever be able to forgive me, or her father. If it's any consolation at all . . ."

Ellie shot to her feet so fast that the floor beneath her yawed alarmingly, and she nearly lost her balance. She righted herself and thought: *Bethanne.* Suddenly, it didn't matter about the past . . . or Kate . . . or what might happen next. A wave of pure understanding smashed through her, leaving a single, perfect shell gleaming on the wet sand of her consciousness: her daughter was in the next room, just beyond those doors.

"I have to go," Ellie said with the urgency of someone running to catch a train or a bus that she might miss if she didn't hurry.

"Please . . ." Kate started to say.

Ignoring her, Ellie turned and walked away, pushing through the swinging double doors to the courtroom.

The first thing that caught her eye was the two lawyers standing in a huddle before the bench—Leon with his arms waving, and the stout woman with the skunk-striped hair. Seated above them, the judge merely looked befuddled, as if he couldn't quite believe this was happening in his courtroom.

Several paces from the respondent's table, Paul stood talking with Georgina. He looked up at her, a tall, somewhat slouch-shouldered man in a tweed jacket and neatly pressed chambray shirt, with finger-combed hair that brushed the folds of his collar . . . and it was the love shining from his eyes, like the beam cast by a lighthouse over stormy seas, that enabled Ellie to continue walking. She kept going, putting one foot in front of the other, until she was face to face with the young woman approaching her with a halting, unsteady gait.

Skyler came to a stop a few feet from Ellie. "Is it true?" she asked. The horror in her voice was like a knife plunged into Ellie's heart.

She doesn't want to know me. The thought boomed in Ellie's head.

"Bethanne." She began to cry again, using her sleeve to wipe away the tears. "I never thought I'd see you again."

Skyler's face blurred, then swam back into focus, mottled with angry red blotches. "I don't believe any of this!" she cried. "You *can't* be my mother."

"I'm just as shocked as you are, believe me," Ellie said softly. "But it's true. Everything fits."

"No ... NO ..." Skyler was shaking her head violently.

"Skyler, listen to me." Ellie spoke softly, though she felt like shouting. "Your real name is Bethanne. You were taken from me when you were four months old. You'd just started teething. And ... and, oh God, this is so hard ..." Her voice choked off, and it was a moment or two before she was able to continue. "I loved you so much, you see. When I couldn't find you, it ... it was like the world had come to an end."

"This is crazy," Skyler protested, her voice rising, tinged with hysteria. "You're making this up so you can take Alisa from me. My mother"—she cast a stricken look at Kate—"is mistaken. She's gotten you mixed up with someone else. My *real* mother walked out on me."

Ellie reeled as if she'd been dealt a blow. "I would never, ever have done that. Oh, God ... you can't imagine what it's been like for me all these years," she choked. "Wondering where you were ... if you were being cared for by people who loved you ..."

Skyler's bloodless face tipped up at her, bone-white, the white of a full moon set adrift on the milky currents of a starless, overcast sky. Something that might have been comprehension gleamed darkly in her eyes. "All I know is what I was told." Her voice was cold ... as cold as the glance she darted at Kate, who hovered just inside the swinging doors, her arms wrapped around her.

"Whatever you were told ... it was a lie. If I'd known where to find you, nothing on earth could have stopped me from taking you back. Nothing."

Ellie took a lurching step forward. She grabbed Skyler by the shoulders and dragged her, stiff and unyielding, into arms that had ached with emptiness for far too long ... arms through which the shock of recognition now traveled, as true and swift as a river.

With a muffled cry, Skyler dropped her head onto Ellie's shoulder. Just for a moment. A single, precious heartbeat.

Then she wrenched free and darted away, her head tucked low. Ellie wanted to run after her ... but she knew better. She stood rooted to the spot, watching in helpless anguish as Skyler brushed past Kate and started to push her way through the doors.

It was Tony who stopped her. Out of nowhere, he grabbed Skyler's wrists and pulled her around to face him. He let her struggle until she collapsed against him, sobbing; then he held her as Ellie had wanted to hold her—with a tenderness that gave solace while asking nothing in return. He stroked her head, murmuring something in her ear that caused Skyler to jerk her head against his shoulder in a nod. She seemed to relax a bit then, and allowed her arms to creep up around his back, her hands fluttering to rest against the broad planes of his shoulder blades.

Ellie saw that her daughter was loved by this man. A small blessing in the midst of all this swirling chaos, but one she was grateful for. If she herself wasn't able to comfort Skyler, at least there was someone who could.

Ellie felt her knees buckle a little, and at that moment, Paul appeared at her side to slide his arm around her waist. All her life, she'd had to be strong, and now it felt like the most incredible luxury in the

world simply to allow her head to sink onto Paul's
shoulder.

I mustn't fall apart, she told herself. Her daughter
was a virtual stranger to her, one she desperately
wanted to get to know. She had only to be patient a
little while longer. When the time was right, Bethanne
would come to her. Yes, *Bethanne* . . . not the young
woman everyone knew as Skyler.

Yet Ellie wanted nothing more at that moment than
to go to her child, the daughter she'd longed for,
ached for.

But she couldn't. Not yet.

Wait until she's ready for you, she told herself. *Wait.*

CHAPTER 18

Skyler clung to Tony, the firm pressure of his arms and body the only thing she could hold on to in a place where everything had been turned upside down.

"Baby, listen to me, it's gonna be okay," he murmured against her ear. "I'm here.... I'm here for as long as you need me."

But Tony's words were drowned out by the roaring of her own thoughts. *They lied to me! Mom and Daddy ... they let me think I'd been abandoned. How could they have done such a thing to their own daughter?*

Well, she wasn't theirs anymore. And apparently she never had been.

Only Tony seemed real, familiar. *I love you,* she wanted to say.

But who was *she*? Skyler Sutton, or—

—or this person called Bethanne. Someone she didn't know. God ... oh God ...

"Skyler, oh, my darling, please let me explain ..."

The evil spell that seemed to have been cast over her was shattered by her mother's voice. Skyler tore herself from the safety of Tony's arms and turned around.

Kate was standing a few feet away, her hands primly folded over the handle of her cane, wearing a look Skyler had never before seen. It was the desperate look of a woman hanging from a cliff by her fingernails. Unable to bear the burning intensity of that gaze, Skyler looked away, past Kate, at her father, seated on the bench with his face buried in his hands.

Staggered by the enormity of her parents' betrayal, Skyler brought her gaze back to her mother, who hadn't moved a muscle, not even to wipe away the tear slowly tracking its way down one cheek. "You lied to me. All along you knew I wasn't abandoned." Her voice, though soft, was pure ice.

"Not at first. When we took you home, we only knew what we'd been told. It wasn't until I saw in the newspaper that your ... your mother—" Kate broke off to take a deep, ragged breath. "Oh, Sky, I know that nothing can ever excuse Daddy and me for not coming forward once we'd put two and two together ... but we—we just couldn't bear the thought of losing you. Believe me, I—"

"Why should I believe you?" Skyler exploded. "Even when I needed your help to get Alisa back, you lied to me. When you turned me down, you told me it was because of Ellie, but that wasn't it at all. You and Daddy ... you were just protecting yourselves!" She wheeled from Kate's anguished gaze, throwing her hands over her face to shield herself from its searing light.

"Oh, darling ..." Kate's voice trembled. "It was *you* we wanted to protect."

Skyler lowered her hands. "You call *this* protecting me—throwing it at me in front of everyone? Why not have the *Times* run the story in their next edition while you're at it?" She gave a bitter laugh.

Any remaining whisper of color drained from Kate's

face. "I'm sorry ... I didn't mean for you to find out like this. I'm sorrier than you can possibly know. For everything. But no matter what you might think of me, you must believe one thing: I love you. I've always loved you ... and I always will. I'm your mother."

Except Kate *wasn't* her mother. Ellie was.

Suddenly, Skyler felt trapped, as if she were in an elevator stuck between floors. No one to hear her screams. And soon she would run out of air.

"I have to get out of here," she said aloud to no one in particular.

But before she'd gotten very far, Verna came bustling over. As if Skyler were a green horse about to bolt, Verna grabbed her by the arm and led her off to one side.

"The judge is granting us a recess—even *he's* never come across anything like this. We have until the day after tomorrow, then he wants to see us all in his chambers. Friday morning, bright and early." Though she spoke calmly, Verna was shaken; she was tugging on her pearls, hard, seemingly unaware of the irritated patch of skin that had appeared along her neck.

"Friday," Skyler echoed dully.

She felt her lawyer's firm hand grip her upper arm. "Go home, lie down ... get your bearings. I may have to do the same." Verna drew an unsteady hand across her forehead and blew out a breath. "I thought I'd seen every kind of tangled family situation there was ... but *this* is one for the books."

Mickey came up to Skyler as Verna hurried off in the other direction. "If you need me for anything ... I'm here," she murmured. But Mickey looked so stricken herself that Skyler, as she hugged her friend, didn't know who was comforting whom.

"Oh, Mickey, none of this makes sense," she cried in a choked whisper. "I feel like if I don't get out of here, I'll explode. I need to be by myself for a little while ... just to think."

But as Skyler was leaving the courtroom, she realized she wasn't alone. Tony fell into step with her as she headed down the corridor to the elevators. They didn't speak, and he didn't try to touch her. Their footsteps clacked in echoing harmony as they crossed the marble rotunda and pushed their way out through the plate-glass doors at the far end of the vaulted entryway.

Feeling the autumn air outside was like diving into cool, sweet water. Skyler shivered, wishing she'd remembered to bring a jacket. She wished a lot of things right now—most of all, that she'd never been granted her lifelong wish to meet her mother. The old Chinese curse came to mind: *Be careful what you wish for . . . you might get it.*

"Let's go someplace where we can talk," Tony said, turning to her at the top of the wide marble steps that led down to the sidewalk.

She started to protest, "Tony, I don't think I can—"

He seized her hand, looking long and hard into her eyes. "Trust me," he said.

Skyler managed a wan smile. "Do I have a choice?"

"Not if you care about what happens to our kid."

She didn't know what he meant by that, but she nodded anyway. In any case, she felt too tired to argue. It wasn't until they'd walked half a block north on Centre Street and were rounding the corner onto Worth that she asked, "Where are we going?"

"Chinatown," he told her. "I know a hole-in-the-wall where we won't run into anyone we know."

The only place Skyler wanted to be right now was home, but the cabin was more than an hour's drive away, and suddenly, the prospect of losing herself in a whole other world seemed vastly appealing. Not only that, to her surprise Skyler realized she was hungry.

But even though it was less than a five-minute walk, Skyler, weakened with shock, was almost staggering by the time they reached Mott Street. Abruptly, she found herself in a crush of mostly Asian pedestrians, their voices blending in what was to her a senseless, high-pitched babble. Tony steered her out of the way of a delivery cart pushed by a man in a dirty white apron, then around a display of produce that spilled onto the sidewalk like some fantastic cornucopia. He came to a halt in front of a storefront so narrow and nondescript that if you'd blinked, you'd have missed it. In its steamy window was an ancient laminated menu, mostly in Chinese. Tony pushed open the door, and she followed him inside.

The noodle shop was packed, every seat and booth occupied by an exclusively Asian lunch crowd. But the owner, a wizened old Chinese man, recognized Tony, and an empty booth in back materialized out of nowhere. Skyler slid gratefully onto the worn banquette.

"They make great shrimp dumplings here," he said as menus were slapped down in front of them.

She only nodded.

"You want to talk about it?" he asked.

Skyler laughed, a bitter laugh that hurt her throat. "What's there to say? Apparently, I have a family that belongs on *Geraldo*. I just have to figure out where I fit in."

"You got yourself a helluva mess, all right," he agreed amiably. That was one thing she loved about Tony—events that shocked most people, he took in stride. Maybe it had something to do with his being a cop. Patrolling the streets, he saw more weirdness in a day than most people did in a lifetime.

"It makes sense, though, in a way," she said thoughtfully, conscious now of something solid taking shape amid the drifting fog in her head. "That feeling I had about Ellie, right from the very beginning—as if . . . as if we knew each other from before. It was almost eerie." She turned her gaze on him in dull wonder. "If I believed in such things, I might even think that none of this was an accident."

"Maybe not ... but you'll never get anywhere with that one. The real question here is, what are you gonna do about it?" Tony's expression turned grave. "Way I look at it, you got two choices," he informed her, holding up the index and middle fingers of his right hand. "One, leave it all up to the judge to decide. Maybe he's the softhearted type and figures Ellie could use a break after all the shit she's been through. Or maybe he decides the best thing is to wait until the smoke clears—and in the meantime, he puts Alisa in a foster home."

Skyler shuddered. Could the judge *do* that? It seemed unlikely, but at this point, anything, absolutely *anything* seemed possible.

Out of the corner of her eye, she saw their waiter approach the table. Tony waved him away.

"What's my second choice?" she asked, the tremor in her voice rising.

Tony sat back, regarding her through half-lowered lids. "We could try and settle this ourselves."

She stared at him. "We?"

"Yeah ... you and me. Sitting in that courtroom, I made a decision of my own. And here it is: I'm not taking a backseat anymore."

"What—what exactly did you have in mind?" she stammered.

"I want us to be a family." His voice, hard, flat, implacable, didn't match his words, and for a moment Skyler wasn't sure she'd heard correctly.

Then his meaning sank in, and she was struck by a thunderbolt that crackled through her, charging her with an electric white heat so exquisite it was almost painful. She grew lightheaded and had to grip the table's chrome edge to keep it from sliding away from her.

Finally, the words forced themselves past the swelling thickness in her throat. "Tony, are you asking me to marry you?"

"It kinda looks that way, doesn't it?" He shrugged, but she could see that there was nothing casual about his feelings.

Skyler rubbed her temples. Her head was reeling. "I don't know what to say," she told him.

"You could say yes." A corner of his mouth lifted.

"And then what? You think the judge is going to be impressed because we made *two* mistakes instead of one?" It all came tumbling loose at once. "You make it sound as easy as me jumping on the back of your horse and riding off with you into the sunset ... but, Tony, getting married could be more of a problem than a solution."

"Problem? Shit, Skyler, in case you don't know it by now, I have news for you—I love you. Don't ask me why. Believe me, up till now none of this was any more my idea than it was yours." He leaned close, so close she could feel his breath against her mouth, warm as a kiss. "You don't feel the same about me, just say so. You won't even see my back, I'll be gone so fast. Just say it. Say you don't want to give it a shot: you, me, our kid."

Skyler dropped her head, holding it pressed between her palms. What was there to say—that she didn't love him? That would be a lie. On the other hand, would it be telling the truth to say she could see them together as husband and wife? They were so different, their lives as separate as two orbiting satellites that had happened to cross paths.

"I just ... I ... I can't think straight," she muttered.

"You were right about one thing, it's not just about us," Tony told her, his voice firm. "You run away from this, you could be letting go of Alisa, too. Grab hold of it, Skyler. *Face* it."

Skyler's head jerked up and she felt something twist in her chest. "How can I? I don't even know who I am anymore. I'm someone named Bethanne. Even my parents aren't who I thought they were. Nothing in my life makes sense right now, but I *do* know one thing: I can't marry you."

Tony was silent for a moment, while around them chopsticks clinked dully against bowls and sizzling rice platters hissed, accompanied by a chorus of Chinese voices rising and falling in ceaseless rhythm.

Finally, in a low, let's-get-down-to-business voice, he asked, "Are you saying not now, or not *ever*?"

She wanted to reach out, grab hold of what was solid. In the shifting, wheeling insanity of the past hour and a half, the only thing that stood clear was how she felt about Tony. She loved him. Madly. Truly. Passionately. She wanted him in her bed ... at her table ... in her shower ... on his horse beside her galloping along the trails behind her cabin.

But wanting something, she knew, wasn't the same as being able to have it. And sometimes even when you got what you wanted, it didn't work out the way you'd imagined. Look at Ellie and her, for instance. Ever since she could remember, Skyler had fantasized about meeting her real mother, but never in a million years could she have pictured it turning out like *this*.

She gazed at Tony across the table, filled with a sorrow so great it momentarily eclipsed every other thought. "All I can promise," she told him, "is that you won't have to take a backseat with Alisa. She needs a father. I was wrong not to see that before."

"You mean like every other weekend, the day after Christmas—that kind of thing?" His black eyes narrowed in anger.

"I ... I haven't thought it through all the way."

"You don't have to," he stated flatly. "I see it every day—the single dads with their kids at McDonald's, in the parks, at the zoo. They're all wearing the same expression, those guys—a look that says, 'Are we having fun yet, kids?' " He shook his head in contempt. "That's not what I want for *our* daughter."

Skyler stiffened. "Tony, let me ask you something.

If I hadn't gotten pregnant, can you honestly say you'd be sitting here now asking me to marry you?"

He stared at her in thoughtful silence before answering. "Maybe not, but that's how life works, isn't it? We don't always get to go face first.... A lot of times it's more like getting rear-ended. What counts isn't everything fitting neatly into place, but how you go about picking up the pieces."

Listening to him, she felt the wisdom in his words. But it would be a long time before she ever got around to picking up all the pieces of her life. Even so, there was one piece, shining and pure, yet sharp enough to draw blood, that she could hold in her hand even while the rest lay scattered at her feet.

Her eyes filled with tears. "I love you," she said.

"Then marry me."

"I can't."

"Because I'm a cop?"

"Yes and no," she told him honestly. "I don't want you to be anything other than who you are. But face it, even your family hated me."

He looked back at her, puzzled. "Where'd you get an idea like that? Carla won't shut up about you. Always after me to ask you over for dinner. The rest of them?" He shrugged. "They got their own lives to deal with. They don't bother with mine."

"You haven't even *met* my family," she reminded him, adding bitterly: "Not that I even know who they are anymore."

"That because you're ashamed to introduce me?" He fixed her with his cold cop's stare . . . the one guaranteed to make even the most hard-ass witness squirm. She must have hesitated just a beat too long, because in the next instant he was cutting his eyes away and saying, "Never mind. Forget I mentioned it."

"Tony ..." She reached for his hand across the

table. "This isn't about my screwed-up family. It's about *me*."

"Isn't that what it's always been about, from the word go?" His voice was hard as he answered his own question. "You."

Skyler drew back as if she'd been slapped. "I can't help what I am, any more than you can change who you are."

"The difference is, I'm willing to live with it."

"I'm sorry, Tony."

God help her, he would never know just how sorry. It hurt just to look at him, knowing that they would never share what she'd so often envisioned, and that even if he remained in her life because of Alisa, she'd always have this feeling of something precious dangling just beyond her reach.

"I wouldn't ask you again," he told her.

"I won't expect you to."

Skyler stared down at the table's marbled gray surface, swamped with an exhaustion more profound than any she'd ever felt. After a minute, she wearily lifted her head and asked, "Do you mind if we skip lunch? I'm not hungry anymore."

With a shrug, Tony was on his feet.

As they stepped outside, Skyler wanted desperately for him to hold her hand. Against all reason, she longed to take it all back, every word she'd said to him. In some parallel universe, they *were* married. A husband and wife, with a child. A family.

But Tony kept his distance, walking far enough from her so that not even their elbows brushed.

Skyler floated past steamy windows in which rows of cured ducks hung like dead soldiers. She barely noticed the outdoor stalls skimming by, with their cheap offerings of scarves, belts, and baseball caps . . . or the tourist shops featuring harmony balls and carved Buddhas and embroidered Chinese jackets. As if in a dream, she stepped around a fishmonger hosing the sidewalk in front of a long metal table on which varieties of sea creatures she'd never laid eyes on before lay on a bed of crushed ice. Through it all, one thought emerged, clear as the patch of sunlight caught between the cramped buildings on either side of her.

I have to be strong . . . for Alisa. She's the only real family I have . . .

CHAPTER 19

The intercom buzzed just as Ellie was putting the baby down for the night.

Knowing it wasn't Paul—he'd fallen back into the habit of using his key, and besides, he wasn't due home from the hospital for another hour or two at least—she pulled a blanket over Alisa and hurried to answer it.

For no reason she could think of, her heart was beating high and fast, and there was a sour taste in the back of her throat. These past two days had taken their toll. Since yesterday morning's surreal courtroom scene, she hadn't been able to sleep more than an hour at a stretch. Meals were only what she could force down whenever it became apparent that if she didn't eat something, she'd pass out.

The only thing that was constant, every minute of every day, was the prayer that kept repeating itself in her head: *Please, God, bring her to me.... Let her want to know me....*

For now it was all up to Skyler (how strange to think of her by that name!). Instinctively, Ellie knew she had to wait for her daughter to come to *her*, in her own way and in her own time ... and that any pressure would only drive her further away. But she'd been patient for twenty-three years, and it seemed unfair, inhuman, to have to wait even another day. And what if Skyler never came around? Because of Alisa, she might decide it was too painful . . . or simply too late . . . or—

I'll thank you to remember that God isn't deaf. Mama's words, thrown at her so often when she was growing up that they'd been permanently seared into her brain. But now Ellie could see the wisdom in them.

Hadn't He heard her prayers about Paul?

And now it seemed that God was about to answer her prayers a second time. For the voice that jumped out from the intercom box was Skyler's.

"Ellie? Can I come in? We have to talk . . ."

Thumbing the buzzer to the outer door, Ellie experienced a surge of wild joy. Her baby, her lost child, had come back to her at last.

But less than a minute later, when Skyler appeared at her open front door with a flat, almost sullen expression, Ellie felt her soaring hope flounder.

"May I come in?" Skyler asked in a polite, cool voice.

"Of course." Ellie held the door open wider. "You came at a good time, actually. I just put Alisa down for the night."

Skyler's eyes lit up, but she didn't comment. "I was hoping you'd have a minute to talk."

A minute! After all these years?

Ellie wanted to scream, to cry, to hold her daughter so tightly her ribs cracked, but instead she forced herself simply to usher Skyler into the living room and offer her a seat on the sofa. Then, without a word, she went into the kitchen to pour them each a glass of chilled Chablis from the refrigerator. *What did Skyler want?* Ellie was filled with anxiety as she carried the glasses into the living room and set them down on the coffee table.

Even so, she couldn't help marvelling at how beautiful her daughter was. How lean and strong and fine-featured. She wanted nothing more at that moment than to hug Skyler tightly and tell her how keenly she'd been missed all these years.

She watched her daughter reach for her wineglass too quickly, and nearly knock it over. But then Skyler caught it, bringing it to her lips with an anxious glance in Ellie's direction.

"Sorry . . . I'm sort of nervous," she said, then paused. "Actually, that's a major understatement. The truth is, on my way over, I almost turned back. That's why I didn't call first—I wanted to leave myself an out in case I changed my mind. Also," she added sheepishly, "I guess a part of me was half hoping you wouldn't be here."

"I'm glad you came," Ellie answered quietly, meaning it with all her heart.

How calm she sounded! How civilized! But Ellie was trembling as she sank down in the armchair opposite her daughter.

"This is so weird." Skyler put her glass down and looked over at Ellie. "The two of us, talking like we're just casual friends who haven't seen each other in a while. The thing is, I don't know how else to act. I mean, I doubt even Ann Landers has ever covered a situation like this."

She offered a wry half-smile that snagged at Ellie's heart—it was so like Jesse's! Over the years, she'd thought of Skyler's father only a handful of times, and when she did, it was usually with disdain. Now she found herself remembering, with a twinge of nostalgia, how endearing he could be, how funny at times.

"I wonder what advice she'd give," Ellie said lightly.

"Oh, probably something along the lines of 'Forgive and forget.' "

Ellie knew she meant Kate, but even so she felt a pang of guilt. She wanted to explain: *It's true I should never have left you with Nadine ... but back then, I didn't feel I had a choice. However much you must have grown up hating me, I never stopped loving you or wanting you back—not once. ...*

They sat listening to the creak of footsteps in the apartment overhead, and the rhythmic *tock-tock-tock* of a pigeon pecking at the courtyard window. Outside, the wind blowing through the dying leaves of the ailanthus trees made a sound like rushing water.

Finally, Skyler took a deep breath and said, "I guess there's no point in beating around the bush. The reason I came here tonight was to see Alisa." Her eyes grew bright with tears. "And to find out if you and I ... if we might be able to work something out."

"What did you have in mind?" Ellie asked slowly.

Ever since she'd learned that Skyler was her daughter, Ellie's whole being had yearned for the two of them to be joined again in some way—one that would include Alisa as well. She didn't know yet what that might entail; she'd purposely kept from thinking that far ahead. And now, seeing the strained look on Skyler's face, she knew why: the danger lay, as it always had, in getting her hopes up.

But even as she was thinking of all that was at stake here, of all the ways Skyler could break her heart, Ellie felt a fierce urge to go to her daughter, to give her what only a mother can: absolute, unconditional love.

"I was hoping—" Skyler stopped, her face reddening. "Oh, I don't know. I guess I was hoping that somehow *you* would have all the answers. God knows I haven't a clue. I'm still getting used to you being my mother."

Mother. That one word, from Skyler's lips, triggered a reaction more powerful than any testimonial. Ellie grew suddenly short of breath; she pressed her palm

to her breast, as if making a pledge. And in a soft
voice, she told Skyler the story ... not stopping until
she got to the end, and the tocking of the pigeon
against the window had given way to a gentle, whispering rain.

"I was so sure I'd find you. Even after everyone
else had given up hope," she finished. "It became an
obsession. Every time I saw a little girl around your
age with blond hair and blue eyes, I'd wonder if she
was mine." Ellie drew a trembling hand across her
eyes. "I don't know when I stopped looking ...
around the time I first met you, I suppose. I might
have seen it then, that day in the hospital ... but your
moth—Kate, that is—she kept me from seeing it. . . .
You see, I simply couldn't imagine anyone loving you
as much as I did."

Skyler's face hardened. "She knew all along. That's
the part I can't forgive. Mom and Daddy—they both
knew."

It wasn't Ellie's place to defend Kate. Not even a
saint could expect her to turn the other cheek. All she
could think of to say was, "Yes, they knew."

"I understand now ... how you must have felt. It's
how I feel about Alisa every minute of the day,"
Skyler told her. "I just don't know if I can ... well ...
if anything will ever make up for all the years you
and I lost."

"We don't have to make up for anything. We can
start from here." Ellie smiled a sweet, sad smile.

Skyler sank back against the sofa cushions, cupping
her wineglass. Reddish patches stood out on her pale
cheeks, and Ellie could see goosebumps on her arms
below the short-sleeved sweater she wore.

"Tell me about my father," Skyler said. "What was
he like?"

Ellie shrugged lightly. "The last I heard, he'd retired
from the army and was living in Minneapolis. But as
you've probably gathered by now, we don't keep in

touch." Casually, she added, "No children that I know of."

"What about *your* parents—are they still alive?"

Ellie nodded, careful to maintain as neutral an expression as possible.

"They're still living in the town I grew up in, about an hour outside of Minneapolis," she said. "But if you're thinking of writing or calling, don't expect much. They have very little interest in me, so I don't imagine they'd get too excited over any child of mine. When I told her I was pregnant, my mother threw me out of the house."

Skyler's gaze grew troubled and distant, as if she were remembering Kate's very different reaction to her own pregnancy. "I guess you haven't had it too easy," she observed softly.

"No," Ellie agreed. "But there's one thing I was never sorry about—having you." Tears rose, flooding her throat. "Even after you were taken from me, when it would have been so much easier just to forget, I never wished you hadn't been born."

Skyler stared at her, and Ellie once again felt the inexorable pull of the connection she'd sensed for the first time that day in the bookstore coffee bar. Yet she was terrified that if she came on too strong, she would frighten her daughter away. She sat there for a minute, helpless.

Then she knew what she had to do. Rising silently from her chair, she walked down the hallway to the nursery, where she found Alisa sound asleep on her stomach, making small mewing sounds as if dreaming of dangers that might lie ahead. Without stopping to think, Ellie gently scooped her up and carried her into the living room. The scent of baby powder clung to Alisa's skin, and the top of her feathery head tickled the underside of Ellie's chin, bringing a blinding rush of love.

And fear, too. What was she exposing herself to?

What if Skyler took one look at her daughter and
decided she couldn't bear to share her after all?

But Skyler, who had stood up to get a better look,
wasn't rushing forward to snatch the baby from her
arms. She stood very still, a rapturous expression
dawning on her lovely, tormented face.

Ellie said softly, "Here. Why don't you hold her?"

The moment Skyler's arms curved around her, Alisa
woke with a start, her eyes flying open. Ellie tensed,
waiting for the baby's face to go all red and bunched.
But Alisa didn't cry; she only lay there, her bright
blue eyes searching Skyler's face.

"She's so beautiful," Skyler whispered in awe.

"Just like her mother."

Just then, Skyler brought her head up, and the two
women shared a look that needed no explaining.

"Thank you," Skyler said, her eyes shining.

"A long time ago, I made a promise to myself,"
Ellie confided. "I told myself that if I ever found you,
I'd make sure you would never again know the feeling
of being torn from your family."

Skyler was silent for what seemed an eternity, but
when she finally spoke, her voice was strong and clear.
"On my way over tonight, I wasn't sure what I hoped
to accomplish . . . but I have a pretty good idea now."
She paused, frowning a little, then took a deep breath.
"I want us to share Alisa. I want her to grow up
knowing *both* of us."

Ellie struggled to absorb Skyler's words, which
seemed to skate over the surface of her mind. It was
as if her heart had stopped beating. She could not
seem to grasp the wondrous gift being offered to her.

Then her heart burst into flight, the earth creaked
on its axis, and she thought: *I can never forgive
Kate . . . but I can be grateful to her for giving me
back a daughter who is wise as well as beautiful, kind
as well as strong.*

For a moment, she allowed herself the luxury of

openly studying the admirable young woman her daughter had grown up to be, before dropping her eyes to the baby nestled in Skyler's arms—a sight that brought a joy so unexpected it caught her by the throat.

"King Solomon," Ellie recalled with a small, tight smile. "He gambled that the real mother would step aside before she'd let her baby be torn in half." She paused to wipe her eyes. "I would step aside, too, if I thought that would happen. What I want isn't half . . . it's *both* of you."

Alisa began to cry just then, and Skyler brought the baby to her shoulder as expertly as if she'd been doing it all along. Yet when she looked over Alisa's head, with its silken tufts that stood up like kitten's fur, the smile she gave Ellie was a tremulous one.

"There's so much I don't know," she said, a hint of nervousness creeping into her voice. "I've never taken care of a baby."

"Don't worry . . . you'll do just fine," Ellie assured her.

As naturally then as one moment flowing into the next, or one heartbeat following another, she rose and went to her daughter, feeling a bright ring form about them—mother, daughter, granddaughter. A whole that was even bigger and stronger than the sum of its parts.

And Ellie, who in her darkest moments never would have believed the sun could rise on such a day as this, felt something stir in her heart that she'd thought long dead—a feeling so unfamiliar that at first she couldn't put a name to it. Then recognition came . . . and she smiled a little at how a concept so simple could have seemed so utterly foreign to her.

She thought: *I am blessed.*

Friday morning at nine, they all met in the judge's chambers—Skyler and her lawyer; Leon Kessler; and Ellie, accompanied by Paul, in whose lanky arms was

cradled a freshly bathed and powdered Alisa dressed
in a flowered smock dress and miniature white Mary
Janes.

The meeting was mostly a formality, as the basic
custody arrangement had been agreed on by Ellie and
Skyler ahead of time. Only the details needed to be
sorted out. Ellie and Paul would have Alisa every
Monday through Thursday, and Skyler would have her
the rest of the week. As far as holidays went, Ellie
and Skyler planned on being together for at least part
of Christmas and Easter, and that meant Alisa would
have them both.

Skyler was going to defer school for another year.
Meanwhile, she planned on giving up the cabin and
moving into the city. Her father had put his pied-á-
terre on the market, but Skyler could stay there until
it was sold. She wasn't too happy about that part of
the arrangement—relations with her parents were
strained, to say the least; in fact, the only one she'd
spoken to was her father, who'd called to insist that
she use the apartment. Skyler had reluctantly agreed,
but only until she could find something of her own on
the West Side, near Ellie and Paul.

Ellie and Skyler agreed that any major decisions
involving Alisa would be hammered out between
them. And when they didn't see eye to eye, a mutually
decided upon third party would be called in to
mediate.

The only remaining question mark was Tony.

But when the judge asked about his role in bringing
up Alisa, Skyler, looking pained, merely said, "He'd
like to be as involved as possible."

Ellie didn't press her, but she was troubled. What
she liked even less was the way Skyler seemed to close
off whenever Tony's name arose, as if she were physically pulling inward. At one point, she even looked as
if she were going to cry.

What was the story with those two? Ellie wondered.

Eventually, she supposed, she would know. In the meantime, the only thing she knew for sure ... the thing that sent her out of Judge Benson's chambers on a carpet of air ... was that, one way or another, and however unorthodox, she would finally have the family she'd always dreamed of.

CHAPTER 20

Four to midnight, Tony reflected, could seem like the longest tour of duty in history when you're standing hospital watch.

Seated beside the bed in Doherty's room at St. Vincent's, he tried to concentrate on the magazine he was flipping through, an old issue of *Field & Stream* that he'd picked up in the lobby. Though it wasn't yet eleven, he was having a hard time keeping his eyes open. He looked over at sandy-haired Doherty, asleep with a cast on his arm; the big guy had taken a tumble off his horse earlier in the day, and had wound up on the operating table with a shattered elbow and several broken ribs. Tony saw the wisdom in the department rule that a cop injured in the line of duty must be placed under twenty-four-hour hospital watch ... but in this case there was about as much of a chance of a perp with a grudge coming after Doherty as there was of Elvis rising from the dead. The only danger facing the big, freckle-faced dope was the possibility that he'd bring the walls down with his snoring.

Sure, Tony could've assigned one of his officers, but with half a dozen of his troop out sick with the flu, the bar would've been short for tonight's all-hands detail—a candlelight vigil being staged by AIDS activists down at City Hall. So here he sat, going stir-crazy, thinking about Skyler.

All week, he'd been itching to call her. He was anxious to see the baby, to be able to hold her without it feeling like a favor he was being granted. Already he was looking ahead into the not-too-distant future—the day when his little girl would see him walk in, and come running toward him with a big smile on her face.

At the same time, he didn't know if he was ready yet to face Skyler. He couldn't even *think* about her without feeling as if his guts had been rearranged by Black & Decker. He couldn't look at her without wanting her—in bed, and everywhere else. He imagined her picture in his wallet, alongside the one he now carried of his daughter. Her reflection in the medicine cabinet mirror, peering over his shoulder in the morning while he shaved. Her muddy riding boots parked in the closet next to his.

No, better if he waited another week or two, until the dust had settled. Why put himself through all that grief? So he could end up with an ulcer, like the one Lou Crawley now claimed to have? Tony allowed himself a flicker of a smile, remembering how he'd finally busted Crawley's ass assigning him that big black brute, Rocky. After several weeks of being tossed time and again—once almost getting his head kicked in—Crawley had officially requested that he be transferred back to his old precinct.

Tony only wished he could resolve his feelings about Skyler as easily. It hurt to think of not having a life with her, and with their little girl. It hurt so bad, sometimes he couldn't sleep at night ... even after eight hours in the saddle in the pouring rain.

"Sergeant? There's a phone call for you—a woman who says it's important."

Tony looked around at the slender black nurse

standing in the wedge of artificially bright light that slanted in through the partly open door.

He nodded to her and started to reach for the phone by the bed before he remembered that all after-hours calls were rerouted to the switchboard. He'd have to take this one at the nurses' station down the hall. Tony heaved himself up from his chair, feeling slightly punch drunk from sitting too long in one place.

Then it hit him. Skyler. It had to be her. Tony, his heart kicking into high gear, hurried out of the room and down the hall. But when he punched the blinking button on the phone, the voice that greeted him wasn't Skyler's.

"Tony—oh, thank heavens I caught you." It was Ellie, and she sounded as if she'd been crying. "Jimmy's housekeeper tried to reach you earlier, and couldn't get through, so she called me instead. I got here as soon as I could, but ..." She stopped, and took a breath. "Tony, I'm sorry ... he's gone."

Tony felt her words slam into him. Dolan dead? God knows he'd been expecting it ... even praying for it, in a way. But hearing it, and realizing he wasn't going to stop by his best friend's place on his way to work tomorrow morning with a fresh bagel and a cup of that designer coffee Dolan liked so much ... Jesus, it just didn't seem—

"Tony?" Ellie's voice filtered through the roaring in his head.

"I'll be right over," he told her.

A quick call to the barn to order Grabinsky, the officer on duty at the wheel, to find someone to take over his watch, and Tony was racing for the elevator. His heart was hammering in his chest as he repeatedly thumbed the down button. There was no reason to hurry, no reason at all, but all of a sudden it seemed urgent that he get to Dolan's, that he ... pay heed.

Pay heed? Where had he gotten that phrase? From a book, probably—nobody he hung around with talked like that, except maybe Skyler. But it fit. Dolan had *counted,* goddammit.

Tony, his breath coming in ragged bursts, was half-way across the parking lot when it hit him anew. *I'll never see him again.* He lurched forward and almost fell, catching himself against the hood of a parked Cadillac DeVille, its cool metal smacking his bare palms. He could feel a pressure gathering in the bridge of his nose—tears he wasn't at all prepared for, tears he didn't fucking need.

"Shit." Tony brought the heel of his hand down on the car hood with enough force to send a bolt of pain shooting up his wrist.

He let go of a gasping sob. No more swapping stories about the old neighborhood ... no more Friday nights spent chasing beers and shooting pool at O'Reilly's Tavern. No more of Jimmy kidding him about how the only reason he'd become a cop was so he could get paid for kicking ass.

And no more of watching his best friend die, inch by inch, until there'd been nothing left for him to hold on to.

Over the next two days, Tony managed to call all the names in Dolan's address book, most of them dancers, along with a few people from the old neighborhood with whom Dolan had kept in touch. After three or four attempts, he finally got hold of Dolan's younger brother Chuckie, the only one in that whole stinking family who hadn't written Dolan off. That left only Dolan's therapy group, but Ellie had said she'd take care of informing them.

On Thursday, as he greeted them all at the door of the flower-decked dance studio on West Nineteenth, Tony couldn't help feeling that his friend had managed to get his way after all, throwing a party in place of a memorial service. All of it had been prearranged by Dolan himself, whose last wish was that he be re-

membered, not with a casket and tears, but with champagne and laughter and good memories. His buddy's
friends filed in one by one and looked around the
mirror-walled space arranged with cocktail tables,
each bearing a centerpiece of freesia and snapdragons.
The caterer's help milled around with silver trays of
canapés and brimming champagne glasses. And what
struck Tony most was how quickly somber looks were
replaced by expressions of relief and, yes, even
gratitude.

Dolan's unerring instinct for knowing how to please
a crowd had not died with him, Tony thought admiringly. He scanned the blowups stuck up on the walls—
his own idea—of Dolan at the height of his dancing career, looking as if he'd managed to defy gravity itself.

Hey, pal, I'm gonna miss you. Tony lifted an imaginary beer to his friend and smiled at his own reflection
in the mirrored wall opposite him.

Several of the men from Dolan's therapy group
came over and introduced themselves. A tall, tweedy
drink of water named Erik Sandsrom, who taught history at Fordham. A young Puerto Rican nicknamed
Mondo, with a red bandanna knotted around his forehead. A Wall Street type, in pinstripes and Ferra-
gamos, who raised a fist in solidarity to the blowup of
Dolan onstage, taking a bow before a standing-room-
only audience at the State Theater.

A number of the dancers from Dolan's old troupe—
lithe, muscled men and wisplike women who seemed
to glide along on invisible casters—clustered around
the piano in the corner, where Dolan's brother was
playing a lively rendition of "Make Someone Happy."
Chuckie, as big and burly as Dolan had been small,
was wearing a checkered blue shirt rolled up at the
sleeves, and a baseball cap that Tony recognized as
Dolan's. Chuckie was grinning, and tears stood out in
his eyes as he thumped the keys.

Tony's sisters, Carla and Gina, showed up as

Chuckie was seguing into "Send in the Clowns." Carla kissed Tony's cheek, looking anything but mournful in tights and a long sweater with a panda bear design. When they were all growing up, she used to tag after him and Dolan like a lost puppy ... but Dolan, she reminded Tony now, had never told her to buzz off. Then Ellie came in, wearing a bright red dress. She folded Tony in a brief, fierce hug.

"Every so often one of them gets under my skin," she told him. "Jimmy was special. I'm going to miss him."

Tony felt his throat start to close up, and he snagged two champagne glasses from a passing tray. Raising his in a toast, he said, "To Dolan—buddy, if you ain't front-center in Heaven, the Catholic church owes you a refund."

"Do you believe in God?" Ellie asked.

"Sure, I do ... every Christmas and Easter, and on some Sundays, depending on my mood. What about you?"

Ellie rolled her eyes. "Growing up, I had so much religion crammed down my throat I never wanted to see the inside of a church again as long as I lived. But lately I've begun to think maybe God was just the victim of bad P.R." Her mouth curved upward.

Knowing she was referring to Skyler—and how blessed she felt—Tony was suddenly conscious of an invisible band tightening about his chest. He stared out the north-facing loft window at the distant spire of the Empire State glimmering above the office buildings along lower Fifth.

"Tony, are you all right?" He felt Ellie touch his arm.

Tony smiled and shook his head. "Must be the champagne," he said. "I'm not used to it. I'm a Budweiser kind of guy ... just ask your daughter."

Ellie looked at him, puzzled. "Are you and Skyler ... ?" She stopped, adding softly, "It's none of my business, I know, but I can't help being concerned."

"Are we an item, you mean?" He snorted. "Yeah, like Martini and Rossi—you can't tear us apart." He gestured at her empty glass. "Want another one?"

She shook her head. "Thanks, but I can't stay. Mrs. Shaw is looking after the baby, and she has a dentist's appointment." Ellie regarded him gravely for a moment before saying, "Tony, there *is* one thing. Normally, I don't give out advice, not even to my patients. My job is to help people find their own solutions. But with you, I'm going to make an exception." Her eyes made him think of Dolan's, their brilliance nearly blinding, like looking directly into the sun. "Tony, if you love her, don't let her get away. Go after her. I've seen the look on her face when she talks about you. But she's young. She doesn't know that life isn't a map you chart for yourself. Sometimes, you have to go wherever it takes you."

Tony shrugged. "Maybe she's right. Maybe we're just too different."

"Do you really believe that?"

"That we're different? Sure." He thought for a moment. "Not that it's stopped us so far."

"Then don't let it stop you now." Ellie held his gaze for a long moment, then turned away.

Tony hung around another hour or so, until the guests began drifting out. Only a few looked as if they'd been crying, and Tony wanted to shake them, even though he felt like crying himself. He could almost hear Dolan in his mind, that mock-contemptuous tone of his as he scolded, "Hey, man, get a life."

Jimmy Dolan sure as hell wouldn't be sitting back, waiting for the person he loved to show up at his door, Tony thought.

So what are you waiting for? Since when do you sit around on your butt when you could be out doing something?

Since I stopped thinking I could fix every damn thing that went wrong, Tony answered himself.

Tonight, he was working the midnight-to-seven . . . and suddenly he couldn't wait to climb onto his horse and ride out into the night, where the streets were ones he could follow blindfolded, and the only shit he'd have to deal with was the kind that had nothing to do with him. He wouldn't have to think about Skyler then. He wouldn't have to think about anything but doing his job.

But at one o'clock the following morning, it wasn't the call of duty that made Tony rein his horse to a stop in front of a scalloped blue awning on Central Park West, the building in which he and Skyler had made love that first time.

Dismounting at the curb, he led Scotty onto the sidewalk. The doorman, a slack-faced kid sporting an Adam's apple the size of a drawer pull, gaped at him as he looped his horse's reins about one of the aluminum poles that supported the awning. But when Tony requested that he page Skyler's apartment, the kid jumped into action as if he'd been booted in the rear.

"If she's there, ask her to please meet me in the lobby," Tony told him. Skyler was probably asleep, he thought. He'd be waking her up . . . and she'd be even less pleased at having to come down here. But Tony couldn't exactly leave old Scotty parked out on the sidewalk all by himself.

Nevertheless, when Skyler emerged from the elevator a few minutes later, her face bleary with sleep, a tan raincoat thrown over her nightgown, he could have kicked himself. She looked worried. And why shouldn't she? She had to be thinking it was some kind of emergency that had dragged her down here in the dark hours of the morning.

"Tony, what is it—is something wrong?" She took his arm and drew him over to a pair of spindly antique chairs flanking a marble console.

"I had to see you, is all," he told her.

"At one-thirty in the morning? Are you *nuts*?" She took a step back and looked at him with an expression that hovered between disbelief and outrage.

Her hair was mussed, and her eyes heavy-lidded. The scent of baby powder drifted toward him. Though he knew their daughter was with Ellie tonight, Tony formed a mental picture of Skyler snuggled in bed with Alisa asleep in the curve of her arm. His heart caught in his chest.

"Yeah, you could say that," he growled in a voice low enough to be almost a whisper. "I'm so fucking nuts I can't stop thinking about you."

"Tony, for God's sake, I was sleep—"

He caught her wrist lightly in his hand. "Yeah? Well, I'm sorry if I woke you. But while we're on the subject, let me ask you this. How many nights lately have you lain awake staring at the ceiling, even when you're so fucking tired you can hardly see straight? Do you wake up at four in the morning feeling like somebody parked a Land Rover on your chest, and the engine is still turning over? Well, I got news for you: if the worst thing that happens to you is being dragged out of bed at one-thirty in the morning by a guy who can't go another hour without seeing you, count yourself lucky."

Skyler was wide awake now. "Do we have to go over it all again?" she asked in a low, distraught voice. "What do you want from me?" It was the plea of someone throwing herself on the mercy of an attacker.

For an instant Tony nearly backed off. *Forget it*, he told himself. *Just forget the whole fucking thing.*

But something in him wouldn't let go.

"I want you to be straight with me," he told her. "If you don't love me, say so, and this'll be the last time we'll ever have this conversation."

"I already told you, I—"

"Yeah, you told me you love me. But what the hell

does it *mean*? There's all kinds of love, Skyler. There's the kind you feel after a couple of beers, when you're horny and somebody just happens to come along at the exact right moment. But that's not the same as the old couple holding hands on the park bench. Or a guy riding his horse around Central Park at midnight, who can't think of a single fucking thing but the woman asleep in the building across the street."

"Oh, Tony . . ." Skyler's eyes filled with tears.

"You just don't see it, do you? How good it could be. You're too busy lookin' at all the negatives."

"Well, *one* of us has to," she told him, an impatient note creeping into her voice. "Look at my parents; they have *everything* in common, and they're barely speaking to each other. And Paul and Ellie—they love each other, but they almost got divorced."

"We're not them. We're *us*."

"Yes," she agreed softly. She took several small, shuffling steps backward, her loafers making whispering sounds against the tile floor. "Listen, I don't think we should see each other for a while. I'll talk to Ellie . . . arrange it with her so you can visit Alisa over at her place. Just for now. It might be better that way. Good night, Tony." With a small, choked cry, she turned and fled.

Watching the elevator doors close on her, Tony felt like the last person aboard a sinking ship that might capsize at any moment.

In a flash, he knew what he had to do. Striding over to the doorman's station, he buttonholed the kid behind the desk. "You know anything about horses?" he asked.

The doorman, who looked all of seventeen, shook his head hard. "All I know is to steer clear of them," he said, obviously scared shitless at the prospect of Tony asking him to keep an eye on Scotty.

Scratch that idea, Tony thought. He'd have to come up with another plan. He couldn't have Scotty bolting on the kid—that aluminum pole wouldn't have held a German shepherd with a mind to take off, much less a thousand pounds of panicky horse.

"This building have a freight elevator?" he asked, stepping outside and untying Scotty's reins.

The doorman nodded. "Down the hall, and to the right. But you need a key," he said, making no move to help.

Tony smiled to himself—the kid had seen too many cop shows. He wouldn't produce the key until he heard the magic words. Happy to oblige, Tony flashed his shield, and in his best imitation of Detective Sipowicz from *NYPD Blue,* barked, "Police business." It wasn't strictly kosher, but why not give the kid his money's worth?

The effect was instantaneous.

Moments later, key in hand, Tony was coaxing his horse into a service elevator large enough to hold the contents of a studio apartment. Even so, he could feel Scotty start to spook as the doors slid shut. He tightened his hold on the bridle, reassuring his quivering horse in a soft voice.

The elevator, creaking slowly upward, seemed to take forever. Tony felt himself break out in a light sweat. Christ, you could find a cure for diphtheria in the time it was taking this old crate to make it up twelve floors.

After an eternity, the doors thumped open. An old woman lugging a bulging Hefty bag on her way to the trash chute—had to be one of those night owls who go into a cleaning frenzy when they can't sleep—took one look at Scotty and let out a yelp.

Leading the horse out of the elevator into the utility passage that ran the length of the floor, Tony raised his hand to her in a two-fingered salute, smiling as he imagined the story this would make for her grandchildren.

"Police business," he explained.

Scotty's hooves clattered against the concrete floor. But the doors facing onto the passageway—they serviced the apartments' kitchens, Tony guessed, which at this hour had to be pretty much deserted—remained closed.

When he knocked at the door of Skyler's apartment, it was a full minute before she answered.

As she stood in the open doorway her astonished eyes moved from Tony to his horse, then back to Tony again. Finally, she managed to croak, "Have you *completely* lost it?"

She'd taken off her raincoat, and in the light that shone from behind her he could see through the thin cotton of her nightgown . . . just the outline of her body, but it was enough to make his knees go weak.

"Let's put it this way, I'm not here on a 911 call," he shot back.

"I'm calling the super," she threatened, growing red in the face. "I'm sure this is illegal."

"You forgetting, I'm a cop."

"You—you—" she sputtered.

Before she could get the words out, Tony calmly hooked his reins over the doorknob and took Skyler in his arms. She resisted him, but only for an instant; then she yielded, the tempting outline he'd caught a glimpse of a moment ago becoming a solid shape that pressed warmly into him, causing the heat in his groin to flare upward.

Kissing her, feeling Skyler's mouth grow soft and dewy under his, Tony was only dimly aware of the old lady at the end of the passageway gaping at them.

Suddenly, Skyler jerked away from him and burst into tears.

"It's okay," he murmured, holding her against him and hearing the soft creak of leather as she buried her face in the folds of his jacket. "It's all gonna work out fine."

"What makes you so sure?" she sobbed.

"We'll *make* it work." He touched her wet cheek,

hoping to lighten the mood. "Hey, aren't you gonna ask me in?"

She looked back at him, unsmiling. "Have you forgotten what happened the last time I did?"

Tony didn't hesitate before replying gently, "What happened was, we made a baby—a beautiful little girl."

Skyler pondered this for a moment, hooking a hank of hair behind one ear. Then it came, the smile he'd been waiting for . . . breaking through her tears with all the radiance of a rainbow following a cloudburst.

"We seem to have a habit of putting the cart before the horse, don't we?" she laughed.

Tony glanced over at Scotty, and grinned. "I don't see any cart."

Her eyes narrowed. "What's that supposed to mean?"

"That it's time for you and me to get married."

She sighed. "Oh, Tony . . . don't you ever get tired of asking me?"

"I was kinda hoping it'd be the other way around—that I'd wear you down into saying yes."

"You were, huh?"

"What can I say? I'm not the kind who gives up easy."

"Neither am I," she told him.

They stood silently facing one another across the threshold while Scotty snorted with impatience. Skyler's arms were folded over her chest, and somewhere in the neat, modern-looking kitchen at her back a clock ticked softly.

Tony took a quick, sharp breath. "So . . . am I in, or what?"

Skyler hesitated long enough to send his already racing heart into maximum overdrive. Then, still smiling, she opened the door wide enough to let in a horse . . . and maybe even a horse's ass of a cop, who knew a good thing when he saw it coming.

CHAPTER 21

Kate rubbed her nose with the back of her wrist. It was the fumes that got to her most when she was stripping furniture—in this case, a little gem of a Pembroke table that she'd picked up at an auction in Maine. The Strypeeze made her eyes water and her sinuses flare, and had already eaten several holes in her rubber gloves. What gnawed at her also was knowing that Leonard would gladly have done this for her, and that she must be raving mad for not letting him.

Is this your idea of a hair shirt? she scolded herself. *Can you really imagine that flagellating yourself will bring Skyler back?*

Nonsense. She was merely doing what had to be done. Leonard had been complaining lately about his arthritis, and she didn't want to overtax him. True, she could have found someone else to do the job. That was what Miranda would have done. In her mind, Kate could see her friend, phone receiver in hand, tapping out numbers with an elegantly tapered and enameled fingernail. But if someone else were doing this, Kate thought, she wouldn't have had an excuse to escape an evening alone with Will. . . .

She rocked back on her heels and considered her progress. She'd finished most of the hinged top, which, stripped of its layers of cloudy varnish, gave off a mellow shine. The table really had been such a find, and she'd gotten it for a song. So why wasn't she more pleased? In the past, she'd have been gloating.

Because, she thought, *because it's hard to gloat when you feel as if you're the one who's been stripped of everything you hold most dear.*

Gone were the cloudy layers of lies and denials. Gone the fear that her path would one day cross Ellie's—her worst nightmare had been realized, and she had survived it. Gone, even, the resentment she'd harbored against Will these past months. He was, like many men she'd known, rock and scissors when it came to his work; paper when it came to family crises.

She pictured Will as she'd left him an hour ago, seated in his favorite easy chair in the small sitting room off the main parlor, his briefcase in front of him, poring over the legal documents for his newest project, a multimillion-dollar development of fourteen acres of Hoboken waterfront that promised an end to the firm's financial crisis. Will should have been excited, but he'd looked listless and gaunt-cheeked, his eyes staring at some distant point beyond her.

"I'm going down to the shop to catch up on some work," she'd told him. "If you get hungry, there's a casserole in the oven. You can heat it up in the microwave."

He'd blinked, looking up at her as if she were a stranger in a train station asking directions. "Oh, sure. That's fine." Then, as if remembering that they were married, and that married people were expected to eat together, he'd asked, "You won't be home for dinner?"

"Probably not." Kate experienced a mild stab that might have been annoyance, but mostly what she felt, she realized, was sad.

She still loved Will—or, at least, she thought she did. Their history was complicated and deep, rooted in their shared love for their daughter and in the life they'd fashioned. But where her love had once been needy, sometimes even clinging, now it was tender, almost maternal. These days, she often thought of Will as a sick child in need of her care.

"Well, then . . . I'm off," she'd said with false briskness. "Call me if . . ." She stopped herself from saying what there was no need to say.

Call me if you hear from Skyler Don't let me spend one moment more than I have to eating my heart out, wondering if she'll ever forgive us.

". . . anything comes up," she ended.

Will, to his credit, understood that she wasn't referring to his needing to know how many minutes in the microwave for the casserole, or to the possibility that one of her friends might call. He nodded, and the flesh around his jaw—it had lately started to sag, like the drooping hem of a coat long out of fashion—tightened briefly. She knew then that he was hurting, too.

And so here she was, kneeling on a varnish-stained dropcloth in the small workroom off her darkened shop, breathing in fumes that were probably giving her cancer, or at the very least poking holes in the ozone.

Life goes on, Kate told herself. *It just doesn't go on as before.*

She would just have to get used to it. She would somehow have to condition herself not to snatch up the phone every time it rang, thinking it was her daughter. She would have to stop leafing through photo albums crammed with pictures of Skyler. Skyler at five, on her new pony. Skyler at the Hampton Classic, with her first blue ribbon. Skyler in her cap and gown, graduating from Princeton . . .

Oh, Lord, would she ever learn to bear it? Knowing she had a daughter and a grandaughter out there . . . but not being able to see them. None of her calls to

Skyler had been returned, and the one time she'd actually gotten through, her daughter had been remote and cold.

Ellie stood it, she reminded herself caustically. *And now you're finding out exactly how it felt. You're getting what you dished out, what you deserve.*

But did it have to hurt so much? Did she have to carry it with her everywhere she went, like a sharp pebble in the bottom of her shoe? Wasn't she to be allowed some credit for the good she'd done, for the honest love that had guided her?

In a fit of despair, Kate tore off her gloves and tossed them at the pegboard on the wall. But when she tried to stand up, pain shot through her hip, so fierce that for a second, as she wavered on her feet, she thought she might be about to black out. Pinpoints of color swarmed before her eyes, and the room seemed to contract, as if she were seeing it through a peephole. She swayed, then caught herself on a Victorian tea caddy.

The room slowly regained its proportions, but her vision remained blurred. Kate brought her hands to her face, and found it wet. Damn. She'd promised herself, she'd *sworn*—no more tears. Crying was so . . . undignified. And so useless. It wasn't going to bring Skyler back. It wasn't going to change a thing.

Kate hobbled cautiously over to the pine workbench against which her cane sat propped. She would rest a while, then head home.

The shrilling of the doorbell startled Kate, causing her to jerk upright and accidentally knock her cane to the floor. Who could it be at this hour? It was too late for a delivery.

The front door suddenly seemed an impossible distance away, the shop a labyrinth of hulking half-lit shapes full of sharp corners and clawed feet waiting to trip her. Through the door's beveled glass oval, she could make out a slender figure in a belted raincoat, half hidden in shadow.

Kate's heart leaped. She would have recognized Skyler anywhere, just from the way she held herself— her weight slung onto one hip, one shoulder dipped slightly lower than the other.

Ignoring her throbbing pain, Kate dashed the last few feet to the door, and hammered open the cranky old bolt latch with the heel of her hand.

"Skyler!" She had to fight to keep her joy from spilling over.

Skyler stepped cautiously inside, leaning forward to kiss Kate lightly on the cheek. It was a polite kiss, nothing more. Kate stood before her daughter, yearning to embrace her, but consciously holding back.

It had been two months since they'd last spoken, and spring no more than a fading memory. The forsythia had come and gone, and so had the daffodils. Her roses were starting to bloom; in the orchard, hard green knobs of fruit were beginning to form. Duncan's favorite mare, Tilly, was due to foal any day.

Kate remembered when the impending birth of a foal would send Skyler running home from the school bus each day in wild anticipation, her book bag thumping against the flat blade of her hip, her hair flying about her head like ribbons on a maypole. Oh, what wouldn't she give to have those years to live over ... her daughter under her roof again, happy to be adored by her!

Kate glanced at her watch, amazed to see that it was almost nine. She hadn't realized it was so late. Time was something she rarely gave much thought to these days.

"Would you like a cup of tea?" she asked Skyler

Skyler nodded, and said, "Tea would be nice."

Kate led the way to the back of the shop, to the corner behind her desk where she kept an electric teakettle atop a two-drawer file cabinet stacked with boxes of tea and packets of sugar. Filling the kettle from the water cooler that stood next to it, Kate was glad for something to keep her busy. She was certain that if forced to stand still she'd have floated right up to the ceiling like one of those balloons delivered in bunches to people on their birthdays.

Skyler, as if not wanting to make herself too comfortable, sat perched on the upholstered arm of a parlor chair, watching her mother with the patient expression of someone biding her time until all the fuss dies down.

Finally, unable to hold back a second longer, Kate blurted, "I'm so glad you're here! You have no idea how much I missed you."

Skyler remained silent, her expression grave.

Kate, her eyes brimming, said the only thing left to say. "I can only begin to imagine what you must think of me. But, believe me, there can't be anything you've held against me that I haven't blamed myself for already. And the really awful part is, I have no excuse. There's no way I can ever make it up to you ... or to Ellie. The only thing I can do is say I'm sorry. I should have told you years ago."

Skyler went on staring at her coldly. "Why tell me at all? You could have just gone on keeping it a secret."

Kate had asked herself the same thing, over and over. And the answer still eluded her. The best she could come up with was this: "It's true that for years I was afraid of what would happen if I confessed ... but I guess what it finally came down to was that I was even more afraid of what would happen if I didn't."

"To Ellie?"

Kate's throbbing hip forced her to sink down onto the chair at her desk. "To me," she said. "I couldn't have lived with myself a second longer if I'd let Ellie walk out of that courtroom not knowing."

"What about Daddy—did he feel the same way?"

Kate was silent. She wouldn't make excuses for Will. But she could see from Skyler's expression that it wouldn't be necessary. Skyler, while loving her father, clearly had his measure.

Maybe I can learn something from her, Kate thought. *I can learn to see Will with wide-open eyes and love him despite his shortcomings.*

The teakettle began to whistle, and she hauled herself to her feet to pour boiling water into two mugs. With her back safely turned, she asked with forced lightness, "How is Alisa? She must be so big by now." Handing Skyler a steaming mug, Kate finished mildly with, "Babies grow so fast."

Skyler's face lit up. "She's just starting to pull herself up onto all fours. It's so funny watching her—she gets this really red face, as if she's doing push-ups."

"Next thing you know she'll be crawling."

"She's already starting. Only a lot of the time, she just scoots around on her tummy. Tony nicknamed her Lizzie, short for Lizard. You should see her!"

I would very much like that, Kate thought.

"Are you and Tony . . .?" she started to ask, then stopped. She'd heard from Will that Skyler and Tony were engaged, but she felt awkward bringing it up. That her daughter should be getting married without Kate being included in any way seemed unthinkable.

"We haven't set a date yet," Skyler hedged.

Or are you just saying that so you won't have to invite me to the wedding? Kate wondered in an agony of despair.

"Oh, well," she said, "I think it's wonderful."

"Do you?" Skyler sounded as if she still might have some doubts about getting married.

"Of course.

"You don't disapprove?"

"Why should I?"

"Well, you know . . .

"Because he's not 'one of us'?" Kate shook her head slowly. "Oh, Skyler, I'm sorry if I raised you to think that way. Believe me, it wasn't intentional. What matters most of all is love and respect. Of course, it's always easier when husbands and wives share similar backgrounds, but it's no formula for happiness. If you love this man, and he loves you, then you can make it work."

Skyler sighed. "It won't be easy."

"No marriage ever is." Kate paused, then added softly, wistfully, "Your father and I hardly ever fought—we didn't have to. We agreed on almost everything. But it would have been better, I think, if we *had* fought. Things wouldn't have been allowed to fester. We might have learned to be more honest with each other."

"You mean about Ellie?"

"About Ellie ... and other things."

Kate tried to sip her tea, but her hand was trembling, and some of the steaming liquid sloshed onto her knuckles, scalding them. She set her mug down, and brought the back of her hand to her cheek, struggling not to give in to the tears that were like a constant waterfall behind her eyes, forever on the verge of leaking through.

"Mom ..."

Skyler's voice made Kate sit up suddenly, and straighten her shoulders. She raised her chin, the way she might have held a brimming glass to keep it from spilling over. Kate waited, not speaking.

Finally, with a deep breath, Skyler continued, "I don't know if I'll ever really be able to forgive you, but the weird thing is ... I *do* understand. If I'd been in your place, if it had been Alisa ... there's no question in my mind that I would have done exactly what you did."

"We do terrible things in the name of love." Kate blinked, and a tear rolled down her cheek.

"I can imagine worse," Skyler said softly, holding Kate in the steady glow of her gaze. "Not to have been loved, not to have grown up knowing that I had a mother I could always count on ... *that* would have been the worst that could have happened to me."

Kate didn't dare breathe; to move even an inch might have shattered the spell. Instead, she simply sat and stared in awe at the borrowed child she had nurtured and loved as her own. *You belong to Ellie,* she thought, *but you have something of me in you, too. Because I loved you with all my heart.*

Kate ventured a shallow breath. "You and Tony must come to the house for dinner next week," she said, adding cautiously, "I'd like to get to know him . . . and Alisa."

"Thursday would be good. . . . I'll have her that night," Skyler said, lowering her gaze with an uncharacteristic shyness. Then she spoke the words Kate had not been able to bring herself to lay claim to. "She's *your* granddaughter, too, you know."

Kate sipped her tea, which was still scalding. She put her mug down on the desk in front of her, and in a voice so soft and choked it was almost a whisper, she answered, "I've never thought of her any other way."

"I know, Mom."

Kate brightened. "Is she really crawling? Oh, I can't wait to see her. I'll make sure I have plenty of film in the camera."

"I only wish I could be as relaxed with her as you were with me," Skyler said with a nervous laugh. "But even when I'm tearing my hair out, wondering what to do next, I can't get over her. It's funny how that works, isn't it? How easy it is to love your child ... even when it seems like half the time you don't know what you're doing."

"Love is the one thing in life you don't need practice for." Kate managed a tremulous smile.

An anxious light crept into Skyler's vivid blue eyes.

"But what if you love your child with all your heart . . . and it still isn't enough?"

Kate retrieved her mug from the desk blotter strewn with paperwork she hadn't gotten around to sorting through, and that Miranda would have a fit over if it weren't cleared away by the time she returned. She cautiously sampled her tea, which was finally the right temperature. Neither too hot, nor too cold—like the single tear that wandered down her cheek, and hovered briefly on the curve of her jaw before dropping into her lap.

"It never is enough," Kate said with a wisdom all too hard won. "No matter how much you might want to, you can't right every wrong, or fix everything that's hurting your child. You can't give her whatever it is you hope she'll one day have." She smiled . . . a smile of exquisite tenderness that was tempered, like a precious metal alloyed with steel, by the kind of heartache only a mother can know. "The secret, you see, is in the trying."